PENGUIN BOOKS

# THE
# COUSINS

## BOOKS BY KAREN M. MCMANUS

# THE
# COUSINS

KAREN M. McMANUS

PENGUIN BOOKS

PENGUIN BOOKS

UK | USA | Canada | Ireland | Australia
India | New Zealand | South Africa

Penguin Books is part of the Penguin Random House group of companies
whose addresses can be found at global.penguinrandomhouse.com.

www.penguin.co.uk
www.puffin.co.uk
www.ladybird.co.uk

Penguin
Random House
UK

First published in the USA by Delacorte Press
and in Great Britain by Penguin Books 2020

001

Printed and bound in Great Britain by Clays Ltd, Elcograf S.p.A.

A CIP catalogue record for this book is available from the British Library

ISBN: 978–0–241–37694–2

All correspondence to:
Penguin Books
Penguin Random House Children's
One Embassy Gardens, 8 Viaduct Gardens, London SW11 7BW

MIX
Paper from
responsible sources
FSC® C018179

Penguin Random House is committed to a
sustainable future for our business, our readers
and our planet. This book is made from Forest
Stewardship Council® certified paper.

For Lynne

# THE STORY FAMILY TREE

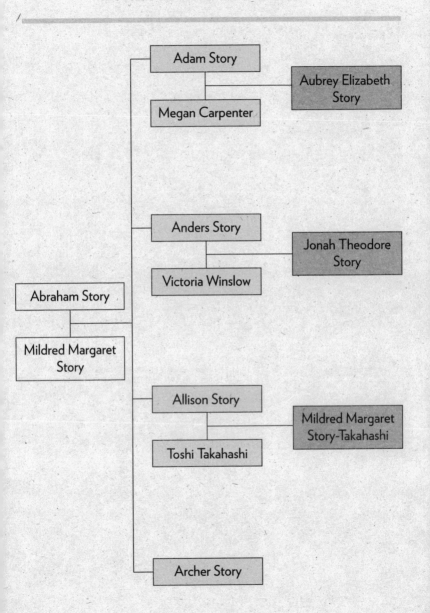

# CHAPTER ONE

## MILLY

I'm late for dinner again, but this time it's not my fault. There's a mansplainer in my way.

"Mildred? That's a grandmother's name. But not even a *cool* grandmother." He says it like he thinks he's being clever. Like in all my seventeen years, no one else has ever noticed that my name isn't the fashionable kind of classic. It took a Wall Street investment banker with slicked-back hair and a pinkie ring to render that particular bit of social commentary.

I sip the dregs of my seltzer. "I was, in fact, named after my grandmother," I say.

I'm at a steak house in midtown at six o'clock on a rainy April evening, doing my best to blend with the happy hour crowd. It's a game my friends and I play sometimes; we go to restaurant bars so we don't have to worry about getting carded at the door. We wear our simplest dresses and extra makeup. We order seltzer water with lime—"in a small glass, please, I'm not that thirsty"—and gulp it down until there's almost nothing left. Then we wait to see if anyone offers to buy us a drink.

Somebody always does.

Pinkie Ring smiles, his teeth almost fluorescent in the dim light. He must take his whitening regimen very seriously. "I like it. Quite a contrast for such a beautiful young woman." He edges closer, and I catch a headache-inducing whiff of strong cologne. "You have a very interesting look. Where are you from?"

Ugh. That's marginally better than the *What are you?* question I get sometimes, but still gross. "New York," I say pointedly. "You?"

"I mean originally," he clarifies, and that's it. I'm done.

"New York," I repeat, and stand up from my stool. It's just as well he didn't talk to me until I was about to leave, because a cocktail before dinner wasn't one of my better ideas. I catch my friend Chloe's eye across the room and wave good-bye, but before I can extract myself, Pinkie Ring tips his glass toward mine. "Can I get you another of whatever that is?"

"No thank you. I'm meeting someone."

He pulls back, brow furrowed. *Very* furrowed. In a behind-on-his-Botox sort of way. He also has creases lining his cheeks and crinkles around his eyes. He's way too old to be hitting on me, even if I were the college student I occasionally pretend to be. "What are you wasting my time for, then?" he grunts, his gaze already roving over my shoulder.

Chloe likes the happy hour game because, she says, high school boys are immature. Which is true. But sometimes I think we might be better off not knowing how much worse they can get.

I pluck the lime out of my drink and squeeze it. I'm not aiming for his eye, exactly, but I'm still a little disappointed when the juice spatters only his collar. "Sorry," I say sweetly, dropping the lime into the glass and setting it on the bar. "Normally I wouldn't bother. But it's so dark in here. When you first came over, I thought you were my dad."

As if. My dad is way better-looking, and also: not a creep. Pinkie Ring's mouth drops open, but I scoot past him and out the door before he can reply.

The restaurant I'm going to is just across the street, and the hostess smiles when I come through the door. "Can I help you?"

"I'm meeting someone for dinner? Allison?"

Her gaze drops to the book in front of her and a small crease appears between her eyes. "I'm not seeing—"

"Story-Takahashi?" I try. My parents have an unusually amicable divorce, and Exhibit A is that Mom continues to use both last names. "Well, it's still *your* name," she'd said four years ago when the divorce was finalized. "And I've gotten used to it."

The crease between the hostess's eyes deepens. "I don't see that either."

"Just Story, then?" I try. "Like in a book?"

Her brow clears. "Oh! Yes, there you are. Right this way."

She grabs two menus and winds her way between white-covered tables until we reach a corner booth. The wall beside it is mirrored, and the woman sitting on one side is sipping a glass of white wine while surreptitiously checking out her reflection, smoothing flyaways in her dark bun that only she can see.

I drop into the seat across from her as the hostess places oversized red menus in front of us. "So it's Story tonight?" I ask.

My mother waits until the hostess leaves to answer. "I wasn't in the mood to repeat myself," she sighs, and I raise a brow. Mom usually makes a point of pushing back on anyone who acts like they can't figure out how to spell or pronounce Dad's Japanese last name.

"Why?" I ask, even though I know she won't tell me. There are multiple levels of Milly criticism to get through first.

She puts her glass down, causing almost a dozen gold bangles to jingle on her wrist. My mother is vice president of public relations for a jewelry company, and wearing the season's must-haves is one of the perks of her job. She eyes me up and down, taking in my heavier-than-usual makeup and navy sheath. "Where are you coming from that you're so dressed up?"

*The bar across the street.* "A gallery thing with Chloe," I lie. Chloe's mother owns an art gallery uptown, and our friends spend a lot of time there. Allegedly.

Mom picks up her glass again. Sips, flicks her eyes toward the mirror, pats her hair. When it's down it falls in dark waves, but, as she likes to tell me, pregnancy changed its texture from smooth to coarse. I'm pretty sure she's never forgiven me for that. "I thought you were studying for finals."

"I was. Before."

Her knuckles turn white around the glass, and I wait for it. *Milly, you cannot exit your junior year with less than a B average. You're on the cusp of mediocrity, and your father and I have invested far too much for you to waste your opportunity like that.*

If I were even a little musically inclined, I'd start a band called Cusp of Mediocrity in honor of Mom's favorite warning. I've been hearing some version of that speech for three years. Prescott Academy churns out Ivy League students like some kind of blue-blood factory, and it's the bane of my mother's

4

existence that I'm always ranked solidly in the bottom half of my class.

The lecture doesn't come, though. Instead, Mom reaches out her free hand and pats mine. Stiffly, like she's a marionette with a novice handler. "Well, you look very pretty."

Instantly, I'm on the defensive. It's strange enough that my mother wanted to meet me for dinner, but she *never* compliments me. Or touches me. All of this suddenly feels like a setup for something I'd rather not hear. "Are you sick?" I blurt out. "Is Dad?"

She blinks and withdraws her hand. "What? No! Why would you ask that?"

"Then why—" I break off as a smiling server appears beside the table, filling our water glasses from a silver pitcher.

"And how are you ladies this evening? Can I tell you about our specials?"

I study Mom covertly over the top of my menu as the server rattles them off. She's definitely tense, still clutching her near-empty wineglass in a death grip, but I realize now that I was wrong to expect bad news. Her dark-blue eyes are bright, and the corners of her mouth are *almost* turned up. She's anticipating something, not dreading it. I try to imagine what might make my mother happy besides me magically A-plussing my way to valedictorian at Prescott Academy.

Money. That's all it could be. Mom's life revolves around it—or more specifically, around not having enough of it. My parents both have good jobs, and my dad, despite being remarried, has always been generous with child support. His new wife, Surya, is the total opposite of a wicked stepmother in all possible ways, including finances. She's never begrudged Mom the big checks he sends every month.

But *good* doesn't cut it when you're trying to keep up in Manhattan. And it's not what my mother grew up with.

A job promotion, I decide. That must be it. Which is excellent news, except for the part where she's going to remind me that she got it through hard work and oh, by the way, why can't I work harder at literally everything.

"I'll have the Caesar salad with chicken. No anchovies, dressing on the side," Mom says, handing her menu to the server without really looking at him. "And another glass of the Langlois-Chateau, please."

"Very good. And the young lady?"

"Bone-in rib eye, medium rare, and a jumbo baked potato," I tell him. I might as well get a good meal out of whatever's about to go down.

When he leaves, my mother drains her wineglass and I gulp my water. My bladder's already full from the seltzer at the bar, and I'm about to excuse myself for the restroom when Mom says, "I got the most interesting letter today."

*There* it is. "Oh?" I wait, but when she doesn't continue, I prod, "From who?"

"Whom," she corrects automatically. Her fingers trace the base of her glass as her lips curve up another half notch. "From your grandmother."

I blink at her. "From Baba?" Why that merits this kind of buildup, I have no idea. Granted, my grandmother doesn't contact Mom often, but it's not unprecedented. Baba is the type of person who likes to forward articles she's read to anyone she thinks might be interested, and she still does that with Mom postdivorce.

"No. Your other grandmother."

"What?" Now I'm truly confused. "You got a letter from—Mildred?"

I don't have a nickname for my mother's mother. She's not Grandma or Mimi or Nana or *anything* to me, because I've never met her.

"I did." The server returns with Mom's wine, and she takes a long, grateful sip. I sit in silence, unable to wrap my head around what she just told me. My maternal grandmother loomed large over my childhood, but as more of a fairy-tale figure than an actual person: the wealthy widow of Abraham Story, whose great-something-grandfather came over on the *Mayflower*. My ancestors are more interesting than any history book: the family made a fortune in whaling, lost most of it in railroad stocks, and eventually sank what was left into buying up real estate on a crappy little island off the coast of Massachusetts.

Gull Cove Island was a little-known haven for artists and hippies until Abraham Story turned it into what it is today: a place where rich and semifamous people spend ridiculous amounts of money pretending they're getting back to nature.

My mother and her three brothers grew up on a giant beachfront estate named Catmint House, riding horses and attending black-tie parties like they were the princess and princes of Gull Cove Island. There's a picture on our apartment mantel of Mom when she was eighteen, stepping out of a limousine on her way to the Summer Gala her parents threw every year at their resort. Her hair is piled high, and she's wearing a white ball gown and a gorgeous diamond teardrop necklace. Mildred gave that necklace to my mother when she turned seventeen, and I used to think Mom would pass it along to me when I hit the same birthday.

Didn't happen. Even though Mom never wears it herself.

My grandfather died when Mom was a senior in high school. Two years later, Mildred disowned all of her children. She cut them off both financially and personally, with no explanation except for a single-sentence letter sent two weeks before Christmas through her lawyer, a man named Donald Camden who'd known Mom and her brothers their entire lives:

*You know what you did.*

Mom has always insisted that she has no clue what Mildred meant. "The four of us had gotten . . . selfish, I suppose," she'd tell me. "We were all in college then, starting our own lives. Mother was lonely with Father gone, and she begged us to visit all the time. But we didn't want to go." She calls her parents that, *Mother* and *Father,* like the heroine in a Victorian novel. "None of us came back for Thanksgiving that year. We'd all made other plans. She was furious, but . . ." Mom always got a pensive, faraway look on her face then. "That's such a small thing. Hardly unforgivable."

If Abraham Story hadn't set up educational trusts for Mom and her brothers, they might not have graduated college. Once they did, though, they were on their own. At first, they regularly tried to reestablish contact with Mildred. They hounded Donald Camden, whose only response was the occasional email reiterating her decision. They sent invitations to their weddings, and announcements when their kids were born. They even took turns showing up on Gull Cove Island, where my grandmother still lives, but she would never see or speak to them. I used to imagine that one day she'd waltz into our apartment, dripping diamonds and furs, and announce that she'd come for me, her namesake.

She'd whisk me to a toy store and let me buy whatever I wanted, then hand me a sack of money to bring home to my parents.

I'm pretty sure my mother had the same fantasy. Why else would you saddle a twenty-first-century girl with a name like Mildred? But my grandmother, with the help of Donald Camden, stonewalled her children at every turn. Eventually, they stopped trying.

Mom is looking at me expectantly, and I realize she's waiting for an answer. "You got a letter from Mildred?" I ask.

She nods, then clears her throat before answering. "Well. To be more precise, *you* did."

"I did?" My vocabulary has shrunk to almost nothing in the past five minutes.

"The envelope was addressed to me, but the letter was for you."

A decade-old image pops into my head: me with my long-lost grandmother, filling a shopping cart to the rim with stuffed animals while dressed like we're going to the opera. Tiaras and all. I push the thought aside and grope for more words. "Is she . . . Does she . . . Why?"

My mother reaches into her purse and pulls out an envelope, then pushes it across the table toward me. "Maybe you should just read it."

I lift the flap and pull out a folded sheet of thick, cream-colored paper that smells faintly of lilac. The top is engraved with the initials MMS—Mildred Margaret Story. Our names are almost exactly the same, except mine has Takahashi at the end. The short paragraphs are typewritten, followed by a cramped, spidery signature.

Dear Milly,

We have, of course, never met. The reasons are complex, but as years progress they become less important than they once were. As you stand poised on the threshold of adulthood, I find myself curious to know you.

I own a property called Gull Cove Resort that is a popular vacation destination on Gull Cove Island. I wish to invite you and your cousins, Jonah and Aubrey, to spend this summer living and working at the resort. Your parents worked there as teenagers and found the environment both stimulating and enriching.

I am sure you and your cousins would reap similar benefits from a summer at Gull Cove Resort. And since I am not well enough to host guests for any length of time, it would afford me the opportunity to get to know you.

I hope you will accept my invitation. The resort's summer hire coordinator, Edward Franklin, will handle all necessary travel and logistics, and you may contact him at the email address below.

Very sincerely yours,
Mildred Story

I read it twice, then refold the paper and lay it on the table. I don't look up, but I can feel my mother's eyes on me as she waits for me to speak. Now I really have to pee, but I need to loosen my throat with yet more water before the words can burst out of me. "Is this bullshit for real?"

Whatever my mother might have been expecting me to say, it wasn't that. "Excuse me?"

"Let me get this straight," I say, my cheeks warming as I stuff the letter back into its envelope. "This woman I have never met—who cut you out of her life without looking back, who didn't come to your wedding or my christening or anything related to this family for the past twenty-four years, who hasn't called or emailed or written until, oh, five minutes ago—this woman wants me to *work at her hotel*?"

"I don't think you're looking at this the right way, Milly."

My voice rises to a near shriek. "How am I supposed to look at it?"

"Shhh," Mom hisses, her eyes darting around the room. If there's one thing she hates, it's a scene. "As an opportunity."

"For *what*?" I ask. She hesitates, twisting her cocktail ring—nothing like the five-carat emerald stunner I've seen on my grandmother's hand in old pictures—and suddenly I get it. "No, wait—don't answer that. That's the wrong question. I should have said for *who*."

"Whom," my mother says. She seriously cannot help herself.

"You think this is a chance to get back into her good graces, don't you? To be—re-inherited."

"That's not a word."

"God, Mom, would you give it a rest? My grammar is not the issue!"

"I'm sorry," Mom says, and that surprises me so much that I don't finish the rant I was building toward. Her eyes are still bright, but now they're watery, too. "It's just—this is my mother, Milly. I've waited years to hear from her. I don't know why now, or why you, or why *this,* but she's finally reaching out. If we don't take her up on it, we might not get another chance."

"Chance for what?"

"To get to know her again."

It's on the tip of my tongue to say *Who cares*, but I bite it back. I was going to follow that up with *We've been fine all this time without her*, but that's not true. We're not fine.

My mother lives at the edge of a Mildred Story–shaped hole, and has for my entire life. It's turned her into the kind of person who keeps everybody at a distance—even my dad, who I know she loved as much as she's capable of loving anyone. When I was little, I'd watch them together and wish for something as perfect. Once I got older, though, I started noticing all the little ways Mom would push Dad aside. How she'd stiffen at hugs, use work as an excuse to stay away until past our bedtimes, and beg off family outings with migraines that never bothered her in the office. Eventually, being chilly and closed off turned into criticizing absolutely everything Dad said or did. Right up to the point when she finally asked him to leave.

Now that he's gone, she does the same thing to me.

I draw a question mark in the condensation of my water glass. "You want me to go away for the entire summer?" I ask.

"You'd love it, Milly." When I snort, she adds, "No, you really would. It's a gorgeous resort, and kids apply from all over to work there. It's actually very competitive. Staff quarters are beautiful, you get full access to all the facilities—it's like a vacation."

"A vacation where I'm my grandmother's employee."

"You'd be with your cousins."

"I don't *know* my cousins." I haven't seen Aubrey since Uncle Adam's family moved to Oregon when we were five. Jonah lives in Rhode Island, which isn't that far away, but my mother and his father barely talk. The last time we all got together was for

Uncle Anders's birthday when I was eight. I only remember two things about Jonah: One, he whacked me in the head with a plastic bat and seemed disappointed when I didn't cry. And two, he blew up like a balloon when he ate an appetizer he was allergic to, even though his mother warned him to stay away from it.

"You could get to know them. You're all the same age, and none of you has any brothers or sisters. It would be nice for you to be closer."

"What, like you're close to Uncle Adam, Uncle Anders, and Uncle Archer? You guys barely talk to one another! My cousins and I have nothing in common." I shove the envelope back toward her. "I'm not doing it. I'm not a dog that'll come running just because *she* calls. And I don't want to be gone all summer."

Mom starts twisting her cocktail ring again. "I thought you might say that. And I realize it's a lot to ask. So I want to give you something in return." Her hand moves up to the chunky gold links gleaming against her black dress. "I know how much you've always loved my diamond teardrop necklace. What if I gave it to you as a thank-you?"

I sit up straighter, already imagining the necklace sparkling at my throat. I've dreamed about it for years. But I thought it would be a gift—not a *bribe*.

"Why wouldn't you just give it to me because I'm your daughter?" I've always wondered but never dared ask. Maybe because I'm afraid the answer would be the same one she gave my dad, not with her words but with her actions: *You aren't enough.*

"It's an heirloom," Mom says, like that doesn't prove my entire point. I frown as she rests one manicured hand on the edge of the envelope. She doesn't *push* it, exactly. Just sort of taps it. "I always thought I'd give it to you when you turned twenty-one, but if you're going to spend your summer in my hometown—well, it just seems right to do it sooner."

I exhale a silent sigh and take the envelope, turning it over in my hand while Mom sips her wine, content to wait me out. I'm not sure which is more frustrating: that my mother is trying to blackmail me into spending the summer working for a grandmother I've never met, or that it's totally going to work.

# CHAPTER TWO

## AUBREY

I stretch my fingers toward the slick wall of the pool. As soon as they touch, I turn and push off for the final lap. This is my favorite part of any swim meet: water rushing over my extended limbs as I glide through it on pure momentum and adrenaline. Sometimes I resurface later than I should, which Coach Matson calls my *derailer:* a tiny flaw in technique that can mean the difference between being a good swimmer and a great one. Usually, I try to correct it. But today? I'd stay down here forever if I could.

I finally break the surface, gasp for air, and settle into the rhythm of the breaststroke. My shoulders burn and my legs churn in welcome, mindless exertion until my fingers brush tile again. I pull off my goggles, panting, and wipe my eyes before looking at the scoreboard.

Seventh out of eight, my worst finish ever for the two-hundred meter. Two days ago, that result would have devastated me. But when I spy Coach Matson staring at the scoreboard with her hands on her hips, all I feel is a triumphant spark of anger.

*Serves you right.*

Anyway, it doesn't matter. I'm never swimming for Ashland High again. I only showed up today so the team wouldn't have to forfeit.

I haul myself out of the pool and grab my towel from the bench. The two-hundred meter was my final event of the day, in the last meet of the season. Normally, my mother would be in the stands posting overly long videos to Facebook, and I'd be poolside getting ready to cheer for my teammates in the relay. But Mom isn't here, and I'm not staying.

I head for the empty locker room, my wet feet slapping the tiled floor, and extract my gym bag from number 74. I drop my cap and goggles into the bag and pull a T-shirt and shorts over my wet bathing suit. Then I put on my flip-flops and send a quick text: *Feeling sick. Meet me at the door?*

The relay is in full swing when I reenter the pool area. My teammates who aren't racing are at the pool's edge, too busy cheering to notice me skulking away. My chest constricts and my eyes prick, until I catch sight of Coach Matson at her usual spot next to the diving board. She's leaning forward, blond ponytail spilling over one shoulder as she shouts at Chelsea Reynolds to *pick up the pace,* and I'm hit with a sudden, almost irresistible urge to barrel forward and shove her straight into the pool.

For a delicious second, I let myself imagine what that would feel like. The Saturday crowd at the Ashland Memorial Recreation Center would be shocked into silence, craning their necks for a better look. *Is that Aubrey Story? What's gotten into her?* No one would believe their eyes, because I'm the Girl Least Likely to Cause a Scene About Anything, Ever.

I'm also a giant wimp. I keep walking.

A familiar lanky figure hovers near the exit. My boyfriend, Thomas, is dressed in the Trail Blazers jersey I bought him, his dark hair buzzed short for the summer like always. The knot in my stomach loosens as I get closer. Thomas and I have been dating since eighth grade—we had our four-year anniversary last month—and collapsing against his chest is like slipping into a warm bath.

Maybe a little *too* like it. "You're soaked," Thomas says, disentangling himself from my damp embrace. He looks me up and down warily. "And sick?"

I might've had one cold the entire time Thomas has known me. I'm weirdly germ-resistant. "You don't take after the Storys," my father always says with a sigh. "The merest hint of a virus can incapacitate us for days." It almost sounds boastful the way he says it, like his side of the family are rare and delicate hothouse flowers, while Mom and I are sturdy weeds that can thrive anywhere.

The thought of my father makes my stomach tighten again. "Just feeling a little off," I tell Thomas.

"You probably caught it from your mom."

That's what I told Thomas last night when I asked him to drive me today; that my mother wasn't feeling well. I didn't tell him the real reason on the ride over this morning, either. I couldn't find the words. But as we reach his Honda I find myself itching to spill my guts, and it's a relief when he turns to me with a concerned look. I just need him to ask *What's wrong?* and then I can say it.

"You're not gonna throw up, are you?" he asks. "I just vacuumed the car."

I tug open the passenger door, deflated. "No. It's a headache. I'll be fine after I lie down for a while."

He nods, oblivious. "I'll get you home, then."

Ugh. Home. The second-last place I want to be. But I'm stuck for a few more weeks, until it's time to leave for Gull Cove Island. Funny how something that was so weird and unwelcome at first suddenly feels like sweet salvation.

Thomas starts the engine, and I pull out my phone to see if either of my cousins added to our group chat since this morning. Milly has; she's posted a summary of her travel schedule and a question. *Should we try to all take the same ferry?*

When I first got my grandmother's letter—which Dad immediately assumed I would agree to, no questions asked—I looked up both my cousins online. Milly was easy to find on social media. I sent a follow request on Instagram and she accepted right away, unlocking a timeline filled with pictures of her and her friends. They're all beautiful, especially my cousin. She's white and Japanese, and looks more like a Story than I do—dark-haired and slender, with large, expressive eyes and cheekbones to die for. I, on the other hand, take after my mom: blond, freckled, and athletic. The only characteristic I have in common with my elegant grandmother is the port-wine birthmark on my right forearm; Gran has one almost the exact size and shape on her left hand.

I have no idea what Jonah looks like. I couldn't track him down anywhere except Facebook, where his profile picture is the DNA symbol. He has seven friends, and I'm not one of them because he still hasn't accepted my request.

Jonah barely posts in our group chat except to complain. He's angrier than Milly and I about getting sent to Gull Cove

Island for the summer. Now, as Thomas pulls out of the Recreation Center parking lot, I distract myself by scrolling through yesterday's conversation.

*Jonah: This is bullshit. I should be at camp this summer.*

*Milly: What, are you a counselor?*

*Jonah: Not that kind of camp. It's a science camp. Very competitive. Nearly impossible to get into and now I'm supposed to miss it?*

*Jonah: And for what? A minimum-wage job cleaning toilets for a woman who hates our parents and most likely hates us too.*

*Aubrey: We're not cleaning toilets. Didn't you read Edward's email?*

*Jonah: Who?*

*Aubrey: Edward Franklin. The summer hire coordinator. There are lots of jobs you can choose from. I'm going to be a lifeguard.*

*Jonah: Well bully for you.*

*Milly: You don't have to be a dick about it.*

*Milly: Also, who says "bully for you"? What are you, 80?*

Then they argued for ten minutes while I ghosted the conversation because . . . confrontation. Not my thing.

The last time I saw any Story relative was right after we moved to Oregon, when my father's youngest brother breezed through for a weekend visit. Uncle Archer doesn't have children, but as soon as he arrived, he dropped onto the floor like a Lego expert to help me with the town I was building. A few hours later, he vomited into my toy chest. It wasn't until recently that I realized he'd been drunk the whole time.

Dad used to call himself and his brothers and sister the Four As, back when he still talked regularly about them. Adam, Anders, Allison, and Archer, born a year apart from one another. They all had distinct roles in the family: Adam was the golden-boy athlete, Anders the brilliant eccentric, Allison the reserved beauty, and Archer the charming jokester.

Uncle Anders, Jonah's father, is the only one who didn't inherit the family good looks. In old pictures he's short, scrawny, and sharp-featured, with eyebrows like slashes and a perpetual thin-lipped smirk. That's how I picture Jonah whenever I read his messages.

I'm about to put my phone away when a new message pops up, from Milly to me. It's the first time she's ever texted me without including Jonah. *Aubrey, important question for you: Is it just me, or is Jonah a total ass?*

A grin tugs at the corners of my mouth as I type, *It's not just you.* I open Thomas's glove compartment, where he keeps a handy assortment of snacks, and dig out a brown sugar–cinnamon Pop-Tart. Not my favorite, but my stomach is rumbling with postmeet hunger pangs.

*Milly: I mean, nobody's thrilled about this. I might not be signed up for Genius Camp, but I still have things I'd rather be doing.*

Before I can respond, another message pops up, from Jonah in our group chat. *That ferry time is inconvenient and I don't see the point in arriving in tandem anyway.*

*Milly: Omg why is he such trash???*

*Jonah: Excuse me?*

*Milly: . . .*

*Milly: Sorry, wrong chat.*

*Milly,* in our private chat: *Fuck.*

I laugh through a mouthful of Pop-Tart, and Thomas glances at me. "What's so funny?" he asks.

I swallow. "My cousin Milly. I think I'm going to like her."

"That's good. At least the summer won't be a total loss."

Thomas drums his fingers on one side of the steering wheel as he turns onto my street. It's narrow and winding, filled with modest ranches and split-levels. It was supposed to be our starter home, bought after my father's first novel was published almost ten years ago. The book wasn't a blockbuster, but it was well reviewed enough that he was offered a contract for a second novel. Which he still hasn't written, even though author is the only job he's had since I was in grade school. For the longest time, I thought he got paid for reading books, not writing them, since that was all he ever did. Turns out he just doesn't get paid at all.

Thomas pulls into our driveway and shifts into park but doesn't cut the engine. "Do you want to come in?" I ask.

"Um." Thomas takes a deep breath, his hand still drumming on the steering wheel. "So, I think . . ."

I lick my lips, which taste like cinnamon and chlorine, while I wait for him to go on. When he doesn't, I prod, "You think what?"

His shoulders tense, then rise in a shrug. "Just—not today. I have stuff to do."

I don't have the energy to ask what stuff. I lean toward him for a kiss, but Thomas pulls back. "Better not. I don't wanna get sick."

Stung, I retreat. Guess that's what I get for lying. "Okay. Text me later?"

"Sure," Thomas says. As soon as I'm out of the car and shut the door, he reverses out of my driveway. I watch him drive up the street with an uneasy flutter in my stomach. It's not as though Thomas waits for me to make it through the front door when he drives me home, but he doesn't usually take off quite that fast.

The house is quiet when I get inside. When Mom is around she always has music on, usually the nineties grunge she liked in college. For one hopeful second I think that means I have the place to myself, but I've barely set foot in the living room before my father's voice stops me.

"Back so soon?"

My stomach twists as I turn to see him sitting in a leather armchair that's too big for the cramped corner of our living room. His author chair, the one Mom bought when his book was published. It would look better in one of those office-slash-libraries with floor-to-ceiling bookshelves, an imposing mahogany desk, and a hearth. Our tabby cat, Eloise, lies stretched across his lap. When I don't reply, he asks, "How was the meet?"

I blink at him. He can't really expect me to answer that question. Not after the bomb he dropped last night. But he just gazes back calmly, putting a finger in the book he's holding to mark his page. I recognize the cover, the bold black font against a muted, almost watercolor-like background. *A Brief and Broken Silence,* by Adam Story. It's his novel, about a former college athlete who achieves literary stardom and then realizes that what he really wants is to live a simple life off the grid—except his rabid fans won't leave him alone.

I'm pretty sure my father was hoping the book would turn out to be autobiographical. It didn't, but he still rereads it at least once a year.

*You might as well,* I think, my temper flaring. *No one else does.*

But I don't say it. "Where's Mom?"

"Your mother . . ." Dad hesitates, squinting as the sunlight streaming through the picture window reaches his eyes. The light brings out glints in his dark hair and gives him a golden glow he doesn't deserve. It makes my chest hurt, now, to think about how mindlessly I've always worshiped my father. How deeply I believed that he was brilliant, and special, and destined for amazing things. I was honored that he'd given me an *A* name. I was the Fifth A, I used to tell myself, and one day I'd be just like them. Glamorous, mysterious, and just a little bit tragic. "Your mother is taking some time."

"Taking time? What, did she, like . . . move out?" But as soon as I say it, I know it isn't true. My mother wouldn't leave without telling me.

Eloise startles awake and jumps down, stalking across the living room with that irritated look she gets whenever her nap ends. "She's spending the afternoon with Aunt Jenny," Dad says. "After that, we'll see." A different note creeps into his voice then—petulant, with an undercurrent of resentment. "This is hard on all of us."

I stare at him, blood pounding in my ears, and imagine myself responding the way I want to: with a loud, disbelieving laugh. I'd laugh all the way across the room until I was close enough to rip the book out of his hands and throw it at his head. And then I'd tell him the truth: *There is no* us *anymore. That's ruined, and it's all your fault.*

But I don't say or do any of that. Just like I didn't push Coach Matson into the pool. All I do is nod stiffly, as though he said something that made actual sense. Then I trudge silently upstairs until I reach my bedroom door and lean my head against the cool, white wood.

*You know what you did.* My grandmother's letter from years ago said that, and my father has always insisted that she was wrong. "I can't know, because *nothing happened*," he'd say. "There's not a single thing that I, my brothers, or my sister ever did to justify this kind of treatment." And I believed him without question. I believed that he was innocent, and treated unfairly, and that my grandmother must be cold, capricious, and maybe even crazy.

But yesterday, I learned how easily he can lie.

And now I don't know what to believe anymore.

# CHAPTER THREE

## JONAH

I'm going to be late.

I've been in this car for almost three hours, driving seventy-five miles through stop-and-go traffic from Providence to Hyannis. It's been the longest, most expensive Uber trip of my life.

"Typical last weekend in June," my driver, Frederico, says as we crawl through Saturday-morning Cape Cod traffic. He brakes as the light we were about to pass through turns yellow. "What can you do, right?"

I grit my teeth. "You could've run that light, for starters."

Frederico waves a hand. "Not worth it. Cops are everywhere today."

Google Maps says we're just over a mile away from the ferry that will take me to Gull Cove Island. But even when we get through the red light, the line of cars ahead of us barely moves. "I'm supposed to leave in ten minutes," I say, hunching forward until my knees bump the seat in front of me. Whoever last rode shotgun in Frederico's car likes a lot of legroom. "Are we gonna make it?"

"Wellll," he hedges. "I'm not positive we're *not* gonna make it."

I suck in a frustrated breath and start stuffing papers back into the folder I'm holding. It's full of press clippings and printouts about Gull Cove and Mildred Story—mostly the island, though, because Mildred's practically a recluse. The only social event she ever shows up for is the annual Summer Gala at Gull Cove Resort. There's a picture of her in the *Gull Cove Gazette* at last year's event, wearing a giant dramatic hat and gloves like she's the queen of England. Donald Camden, her lawyer and sender of the infamous *you know what you did* letter, is standing next to her. He looks like the kind of smug asshole who would enjoy the job.

Mildred is now best known for being a patron of the arts. Apparently she's got a massive private collection of paintings and sculptures, and she spends a ton of money supporting local artists. She's probably the only reason there's still an artist community on that overpriced pile of rocks they call an island. So she has that going for her, at least.

The back of the folder has a few things related to Aubrey, Milly, and their parents. Old reviews for Adam Story's book, coverage of Aubrey's swim meets, an article about Toshi Takahashi making partner in one of New York's biggest law firms. I even dug up an old *New York Times* Vows column on his and Allison Story's wedding almost twenty years ago. Nothing about their divorce, though.

It's a little weird, maybe, to be carting all this around, but I don't know these people. And when I don't know something, I study it.

26

I shove the folder into my duffel bag and zip it up. It's one of those oversized bags meant to see a kid through two weeks of summer camp. It has to last me two months, but I don't have much. "Don't you know any back roads?" I ask Frederico. We're down to eight minutes.

"These *are* the back roads," Frederico says, glancing at me in the rearview mirror. "How fast are you?"

"What?"

"Can you run a five-minute mile?"

"Shit." I exhale as his meaning hits me. "You can't be serious."

"We're not moving, kid. If I were you, I'd make a run for it."

Desperation turns my voice into a snarl. "I have a *bag*!"

Frederico shrugs. "You're in good shape, aren't you? It's either that or miss your ferry. When's the next one?"

"Two and a half hours." I look at his dashboard—seven minutes to go—and make up my mind. "Fuck it. I'm going." A mile isn't that long, right? How bad could it be? Better than being stuck at a dock for almost three hours. Frederico brakes so I can get out, and I loop the straps of my bag around my shoulders like an oversized backpack.

He points out the window. "GPS says it's on the right. Should be a straight shot along this road. Good luck."

I don't answer, just take off for the grass at the side of the road and start running. For about thirty seconds it's fine and then everything goes to hell: the bag's thumping too hard against my back, I can feel rocks through the thin soles of my cheap sneakers, and my lungs start burning. Frederico was wrong; I'm not in shape. I look it, because I spend hours every day hauling boxes, but I haven't flat-out run in a long time. My lung capacity sucks, and it's getting worse by the second.

But I keep going, lengthening my strides because it doesn't feel like I'm getting anywhere near fast enough. My throat is so dry that it aches, and my lungs feel ready to explode. I pass a cheap motel, a seafood restaurant, and a minigolf course. The air is hot and muggy, the kind that settles over your skin even when you're standing still, and sweat coats my hair and pastes my T-shirt to my chest.

This was a big mistake. Huge. How am I going to explain collapsing on the side of a Cape Cod road to my parents?

Somehow I'm still running, my bag whacking me painfully with every step. My eyes sting with sweat and I can barely see, but I keep blinking until I make out the edge of a squat white building. It looms closer, and I spy a cobblestone path and a sign that reads STEAMSHIP AUTHORITY. I don't know how much time has passed, but I'm here.

I drag myself to the ticket window, panting. The woman behind the glass, a blonde with heavy makeup and teased bangs, looks at me with amusement. "Ease up on the heavy breathing, handsome. You're too young for me."

"Ticket," I gasp, digging in my pocket for my wallet. "For . . . the . . . one . . . twenty."

She shakes her head, and my pounding heart drops to my feet. Then she says, "You like to cut things close, don't you? You almost missed it. That'll be eighteen dollars."

I don't have enough breath left to thank her. I pay, grab my ticket, and push through the doors into the station. It's bigger than I thought, so I pick up my pace to the exit, one hand pressing against the stitch in my side.

There's a fifty-fifty chance I'm going to hurl before I get on this boat.

When I reach the dock there's hardly anyone on it, just a few people waving at the ferry. A guy in a white shirt and dark pants is standing at the entrance of a walkway connecting the dock to the boat. He checks his watch and grasps a chain that dangles to the ground, fastening it across the two posts on either side of the walkway. Then he looks up and catches sight of me lunging toward him with my ticket outstretched.

*Don't do it,* I think. *Don't be a dick.*

He takes my ticket and unclips the chain. "Made it in the nick of time. Bon voyage, son."

Not a dick. Thank Christ.

I stagger up the pier and through the ferry's entrance, almost groaning with relief at the air-conditioned chill that greets me, and collapse in a bright-blue seat. I dig inside my bag for my water bottle, unscrew the top, and drain almost the entire thing in three long gulps. Then I pour the rest over my head.

Note to self: take up running this summer, because that was pathetic.

My fellow passengers all ignore me. They look primed for vacation, wearing baseball caps, flip-flops, and T-shirts with what I've come to realize is the unofficial Gull Cove Island logo: a circle with the silhouette of a gull inside and the letters *GCI* above it.

I keep still until my breathing returns to normal, then pull a Gull Cove Island tourist brochure out of my bag and flip to the transportation section in the middle. The ride is two hours and twenty minutes, and we'll pass Martha's Vineyard and Nantucket along the way. Gull Cove Island is smaller than either of them— which is saying something, since Nantucket is only fourteen miles long—and what the brochure calls "more remote and rugged."

Translation: fewer hotels and worse beaches.

I put the brochure away and survey the crowd. It looks like people are just leaving their luggage wherever, so I stuff my bag under my seat and get up. Might as well check the place out. I head for a staircase next to the snack bar, and my stomach instantly growls. I haven't eaten anything since breakfast and that was five hours ago.

Upstairs looks almost the same, with a staircase that goes to the top deck. That's open air, and everyone is clustered around the railings that overlook the ocean. It's overcast, threatening rain, but the air that was choking me onshore is crisp and salt-scented here. Seagulls circle above the boat with noisy cries, water stretches smoothly on every side of us, and for the first time in a month this doesn't seem like the worst idea I've ever had.

I'm more thirsty than I am hungry, so I decide to head back downstairs and get something to drink from the snack bar. I'm preoccupied, digging for my wallet to check how much cash I have on me, and almost bump into somebody who's heading up as I'm going down.

"Watch it!" says a girl's voice.

"Sorry," I mumble. Then I look up and gulp. "I mean, hey. Hi."

At first, all that registers is that this girl is drop-dead gorgeous. Dark hair, dark eyes, and full lips curved in a smirk that should probably be annoying but isn't. She's wearing a bright-red sundress and sandals, with sunglasses holding back her hair and a large, man-sized watch on one wrist, and—*oh*.

Oh, shit. I can't believe I blanked for a second. I know exactly who this is.

"You mean *hi*?" she asks. The smirk gets bigger. Possibly a little flirty. "Are you sure?"

I step back, forgetting I'm on a staircase, and nearly fall. I take a few seconds to consider my predicament while I grasp the rail to steady myself. I was hoping to avoid this particular person, at least until we got to Gull Cove. But now that I've almost literally run into her, I guess there's no going back.

"I'm sure," I say. "Hello, Milly."

She blinks in surprise. Behind us, someone clears his throat. "Excuse me," calls a gruff voice. "I'm trying to get downstairs." I turn to see an old guy in plaid shorts and a Red Sox baseball cap hovering behind me, one foot on the top step.

"Hang on. We're going up," I say, and reverse course. He steps aside to let me pass, and I lean against the wall of an alcove beside the staircase.

Milly follows, her hands on her hips. "Do I know you?"

Crap. I can't believe I was just checking her out. I don't think she minded, either. Awkward. "Yeah. Well, sort of. I'm Jonah." I hold out my hand. Her eyes widen, and she doesn't take it. "Jonah Story."

"Jonah Story," she repeats.

"Your cousin," I clarify.

Milly stares at me for a beat. Then she takes my hand so gingerly that her fingers barely graze mine. "*You're* Jonah?"

"Yes."

"Really?"

I let annoyance edge into my voice. It's my trademark, after all. "Do you have auditory issues? I've responded affirmatively multiple times."

Her eyes narrow. "Oh, *there* you are. I got a little confused by this whole"—she waves a hand near my face—"J. Crew model look you have going. I have to admit, that's unexpected.

31

I thought you'd look how you talk." I'm not going to rise to the bait and ask her what she means, but she keeps going without prompting. "Like a constipated gnome."

Points for creativity, I guess. "Nice to meet you too."

Her nose wrinkles as she looks me up and down. "Why are you all sweaty?"

I resist the urge to sniff myself to see if I smell. From the look on her face, I probably do. "I don't see how that's any of your business."

"Why are you even here? I thought you didn't see any point in *arriving in tandem*?"

I fold my arms, wishing I'd never come upstairs. Talking to her is wearing me out. I'm not sure how much longer I can keep it up. "My schedule changed."

Milly clucks her tongue a few times before lifting her hand in a beckoning motion. "Come on, then. You might as well meet Aubrey." I'm not in the mood for more people, and it must show on my face because she rolls her eyes and says, "Trust me, she's not going to enjoy it any more than you are."

"I don't think—"

"Hey!" Another voice breaks in. "There you are! Thought I'd lost you." It's a girl my age wearing a short-sleeved blue hoodie and gym shorts, her blond hair pulled back into a low ponytail. She has serious freckles, the kind that cover not just her nose and cheeks, but her entire body. I've seen her face throughout the news clippings in my folder, although she's usually wearing a swim cap. Aubrey's smile, aimed at Milly, widens when she notices me. "Oh, sorry. Didn't mean to interrupt."

"You're not," Milly says quickly. She gestures toward me

like she's a game show host giving away a prize nobody wants. "Guess what? *This* is Jonah."

Aubrey's brows shoot up. She glances uncertainly between Milly and me. "Really?"

Milly shrugs. "Apparently."

Aubrey's eyes are still ping-ponging between us. Even when she's not smiling, there's something friendly about her face. And honest. She looks like she'd be a terrible liar. "Are you guys messing with me?"

Time for me to talk again. "Sorry I don't splash my face all over social media like a mindless lemming desperate for attention."

"Oh." Aubrey nods. "Okay, then. Hi, Jonah." She looks back at Milly, whose eyes keep wandering to the ocean like she's weighing the pros and cons of pushing me overboard. "You don't really look like a Story."

"I look like my mother," I tell her.

Aubrey sighs and brushes a strand of windswept pale hair out of one eye. "Me too." Then she takes a deep breath and steadies herself, like she's about to dive into a frigid pool. "Come on. Let's go downstairs and sit for a while. Might as well get to know one another."


Half an hour later, Milly's had it. I don't know her well enough to be sure, but I'd bet everything I have that she's taken an instant, profound dislike to me.

Mission accomplished, I guess.

"I'm getting a drink," she says, rising from our window

booth on the first floor. "Aubrey, do you want anything? Or to come with?"

I expect Aubrey to take off too, but she's distracted. Every once in a while—like right now—her entire face droops as she stares intently at her phone. She's looking for something, and she keeps getting disappointed. "No thanks," she murmurs. Milly heads for the stairs, and silence descends as Aubrey swipes methodically at her phone. Mine buzzes in my pocket, and I dig it out to a text from a contact I've saved as JT.

*How's everything going?*

Every muscle in my body tenses as I reply, *Fine.*

*That's all you have to say?*

*I could say fuck you,* I think. But all I type back is *Yep. Gotta go.*

I ignore the buzz of a new text and stuff the phone back into my pocket as Aubrey lifts both hands to tug on her ponytail, pulling it tighter. "Sorry about Genius Camp," she says.

"What?"

She tilts her head. "That's what Milly and I call that science camp you wanted to go to. Do you think you'll get another chance? Like next summer, maybe? Or is that too late?"

"Too late," I say. "The whole point was to enhance the college application process." Without Milly here, I can't inject as much disdain into my words as I want to. Being sarcastic to Aubrey feels like kicking a puppy.

"That's too bad. I wasn't sure you'd come, to be honest. You seemed pretty determined not to."

"Turns out I didn't have a choice."

"I guess none of us did," Aubrey says. She crosses a leg over one knee and jiggles her foot, staring out the window at the darkening sky. It's thirty-five miles from Hyannis to Gull Cove Island, and it looks like we're headed for stormier weather. "What's your dad like? *Uncle Anders.*" She says the name like he's a movie character. "I think I last saw you guys when I was five? I can't remember him at all."

"He's—intense."

Aubrey's blue eyes take on a faraway expression. "My dad talks about yours the least of anyone. Like, he probably has the most in common with Aunt Allison, and he seems to feel sort of protective about Uncle Archer, but your dad? He barely mentions him. I don't know why."

I swallow and lick my lips. I'm on unsteady ground, and not sure how much to say. "My dad . . . he was always kind of the odd man out, you know? I think he felt that way, at least."

"Are you guys close?"

*To that asshole? No way.* I swallow the truth and try for a nonchalant shrug. "Ish. You know how it is."

"I do. Especially lately." Rain starts spattering against the window next to us, and Aubrey cups her hand against it to peer outside. "Do you think she'll meet us at the dock?"

"Milly?" I ask. "What, you think she found better company till then?" Here's hoping.

"No," Aubrey says, laughing a little. "Gran."

The laugh catches me off guard. Aubrey and I are getting comfortable with one another, and that's not good. In the words of every reality contestant ever: *I'm not here to make friends.* "Yeah, right," I snort. "She never even bothered to send a follow-up letter."

Aubrey's face clouds. "You too? I wrote her six times and heard nothing."

"I wrote zero times. Same result."

"It's so *cold*." Aubrey shivers a little, but I know she's not talking about the temperature. "I don't understand. It's bad enough that the first time she ever contacted us, she made a *job offer*. Like we're hired help instead of family. But then she can't even be bothered to stay in touch? What's the point of all this, if she's not interested in getting to know us?"

"Cheap labor." I mean it as a joke, but Aubrey's mouth just turns down further. I'm about to make an excuse to leave when I catch a flash of red on the stairs: Milly's back. That should get me moving even faster, but for some reason I stay put.

"Here you go, cousins." Milly is balancing four plastic cups: one full of clear liquid and garnished with a lime wedge, and three that are empty except for ice. She settles next to Aubrey and starts evening out the cups, pouring the full one into the other three until it's empty. When she's finished, she hands one cup to me and one to Aubrey. "Cheers to—I don't know. Finally meeting the mysterious Mildred, I guess." We all clink cups, and Aubrey takes a long swig of hers.

"Ugh!" She spits it right back out. "Milly, what *is* this?"

Milly hands her a napkin, unfazed. She plucks the lime garnish from the empty cup and squeezes juice into each of ours. "Sorry, forgot the lime. A gin and tonic."

"Seriously?" Aubrey grimaces and sets her cup down on the table. "Thanks, but I don't drink. How'd you get alcohol?"

"I have my ways." Milly watches as a line of people stream down the staircase from the upper deck to escape the rainstorm, then focuses her attention on Aubrey and me. "So. Now that we've covered all the surface stuff, let's get real. What *aren't* we telling each other?"

My throat gets dry. "Huh?"

Milly shrugs. "This entire family is built on secrets, right? It's the Story legacy. You guys probably have some juicy ones." She tilts her cup toward me. "Spill."

I glance at Aubrey, who's gone pale beneath her freckles. I feel a muscle in my jaw start to twitch. "I don't have any secrets," I say.

"Me either," Aubrey says quickly. Her hands are clenched tight in her lap, and she looks like she's about to either throw up or cry. I was right; she's a terrible liar. Even worse than I am.

Milly isn't interested in going after Aubrey, though. She pivots toward me and leans forward, her big watch sliding down her arm as she cups her chin in her hand. "Everybody has secrets," she says, taking a sip of her drink. "That's nondebatable. The only question is whether you're keeping your own, or someone else's."

A bead of sweat gathers on my forehead, and I resist the urge to wipe it away as I gulp down half my drink. I don't like gin, but *any port in a storm* seems like a solid metaphor right now. I try for a half-bored, half-irritated expression. "Can't it be both?"

Rain lashes the window behind Milly as her eyes lock on mine. "With you, Jonah?" she asks, raising one perfectly arched brow. "I'm guessing it can."

# CHAPTER FOUR

## MILLY

"Doesn't look like much, does it?" Jonah asks.

I steal a glance at him across Aubrey. The rain has cleared, and we're on the upper deck watching our approach to Gull Cove Island. Jonah rests his forearms against the rail and leans forward, the wind tousling wavy, dark brown hair that's halfway between Aubrey's blond and my near black. The pointed chin I remember has morphed into a square jaw, and braces did him a world of good. Not that he smiles much.

"I think it's pretty!" Aubrey says, raising her voice to be heard over the roar of the ferry's motor. The boat pitches sharply to one side, sending a spray of white foam into the air. I hold tightly to the rail with one hand and use the other to indulge in a nervous habit my mother hates—bringing the knuckle of my thumb between my teeth. My damp skin tastes like salt, but it's better than the exhaust-filled air we're breathing.

"Me too," I say.

My words are automatic, a reflexive desire to disagree with Jonah, but he's right. Even from a distance the island looks flat and unremarkable, surrounded by a strip of pale-yellow beach melting into an ocean that's almost the same shade of gray as the dense, low-hanging clouds that surround us. Tiny white houses dot the shoreline against a backdrop of short trees, and the only spot of color is a squat tan lighthouse striped with jaunty blue.

"It's so small," Aubrey says. "Hope we don't get island fever."

I pull my knuckle from my mouth and lower my arm, feeling the heavy weight of my watch slide to my wrist as I do. My grandfather's battered old Patek Philippe is the only memento my grandmother passed along to my mother before she cut off contact. No matter how many times Mom's tried to have it repaired, the watch refuses to tell time. It always reads three o'clock, so twice a day—like about now, probably—it's right. "Maybe Mildred will work us so hard that we won't even notice," I say.

Aubrey glances at me. "You call her Mildred?"

"Yeah. What about you?"

"Gran. My dad always says 'your gran,' so I guess I just went with that." She turns toward Jonah. "What do you call her?"

"Nothing," he says briefly.

We're silent for a few minutes as the ferry continues its progress toward shore. The white houses get bigger, the yellow strip of sand more defined, and soon we're passing so close to the lighthouse that I can see people walking around its base. The dock is crowded with boats, most of them much smaller than the one we're on, and we neatly slot into a space between two of them. "Welcome to Gull Cove Island!" the captain calls over the intercom as the noise of the engine abruptly stops.

"It's packed," Aubrey says nervously, scanning the crowd on the dock below us.

"Tourist trap central," Jonah says, turning from the rail and toward the staircase. "Have you looked up how much rooms cost at Gull Cove Resort? People are out of their minds." He shakes his head. "The beaches are way better on Martha's Vineyard or Nantucket, but somehow being the worst, smallest island has become a selling point. Because it's 'off the beaten path.'"

When we near the ferry's exit, Jonah veers off to one side and hauls a battered duffel bag out from under a bench. "Where's your stuff?" he asks Aubrey and me.

"We checked it when we came on board," I say, eyeing his bag. "Is that all you brought?"

Jonah slings the duffel over one shoulder. "I don't need much."

We enter the stream of people leaving the ferry, following the narrow walkway from the boat to the dock. It's a full-on vacation crowd; despite the cloudy weather everyone is decked out in shorts, sunglasses, and baseball hats. My red dress looks completely out of place, even though I wore it for a reason. It was my mother's in high school, one of the few things she held on to that I can get away with wearing today. Putting it on felt like getting a subtle dig in at my grandmother for bringing us all this way without acknowledging her children first. *They still exist, Mildred, whether you want to admit it or not.*

The ferry walkway exits onto a wide cobblestone path flanked by shingled buildings in alternating shades of white and gray. As soon as we reach the road I take a deep breath, then startle a little as I smell honeysuckle mixed with the salty air. Mom's signature fragrance, but I've never smelled it live before.

A row of luggage tents on wheels line one side of the cobble-stone path. Aubrey and I find number 243, as we were instructed when a valet took our suitcases, and open the flap. "Here they are," Aubrey says, sounding relieved as she pulls out a suitcase and backpack.

I go in for mine. Behind me, Jonah lets out a snort of disbelief as I extract two large rolling suitcases, a smaller carry-on, and a bulging laptop bag. "That can't all be yours," he says. When I don't reply, he adds, "Did you pack your entire closet?"

Not even close, but he doesn't have to know that. Or that the smaller suitcase is nothing but shoes. "We're going to be here for two months," I say.

Jonah narrows his eyes as he takes in my suitcases. They're Tumi with pearlized aluminum casing, and I suppose if you didn't know my mother bought them secondhand on eBay, they might look a little ostentatious. Especially in the middle of this shorts-and-T-shirt crowd. Gull Cove Island visitors have money—lots of it—but they don't flaunt it. That's part of the alleged charm of this place. "Guess Aunt Allison is doing all right," Jonah says.

"Oh please," I snap. "You were going to go to some fancy-ass science camp all summer, so don't judge me for bringing wardrobe options."

"Except I couldn't afford it," Jonah says. Something almost like anger flashes across his face before he composes his features into their usual expression of half-boredom, half-disdain. "And now I get to be here instead."

I pause before the reflexive response *lucky us* crosses my lips. I don't know a lot about my cousins' financial situations. I know Aubrey's mom is a nurse and her dad has spent the past ten years trying to write another book, so they're probably comfortable but not rolling in it. Jonah's parents' situation is murkier. Uncle Anders is a financial consultant, supposedly, but the kind who works for himself instead of an actual company. A couple of weeks ago, when I was trying to find any information I could about Jonah's family online, I stumbled across a short article in the *Providence Journal* about Uncle Anders in which a disgruntled former client called him "the Bernie Madoff of Rhode Island."

I didn't know who that was, so I had to look him up. Apparently Bernie Madoff was a financial adviser who went to jail after cheating thousands of investors in a giant Ponzi scheme. I'd felt a shocked little thrill then—our family had always been strange, but never *criminal*—until I kept reading. Ultimately, even though a couple of former clients reported him for fraud, all that could be proved was that Uncle Anders gave bad financial advice. It wasn't a big enough story to make the New York papers, so my mother hadn't seen it. She didn't seem especially shocked when I told her. "Nobody with an ounce of common sense would ask Anders to help manage their money," she'd said.

"Why?" I asked. "I thought he was supposed to be brilliant."

"He is. But there's only one person whose interests Anders has ever looked out for, and that's Anders himself."

"What about Aunt Victoria? Or Jonah?" I'd asked.

Mom's lips had thinned. "I'm talking about business, not family." But from the look on her face, she didn't think much of those relationships, either. Which might have something to do with the bitter expression Jonah's wearing right now.

Aubrey gazes around at the teeming crowd surrounding us. "No Gran," she says sadly, like she honestly expected Mildred to be waiting for us. "Should we just grab a cab?"

"I guess. I don't see any, though." I squint against the emerging sun and pull my sunglasses from the top of my head, settling the large tortoiseshell frames across my nose.

"Allison." It takes the name being repeated a few times—plus Jonah's furrowed brow—before I look for the source. An old man, white-haired and frail, stands beside me, with his watery brown eyes fastened on my face. "Allison," he repeats in a low, wavering voice. "You came back. Why did you come back?"

"I . . ." I glance between the man and my cousins, at a loss for words. People have told me I look like my mother—"surprisingly like her," they sometimes add with a sideways glance at my dad—but I've never been mistaken for her before. Is it the dress? The sunglasses? Or is this guy just senile?

"Does Mildred know?" the man says, sounding agitated. "She wouldn't like this, Allison. She wouldn't like it at all."

The back of my neck prickles. "I'm not Allison," I say, pulling off my sunglasses. The old man startles and takes a step back, the heel of his shoe catching on a cobblestone. He nearly stumbles, but Aubrey darts forward lightning-quick and catches hold of his arm.

"You okay there?" she asks. He doesn't reply, still looking at me as though he's seen a ghost, and she adds, "It sounds like you know our grandmother? Mildred Story? This is Milly, Allison's daughter, and I'm Aubrey. Adam Story is my father." She gestures toward Jonah with her free hand. "And this is Jonah, he—"

"Adam," the man says faintly. "Adam is here?"

"Oh no," Aubrey says, smiling brightly. "Just me. I'm his daughter."

The man looks forlorn and lost, one hand fumbling at the empty pocket of his cardigan like he just realized he left something important behind. "Adam had seeds of greatness, didn't he? But he wasted them. Foolish boy. Could've changed it all with a word."

Aubrey's smile slips. "Could have changed what?"

"Granddad!" A harried voice floats our way, and I turn to see a girl around our age striding toward us. She's short and muscular, with brown skin, freckles, and a cloud of dark hair. Both of her wrists are piled high with braided leather bracelets. "I told you to wait in front of Sweetfern! Parking was impossible because of all the damn tourists—" She pauses as she takes in the three of us surrounded by suitcases, with Aubrey still propping up her grandfather. "I mean *new arrivals*. Is he all right?" she asks, a note of anxiety creeping into her voice.

The man blinks slowly a few times, like he's trying to bring her into focus. "Fine, Hazel. Just fine," he murmurs. "A little tired, is all."

Hazel takes hold of her grandfather's arm, and Aubrey steps back. "I think we startled him," she says apologetically, even though it was the other way around. "He seems to know our grandmother."

"Really?" Hazel asks. "Who's your grandmother?"

"Um, Mildred Story?" Aubrey says it like she's not sure the name will register, but the girl's eyes immediately widen. Her face, which had been tense and preoccupied, breaks into a wide smile.

"No way! You guys are Storys? What are you doing here?"

"Working at our grandmother's resort for the summer," Aubrey says.

Hazel's gaze bounces between the three of us with avid interest. "Wow. Is this your first time on Gull Cove Island?" Aubrey and I nod, and she squeezes her grandfather's arm. "Granddad, how could you not tell me the Story grandkids were spending the summer here? You must've known, right?"

"No," the old man says, plucking at the pocket of his cardigan again.

"Maybe you forgot." She turns to us and adds in a lower voice, "Granddad has early-stage dementia. Sometimes he's fine, but other times he gets really confused. He's friends with Mrs. Story, though, and he was her family doctor, so he knew your parents really well. I'm Hazel Baxter-Clement, by the way. My grandfather is Dr. Fred Baxter."

I recognize the name instantly. "Of course! My mother used to say he must've been the only doctor alive who still made house calls."

Hazel grins. "Well, for *your* family."

"My dad said the same thing," Aubrey says. "And also that your grandfather got him playing lacrosse again in high school after he'd injured his knee."

We all look at Jonah to see whether he'll weigh in with a memory, but he just stares at his phone, rude as ever. Then he thrusts the screen toward Aubrey and me. "Yelp says we should go to Hurley Street to find a cab."

"Hurley is right around the corner," Hazel says, pointing to our left. I grasp the handle of my carry-on as she adds, "Hey, so this might be kind of weird and random when we just met, but—I actually did a school project that included your family last semester. I'm a history major at BU, and my independent study is about early colonists whose descendants are thriving in the information age. My professor really liked the initial write-up and wants me to expand on it next fall. Is there any chance I could interview you guys?" She smiles ingratiatingly when none of us respond right away. "Total softball questions, I promise."

"Um." I put my sunglasses back on to avoid Hazel's gaze. Even softball questions are loaded when you're a Story. "We might be kind of busy for a while."

"I understand. Could I give you my number in case you find the time? Or if you just want to know what's fun to do on the island. I'd be happy to show you around." She looks at Jonah, who still has his phone out, and quickly recites her number. I can't tell whether he actually adds it, or just pretends to.

"Enjoy your first day," Hazel says. "Come on, Granddad, let's get some ice cream."

Dr. Baxter has been quietly leaning on his granddaughter's arm while we talk, but Hazel's voice seems to shake him out of his reverie. He focuses on me again, a frown tugging down the corners of his mouth. "You shouldn't have come, Allison."

Hazel clucks her tongue. "Granddad, that's not Allison. You're confused." She offers us a smile and wave before steering him toward the café behind us. "See you around."

Aubrey stares after them as they disappear into the café. "Well, that was strange," she says. Then she hitches her backpack over her shoulder, grabs the handle of her suitcase, and starts toward Hurley Street. I pause, eyeing my suitcases, until Jonah heaves a deep sigh and grabs hold of the two big ones.

"Can you handle the rest, princess?" he asks over his shoulder as he drags them across the cobblestones.

"Yes," I mutter ungraciously. I would've thanked him without the princess comment.

\* \* \*

46

"Whoa," Jonah says when our taxi driver pulls to a stop.

Gull Cove Resort is on the opposite side of the island from the ferry dock, or we never could've missed it. The architecture is Victorian mansion meets modern luxury beach spa, which works a lot better than you'd think. It's also the biggest building I've seen here so far, four stories high and I don't know how many rooms across. The paint is pristine white, the flowering shrubs are perfectly shaped and bursting with color, and the grass is impossibly green. Even the driveway feels smooth and newly paved.

"Enjoy your stay," the driver says, getting out of the cab so he can help pull our suitcases from the trunk. "Gonna be a long one, huh?"

I hand him a ten-dollar bill for our seven-dollar ride. "You could say that."

Aubrey is consulting her phone. "We're supposed to pick up registration packets in Edward Franklin's office," she reports. "First floor, near the lobby."

"Let's leave this crap here," Jonah says, dragging all the suitcases and duffels off to one side. He rolls his eyes at my dubious expression. "Oh, come on. Rooms here start at eight hundred dollars a night. Nobody's taking your stuff."

"Shut up," I grumble, grabbing my laptop bag and brushing past him toward the front door. Every time Jonah opens his mouth, I wonder if this entire summer was a mistake.

A smiling concierge in the spacious, airy lobby directs us to Edward Franklin's office. We pass the elevators and turn down a narrow hallway with plush carpeting. I'm so busy looking at the framed photographs hanging on the walls—eager for a glimpse of my grandmother, or maybe even my mother, among the smiling guests—that I nearly bump into Aubrey when she stops short. "Hello?" she calls, rapping on a door. "Is this where we get orientation stuff?"

"It is," calls a cheerful voice. "Come in, come in."

We step into a small office dominated by a large walnut desk. A smiling man sits behind it, surrounded by haphazardly stacked folders. He has Draco Malfoy white-blond hair swept to one side, and he's wearing a crisp white shirt and a tie patterned with bright-blue fish. "Hello, and please excuse the mess," he says. "We're a little disorganized at the moment."

"You must be Edward," I say.

It's a logical assumption, given that he's sitting in Edward's office. But Friendly Draco shakes his head. "I am not. I'm Carson Fine, head of hospitality for Gull Cove Resort. Doing double duty until we find Edward's replacement."

"His what?" I frown. "He's not here?"

"He left two days ago," Carson says. "Bit of an abrupt departure, but don't worry. The summer hire program continues without him. I just need your names, please."

"Milly Story-Takahashi, Aubrey Story, and Jonah Story," I say.

Carson's hands pause over his keyboard. "Really? Did you guys know you have the same last name as the resort's owner? What a coincidence. I don't think we've ever had another Story here before, and now we've got three of you." His blue eyes crinkle. "Too bad you're not related, huh?"

Jonah clears his throat as Aubrey and I exchange startled glances. How can this guy not know who we are? It seems like the sort of thing people would talk about here, even if they're not running the summer hire program. "We *are* related," I say. "We're her grandchildren."

"Right, wouldn't that be nice," Carson chuckles. When no one else cracks a smile, his vanishes. "Wait. Are you serious?"

"Didn't Edward tell you?" I ask. "We've been talking to him about it since April." And then, because I feel a sudden urge to prove myself, I pull a folder full of our correspondence out of my laptop bag. "It's all here, if you want to see."

Carson takes the folder, but barely glances through it before handing it back. "He never said a word. I can't believe him! Oh, Edward, you utter incompetent. If you hadn't already quit, I'd fire you. Let me see if he left some notes." He taps furiously at the keyboard while we stand in uncomfortable silence. Then his expression brightens. "Okay, I'm not seeing any background, but the good news is, your grandmother is actually at the resort as we speak. We just finished renovating the ballroom for the Summer Gala, and she's conducting a site visit. So if you can hold tight for just a few minutes, I'll bring her right by."

Aubrey's eyes widen in alarm. "What, now?"

Carson jumps to his feet with the energy of someone determined to right a grievous hospitality wrong. "No time like the present. Be right back!" He darts into the hallway, leaving the three of us standing awkwardly around his desk.

I swipe suddenly damp palms against the skirt of my dress. I thought I was prepared to meet my grandmother, but now that it seems imminent, I'm—not. My mind goes blank, and the room falls silent except for tinny Muzak piping from a speaker somewhere. After a few seconds I recognize a familiar chord, and almost laugh out loud. It's "Africa," by the band Toto, and it was my mother's favorite song growing up. The only family video she has, which I've watched dozens of times, is of her and my uncles singing "Africa" on the beach when they were kids.

The music seems like a strangely fitting backdrop as footsteps approach, accompanied by Carson's eager voice. "So lucky that I caught you before you left, Mrs. Story!"

I hear Aubrey gulp and then—there she is. Standing directly in front of me for the first time in my life. The elusive, eccentric, mysterious Mildred Story.

My grandmother.

I take her in bit by bit: First the jewelry, because of course I would notice that. Mildred is wearing a double strand of lustrous gray pearls, striking against her sharp black suit, and matching drop earrings. Her heels are impressively high for a woman in her seventies, and she's topped off the outfit with a small netted hat. She looks like she's going to some elder statesman's funeral. Her purse is gleaming black crocodile, with a distinctive gold lock on the front. I've seen enough fake Birkins in New York to recognize the twenty-thousand-dollar real deal.

Mildred's famously high cheekbones have softened with age, but she's still as impeccably made up as she was in every photo I've seen of her as a younger woman. The most eye-catching thing about her, though, is her hair. It's tied back in a low bun, and is such a pure, snowy white that I can't believe it's her natural color.

Her gaze flits between Aubrey and Jonah—neither of whom look anything like their fathers—before settling on me with a spark of recognition. "So it's true," she says in a low, throaty voice. "You really are here."

I have to fight off the irrational urge to curtsy. "Thank you for inviting us."

Mildred inhales sharply, her brows drawing together. "Inviting you," she repeats. We stare at one another until Carson nervously clears his throat, and our grandmother's face transforms into a smooth, expressionless mask. "Indeed," she says, transferring her Birkin from one arm to the other. "You must be exhausted after your travel. Carson, please bring them to the dormitories. I'll have my assistant reach out to arrange a more fitting time for us to talk."

Over her shoulder, Carson looks crushed. "Right, of course," he says. "I'm so sorry. I should have taken them there first thing."

"Please don't trouble yourself," Mildred says coolly. "It's perfectly fine."

But I know better. In the seconds before my grandmother regained her composure, one of my tangled thoughts separated from the rest with total, piercing clarity.

She had absolutely no idea that we were coming.

## ALLISON, AGE 18

### JUNE 1996

The ferry approached from the opposite side of Gull Cove Island, so when Allison sat on the upper deck of Catmint House, all she saw in front of her was smooth water melting into blue sky. But the buzzing activity around the house made it clear: the summer season was about to begin, and her brothers would be home soon.

Their mother had wanted to throw a party for Adam and Anders's return, but before she'd even started planning, she'd become overwhelmed at the amount of work involved. So her assistant, Theresa, had stepped in like the quietly efficient savior she'd become ever since Allison's father died six months ago. Now a small army of people was setting up for the party tonight: stringing fairy lights on every available tree, building a temporary stage for the live band, and constructing white tents along the side lawn where guests would dine on lobster, mussels, and the Gull Cove Island specialty of quail eggs à la russe.

Allison couldn't see the beach below, but she knew a crew was down there getting ready for a fireworks show that would put the Fourth of July in most major American cities to shame.

"Think we'll get this kind of homecoming when we come back from college?"

Allison's younger brother, Archer, flopped onto the patio chair beside her with a grin. His legs dangled awkwardly off the end; at seventeen, Archer had gone through his growth spurt late, and had only recently reached the same six-foot height as Adam. He still didn't know what to do with his newly long limbs.

"Well, it's not like Mother did this for Adam last summer," Allison pointed out. Their oldest brother had started at Harvard two years ago, and the next oldest, Anders, had joined him there the past fall. Allison was breaking family tradition by going to NYU in September. "I think it's just that things are different this year."

"I know." Archer hunched his broad shoulders, looking suddenly much smaller and younger. "It's weird, isn't it, how the house can be so full right now but still . . . empty."

Allison's throat tightened. "It doesn't feel like a Story party without Father here," she said, and Archer smiled ruefully.

"Especially since they're serving mussels as a main dish. God, he hated those." Archer deepened his voice as Allison joined in his imitation of their father: "Snot of the sea." They both huffed out almost laughs, and Archer added, "I mean, he wasn't wrong. You can put all the butter and cream and salt or whatever you want on those things, but they're still disgusting."

Most days since their father's death, Allison felt as though the void left by his larger-than-life presence was unfillable; the kind of loss she'd ache with her entire life. But every once in a while—usually in a quiet moment like this with Archer—she could imagine a time in the future when the memories became more sweet than bitter. Part of her wanted to keep reminiscing, but she'd learned over the past few months that you could only stay so far ahead of grief. If she let herself wallow before Mother's big night, it would be hard to put on the kind of bright face expected of her.

Archer seemed to be thinking the same thing. He leaned back in his chair, clasping his hands behind his head and crossing his legs at the ankle, the new position signaling an abrupt change of subject. "On a scale of one to ten," he said, "how much more obnoxious do you think Harvard has made Anders?"

"Twenty," Allison said, and they both laughed.

"Probably. It'll be good to see Adam, though," Archer said. He worshiped their oldest brother to a degree Allison didn't quite share, but she was still happy at the thought of him coming home. There was no one on earth who could make their mother smile like Adam. "I talked to him right before he left, and he said he's down for Rob Valentine's party next Saturday. We just have to convince Anders."

"I never said *I* was going," Allison reminded him. All the Story children had attended boarding school outside Boston since they were twelve years old, and only Archer had maintained—and grown—the friendships he'd made at Gull Cove Elementary School. For the past few years, he'd spent every school vacation trying to convince his siblings to accompany him to one party or another. None of them blended as well as he did.

"C'mon, it'll be fun," Archer urged.

Allison rolled her eyes. "Did you learn nothing from the Kayla-Matt debacle?"

"That's ancient history," Archer said.

"Not to Anders." Allison straightened suddenly, tilting her head. "Is Mother calling me?"

"I don't think—" Archer started, pausing when a faint but clear "Allison!" floated toward them from inside the house. "I stand corrected. Your supersonic ears strike again."

Allison got to her feet and crossed the patio, opening the sliding glass door just as their mother stepped into the connected parlor. "Oh, Allison, thank goodness. There you are."

Mother was already dressed for the evening in a white sheath, silver sandals, and canary diamond jewelry. She'd pulled her dark hair back into a loose chignon, a few well-placed wisps softening the sharp planes of her face. Her lips were signature red, her smoky eye shadow as flawless as ever. You'd have to look closely to notice the tightness in her expression. Mildred Story wasn't a natural hostess; she'd always relied on her husband's gregariousness to get her through social gatherings. "Could you go to the tents and let me know what you think about the flowers?" she asked. "Theresa ordered them from the new place on Hurley Street—Brewer Floral, I think? Something like that. We've never used them before, and I'm worried she only chose them because Matt works there now. I just had a look at the arrangements, and they feel a touch unbalanced to me."

"Unbalanced?" Allison asked.

"Too heavy on the calla lilies," Mother said. She twisted her hands together, looking down at them with a frown. That was another new anxiety; Mother had recently become convinced that her hands betrayed the fact that she was nearing fifty in a way her face still didn't. Allison pried them gently apart with a reassuring squeeze.

"I'm sure they're beautiful. But I'll take a look," Allison said, slipping through the door and closing it behind her.

She knew what her father would say if he were here: "Your job at this moment, Allison, no matter what your actual opinion might be, is to reassure your mother that each vase contains precisely the right amount of calla lilies." This, she could do.

She padded on bare feet across the polished hardwood and marble floors of the house, stopping at the side entrance to slip on a pair of sandals she'd left by the door. The noise level was much higher when she stepped outside than it had been on the patio, voices mixing with the sounds of light construction and the occasional strum of a guitar from the band's sound check. The smell of honeysuckle was everywhere, wafting from the bushes that nestled against the side of Catmint House. Allison turned the corner and nearly bumped into two people standing side by side, surveying the sea of white tents in front of them.

"Hello, Allison." Her mother's lawyer, Donald Camden, put a hand out to steady her. "Where are you running off to?"

"Oh, well . . ." Allison trailed off as she took in Mother's assistant, Theresa Ryan, standing beside him. She couldn't very well say that she was here to make sure Theresa hadn't selected a subpar florist due to nepotism. "I just wanted to look around."

Theresa smiled warmly. She was a widow too, but unlike Mildred, Theresa wasn't afraid to show her age. She was gray-haired and a little plump, known for wearing simple dresses and comfortable shoes no matter the occasion. "Let me know what you think," Theresa said, lowering her voice to a conspiratorial tone as she put a hand on Allison's arm. "Between you and me, your mother's standards are a bit terrifying."

"Tell me about it," Allison said with a laugh, relieved at the excuse to poke around.

Allison felt her spine stiffening and her shoulders straightening as she walked across the lawn through the deferential path that opened when people recognized her. Usually she tried to blend into the background at her parents' parties, but tonight would be different. Her mother needed her to be a hostess, not a shy teenager.

When Allison stepped inside the nearest tent, she took a moment to appreciate Theresa's skills. Everything was beautiful: the crisp white tablecloths, the cushioned chairs with gauzy white bows tied across their backs, the shining silverware, the sparkling crystal, and, yes, the flowers. They stood in gleaming white vases at the center of each table, bursting with creamy roses, lime-green orchids, some sort of feathery succulent Allison couldn't identify, and striking magenta calla lilies.

She couldn't imagine anything more perfect.

"Meet with your approval, Allie?" asked a voice behind her.

Allison turned to see Theresa's son, Matt, wearing a Brewer Floral T-shirt, and all the carefully constructed poise she'd imagined for herself vanished. "Nobody calls me that," she blurted out.

"Too bad," Matt said. "It suits you. Maybe I can make it catch on." Allison remained tongue-tied until Matt added, "Seriously, is everything okay? My mom is freaking out about this party. If I have to return fifty floral arrangements, she might have a heart attack."

"They're beautiful," Allison said, and Matt wiped imaginary sweat from his brow.

"You just made her year."

Allison bit her lip to swallow a smile. Matt was cute, charming, and—despite his relationship to Theresa—currently persona non grata among the Story siblings. He'd been friendly enough with all of them until last Christmas, when he'd hooked up with Anders's on-again, off-again Gull Cove Island girlfriend, Kayla Dugas. Matt and Kayla's relationship barely lasted two months, but it was enough to turn Matt into Anders's sworn enemy for life. It had been a while, come to think of it, since Allison had heard Matt referred to as anything other than "fucking Matt Ryan."

"Anders is going to be here soon," she found herself saying, and Matt's smile dropped.

"Thanks for the tip," he said. "Better make myself scarce." He looked around at the glittering surroundings and added, "After all, it's not like I'm a guest or anything."

"No, don't . . . I didn't . . ." God. She hadn't meant to chase Matt off. She should have been mad at him on Anders's behalf, but the thing was, Anders put as much effort into being Kayla's boyfriend as he did everything else in life that wasn't directly about being Anders Story. In other words: minimal. And Matt was . . . Matt.

Matt gave her a crooked smile. "Hey, don't worry about it. My job here is done anyway, as long as you like the flowers." Then he stepped a little closer, blue eyes crinkling as they swept over her faded T-shirt and athletic shorts. "You wearing that tonight? I like it. Very GCI casual."

Allison knew he was kidding, but she still couldn't help saying, "My mother would die a thousand deaths and then come back to kill me."

Matt moved closer still. "Would she kill you if you had coffee with me next week?"

Wait. Was Matt Ryan asking her out? Allison opened her mouth to reply—with what, she had no idea—then closed it as a familiar face swam into focus at the tent's opening. Handsome, expectant, and a little bit arrogant. *Adam.* Her oldest brother had made it back from Boston, which meant Anders must be right behind him. So Allison straightened her shoulders once again, gave Matt her most practiced Story smile, and said, "I'm sure she wouldn't mind at all. Let's set that up sometime. But I have to go now. Please excuse me."

Abraham Story might not be here anymore, but Allison knew exactly what he'd say if he found her caught between her brothers and her crush.

*Family first, always.*

"Guys! You're back!" Allison called, stretching her arms out wide to greet her brothers.

# CHAPTER FIVE

## AUBREY

"How do I look?" Milly asks, half turning in front of her closet with one hand on her hip. Her long dark hair is loose, and she's wearing cropped white jeans and a floaty tank top patterned with vivid pink and silver flowers.

"Gorgeous," I say truthfully.

I run a hand over the threadbare green blanket covering my twin bed while I wait for my cousin to finish getting ready. The summer hire dorms aren't nearly as luxurious as the resort itself. Milly and I are sharing a small, bare room simply furnished with beds, built-in dressers topped with mirrors, and two desks with wooden chairs. Bathrooms are down the hallway, and if we want to watch big-screen television or sit on something with an actual cushion, we have to go to the common room. The space between our desks has been overtaken by Milly's suitcases, which wouldn't fit into her narrow closet.

Still, if all her clothes are like what she's wearing now, I can't blame her for bringing them. "I love that shirt," I say.

"Thanks. Baba bought it on that same trip to Japan when she got your gamaguchi," Milly says, carefully running a brush through her already-shining hair.

"That was really nice of her," I say. When we first got to our room and started unpacking, Milly handed me a gift from the grandmother she calls Baba. It was a beautiful little clasp bag with a pattern like blue waves, because, Milly said, "She knows you like to swim." That put a lump in my throat. My mother's parents are dead, so Gran is my only living grandparent. And yet, a woman I'm not even related to is a hundred times more thoughtful toward me.

It's been four days since that strange, awkward introduction in Carson Fine's office. As soon as Milly and I got to our dorm room, my cousin insisted that Gran didn't know we were coming. "Didn't you see her face?" she asked. "She was shocked."

"Well, yeah," I said. "She was unprepared. I'm sure she had something more formal in mind for our first meeting. But of course she knew we were coming, Milly. She invited us."

Milly sniffed. "*Someone* invited us. I'm not so sure it was her anymore."

"That makes zero sense," I replied, and I meant it. I assumed Milly was just being dramatic. But since then we've heard from Gran exactly once—a short, impersonal note to let us know she'd been called away to Boston on business. *I'll be in touch upon my return,* she wrote.

I still think Milly is overreacting, but . . . yeah, it's weird. Who brings their grandchildren to visit for the first time ever, and then takes off?

Milly's hairbrush strokes get more aggressive as she glares into her mirror. "Maybe Baba should've gotten us T-shirts that say 'My Other Grandmother Is a Bitch Who'll Stand You Up,' but she's not clairvoyant."

I can't help but snicker, which makes me feel guilty, so I quickly change the subject. "I wonder if Gran saw the article?" I say. On Sunday, the *Gull Cove Gazette* ran an article with the headline A NEW CHAPTER TO THE STORYS: GRANDCHILDREN RETURN TO GULL COVE. We're not sure who tipped them off. Milly thinks it was that Hazel girl from downtown, but I'm guessing Carson Fine. He's been treating us like island royalty ever since we arrived, offering us perks like use of the resort Jeep and giving us all the best shifts. I'm one of the lifeguards at a pool that opens at six a.m., but I've never had to be there before ten. Jonah and Milly work at two of the resort restaurants, and while I haven't talked to Jonah much since we arrived, I know for a fact that Milly barely works three hours a day.

Milly snorts. "Well, we know *someone* did."

Yesterday afternoon, creamy white envelopes appeared in our mailboxes. I thought it might be Gran again, but the note inside was something else entirely:

To: Aubrey Story, Jonah Story, and Milly Story-Takahashi

Donald S. Camden, Esq., requests the pleasure of your company at lunch Wednesday, June 30, 1:00 p.m.
 L'Etoile Restaurant
 RSVP to Melinda Cartwright
 mcartwright@camdenandassociates.com

"Oh my God," Milly said when we read it. "Donald Camden. He's going to banish us from the island, isn't he? Just like he did with our parents." Her voice dropped an octave. *You know what you did.*

"He can't do that," I'd protested weakly, but I'm honestly not sure. The longer we go without hearing from Gran, the less confident I am about anything. At least we'll find out soon, though. It's twelve-forty-five, and the car Donald Camden is sending for us should be arriving any minute.

Milly fastens on her second earring. "Let's talk about something more cheerful. How is your boyfriend? Is he pining away for you already?"

Instinctively, I pull my phone out of my pocket. Right before my plane took off from Portland last Friday, Thomas texted *Have a great summer!* with a GIF of rolling waves. It felt weirdly . . . final. I haven't heard from him since, even though I've been sending constant updates and left a couple of voice messages. I know there's a time difference, and he can't use his phone at his summer job, but still. "Thomas isn't really the pining type," I say.

My cousin darts a quick glance toward my reflection in her mirror, like she's weighing the pros and cons of a follow-up question, before picking up a tube of lip gloss. "Well, you have my permission to flirt with anyone in this . . . Tory program," she says, stumbling over the word.

"Towhee," I correct. That's what Gull Cove Resort calls those of us in the summer hire program who are still in high school. We have separate housing with resident assistants plus extra team-building activities—so far a beach bonfire party our first night, and a volleyball tournament yesterday. We even got T-shirts with TOWHEE emblazoned on the front in cursive letters, which I was wearing until a few minutes ago when I changed to go to lunch. Milly shoved hers in the bottom drawer of her dresser as soon as she got it.

Most of the Towhees don't really need to work. Jonah's roommate, Efram, is the son of an R&B star from the early aughts. Another guy's mother is a senator, and our next-door neighbor Brittany's parents developed the messaging app that my entire school uses. Almost everyone in the summer hire program is here for the experience, or the prestige, or a chance to get away from their families.

Milly frowns into the mirror. "I don't get that name. What's a Towhee?"

"It's a bird," I remind her. She must not have read the welcome packet as closely as I did. "It only shows up on Gull Cove Island in the summer."

"Cute," Milly says flatly.

I can already tell that Milly isn't the team-building type. But I am. I've been part of a team almost my whole life—lots of different sports until middle school, when I started focusing exclusively on swimming. Now, as I watch my cousin get ready, it hits me that even though the swim team and Thomas have been the twin pillars of my existence since I was thirteen, I feel miles away from either of them. And not just literally. The loneliness of that settles over my shoulders like a heavy blanket.

I stand and shake myself like I do before the start of a meet, trying to chase away my gloomy thoughts. "Should we get Jonah?"

"Let's not," Milly says dryly. "We'll see him soon enough."

"He's not as bad as I expected," I say, peering into the mirror above my dresser. My ponytail is still intact, so I'm good to go. I went through a brief phase of "getting ready" when I first started high school, until Thomas told me he couldn't tell the difference. "Every once in a while, he forgets to be rude."

Milly makes a face. "And then he remembers."

My phone buzzes and I look down hopefully, but it's just a message from my father. *Again.* Mom sent a string of texts earlier asking about the trip, my cousins, and the resort. She also told me she'd be staying with her sister "for a while." Dad, on the other hand, only sends variations on the same question:

*What's going on with your grandmother?*

I ignore the message and stuff my phone into my pocket. My entire life, I've dropped whatever I was doing to answer when my father calls. This time, he can wait.

The car that Donald Camden sends for us is a spacious Lincoln, but fitting three in the back would be tight. Jonah volunteers to take the front seat—and then, I suspect, has instant regrets when it turns out our driver is a chatterbox.

"You seen much of the island yet, or are they keeping you too busy for that?" he asks as we pull onto Ocean Avenue. It's the not-very-originally-named road that runs alongside some of the biggest beaches on Gull Cove Island.

Jonah just grunts, so I lean forward. "Well, we've only been here four days," I say. "We've gone to the beach closest to the resort, and we've been downtown a couple of times."

"Did you notice anything missing?" he asks, in the tone of someone about to reveal a delightful secret. Before I can reply, he adds, "Not a single chain store or restaurant. And don't think they haven't tried. Starbucks, especially. But we're big supporters of local business here."

Jonah, who's been staring at his phone, revives briefly. "That's great," he says, with more enthusiasm than he's shown for anything so far.

Milly pokes the back of his seat. "Do you hate Starbucks as much as you hate . . ." She screws her face up, as if deep in thought. "Everything?"

He doesn't bother answering, and our driver just keeps on talking. "We're gonna pass a few beaches on your right before we get downtown. That's Nickel Beach, very popular with families. It got the name because you used to find loose change in the sand all the time. Rumor has it that the man who founded Gull Cove Resort used to bury hundreds of dollars' worth of coins there every summer so kids could have treasure hunts. I don't know if that's true or not, but people did stop finding change shortly after he died."

*It is true,* I almost say. It's always been my mother's favorite Story tale, how my tycoon grandfather would sneak out in the dead of night every few weeks to replenish the supply of beach change. My father told it to her when they met at a mutual friend's party after college, and Mom always used to say that she fell halfway in love with him right then and there. It didn't occur to me until just now that the first thing that attracted her to Dad was the reflected glow of someone else's generosity.

I exchange glances with Milly, and can tell she's heard about Nickel Beach from her mother too. But neither of us say anything. It's too complicated a subject for a short trip.

We pause at a red light, but the driver's monologue doesn't

stop. He gestures toward a strip of flat, gray sand to our right. "And over here, we have Cutty Beach—"

"Wait," I interrupt, the name catching my attention. "Did you say Cutter Beach?"

"No, Cutty. With a *y*."

"Can we . . . can I look at it?" I ask. "It was, um, my father's favorite."

"Really?" Milly asks, just as our driver good-naturedly says, "Sure." He pulls over to the side of the road. "Not our prettiest beach, in my opinion, but go ahead and take a gander."

I get out of the car, Milly at my heels. There's a strip of grass between the road and the beach, which is small with a crescent shape in the middle. The sand is coarse and rocky, the vegetation surrounding us sparse and dry-looking. Beachgoers with bright towels are scattered here and there, but it's not as crowded as I would have expected for the middle of the day.

Milly adjusts her sunglasses. "*This* was Uncle Adam's favorite beach?"

I turn to her. "Did you ever read his book? *A Brief and Broken Silence*?"

"Ah, no," she says. "I tried, but it was kind of . . ."

"Boring," I say. "I know. But the main character—who's a stand-in for my dad, I always thought—constantly talks about a beach in his hometown. Cutter Beach. And one of the lines he repeats, over and over, is: *That's where it all started to go wrong*."

"Huh." Milly is quiet for a few seconds, then points out, "But this is *Cutty* Beach."

"I know," I say. "My dad isn't the most original thinker, though. His main character has a wife named Magda, and my mom is Megan. And his daughter's name is Augie."

67

Milly wrinkles her nose. *"Augie?"*

"Short for Augusta," I explain.

"Okay, so—what? You think something happened to your dad at this beach?"

"Not necessarily," I say slowly, because that's exactly how my dad would put it. Things happen *to* him, like they're out of his control. But that's not how life really works; or at least, it's not how it's ever worked for him. "I just think it's interesting."

There's a loud *ahem* noise behind us, and when we turn, Jonah is glaring out the window. "You done sightseeing?" he asks. "Or should we skip lunch so you can keep staring at the world's ugliest beach?"

"Three more days," Milly mutters as we start back toward the car. "That's it. That's how long until I kill him."


L'Etoile is a classic old-person's restaurant. The wallpaper is floral, the chairs are low and cushiony, and everything on the heavy, gilt-edged menu is baked and costs at least thirty dollars.

"If you want something that's not on the menu, by all means let me know," Donald Camden tells us as a server fills our water glasses. "The chef is a personal friend."

"Thanks," I murmur, studying him surreptitiously over the top of my menu. He's about Gran's age and equally well preserved, with thick silver hair and a deep tan. There's a ruddiness to his cheeks, either from the sun or his already being on his second drink. Ever since we arrived at the restaurant he's been affable and seemingly at ease, asking questions about our jobs and how we like the Towhee program. Meanwhile I'm getting more and more nervous, because I still have no idea why we're here or what he wants from us.

"Can I get my hamburger *with* a bun?" Jonah asks, frowning as he studies his menu. He's the least dressed-up person in the room, in a threadbare T-shirt, jeans, and ratty Van sneakers. At least Milly and I put some effort into our clothes after we looked up the restaurant online. But if Donald is annoyed by Jonah, he doesn't show it.

"Of course," he chuckles. "The regulars here are very carb-conscious, but that's not something you need to worry about." The server returns to take our orders, and when he's finished, Donald leans back in his chair and sips amber liquid from a crystal tumbler. "Have you had a chance to enjoy our beaches yet?"

His glance around the table lands on Jonah, who slouches lower in his seat. "I'm not really a beach person," he mutters.

As far as I can tell, Jonah isn't an *anything* person. He hasn't taken part in any of the Towhee activities so far. A lot of the girls on our hallway think he's cute—Brittany in particular makes a point of inviting him everywhere—but if he's interested in anyone, he doesn't show it.

"I've heard Catmint Beach is nice," Milly says. "You know, the one in front of our parents' house." She tosses her hair and adds, "It was my mother's favorite."

I can feel myself go red. Gauntlet thrown, before the entrées have even arrived. But Donald barely reacts except to take another sip of his drink. "Catmint Beach is lovely," he says smoothly. "Exquisite sunrises."

"What about Cutty Beach?" I ask.

*That's where it all started to go wrong.* I watch Donald Camden's face carefully for some sign that Cutty Beach matters—that maybe it's even tied to why my grandmother disinherited our parents—but he just shrugs. "Unremarkable."

Milly shifts restlessly in her seat. I think Donald picks up on the fact that she's getting antsy with all the polite conversation, because he settles his glass on a coaster and leans forward, hands folded in front of him. "I could talk about our lovely beaches all day, but that's not why I asked you here. May I be frank?"

"Please," I say, just as Milly says, "I wish you would." Jonah mutters something that sounds like "I don't know, can you?" but it's too low for me to be sure. The server reappears just then with our food, and Donald waits until he's handed all the plates around before continuing.

"Your grandmother isn't in the best of health. There's no imminent crisis, but she's increasingly delicate, and in my opinion, any disruptions in routine should be avoided. I fear she's overextending herself with the hospitality she's shown toward the three of you to date, and that burden will only increase as the summer progresses."

"Burden?" Milly says, looking affronted. "And what *hospitality* are you talking about, exactly? We've barely seen her since we got here."

Donald acts like she hasn't spoken. "At the same time, an interesting opportunity has presented itself, and I wanted to share it with you. Are you familiar with the *Agent Undeclared* movies?"

"Well, yeah," I say. "Of course." The first *Agent Undeclared* movie—about two college students turned high-tech spies— came out when I was in eighth grade, and was such a surprise hit that there have been two more since. I've had a crush on the lead actor, Dante Rogan, for years. Sometimes when Thomas is kissing me, I close my eyes and picture Dante.

"I don't know if you've heard, but the fourth one is filming in Boston this summer," Donald says. "An old friend's law firm does legal work for the franchise, and he shared that they're in need of some help on set. Young people who could assist with gopher tasks and occasionally be present as stand-ins or perhaps even extras in crowd scenes. I wondered if you three would be interested."

"Would we ever," I blurt out without thinking.

"No promises," Donald says, cutting into his baked scrod. "But if you'd like me to look into it, I'm happy to. Housing will be provided, and the pay is quite good, I hear. More than the going rate for resort work. It would be quite a win-win." He pauses to take a careful bite of fish. "You three get the experience of a lifetime, and your grandmother, who's not in the best shape to play hostess at the moment, can enjoy a quiet, uneventful summer."

"But we already have jobs," Jonah says, looking pensive. "We can't just leave."

Donald waves a dismissive hand. "The summer hire program at Gull Cove Resort always has more applicants than it can accommodate. There's quite a lengthy wait list. I'm sure your spots could easily be filled."

"Would we get to work *with* Dante Rogan?" I ask breathlessly.

Milly stands abruptly and drops her napkin on her chair. "I need the restroom," she says. "Want to come with, Aubrey?"

"I don't have to go."

She smiles through gritted teeth. "So *keep me company.*"

I don't have much choice when she latches onto my arm and pulls. I follow her through the restaurant, weaving among mostly empty tables. Milly pushes through the door to the ladies' room, steering me in front of a gilt-framed mirror above double sinks. The entire room smells like we just tumbled into a vat of potpourri.

My cousin leans against the pink-tiled wall and crosses her arms. "Don't you think this is a little weird?"

Half of me registers her skeptical tone, but the other half is still imagining bonding with Dante Rogan over the coffee I'm going to fetch him this summer. "Working on a movie set? I think it's amazing."

"Really?" she asks. "Because it feels like a bribe." I frown, stubbornly resistant to her ruining my fantasy, and she sighs. "Come on, Aubrey. This is Donald Camden we're talking about. Our parents' archnemesis. He doesn't have our best interests at heart."

"Archnemesis?" I almost laugh, but . . . she's right. My father talked about Donald Camden constantly when I was growing up, always with a note of bitter resentment: *Donald won't return my emails. Donald says Mother's decision hasn't changed. Donald says it doesn't matter that Father wouldn't have wanted his children disinherited. All that matters is that he didn't put it in writing.* "So what are you saying? That Mr. Camden's trying to get rid of us?"

"That's exactly what I'm saying. It's what I've *been* saying, remember?"

"But why?"

Milly taps a finger on her chin. "I don't know. But it's interesting that he *can't*, isn't it?"

As usual, I feel like Milly is three steps ahead of me. "Huh?"

"Clearly, if it were up to him we'd already be gone. He wouldn't need to dangle a plum job. He'd just have us fired. So whatever's going on around here, Donald Camden and Mildred Story aren't in sync this time. He can't send a *you know what you did* letter and be done with it." She peers into the mirror to smooth her hair, a small smile playing at her lips. "Which is kind of satisfying, isn't it?"

"So, what?" I ask. "Now you think Gran *did* invite us?"

"No. Just because she's willing to let us stay doesn't mean she brought us here."

I sigh. "You make my head spin, Milly."

She grins and loops her arm through mine, pulling me toward the bathroom door. "Don't worry. You'll get used to it."

# CHAPTER SIX

## JONAH

Two days after lunch with Donald Camden, Mildred Story still hasn't bothered to grace us with her presence.

It's four o'clock on Friday, an hour before it starts getting busy at The Sevens, which is what passes for a sports pub at Gull Cove Resort. I'm a busboy here, and it's not the worst summer job I've ever had. Especially since it comes with free food.

"What's new, Jonah?" Chaz the bartender asks as I slide onto a stool across from him. Chaz isn't nearly as much of a dick as the nickname implies. He's an okay guy, actually, although he has a thick, dark, mountain-man beard that I'm surprised passed the Gull Cove Resort dress code. "You want the special today?"

"What is it?"

"Shrimp linguine."

I nod vigorously, and Chaz taps on the iPad in front of him. "You're in luck," he says, squinting at the screen. "No waiting.

The kitchen just made an order for a customer who changed their mind. Someone will bring it by in a sec."

He turns and starts pulling glasses from a low shelf, arranging them in neat rows on the bar. The Sevens is a mix of high-tech and old-school; the televisions that line each wall are the biggest, most high-definition screens I've ever seen, but the interior of the restaurant is all dark polished wood, recessed lighting, and leather chairs. The bar is massive, propped up by two pillars on either end, with seating all the way around. Summer staff usually starts congregating here around four-thirty to eat, but I'm always hungry way before then.

"First one here, as usual?" asks a dry voice behind me.

I turn to see Milly in her work uniform: a black cocktail dress, black apron, trendy black sneakers, and dark-red lipstick that must be mandatory, because every waitress who works at Veranda—Gull Cove Resort's fine dining restaurant—wears the same shade. Her hair is pulled into a high ponytail, her lashes thick with dark mascara. Or maybe she just has a naturally intense eyelash situation happening at all times.

"I like the food," I say, eyeing her warily as she slips onto a stool beside me. Other than the ferry ride and that weird lunch with Donald Camden, Milly and I haven't spoken much since we got here. Which is exactly what I thought she wanted, so I'm not sure why she's sitting next to me all of a sudden.

The television in front of us is turned to CNN for a change—Chaz likes to get the news in before he's forced to make it all sports when happy hour starts—and Milly's eyes flick over the reporter on-screen. "Some investment banker's been arrested for fraud *again*," she says, a little louder than necessary. "Seems like a rampant problem in the financial industry. Has Uncle

Anders ever come up against anything like that? Like, oh, I don't know . . . a Bernie Madoff in Rhode Island, maybe?"

Shit. I don't have to look at her face to know she somehow stumbled across that little write-up in the *Providence Journal* from earlier this year. *One disgruntled client lost the entirety of his retirement savings, his child's college fund, and is now in danger of losing his family's small business. Frank North, who recently filed for bankruptcy, called Anders Story "the Bernie Madoff of Rhode Island." "His investment strategy was nothing more than a pyramid scheme," says Mr. North. "And I was the last fool standing."*

I wonder, though, if she knows that it's true.

Chaz saves the day without realizing it, clicking from CNN to ESPN. "The entire financial industry is a joke," he says. "Bottom line is, nobody's ever gonna care as much about your own money as you do." His cheeks crease in a tired smile. "Says the guy who has none. You kids keep that in mind, though, when you're out running the world. Either of you want something to drink?"

"I'm all right," Milly says.

"A Coke would be great," I say. I watch Chaz disappear behind one of the pillars before turning to Milly. "What do you want?" I ask bluntly.

"You're so touchy, Jonah." Her brows draw together in an expression of mock hurt. "Can't I just enjoy the pleasure of my cousin's company?"

"I doubt it."

She drops the pretense and pulls a cream-colored envelope out of her pocket, her tone turning businesslike. "Did you get one of these?"

It looks exactly like the envelope that Donald Camden sent

with his invitation to lunch. "Yeah. I was there. Hamburger without a bun. Remember?"

"No," she says impatiently, opening the flap and pulling out a card. "It's a follow-up." She hands it to me and I read the short note inside.

I strongly urge you to reconsider my offer.
The terms of employment are more generous than I realized.
See below.

Donald S. Camden, Esq.

I stare at the number written at the bottom. It's easily three times what I'd make at Gull Cove Resort. Then I turn the card over, but there's nothing else. "I don't know if I got one of these or not," I tell Milly, handing it back to her. I have to fight to keep my voice normal, because that's *a lot* of cash. "I haven't checked my mailbox in a while."

"Hey, Jonah." A girl's voice, sweet and just a little seductive, interrupts us. It's Brittany, one of the servers and a fellow Towhee. She smiles coyly and bats her eyes at me, like she's been doing ever since we got here. Which is a problem. Brittany is cute, but I'm trying to keep a low profile. "I hear you're the lucky recipient of buyer's remorse." She slides the plate in front of me and flips her thick blond braid over one shoulder at the same time. Milly folds her arms, watching us.

"Thanks, Brittany." The smell of garlic and seafood hits me and I'm instantly starving.

She beams at me. "Anytime." Her eyes shift to my right. "Hi, Milly. What's up?"

"Not much," Milly says. "Just talking to my cousin. About family stuff." The unspoken *And you're interrupting* is so obvious that if I were trying to make something happen with Brittany, I'd be annoyed. But since I'm not, I just drop a napkin onto my lap and pick up my fork.

"Okay, well." Brittany twists her braid. "I have to get back to my tables, but . . . a bunch of people are going to Dunes tonight when their shifts are over." At my blank look, she adds, "It's a beach bar type of place? Well, not just a bar. You don't have to be twenty-one to get in. They serve food, and there's music and games. And it's right down the street, so we can walk there. Do you want to come?"

Not really. Again: nothing personal. But the less I socialize here, the better. "I don't know," I say. "I get really tired at the end of my shifts, so . . ."

"Also, Jonah hates people," Milly puts in, with the air of somebody who's offering a helpful tip.

Brittany blinks as I glare. "Can you mind your own business for once?" I growl.

Milly spreads her hands. "Like I was saying."

"Well, let me know if you're up for it," Brittany says with a strained smile. She heads back into the kitchen, and I dig my fork into the pile of linguine in front of me with a vengeance.

"You can leave anytime," I tell Milly.

She looks at my plate, brow furrowed. "That's shrimp."

"No shit," I say, taking as big a mouthful as I can manage. Milly just keeps staring, which is kind of weird and rude, until

Chaz returns and sets a Coke in front of me. Her eyes stray to the thick silver band on his right index finger.

"I like your wedding ring," she says.

"Not a wedding ring," Chaz says. He pulls off the silver band and holds it up so a thin line that looks like a zipper is visible. "Guitar string," he explains. "I used to play a lot. Still do, sometimes."

"Cool." Milly gives him a half smile. "Are you any good?"

Chaz puts the ring back on and makes a sweeping gesture around the bar. "Well, I work here, don't I?" he says. "So . . . not good enough."

I've been inhaling my food during their entire conversation, and Milly keeps watching me. "Enjoying your dinner?" she asks when I stop for air.

Chaz grins, stroking his beard. I can't tell how old he is; he could be anywhere between twenty-five and forty-five. "You have to ask?" he says.

"You guys need a new hobby," I snap. Meals are a highlight of this weird place, and their hovering is ruining mine.

Milly slides off the stool. "I changed my mind," she says. "I want a drink after all. I'll get it myself, though."

"Something nonalcoholic," Chaz calls as she disappears behind one of the bar pillars. "I know the exact level of every bottle and I *will* check." He shakes his head, picking up a towel and a wineglass. "That kid knows her way around a bar."

*She's not the only one,* I think, watching him polish the glass with slightly trembling hands. My favorite aunt, my mother's youngest sister, has hands that do the exact same thing when she's gone too long without a drink. She's one of those high-functioning alcoholics who's always slightly buzzed, but rarely drunk. Or maybe I'm just in denial about that. "I guess," I say, pushing the last of my pasta away.

"You guys are cousins, right?" Chaz asks. Like the entire island doesn't know exactly who we are. I nod, and he asks, "You close?"

"No." Chaz raises his brows at my swift reply, and I add, "I mean, I hadn't seen her for years before we started working here. Our families don't exactly hang out."

"Well, now's your chance to get to know one another, right? Family's important. Or it should be, anyway." Chaz's lean face looks suddenly tired. He's still polishing the same wineglass, which is streakier than when he started.

Milly returns with a glass of water and hops back onto the stool beside me, putting the card from Donald Camden down on the bar. I can't help myself; I pick it up again and look at the number inside. "So, listen," I say. I lower my voice, but Chaz is already turning away to finish stocking the bar. "Are you thinking of doing it?"

"No. Not when he wants to get rid of us that badly." For a second our eyes meet in solidarity—despite the lure of the money, I don't want to leave either—and then something in her face shifts. "It's funny that Brittany mentioned Dunes. Aubrey and I were just thinking that the three of us should go out. Have a cousins' night."

Her eyes get wide and guileless, and I roll mine. "Bullshit." Milly doesn't seem surprised by the response, but she does look like she's waiting for more, so I add, "In case it wasn't clear, that's a no."

"Come on," Milly says, in a persuasive tone that probably

works for her ninety-nine percent of the time. "Aubrey needs a night out. Something's going on with Uncle Adam, but she won't tell me what. Maybe you can get her to open up."

I snort. Now she's flat-out lying, because there's no way Aubrey would tell me anything she's not willing to tell Milly. "Drop the act. We both know you don't really want to hang out with me. So what *do* you want?"

Milly's face hardens. "Show up tonight and find out."

We stare at one another for a beat. "Maybe I will," I finally say.

Dunes is packed when I get there. The restaurant is dim, paneled with the same kind of wood as my parents' hasn't-been-touched-since-the-seventies basement, which gives it a closed-in feel despite the large space. There's a dining area with a few dozen full tables, a bar strung with twinkling white lights, and a small stage off to one side where a girl with a guitar and a guy with a keyboard are starting to set up. The back of the room is filled with pool tables, dartboards, and a bunch of high-top tables.

I spot a lot of familiar faces as I approach; it looks like Towhees have taken over two pool tables and all the surrounding seats. Brittany waves wildly from a corner where she's clustered with a group of girls, and my roommate, Efram, steps away from a pool game to drop his jaw in mock surprise. Efram is one of those relentlessly friendly guys who invites me everywhere he goes, even though I never accept.

"Is there a fire in the dorms?" he asks. He puts one hand over his heart and the other on my shoulder. "Are you okay? And more important, did you save my laptop?"

Milly materializes beside him with an arch smile. "Jonah is being social tonight," she says. I don't like the triumphant gleam in her eyes. At all. I'm half tempted to turn and leave when someone grabs hold of my arm. It's Aubrey, smiling widely and holding a pool cue.

"Perfect timing," she says. "You and Milly can play me and Efram."

I narrow my eyes. Is she in on whatever Milly's up to? But I stand by my original impression of Aubrey: the girl can't lie to save her life. She might actually be happy to see me. Which is weird, but then again, I haven't seen Aubrey hang out with anyone except Milly and Efram, who's also a lifeguard, since she's been here. She fits in only a little better than I do.

"Great," I say blandly, grabbing a cue from the rack on the wall. "I'll break."

Efram, who's been gathering balls from the pockets, tosses the last of them into the rack. "We should probably warn you that Aubrey and I are undefeated, and that includes a game against a couple of townie dudes who are now drowning their humiliation at the bar," he says, pulling the triangle away with a flourish. "But let's see what you can do, hermit."

I run my eyes over the table, then focus on the cue ball as I position myself to take aim. For a few seconds, I barely move except for a couple of micro adjustments to get my stick angled exactly how I want it. Then I draw back and strike fast. The balls explode against each other with such a loud crack that Aubrey gasps beside me. Striped balls start dropping into the pockets one after the other, while the solid balls spin harmlessly against the sides of the table. When the balls stop moving, only two stripes remain along with all but one of the solids.

I glance up to meet Milly's shocked expression and try not to look smug. I probably fail. "We're stripes," I say.

Efram raises and lowers his arms in a *we're not worthy* gesture. "Why didn't you tell me your cousin was a shark, Aubrey?" he asks.

"I had no idea," Aubrey says, blinking like she's seeing me for the first time.

Which is disconcerting. Maybe I should've stuck with my first instinct and left, but the thing is, as soon as I saw the pool table, my hands itched to hold a cue again. I grew up around a billiards hall and used to hang out there every afternoon. One of the regulars taught me how to play, and after he died—dropped dead from a heart attack in his early fifties, which my father used to call "the blue-collar guy's retirement plan"—I kept playing by myself. When I was twelve years old, I started challenging adults to play for money. They thought it was cute until I beat them.

Milly jostles against me in a surprisingly friendly way. "Well, well, well," she says. "Looks like we've discovered your secret talent."

She cheers me on for the rest of the short game—I clear the table before Aubrey and Efram get a turn—and then she leans her pool cue against the wall. "I need the restroom," she says over her shoulder to Aubrey and Efram. "But we challenge you suckers to a rematch. You can break this time, to give you a fighting chance."

"Only if Jonah ties one hand behind his back," Efram mutters as he starts gathering balls.

"Where did you learn to play like that?" Aubrey asks.

"Just around," I say, my eyes straying to one of the Towhee tables behind us. It's full of guys Efram calls the Prep Squad—

they're all tall and blond and wear stuff like whale belts unironi-cally. Their unofficial leader is Reid Chilton, whose senator mother might be running for president in the next election. I don't see much of the guy except when he bangs on our door to borrow toothpaste, but I already know I don't like him.

Reid pauses midconversation to watch Aubrey lunge awk-wardly across the table for the triangle, and says something that makes the Prep Squadder next to him laugh. My hand curls more tightly around my pool cue. The more I see of Reid and his friends, the more I wonder whether there was some kind of method to Mildred's madness. Maybe she saw her kids turning into assholes and took extreme steps to stop them.

"You." The voice at my elbow is ice cold, and when I turn, so is the look in Milly's eyes. "Come with me. *Now.*" She snatches the pool cue out of my hands and leans it next to hers against the wall. "Game delay," she says to Aubrey. "I need to talk to Jonah."

"About what?" Aubrey asks, but Milly has already fastened her fingers around my wrist like a handcuff as she drags me toward the back exit. All of her earlier friendliness is gone. I'm not surprised, exactly, but I'm still thrown off by how fast she flipped the switch.

"What's your problem?" I ask, my irritation mounting as I pull away from her grasp. "Stop *yanking* me. I'm already coming with you."

"Oh, you should thank me that this is all I'm doing," Milly says in a low, threatening voice as she leans one shoulder into the door. It opens, and we spill outside into the cool night air. I take a deep breath to clear my head, but almost gag when I'm hit with the sour stench of garbage. We're right next to a dumpster. Milly stops, hands on her hips as she turns to face me.

"Can we move away from the trash—" I start, but that's all I get out before Milly reaches both arms out and shoves me as hard as she can.

I stumble backward, unprepared for both the action and the force behind it. That girl packs a lot of strength into a small frame. "What the hell?" I growl. My hands are up in a gesture of surrender, but my temper spikes.

Milly pulls something small and square out of her pocket and waves it in my face. "What the hell indeed?" she says.

A light over the door behind us throws enough of a glow to illuminate what she's holding. My stomach twists as I stare at the familiar card, and all the anger drains out of me in an instant. I reach behind me for the wallet in my back pocket. Or rather, the wallet that *should've* been in my back pocket, but isn't.

So that's why she was acting so friendly while we played pool. She took it. Snaked it right out of my pocket while I was showing off. I could punch myself in the face for being so stupidly focused on the game I was playing that I missed the one *she* was playing.

"Give me back my stuff." I try to sound authoritative and unbothered at the same time, but sweat is already gathering at my hairline.

Shit. Shit, shit. This is bad.

Milly waves my driver's license again, looking up at me from under those mile-long lashes. "Gladly. Just as soon as you tell me who the hell you are, Jonah North, and why you're pretending to be my cousin."

# CHAPTER SEVEN

## MILLY

I don't know whether it's to his credit or not that he doesn't try to deny it.

"Why did I even bring that damn license," Other Jonah mutters. He looks furious, but I think it's mostly at himself.

"Yeah, well, this was only confirmation," I say. I pull Jonah's thin black wallet from my jeans pocket and stuff the license inside. It's served its purpose now—and I already took a picture with my phone—so I hand the wallet to him. "Your polishing off an entire plate of shrimp linguine when you have a *shellfish allergy* is what tipped me off."

As soon as Jonah started eating his dinner at The Sevens, I waited for his face to swell up like it did when he ate a shrimp wrapped in bacon nine years ago at our house. I was shocked that he didn't even turn a little red. When I went to get my drink, on the opposite side of the bar, I Googled *can you grow out of a shellfish allergy* and learned that while it's not impossible, it's highly unlikely, and there's usually still at least some reaction. Enough that most people would avoid inhaling an entire plate of them in under five minutes.

Maybe I could've accepted my alleged cousin as one of the lucky few, if it weren't for the fact that this boy has *never* fit as Jonah Story. From the first time I saw him on the ferry, he didn't make sense. For one thing, he's a lot better-looking than I remember, even allowing for the space of nine years. For another, although he made a solid early effort at copying my cousin's obnoxious mannerisms, he hasn't been able to keep it up. This Jonah is annoying in his own way—he has a bad attitude and a chip on his shoulder about *something*, clearly—but he doesn't have the same analytical, academic tone as Jonah Story.

"Are you kidding me?" Jonah's tense expression turns to outraged disbelief. "A shellfish allergy? Thanks, JT. That would've been useful information to have."

"Who's JT?" I ask, although I think I know.

Jonah's jaw ticks, and he regards me in silence for a few seconds like he's weighing how much to say. "Your cousin," he finally admits. "We go to school together, and people call him JT so they don't get us confused. His middle name is Theodore. But I guess you already know that."

I don't—or if I ever did, I've forgotten—but Jonah North doesn't need to know that. I can't help a satisfied smirk at the idea of my cousin being the secondary Jonah somewhere. I'll bet that bugs the crap out of him. "So he knew you were doing this?"

Jonah hesitates again, rubbing the back of his neck with one hand as conflicting emotions skitter across his face. "He asked me to do this," he says.

"He asked you to *pose* as him?" My voice edges upward in disbelief.

"Shhh," Jonah says, even though we're the only ones out here. He looks at the dumpster beside us, his mouth twisting. "Look, I can't think straight with this stench. I'm moving. You can come with or not."

"Oh, I'm right behind you," I say, secretly relieved as Jonah heads for the back of the parking lot. When we reach the edge of a grassy path, I grab his arm. "This is far enough. Spill the rest. Why did Jonah—or JT, or whatever—ask you to pose as him?"

Away from the lights of the restaurant, Jonah's face is nothing but shadows. "I'll tell you everything, but I have one condition." He raises his voice to cut off the protest I'm about to launch. "You don't tell anybody who I really am. Well, you can tell Aubrey. But that's it."

"I'm sorry, *what?*" Jonah doesn't answer, and I fold my arms tightly across my chest. It feels like the temperature dropped by at least fifteen degrees since we arrived at Dunes, and the sleeveless top that was fine inside the crowded restaurant isn't doing me any favors out here. Jonah, on the other hand, looks perfectly comfortable in a flannel shirt over his usual faded T-shirt. "You don't get to make the rules when you're the one committing fraud."

Jonah shrugs. "Okay, then. Have a good night."

He turns away, and I lunge for his arm. "You can't just leave!"

"I can if we don't have a deal."

"That's—" I sputter for another few seconds until it occurs to me that lying to a liar isn't the worst sin I could commit. "Okay, fine. I won't tell."

Jonah turns so he's fully facing me once again. "I don't really believe you," he says, almost to himself. "But I can always drag you down with me if I get caught, so there's that."

"No wonder you and JT are friends," I snap. "You have a lot in common."

"I never said we were friends," Jonah says coldly. "This is a business arrangement." I force myself to keep quiet, and after a few seconds he blows out a sigh. "Here's the thing. JT wanted to go to science camp. Which you knew, right?" I nod. "His father said no once they got the invitation from your grandmother. JT was pissed, because he got a scholarship and everything, which is tough to do, and Anders still told him he had to come here. I got into the same camp, but I didn't get a scholarship. So I couldn't go."

A note of bitterness creeps into Jonah's voice as he adds, "The whole thing was JT's idea. He heard me talking at school about not being able to go to camp and cornered me in the cafeteria one day, saying we could help each other out." His jaw ticks. "For a second, I thought he was gonna offer me his scholarship. Which was stupid. JT's not that kind of guy, and anyway, it probably wasn't transferable like that. But he said he'd pay me to go to Gull Cove Island in his place and not tell anyone. He'd go to science camp, and I'd get this sweet summer job with an extra bonus from him."

"Extra bonus?" I raise a brow. "How much? What's the going rate for impersonation these days?"

"Enough," Jonah says shortly.

The wind picks up, and I shiver as I clutch my arms more tightly. Jonah starts taking off his flannel shirt, but I stop him with an upraised hand. "Don't bother, Lancelot. I'm good. Did you guys even think this through? I mean, to be perfectly blunt, we're all here to get into Mildred's good graces. What did Jonah—or JT, or whatever—think was going to happen when she realized he sent a fake?"

Jonah shrugs his shirt back on. "He didn't believe your grandmother actually planned to do anything for you or your families. He thought it was just some weird game she'd decided to play that would mess with his future for no good reason. Which, given how things are going so far, seems about right."

Ugh. I hate that JT Story didn't harbor any pointless hopes like me and Aubrey. The fact that we were gullible and he's spending his summer exactly how he wanted sharpens my tone. "And how did you expect to pull this off for two months? I figured it out in less than a week and I wasn't even trying."

Jonah rakes a hand through his hair. "God, I don't know right now. It seemed logical at the time. JT and I are the same age, from the same town, and we have the same first name. We have the same coloring. The resort never asked for photo ID, just a birth certificate. JT has, like, zero social media presence, so it's not like anybody would expect him to be posting about his summer. He hadn't seen you or Aubrey in years, and his grandmother ever. And he gave me lots of background on your family—that whole *you know what you did* letter, plus stuff about your and Aubrey's parents, and the different ways everyone tried to get back in touch with Mildred over the years. I thought I had all the information I needed." He shakes his head in disgust. "*Shellfish allergy.* God damn him."

"So was that you messaging me and Aubrey, back when we first got the letters?" I ask. "Or was that JT?"

"It was JT. When you guys started the group chat—that was all real—he thought he'd have to go to the island with you.

Then, once I agreed to take his place, he just played along like nothing had changed. He gave me printouts of all the chats so I'd know what you talked about."

"What's your deal, then? Who *are* you?"

"You saw the license. I'm Jonah North. I live in Providence and go to high school with your cousin. I needed the cash, so I posed as him when he asked me to. That's it."

"What do you care if I tell, then?" I ask. "You got your money."

"It's an installment plan," Jonah says. "I only got the first third. Plus, Gull Cove Resort pays way better than what I'd make working at my parents' place."

"Is it more than you would've made on the *Agent Undeclared* set?"

Jonah's tone gets wistful. "No. But I couldn't say yes to that. I'm supposed to send pictures of the resort every week so JT can convince his father that he's working here."

"Where do your parents think you are?"

"Here. At a cushy summer job I lucked into. They just don't know what name I'm using."

"You said you used to work for them? What kind of place do they have?"

"It doesn't matter." Jonah takes a step back, and I can see him clearly in the moonlight. I'm not sure why that particular question was his breaking point, but he looks entirely done—tense and exhausted, every angle of his face pronounced. "Listen, I'm going back to the dorms. I know I can't make you keep your word about this, but I hope you do." Then he turns and starts walking away. I contemplate following him, because I have plenty more questions, and he owes me some answers. But in the end I retrace my steps toward Dunes, heading inside to the only person currently on the island who's related to me.

I'm halfway there when something warm and soft materializes in my hand, and I turn to see Jonah North in a T-shirt, shoving his flannel at me.

"For the walk home," he says, before disappearing back into the shadows.

The next night I'm still preoccupied, waiting tables in Veranda on autopilot. I'd lifted my phone a dozen times today to text my mother: *Jonah is a fake!* But I didn't do it. I told Aubrey—who was almost comically shocked—but so far, that's it. I'm not sure what's stopping me. Except, maybe, that I can't untell the truth once it's out.

Luckily, I'm not busy tonight. Head of hospitality Carson Fine is supervising the dining room, and he's been insisting I get lengthy breaks between tables because I'm so new. Although I think his real reason is that he wants to gossip with me at the bar.

We're sitting there now, his chin in his hands as he peppers me with questions about Mildred. "So you never met her at all before last weekend?" he asks. Tonight, his tie is patterned with bright-pink seashells against a purple background.

"Never," I say. There's no point in pretending otherwise. The Story kids' disinheritance isn't a secret. Every time Mom or her brothers tried to claim their legal right to some of my grandfather's fortune, they had to release more details about how they'd been cut off.

"It's all so *gothic*," Carson says, in a tone of hushed awe.

"And so strange. Mrs. Story couldn't be lovelier to her employees and people around town. Why would she be so ruthless with her own children?"

That's the one part of the story Google can't tell you, and Carson is clearly hoping that I can. "No idea," I say. "We've never known."

He visibly deflates. "Well, at least she brought you here. That's something."

"And then she took off." That can't have escaped Carson's notice, and maybe I can use his avid curiosity to my advantage. The longer Mildred goes without contacting us, the more convinced I am that there's something off about this entire summer. And it all started with a letter telling us to coordinate with Edward Franklin.

"I wonder if we might've gotten our dates mixed up." I deliver the lie with a faintly perplexed smile, draining the last of my water. Marty, Veranda's bartender, appears out of nowhere to refill my glass. Everyone at Gull Cove Resort is under the impression that my cousins and I have some sort of pull with Mildred, so we get better service than the guests. "I was thinking about touching base with Edward Franklin to double-check, but the only contact information I have for him is his resort email address." I wait a couple of beats, like I'm lost in thought. "I don't suppose you have, like, a personal email on file, do you? Or a phone number?"

"I'm sure we do," Carson says, flicking a strand of white-blond hair off his forehead. "But I can't give it to you. Privacy laws and all that."

"Right," I say, crestfallen. I'm debating whether I can convince him to trade the information for some sort of salacious, made-up Story gossip, when Carson's phone buzzes in his pocket. He pulls it out and frowns at the screen.

"Hmm, they need me out front for something. Be right back."

I watch him wind his way through the dining room until Marty clears his throat. I hadn't realized he was still standing there. "Hey, if you want to reach Edward, you could maybe try Chaz," he says.

I wrinkle my brow. "Why would I try Chaz?"

"He and Edward were a couple for a while. They might still be in touch."

"Ah, okay," I say, absorbing that. It hadn't occurred to me that Chaz was gay. Or dating. He seemed eager to get off the subject of his love life the one time we'd touched on it. "Thanks, I'll check with him. Is he working tonight, do you know?"

"No. Sick day. He'll probably be sick for a while, if you know what I mean," Marty says, miming tipping a bottle to his lips.

"Oh no." It hasn't escaped my notice how much liquor Chaz sneaks while he's working; people don't usually pick up on *my* bar tricks unless they have a few of their own. But he's always so professional that I assumed his drinking is under control. "Does that, um, happen often?"

"More than it should. Worst-kept secret at the resort. Everyone knows except Carson." Marty's gaze turns toward the dining room, where Carson's blond head gleams beneath the restaurant's dim lighting as he makes his way back toward us. "Chaz is a good guy, though, and a great bartender when he's sober. So we try to look out for him."

"Understood," I say as Carson lifts his hand in a wave. He's not alone, and my heart stops for a second when I realize there's an older woman walking beside him. Is Mildred finally making an appearance? But when they get closer, I realize my mistake. This woman is around the same age as my grandmother, but her hair is gray, not pure white, and she's wearing a simple brown dress and clogs. Carson looks delighted to be by her side, though, and steers her my way with a wide smile.

"Milly, I have an introduction to make. Your grandmother's assistant, Theresa Ryan, is here to see you. She has *news.*"

Carson says it with breathless anticipation, earning a low chuckle from Theresa. She holds out her hand, clasping warm fingers around mine when I take it. "That makes me sound very exciting, doesn't it? Hello, Milly. Lovely to meet you."

"You too," I say, my pulse quickening. My mother had always gotten along well with Theresa—they were the only Yankees fans in a house full of Red Sox fanatics, she used to tell me—and they'd stayed in touch for a few years after Mom's disinheritance. Theresa was always kind, Mom said, but firm that Mildred hadn't shared her reasons with anyone except Donald Camden. Eventually, my mother got frustrated and stopped speaking with her, too.

"Mrs. Story asked me to come by. She'll be back on the island soon, and wanted to have the three of you over to Catmint House for brunch on Sunday. Not tomorrow," she adds when my eyes widen. "She'll still be in Boston, and anyway, that's the Fourth of July. You children should stay close to the resort; there are always such lovely events planned for staff and guests, and a truly breathtaking fireworks display. I'm sure Carson has told you all about it."

I glance at Carson, and can read the plea in his fixed smile. *Please, Milly. Pretend just this once that you didn't tune me out when I started talking about Towhee activities.* "Oh yes, of course," I say. "Looking forward to it."

"Wonderful. I do hope you enjoy," Theresa says. "At any rate, your grandmother would like to have you over for brunch the following Sunday, on July eleventh. I'm hoping that won't be a problem with their work schedules?" she adds, turning to Carson with a smile.

"Of course not," he assures her.

"Okay," I say, searching Theresa's gaze for a hint of anything behind her words. Does my grandmother *want* to see us? Or does she just feel like she has to, in order to keep up appearances? But Theresa's pleasant expression doesn't change.

"Mrs. Story also wanted to make sure that you leave July seventeenth open. That's a Saturday, the night of the Summer Gala, and she'd like you to attend as her guests." An image flashes through my mind of my mother at age eighteen, wearing a white ball gown and her diamond teardrop necklace. The one I wanted so much that I gave up my summer for it.

Except, I've realized, it's not quite that simple.

Yes, I want the necklace. But more than that, I want Mom to *want* to give it to me. I want her to be the kind of person who would care about passing along something meaningful from mother to daughter, no strings attached. But she's not. So if I can't have that, then what I really came for is this: the chance to be in the presence of my grandmother, her circle of confidants, and all these Gull Cove Island people who remember Mom as a child and teenager. Because surely, one of them has to know what happened twenty-four years ago to make Mildred Story sever ties with all four of her children and never look back. And maybe if I know *that,* I'll finally be able to understand my mother.

Theresa is still talking, and I refocus my wandering attention on her. "It's a formal affair—tuxedos for the men and gowns for the women," she explains. "We realize you probably don't have the appropriate attire on hand, so you and your cousins should feel free to shop at any of the island's boutiques and charge your purchases to the Story account."

Despite the weirdness of the situation, I feel a little thrill. It's *almost* like my childhood shopping fantasy, except for the part where Mildred delegates the details to her assistant. Plus . . . "Nothing will fit," I say. When Theresa raises her brows again, I flip a hand toward my torso. "I'm too short to wear anything full-length off the rack."

Theresa lets out another soft chuckle. "Don't worry. Your alterations will be a priority for whichever shop you choose," she says, like that settles the matter.

And I guess it does.

# CHAPTER EIGHT

## AUBREY

"So." Milly looks at me expectantly. "Should we tell about Fake Jonah before we have brunch with Mildred, or not?"

I swallow the last of my Plumwich before answering. We're in downtown Gull Cove on a Tuesday afternoon, trying the signature dessert at Sweetfern Bakery: an ice cream sandwich made with beach plum ice cream and fried doughnut halves. It sounds better than it tastes, but that didn't stop either of us from finishing.

"I don't know," I admit. "Who would we tell?"

"Our parents?" It comes out uncertainly from the usually decisive Milly. "Or Theresa."

"We could, but . . ." I hesitate. Unlike Milly, I know what it's like to need money. And I don't care all that much that Jonah North replaced Jonah Story. The new Jonah is kind of prickly, but overall he seems like an upgrade from our actual cousin. "He's not really our biggest problem right now, is he?"

Milly laughs, but I'm not kidding. Jonah North is a distant fourth on the list of things I'm worried about. Number one is my dad. Number two is having to go to brunch and a fancy-dress ball with a grandmother who's still barely acknowledging my existence. Number three is Thomas's weird silence, and the fact that I don't miss him nearly as much as I thought I would. I've stopped texting him, and occasionally I stare at my dark phone and wonder if this means we're broken up. And why I can't summon the energy to care if we are. It almost seems inevitable, like there's not a single thing in my formerly comfortable, predictable life that gets to stay the way it used to be.

The Fourth of July was two days ago, and between the fireworks and a Towhee after-party, I stayed up much too late. Then I couldn't sleep. While Milly breathed steadily on the other side of our room, I lay in bed tracing a crack in the wall with one finger and thinking about unintended consequences. About how I did something last year that, at the time, seemed even smaller and less significant than this tiny imperfection on an otherwise pristine area. And how it set off a chain reaction that made my family implode.

The guilt of that has kept me from talking to my mother as often as I usually do since I got here, but I did text her a question on Sunday when my insomnia was at its worst. *Does Dad ever talk about Cutty Beach?*

Mom, who always falls asleep early in front of the television, didn't reply until yesterday morning. *Cutty Beach? Why do you ask?*

I wasn't sure how to answer that, so I settled for vague. *I went there a couple days ago. It made me think of him.*

She took her time responding. *He's mentioned it occasionally.*

*I never thought he liked it much, although I couldn't tell you why. Just the impression I got. But it's been a long time since your dad and I talked about his time on the island.*

That made my stomach roll with uneasiness. Not only because it added to the weird Dad–Cutty Beach connection that's been forming in my brain, but because it reminded me how tense things are between my parents. Now, and probably for much longer than I recognized. So I made an excuse to sign off.

When I showed the texts to Milly, she'd just shrugged. "Well, it's an ugly beach," she said. "I didn't like it much either."

My cousin's voice pulls me back to the present, and I have to give myself a mental shake to remember what subject we're on. Right: Fake Jonah. "He can't keep this up forever," she says. "When he gets found out, we'll look bad for going along with him."

"We need more caffeine for this discussion," I say, standing up and gathering our empty iced coffee cups. "Do you want the same thing?"

"Yeah, thanks."

The line to order is shorter than when we arrived, but there are still three people ahead of me, so I gaze around while I wait. Sweetfern looks like the inside of a candy cane: red-and-white striped walls, white wrought-iron tables and chairs, and a shiny, cherry-red floor. The air is warm despite the hum of air-conditioning and thick with the smell of sugar and chocolate. A dozen black-framed photos line the wall behind the cash register. I look them over absently, then snap to attention as I recognize a familiar face in the picture over the cashier's right shoulder.

It's my father in all his youthful glory, dark-haired and handsome, one arm cradling the ugliest painting I've ever seen.

It looks like a preschooler dragged a ball of yarn through mud. Dad's other arm is draped casually across the shoulders of an older woman whose palm rests affectionately on his cheek. Even from a distance, I can see the distinctive port-wine stain on her hand. My elusive grandmother, showing up in the most unexpected places.

I step a little closer to read the plaque beneath the photo: MILDRED AND ADAM STORY WITH THE FIRST-PLACE WINNER OF THE 1994 GULL COVE ISLAND LOCAL ARTISTS COMPETITION. Hard to believe that a woman with a world-renowned art collection would've given a blue ribbon to *that*.

When it's my turn to pay I swipe my credit card left-handed, even though I know it's silly to imagine that the teenage cashier, who's barely looking at me, would see the birthmark on my arm and realize I'm a Story. Still, not waving it in front of her gives me the courage to ask, "Are any of those pictures on the wall for sale?"

"What?" The cashier finally meets my eyes, her thinly plucked brows raised in surprise. "I don't think so. They're, like, decoration."

"Okay," I say, feeling foolish. My father was a senior at Harvard when Mildred disinherited him; he was living in Cambridge with no opportunity to return to Catmint House and gather personal effects. Someone boxed his room up and had the contents sent to him, but there were hardly any family photos included. It would be nice to have something like a picture, but there's no way I can explain all that to a bored cashier.

I turn and nearly bump into the person behind me. "Nice picture, huh?" says a familiar voice. "Terrible painting, though." It's Hazel Baxter-Clement, who gestures at the next person in line to go ahead of her as she steps closer to the wall with photos. Her grandfather is nowhere in sight. "That was the first annual local artist competition. I like to think we've improved since then."

"Are you an artist?" I ask.

"Me? No. Just interested in Gull Cove Island history." Hazel pushes her stack of leather bracelets up her arm. "How's everything going?"

"Pretty good. How's your grandfather?"

"He's fine." She tilts her head and smiles. "I'd hoped to hear from you guys."

"We've been really busy," I say limply. Over Hazel's shoulder, Milly is pointing toward that big gold watch of hers that doesn't work and then toward the door. "We're just heading out, actually. Time to get back to work."

"Well, let me know if your schedules open up. Granddad is doing much better lately, so he could probably tell you a few stories about your parents."

I pause, because that's actually tempting. "Will you give me your number again? I know Jonah has it, but he's kind of disorganized."

"Sure," Hazel says, brightening. She recites it and steps aside to let me pass. "Text me anytime."

Milly is standing beside the door, holding it open with one foot while the other taps impatiently. "What did she want?" she mutters under her breath when I join her.

"She still wants to talk to us," I say, handing her an iced coffee as we pass through the doorway. "She said her grandfather's doing better. Maybe he could explain all the weird stuff he said when we met him."

Milly looks skeptical as she puts on her sunglasses. "Or maybe she's just saying that so she can turn us into a term paper."

We head up the sidewalk, away from the ferry dock, passing a row of shops and restaurants. "It's like a mini Fifth Avenue around here," Milly says, pausing to look into the window of a store with KAYLA'S BOUTIQUE lettered across it. "Ooh, this looks cute. We should go dress shopping here."

"Okay," I say, still preoccupied with the picture on Sweetfern's wall. I owe my father a call, and for the first time since I got here, I find myself wanting to talk to him. Something about seeing him so relaxed and happy with Gran reminds me of what it feels like when he turns that blinding smile on me. Before I can think too much about what I'm doing, I take out my phone and hit his number. "I'm just going to make a quick call," I murmur to Milly.

It takes four rings for my father to answer, and when he does, his voice is clipped. "Aubrey."

"Hi, Dad." I start walking again and make a sharp turn down a less crowded side street, where tall trees behind a stone wall shade the sidewalk. Behind me, I can hear the tap of Milly's sandals as she follows. "How've you been?"

"Fine," he says coolly. And then he goes so silent that I'd think the call dropped if I didn't know better. He's punishing me for avoiding him all week. This is what my father does when he's annoyed: withholds affection and approval to make his disappointment clear. I know that, and yet . . .

"I'm going to brunch with Gran next weekend," I blurt out. "Did Mom tell you?"

"She did." Another long pause. "That certainly took long enough."

"Gran had to go to Boston," I say, hating the defensive note creeping into my voice. I take a sip of iced coffee and almost gag. The cashier gave me hazelnut by mistake, and that's my least favorite flavor in the world. I toss the nearly full cup into a trash can as I continue to walk.

"I heard," Dad says. "I'm surprised you let that happen."

I plug my free ear with an index finger, not sure I'm hearing him right. "What do you mean? I didn't *let* anything happen. She just—went."

"Of course she did. Because you weren't proactive enough."

"Not proactive enough," I echo, stopping in my tracks. Milly pauses too. We're beside an arched stone entranceway, the gold-rimmed plaque beside it indicating that whatever's inside is either touristy or historically significant, but my vision goes too hazy for me to know which. "You think I should've been more proactive."

"Yes. This is your biggest problem, Aubrey. You're passive. You'd rather waste an entire summer than take matters into your own hands." He gathers steam, like this is a topic he's been meaning to address with me for a while, and I've finally given him the perfect opening. "Did it ever occur to you to get in touch with your grandmother yourself, or speak with her assistant?" I don't reply, and his voice turns even more condescending. "I didn't think so. Because you don't act, you react. That's what I mean by *proactive*."

For a few seconds, I can't reply. I'm rooted to the sidewalk, the words spoken by Dr. Baxter my first day on Gull Cove Island flashing through my head. *Adam had seeds of greatness, didn't he? But he wasted them. Foolish boy. Could've changed it all with a word.*

I wonder which word that was, and if it's half as enraging as—

"Proactive?" I say. It bursts from me like an icicle, sharp and cold and deadly. "Do you mean *proactive* like when you fucked my swim coach and knocked her up? Is that the kind of *proactive* I should be shooting for?"

Milly makes a strangled little noise as she presses both hands against my side, pushing me away from the scattered pedestrians on the sidewalk and through the stone archway. We're someplace quiet and green, but nothing else registers beyond my father's harsh, incredulous words thundering in my ear. "*What* did you say?"

I'm shaking all over as I walk blindly forward, Milly by my side. My throat has closed to a pinprick, and I can barely squeeze the words out. "You heard me."

"Aubrey Elizabeth. How dare you speak to me like that? Apologize immediately."

I almost do. The urge to please him is so strong, ingrained over seventeen years, that despite everything, I feel a desperate need to make the anger in his voice go away. Even though *I'm* the one who should be angry. And I am, but it's not the hard, relentless anger he deserves. It's the kind that will crumble into a pathetic apology if I stay on the phone. "No," I manage to choke out. "I'm hanging up now. I don't want to talk to you anymore."

I disconnect and immediately power down my phone. Then I stuff it in my pocket, drop like a stone onto the grass, and cover my face with my hands.

There's a rustling sound beside me, and a tentative hand pats my arm. "Wow. That was—wow. I did not see that coming.

Any of it," Milly says. I don't reply, and she adds, almost to herself, "I didn't think you had it in you to go off like that."

I lower my hands with a reproachful look. "Really? So you're basically agreeing with my father that I'm a do-nothing loser? Thanks a lot, Milly."

My cousin's eyes widen in horror. "No! Oh God. I didn't mean that. I just . . . I'm sorry. I'm bad at comforting people. Obviously." She's still patting my arm mechanically, and she's right. There's nothing even a little bit comforting in the gesture. "Uncle Adam is a rat bastard and I'm glad I threw up on him when I was two," she adds, and I snort.

"You did?"

"According to my mother."

"He's never mentioned it. Not that I'm surprised. We don't talk about anything that might make him look less than perfect. I wasn't supposed to say anything about *this*." A lump forms in my throat, and I swallow against it. "It's bad enough that he cheated on my mom. But he did it with *her*. Coach Matson has been my coach since middle school! I idolized her. I wanted to *be* her. I even . . . God, I'm the idiot who introduced them."

The image has been playing across my mind all month: me dragging Dad to the edge of the pool sophomore year, insisting he finally meet the woman who'd been training me for years. Standing proudly between my young, pretty coach and my handsome, distinguished father, pleased to be the connecting thread between the two people I admired most in the world. It never occurred to me that they'd think of one another in any way except in relation to me.

There are a lot of shitty things about this situation, but one of the worst is realizing that neither of them ever thought much about me at all.

Tears start pooling in my eyes and slipping down my cheeks. I haven't cried properly since my father broke the news last month. At first I was too shocked to react, and then—like I've been doing my whole life—I took my cue from him. He didn't want to talk about it, so I didn't. He acted like this was something that happened *to* our family, instead of something he caused. Like it was a random natural accident that nobody could have predicted or avoided. It took being three thousand miles from him to realize how colossally messed up that was.

I take a deep breath, trying to get myself back under control, and end up letting out a loud, choked sob. Then another one.

"Oh. Oh no. It's, um, going to be all right," Milly says as I cry harder. "I have a tissue in here somewhere, hang on. . . ." I can hear her rooting around in her bag, and then her voice turns a little desperate. "Okay, it's not a tissue, it's one of those cloths you use to get smudges off your sunglasses. But it's nice and soft. And clean, mostly. Do you want it?"

I take it from her with a strangled half laugh and swipe it across my eyes. "You weren't kidding. You're terrible at this."

"At least I made you laugh. Sort of." Milly takes one of my hands in both of hers and gives it a decisive pump. It feels more like she's running for office than consoling me, but I let it slide. "I'm really sorry," she says earnestly. "None of this is your fault. It's totally normal for you to want people you care about to get along."

"Did they ever," I say hollowly. "The worst thing is, I thought they liked each other because of *me*. Pathetic, huh?"

"Yes," Milly says. I give her another reproachful look until she adds, "I assume you're talking about Uncle Midlife Crisis and Coach Home-wrecker? Ugh, he's such a gross cliché, isn't he? And she's no better."

I blink back fresh tears. "Everything is a mess. I feel so guilty that it's hard talking to my mom like normal, even though she's said a million times that this has nothing to do with me. I stopped swimming with my team because I couldn't stand being around Coach Matson. I don't think I can ever go back. I can't imagine what meets will be like next year once the team finds out. Nobody at school knows yet."

Including Thomas. I'd wanted to tell him, but the timing never felt right. I'm not sure what it says about our relationship that I told the cousin I've known for less than two weeks before the boyfriend I've known four years, but it probably explains the silent breakup we're having.

"What's going to happen?" Milly asks. "With the baby and everything?"

"Well, she's keeping it. So I'll have a half sibling at some point this fall. Maybe it'll be the boy Dad always wanted." Milly squeezes my hand harder as I add, "I don't think my parents are going to make it through this. I don't see how they could. And my father refuses to get a real job and support himself, so . . . worst-case scenario, I guess my swim coach becomes my step-mother." The thought gives me a full-body shudder, and I let it run through me before darting an apologetic look at Milly. "I mean, I know you have a stepmother and all, but—"

"Not even close to the same thing," she says quickly. "There was no cheating involved. My dad didn't meet Surya until the divorce was finalized. And he wasn't the one who wanted it in the first place."

I drop my head. "What is *wrong* with my father? He could've been so much more. It's like Dr. Baxter said—he had all this potential, and he wasted it. He turned out . . . so small."

"I know," Milly says. "I feel the same way about my mom. Well, she's not horrible like your dad, but . . . she's so cold. She doesn't let anybody in. My father could never do anything right with her, and he tried so hard. It makes me feel like—what's the point? If he couldn't get through, I have no shot. He's way nicer and more patient." She gives my hand one last squeeze, then leans back on her elbows with a sigh. "The Story family is seriously messed up."

The simple truth of that hits me with more surprise than it should. Even though I've always known my father's family wasn't exactly normal, I used to think there was something . . . romantic, I guess, about their particular brand of dysfunction. But truth is, my dad and his siblings are all miserable: him ripping our family apart out of a deep-seated need to feel special without working to accomplish anything; Aunt Allison pushing Uncle Toshi away and keeping Milly at arm's length; Uncle Anders having such a bad relationship with his only son that JT paid an imposter to defy him; and Uncle Archer falling out of touch for years on end due to one addiction or another. For a second, I wish I still had my father on the phone. *You need to face up to whatever you did that turned Mildred against you,* I'd tell him. *Before the person you could've been is gone forever.*

It would be pointless, though. If there's one thing my father has an unshakable belief in, it's himself as a misunderstood genius.

I blink the last of my tears away, and our surroundings finally come into focus. "Are we in a . . . graveyard?" I ask Milly.

"Oh. Yes. It was, you know, a little more private here." A small grin tugs at the corners of her mouth. "Check out who we ended up next to. It's a family reunion."

I follow her gaze to the letters etched across the gravestone beside us:

Abraham Story
Beloved husband, father,
and philanthropist
"Family first, always"

"Ironic quote," Milly says, and I manage a short laugh.

"You know what?" I say. "My father was right about one thing. *Only* one thing," I add as Milly raises a skeptical brow. I feel lighter after finally letting my pent-up tears out, and sharper, too, as though I've shed blinders that were forcing me to miss half of what's around me. "We shouldn't just sit back and wonder what's happening. We should do something."

"Like what?" Milly asks, shifting immediately into problem-solving mode. "Talk to Chaz? Maybe he can put us in touch with Edward Franklin."

"That's one idea, but I was thinking of something else." I stand and brush off my shorts. "Let's give Hazel that interview she's been after. And ask some questions of our own."

Allison paused outside the door to her mother's study at the sound of familiar voices. "Rest and exercise, Mildred. Both will do you a world of good," Dr. Baxter said as he zipped up a medical bag. Dr. Baxter didn't typically do house calls, let alone appointments at nine o'clock at night, but he'd always made an exception for the Storys. Especially in the six months since Father had died unexpectedly of a heart attack, and Mother was suddenly hyperaware of her own heartbeat.

"It feels erratic," she'd say, one hand clasped tightly over her chest.

But Allison knew what the problem was with her mother's heart: it was broken.

"I keep telling her that," came another voice. Theresa Ryan, Mother's assistant and Matt's mother. "Let's bring a yoga instructor here, Mildred. It's calming *and* an excellent workout. We could both use it."

Theresa sounded more stressed than usual. She'd moved into Catmint House a few months ago at Mother's insistence—"temporarily, just until I get on my feet," Mildred had promised—and Allison was sure Theresa found the proximity tiring. Mildred's constant fearfulness and her inability to make even the simplest decision wasn't surprising at this point in the grief cycle, but it was disconcerting for everyone who was used to the Story business running like a well-oiled machine. Allison knew Adam was feeling pressured too, as their mother kept hinting that she'd like him to come home more often next semester and take an active role in managing some of their properties.

"The whole point of going away to college is to *go away*," he'd complained yesterday while the four Story siblings were sprawled on oversized towels on the beach in front of Catmint House. "I don't want to be back here every other weekend like some kind of townie."

"Someone's unclear on the definition of a townie," Anders said, his voice muffled from beneath the Indiana Jones–style hat he'd placed over his face. The rest of him looked just as ready for an archaeological dig in linen pants and a long-sleeved shirt. Unlike his siblings, Anders burned to a crisp in the sun, no matter how much sunscreen he put on. But that day he looked less out of place than usual, because it was a cool sixty-nine degrees. Allison was in a sweatshirt, and kept wishing she hadn't worn shorts.

"You could step up, you know," Adam said peevishly. "Offer to come back occasionally. If we split things up, it might not be that bad."

"No thanks." Anders yawned. "Mother is finally cashing

those golden-boy chips you've been coasting on all these years. This is all you."

"That metaphor doesn't even make sense," Adam grumbled.

Now, Allison rapped lightly on the doorframe to Mother's study before poking her head in. "Hello," she called as three heads turned her way. "Nice to see you, Dr. Baxter."

"You as well, Allison."

"We're headed out, Mother." At her mother's blank look, Allison added, "To Rob Valentine's. Remember?" Archer had successfully convinced his siblings, even Anders, to show up at his friend's party tonight.

"All four of you?" Mother asked.

"Yes. I told you that earlier," Allison said, trying to keep the impatience out of her voice. She'd mentioned it twice in fact, but lately Mother ignored anything she didn't want to hear.

Mother's face sagged with disappointment. "I forgot about that. I thought we could have a family game night. I've been looking forward to it all day."

"Well . . ." Allison wished Adam were here. He was so much better at handling Mother's moods. "Archer hasn't seen Rob in a while, and we promised . . ."

"Oh, Mildred, let them go," Theresa urged. "It's Saturday night. You have them all summer." Mother still looked doubtful, but she sighed in a resigned sort of way as Theresa gave Allison a warm smile. "I think Matt will be there, too. Tell him I miss him, and I hope he's eating something besides ramen noodles while he has the house to himself."

Allison's heart skipped a beat. The coffee date Matt had mentioned last week during the party setup hadn't happened, but she'd been hoping to see him at Rob's. "I will," she said, and ducked back into the hallway before Mother could protest.

"This summer sucks," Anders complained as the four Story siblings crossed the street from the parking lot at Nickel Beach to Rob Valentine's house. He zipped a thick Harvard sweatshirt all the way up to his neck and added, "It's been freezing since we got here."

"Coldest summer in ten years," Adam said, in that voice he used whenever he was sharing information he thought people should already know. "It's wreaking havoc with coastal tide patterns."

"Fascinating," Anders grumbled, then stopped short as they passed a distinctive, bright-green moped. "Oh hell. Fucking Matt Ryan is here."

"I think everyone is here," Archer said diplomatically. He couldn't resist elbowing Anders and adding, "We live on a twelve-mile island, remember? Nightlife is kinda limited."

Allison was silent. She'd hoped that Anders's ire toward Matt might have cooled after a semester away, but apparently not.

"Forget that guy," Adam said, jogging up the front steps two at a time. He pulled the door open with a flourish and looked back. "He's no one."

Rob Valentine had graduated from Gull Cove Island High last year, and he'd just moved into a new place—one of those rental bungalows that tourists wouldn't touch because the owner couldn't be bothered to invest in any upkeep. The beach grass in front was long and yellow, the paint was peeling, and one of the front windows was taped over with cardboard that did nothing to keep the cool air out. It was dim inside, filled with pulsing music and what looked like half of Gull Cove Island High's current and recent student body. Allison couldn't help but compare the noisy scene with the much more sedate parties she'd gone to at boarding school before graduating last month. Students lived on campus at Martindale Prep, as did a lot of teachers, which effectively dampened everyone's social lives.

A pretty blonde wearing a Burger King crown and holding a wine cooler swayed in front of the Story siblings' path as soon as they stepped inside. "It's my birthday," she slurred, poking Adam's chest with her bottle. "Are you my present?"

Adam smirked, sliding an arm around the girl's waist. "I could be."

"Archerrrrr!" A boy Allison vaguely recognized as Rob Valentine waved wildly from a corner where kids were sitting on pillows around a low table. "Come play quarters."

"They're dropping like flies," Anders said as Archer sprinted toward his friend. "Come on," he added to Allison, who watched in disbelief as Adam and the birthday girl started making out against a wall. Thirty seconds after arrival; a new Adam Story record. "Let's get a drink."

Allison didn't particularly want to hang out with Anders, but she didn't recognize anyone else here, so she followed him into the bungalow's run-down kitchen. "Beer?" he yelled over his shoulder, then grabbed two Solo cups from a stack on the counter without waiting for an answer. The line for the keg was ten people deep, but Anders pushed his way to the front as though he didn't notice and wrestled the tap away from the startled boy who'd been filling his cup.

"Some things never change, huh?" asked a wry voice.

Allison turned to see Kayla Dugas, Anders's ex, and the third point of the infamous Matt-Anders-Kayla love triangle. Kayla's signature waist-length hair—she'd never cut it in her entire life—was hanging over her shoulders in loose curls. She looked effortlessly sexy in a black tank top and jeans, no makeup except for wine-colored lipstick on her rosebud mouth. Allison, who'd agonized about what to wear before settling on the kind of sweatshirt-and-shorts combo that Matt had deemed "GCI casual," suddenly felt ten years old.

Kayla had that effect on people. She wasn't unfriendly, exactly, but she was aloof in a way that Allison found frustrating. If life were a movie, Anders's on-again, off-again townie girlfriend would have been eager to impress his wealthy family, but Kayla always acted as though she was the one who needed to be won over. As a result, none of the Storys had ever really warmed to her except for Allison's father, who'd considered her a breath of fresh air. "I do believe your father has a *crush*," Mother had once said acidly, which made Allison certain that she celebrated Anders and Kayla's frequent breakups more than anyone.

This last one, after the Matt hookup, had been the longest ever. Anders had gone back to his second semester at Harvard swearing he'd never speak to Kayla again, and Allison hadn't heard him mention her name since. Until—

"Kayla." Anders handed Allison's beer to his ex, as though he'd intended it for her all along. "What a delightful non-surprise."

"Anders." Kayla accepted the cup with a sly smile. "Thought you weren't talking to me?"

Allison slipped away before Anders could reply. She'd never understand their dynamic: how her haughty, imperious brother could practically grovel for Kayla's affection until she gave it, and then promptly ignore her. Allison waited her turn at the keg, feeling invisible as Anders and Kayla kept inching closer together, becoming the center of the room's attention even as everyone pretended not to notice them.

"Disaster waiting to happen," someone murmured in her ear.

Allison turned to see Matt Ryan holding two full cups of beer. He handed her one, and she pushed his chest with alarm that was only half joking. "Run away before Anders sees you!" she said in an urgent whisper, but Matt just laughed.

"Anders only has eyes for Kayla," he said, but let Allison lead him out of the kitchen anyway. "I was hoping you'd be here," he added once they were out of sight in a corner beside the stairs.

Allison looked up at Matt, taking in his flushed cheeks, disheveled hair, and lopsided smile. It looked as though he'd been at Rob's party awhile. "Thanks for calling about getting coffee," she said sarcastically.

Whoops. That's not what she'd meant to lead with. She'd wanted to play it cool, like she hadn't thought about Matt's invitation every day since he'd made it. Her cheeks burned, but Matt just grinned. "Come on, you know I can't call your house. Everyone except you would hang up on me." He gave a rueful little chuckle. "Well, and maybe my mom."

"She says hi and hopes you're eating well," Allison reported dutifully, then wanted to sink through the floor. Nothing sexier than passing along a message from a guy's mother.

But Matt just laughed. "I'm not, but don't tell her that. She'll probably freak out and ask her sister to come stay with me. The last thing I need is my aunt Paula as a roommate. Hey, you want to play quarters?"

Allison drank half her beer as a stalling tactic. She didn't, particularly. She wanted to talk to Matt alone, but she wasn't sure how to make that happen at a party filled with people he knew and she didn't.

Unless she borrowed one of Adam's patented moves. Allison fanned herself and frowned. "It's so hot in here. I was thinking about taking a walk. Want to come?"

"Sure," Matt said, easily swallowing the line that, Adam liked to brag, had gotten him laid on every beach on Gull Cove Island. *Not that that's what I'm doing,* Allison told herself, draining the rest of her beer as she and Matt wound their way through the crowded living room. She just wasn't good at parties. And even though her brothers had all deserted her almost as soon as they'd arrived, she didn't want any of them seeing her with *fucking Matt Ryan.*

Plus there was the problem of Kayla. If she got bored with Anders, she might turn her attention back to Matt. And Allison couldn't compete.

She'd forgotten how cold it was, though, and started shivering as soon as the front door closed behind them. "Maybe this was a bad idea," Allison said as the wind picked up and goose bumps sprouted on her bare legs.

"Nah, we just need reinforcements." Matt unzipped his leather jacket and pulled a small bottle of bourbon from the inside pocket. "Liquid warmth," he said with a grin, unscrewing the top and handing it to Allison. She hesitated, and he cocked a teasing eyebrow. "Unless you're backing out on me?"

Allison had the feeling that he knew exactly what had been on her mind when she invited him outside, and her first instinct was to dart back into the bungalow. Until she took a small sip of bourbon, which was so warm and spicy and welcoming that she took a much larger one, and suddenly the last thing she wanted to do was play it safe. *Kayla wouldn't,* she thought, and then mentally kicked herself for thinking about Matt's ex at this particular moment. That girl took up far too much of her family's headspace as it was.

"Definitely not," Allison said.

"Good." Matt's smile widened as he slipped an arm around her shoulders. "I was hoping you'd say that."

# CHAPTER NINE

## JONAH

No matter how many times I stare at my phone, the numbers in my bank account never change.

*Checking: $10.71,* although that'll finally go up when I deposit my first paycheck from Gull Cove Resort. Nobody in accounting blinked, earlier in the summer, when I told them to use the name North. "My checking account is under my mother's maiden name," I said, and all they cared about was that I returned the paperwork in time.

The number that kills me is my savings account: *$0.00.* Five months ago, it was enough to cover two years of community college, where I planned to kick ass, grade-wise, while working part-time until I could transfer to a four-year university. I'd become the first college graduate in our family, and I'd do it with minimal loans because I'd saved every birthday check, every cent I'd ever made at my parents' billiards hall, and all the money I'd made tutoring over the years. I was still hoping for scholarships, but I wouldn't *need* them. Anything I got would just be icing on the cake.

Then I handed the entire account over to my dad, for a "can't miss" investment opportunity that was going to double everything we had. Maybe even triple it. And here we are now: a zero balance for me, and my savings account was hardly the biggest gamble the North family took with Anders Story.

*One disgruntled client lost the entirety of his retirement savings, his child's college fund, and is now in danger of losing his family's small business.*

It's ironic, I guess, that the son of the biggest victims of Anders Story's scam is now masquerading as *his* son. But it's also intentional. I had big plans for this summer, all of which I probably shot to hell by eating a plate of shrimp linguine.

"Dude." Efram's voice yanks me back to our dorm room at Gull Cove Resort. There's no air-conditioning, so Efram's giant fan is whirring noisily on his desk, sending a burst of air every time it rotates. Warm air, but better than nothing. "Do you seriously not hear the door?"

I blink at him as the knocking finally registers. "Why don't you get it?"

"Dude," Efram repeats, gesturing between me and the door. I'm at my desk, and he's prone on his bed with his laptop propped against his knees, a pair of oversized headphones looped around his neck. "You're closer."

Responsibility by proximity is one of the unspoken rules of guys rooming together, so I get to my feet without further complaint. When I open the door, Milly's standing there with Aubrey at her side, her fist half raised. "About time," she says, walking into the room.

"Hey, guys, what's up?" Efram says, a confused expression crossing his face. My "cousins" haven't visited me here once since we arrived a week and a half ago.

"We're borrowing Jonah," Milly says, spinning a set of keys on one finger. I force myself to keep my eyes on her face instead of the uncharacteristically short shorts she's wearing, because I'm not supposed to notice that kind of thing. "Carson is letting us use the resort Jeep for the afternoon. We're going to meet Hazel."

She says it like I'm supposed to know the name, but my mind is blank. "Who?"

"Hazel Baxter-Clement. The girl from town who's doing a college project on the Story family. Remember? With the grandfather?" My stomach clenches then, because *yeah,* I remember. I could barely stand to look at that girl while she was talking to us. I kept expecting her to blow my cover before I'd even gotten to the resort.

"Right," I say, aiming for a casual tone. "Why are we meeting her?"

"For the interview," Milly says brightly. "Aubrey and I decided to do it. And we *all* have to go. It's a family thing."

She's still spinning the keys, and I can read the challenge in her eyes loud and clear. I've barely seen Milly since she found me out, but I've been on edge the whole time, waiting for her to tell me she's sending me home. Now, it looks like she's decided not to—as long as I play along with whatever she wants.

And I will, but it's not a great situation. Especially since that Hazel girl literally studied the Story family. JT gave me background information before I left, but considering he couldn't be bothered to tell me he's allergic to shrimp, I'm not counting on his thoroughness. "I thought you didn't want to talk to her," I

122

hedge. Efram's still lying on his bed with his headphones around his neck, not even pretending that he's not listening.

"We changed our minds," Milly says. "Are you coming or not, *Jonah*?"

The way her voice hardens on my name decides it for me. "Fine," I mutter, grabbing my room key off the dresser. "But I won't have much to say."

She rolls her eyes. "You never do. See you, Efram."

"Later, cousins," he says, settling his headphones over his ears.

I follow Milly and Aubrey into the hallway, but wait until we're in the stairwell with the door closed behind us to ask, "Does this mean you're not gonna tell?"

Milly faces me, eyes wide. "Tell what? We don't know anything about anything. If something strange is going on around here, we'll be just as surprised as the rest of the world once it comes to light." Her lips press into a thin line. "Which it *will*."

She turns and heads down the stairs, and Aubrey pats me on the shoulder. "You're not very good at being our cousin," she says, not unkindly. "Go ahead and keep trying, though."

She follows Milly, and I'm at her heels with a growing sense of relief. "But you guys aren't gonna say anything?" I repeat. Just to be sure. "To Carson, or your parents, or JT, or . . . anyone?"

Milly makes me wait until we've made it all the way down the stairs before she lets me off the hook. "Your secret is safe with us, Jonah North."

Milly drives the resort-loaned Jeep while I scroll through the latest texts from JT. I hadn't told him about Milly catching on to us, hoping for a reprieve like the one I just got, but I did keep him in the loop about Mildred's invitations. He's not happy, at all, about the prospect of me hanging out with his grandmother. I can tell from his increasingly irritable messages that he never thought things would get this far.

*You should pretend you're sick for brunch*
*And the gala*
*Lie low till she gets bored*
*This is all just a game to her anyway*

I feel a rush of bitter satisfaction when I put my phone away without answering. Because here's the thing: if Mildred *isn't* playing a game—if she's actually interested in letting her grandchildren be part of her life—then JT is one degree of separation from a Bruce Wayne fortune. I go to school with a few people like Milly, who have the kind of money that pays for a big house, nice cars, and college. But Mildred Story is next level. She has fuck-you money and then some. If JT gets ahold of even a little of that, his entire family will be set for life.

And I promised myself, when I agreed to do this, that I wouldn't let that happen.

I didn't tell Milly the whole truth when she confronted me with my license. If I had, she would've sent me packing immediately. The reality is, I didn't go along with JT's plan for the bonus payment, or the free vacation. I agreed because it's not every day you get to screw people out of becoming megamillionaires, especially when those people are the Providence branch of the Story family. Nothing personal against JT, who's an ass but mostly harmless. He dangled this job like the privileged little prick he is: a consolation prize for what my family lost because of his father. *No hard feelings, right, Jonah? Shit happens.*

Shit doesn't happen unless it's stirred. I can give JT a pass. But his father?

I fucking hate that guy.

Which JT *has* to know. The fact that he asked me to take his place anyway proves that he's book smart, not people smart. He saw a cushy summer job for a guy who needs the money, and I saw the chance to make sure Anders Story stays cut off from his family fortune forever.

I'd have done that for free.

As soon as JT and I shook on this plan, I started dreaming about what I'd do if I ever got in front of Mildred Story. How I'd be a complete and utter asshole, so insulting that whatever door she might've been thinking about cracking open to the Providence Storys would slam shut. How Anders Story would know it happened because of me, and would wish he'd never messed with our family.

When I met Mildred that first day in Carson Fine's office, I was too caught off guard to say anything before she dismissed us. Then I blew my cover, and thought I was done for. Now it looks like I'm getting another chance. Except . . .

Some of my satisfaction ebbs away as I watch wind from the half-open window loosen strands from Milly's ponytail. I wasn't counting on having to worry about her and Aubrey this summer, because I didn't think I'd care about them. But Aubrey is one of the nicest people I've ever met, and Milly . . . well. She's given me nonstop grief since I met her on the ferry, but I can't blame her for that, and it hasn't stopped me from liking her a little too much.

I don't want to mess things up for either of them. What if

my selling out JT and Anders ruins their chances with Mildred too? What if they hate me for it?

"Oh my God." Milly sounds so startled that for a second, I'm sure she's read my mind. Then she slows the Jeep and says, "I think that's Catmint House."

I look up as Milly pulls the Jeep to a stop, giving us a clear view of the curving seaside road we're on and—holy hell. There's a huge house built at the edge of a steep bluff rising directly out of the ocean, its clean white lines a sharp contrast to the jagged black rocks. The part we're looking at is practically all floor-to-ceiling windows that sparkle in the summer sun. A shimmering metal widow's walk surrounds the roof, and a metal rail runs in front of a flat section to one side of the house. If I had to guess, I'd bet there's an infinity pool there. The view would be unbelievable.

I'm not really an architecture guy, but even I can appreciate how dramatic everything is. Not to mention massive. The place looks almost as big as Gull Cove Resort. For *one* person. My chest tightens, and once again, there's nothing on earth I want more than to keep Anders Story from ever making his way back here. I hope he dies before he sets foot in the oceanfront palace he grew up in. Even if I have to kill him myself.

"Unbelievable," Milly breathes, and my murderous thoughts evaporate. Mostly.

"I wonder what it's like inside?" Aubrey says wistfully. The more time I spend around Aubrey, the more I think she couldn't care less about the money. She just wants somebody in this messed-up family to give a shit about her.

"Guess we'll find out Sunday," Milly says, putting her foot back on the gas. Her words are casual, but her voice is tense as

Catmint House disappears from view. Milly's feelings about the Story family are harder to read. When she told Aubrey and me on the ferry that her mother bribed her with a diamond necklace, my first thought was: *She's shallow. She likes chasing shiny things, just like Anders Story.* But she could've easily joined the über-rich Towhee crowd—that smarmy senator's kid Reid Chilton obviously has a hard-on for her—and she hasn't.

We drive a few more minutes in silence until Milly turns into a driveway, so long and winding that we can't see the Baxterses' huge colonial until we're halfway down it. "Ooh, nice," Aubrey says as we approach. "I saw online that this place used to belong to a whaling captain. It's a historic landmark."

"You *saw online*?" I echo, amused. "Doing a little light stalking?"

She shrugs. "Hazel seems to know a lot about *us*. It's only fair."

Milly eases the Jeep next to a black Range Rover and shifts into park. "So you guys will do all the talking, right?" I say as we climb out of the car.

"Oh, I don't know," Milly says airily. "It depends on what kind of questions Hazel asks, doesn't it? Uncle Anders is a fascinating branch of the Story family tree."

She's enjoying my discomfort way too much.

Aubrey presses the doorbell, and we hear a muted "Be right there!" and the sound of footsteps before the door swings open to reveal Hazel. "Hi!" she says, stepping aside to let us in. Her eyes rove across each of us in turn, and I quickly drop mine. "You guys are right on time. I thought we could do the interview in our living room, if that's okay? Granddad is already there."

"Sure," Aubrey says. We follow Hazel down a hallway that's filled with what look like family pictures spanning several generations.

"Do you live with just your grandfather?" Milly asks.

"No, my mom lives here too. She moved back in after she and my dad got divorced a couple of years ago," Hazel explains. We pass a formal parlor, and I'm glad we're not talking there because all the chairs look like they belong in a museum. This conversation is going to be uncomfortable enough as it is. "She travels a lot in the summer, though. It works out, because I'm home then to spend time with Granddad." She lowers her voice. "We have a live-in nurse, but his dementia seems to get worse with no family around."

"You said he's doing better today, though?" Aubrey asks in a hopeful whisper.

"Totally," Hazel says as we step into a sun-filled room. It's much more casual than the rest of the house, with couches lining the brightly painted walls. Her grandfather is sitting in a corner of the biggest couch, a wooden tray with a teapot and a cup in front of him. As soon as he lifts his eyes, I can see the difference from the guy we met downtown. His gaze isn't sharp, exactly, but it's a lot more focused. "Granddad, the Story kids are here," Hazel says, crossing in front of him and pouring more tea into the cup. "This is Aubrey, Jonah, and Milly."

"So nice to see you again, Dr. Baxter," Milly says brightly. Aubrey echoes her greeting, while I shove my hands in my pockets and look at the floor. Operation Invisible, commenced.

"My goodness." Dr. Baxter's voice is faint. "I thought I must have misunderstood you, Hazel. But they really are here." I look up then, catching an expression of mild alarm on his face before he forces a stiff smile. "How wonderful. Please excuse me for not getting up to greet you properly. I'm not as steady on my feet as I once was."

"Do you guys want anything to drink?" Hazel asks. I shake my head as Milly and Aubrey murmur "No thanks," and Hazel gestures around the room as she settles in next to her grandfather. "Have a seat wherever."

I sit as far from Dr. Baxter as I can manage, but Aubrey does the opposite. She perches at the edge of the sofa that's at a right angle to Dr. Baxter's, so there's just an end table between them. "I'm Adam's daughter," she says with a friendly smile. "He talks a lot about how you helped him get back in shape after he blew out his knee in high school."

"Oh well." Dr. Baxter wets his lips. "Adam was a very determined young man. Yes. He certainly was."

Aubrey looks like she wants to say more, but Hazel picks up a notebook from the cushion beside her and speaks first. "So, I'm really curious," she says, flipping the notebook open and pulling a pen from its spine. "What was it like growing up knowing that you would've had a completely different life if your parents hadn't been cut off?"

"Wow." Milly blinks, giving the full Milly Story-Takahashi eyelash effect. "You're getting right to it, aren't you?"

Hazel smiles apologetically, but keeps her pen poised. "It's really interesting, from a sociological perspective, how the knowledge of a theoretical parallel life might affect the goals and aspirations of a new generation."

I slouch deeper into the armchair, but Milly straightens beside me. "You know what else is interesting?" she asks. "What people on Gull Cove Island think about what happened between my grandmother and our parents. I'd love to know what the local theories are."

"Oh gosh." Hazels lets out a guilty little laugh. "Do you really want to know? Some of the things people say are pretty out there." There's a clattering sound to my left as Dr. Baxter, who just took a noisy sip of tea, puts his cup back down and almost misses the saucer.

"I really do," Milly confirms.

Hazel tugs at her earring. "Well, the most common theory is that your grandmother had a breakdown after your grandfather died. Like, she was practically a hermit for a while, refusing to see anybody except her kids. And then she wouldn't see *them*, either. But Granddad has known Mrs. Story for years, and he never thought she was actually unstable," Hazel adds, turning to Dr. Baxter. "Did you, Granddad?"

"Well, no," Dr. Baxter says hesitantly. He looks even more uncomfortable than I feel, which is . . . interesting. I forget my disappearing act and lean forward for a better look at his face. The motion makes him turn my way, and his forehead creases in a deep frown. "You look nothing like Anders," he says abruptly.

Shit. I slouch right back into the shadows as Milly quickly says, "What are some of the other theories, Hazel? The ones that are 'out there.' " She puts the last two words in finger quotes.

Hazel glances my way, and I rub a hand over my face like I'm thinking. Even though what I'm really doing is hiding. "Well, it's funny what Granddad said about Jonah," she says slowly. "He *doesn't* look like Anders, does he? And Anders never looked like anybody else. Some people think Anders wasn't actually Mildred's son, that Abraham had a love child he forced his wife

130

to raise as their own." Aubrey's eyes pop as Hazel adds, "They say Mrs. Story tried to disinherit only Anders when her husband died, and the other kids left the island with him in solidarity."

"That wouldn't happen," Aubrey says, so quickly that I snort.

"Hell no," Milly agrees.

"And some things are just creepy," Hazel says. "Like, there's this gross rumor that one of Allison's *brothers* got her pregnant, and the rest of them tried to cover it up. But Mildred found out, and went ballistic on all of them. And that the baby is still—"

"*What?*" Milly interrupts in a piercing shriek. The look on her face is flat-out murderous. "People actually say that? That's completely and utterly disgusting!"

Hazel looks like she wants to crawl under the couch. I think she might've legitimately forgotten, for a few minutes, that she was talking about a real family. "I know. I'm sorry," she says, slamming the cover of her notebook closed. "I didn't mean—Look, no one actually believes it. Honestly. People just like to gossip and make shit up."

Milly stares blankly at Hazel, like she's about to burst into furious tears, and I have the irrational urge to punch someone. Not Hazel, obviously. Or her grandfather. But *someone.* Even Aubrey, who always struck me as the kind of person who'd release bugs outdoors instead of squashing them, looks ready to fight. Her hands are curled at her sides as she says, "I'd more easily believe they all killed somebody than *that.*"

There's a crashing sound then, as Dr. Baxter's knee knocks heavily into the tray table in front of him. The three girls turn toward him in unison as he fumbles for his teacup, staring at the bottom like it's disappointed him. "Where's my hot chocolate?" he asks, moving his watery gaze somewhere over Hazel's shoulder. "Katherine, it's time for hot chocolate."

"No it isn't, Granddad. You aren't supposed to have refined sugar. And Mom's not here," Hazel says with a sigh. She gets to her feet and moves the tray table a safe distance from the couch. "Katherine is my mother," she adds over her shoulder. "I think I'd better get him settled upstairs. It's not a great sign when he starts mixing us up."

She helps her grandfather stand, and holds him steady as they begin a slow shuffle across the room. He's still mumbling about hot chocolate when he passes Milly and Aubrey, both of whom look deeply unsettled. I'm pretty sure neither of them noticed that Dr. Baxter had clear, alert eyes on Hazel the entire time she was talking—right up until he deliberately bumped the table with his knee.

# CHAPTER TEN

## MILLY

I'll admit, I overpacked for the summer. But when I got dressed for my visit to Donald Camden's office this morning, I was glad for my navy sheath and high-heeled sandals. I was heading for the closest thing Gull Cove Island has to a corporate environment, and I wanted to blend in. Now that I'm seated in the plush waiting area, though, I'm not sure why I bothered. I haven't seen a single other person except the receptionist, who's currently filing her nails.

I listen to the receptionist answer an incoming call—it sounds like someone is trying to sell her a new copy machine—as I smooth out the flyer that I grabbed from the GCI HAPPENINGS bulletin board I passed on my way here.

**Friday, July 9**
**Rock on with the Asteroids**
**Gull Cove Island's Premier '80s Cover Band**
**9:00 p.m. at Dunes**

It's super cheesy, and I only picked it up because of the small lettering at the bottom: FEATURING ROB VALENTINE, JOHN O'DELL, CHARLIE PETRONELLI, AND CHAZ JONES.

I don't know Chaz the bartender's last name, but there can't be that many people named Chaz on Gull Cove Island. He hasn't come back to work yet, so I haven't had a chance to ask him for Edward Franklin's contact information. I'd love to track Edward down before brunch with Mildred on Sunday, so . . . it looks like I'm headed to eighties night at Dunes. Maybe I can rally a few Towhees to come with me.

"Miss Story-Takahashi? Mr. Camden will see you now," the receptionist calls. She stands and gestures for me to follow her down a marble-floored hallway. Trailing behind her, I pass a row of empty offices until I finally spot a young woman hunched over a phone, taking furious notes on the legal pad in front of her. It must be a big vacation week at Camden & Associates.

The receptionist pauses in front of an office with one wall that's nothing but windows, showing off a view of Gull Cove Harbor. She gestures for me to enter, and I step through the doorway. "Milly, hello," Donald Camden says. He gets up from behind a black desk with such a high-gloss finish that I can see my reflection when I lean forward to shake his hand. The entire office is decorated in black, white, and chrome, including the futuristic-looking desk chair that Donald settles back into once I'm sitting across from him. "How wonderful to see you again."

"You too."

"Thank you, Miranda," Donald tells the receptionist, who leaves without a word, shutting the door noiselessly behind her. My eyes stray to the large, silver-framed photo on the corner of Donald's desk, expecting to see a bunch of artfully posed blond grandchildren. Instead, it's a picture of Donald, Dr. Baxter, and Theresa Ryan, all dressed in formal wear, standing on what looks like the sweeping marble staircase at Gull Cove Resort.

*My grandmother's surrogate family,* I think, leaning in for a closer look. "That's a nice picture. Is it from the Summer Gala?"

"Yes, last year," Donald says, steepling his fingers beneath his chin. The sun streams through the window behind him, glinting off his gold cuff links. "I was so pleased to hear you're reconsidering my job offer, Milly. What else can I tell you about the opportunity?"

*Hell if I know.* I didn't come here with much of a plan beyond getting in the same room as Mildred's favorite guard dog, to see whether he'd let something interesting slip. Or whether I could pry it out of him. "I was curious about, um, what kind of work your friend's firm is doing for the movie? Because I'm interested in law as a career. I thought maybe I could help on that end of things."

An indulgent expression crosses his face. "I'm afraid their legal work is very specialized, and also very dry. A young lady like you wouldn't enjoy it at all."

Ugh, what a condescending jerk. I know plenty about specialized legal work from my dad's practice. But Donald seems like the type who might let his guard down if you encourage him to play the expert, so I ask, "Is it, like, contract stuff?"

Donald launches into a long-winded explanation that I only half listen to, because I don't actually care. Yesterday's conversation with Hazel left me seriously shook. Last night I kept tossing and turning, sickened by the perverted rumors about my mother floating around Gull Cove Island, unchecked by the people who know what really happened.

Including this guy, who's willing to pay a small fortune to get rid of us.

"That's so interesting," I say brightly when Donald finally stops for a breath. "It sounds like a great opportunity. I'm just torn because, you know . . ." I bite my lip. "I was excited at the chance to get to know my grandmother. I've never understood what happened between her and my mom. If I did, it would be much easier to leave."

"Milly." Donald shakes his head. "This is exactly the sort of conversation you shouldn't be having with your grandmother. It will upset her and threaten her fragile health."

"That's why I'm not asking her. I'm asking you." I deliver the words with as much wide-eyed innocence as I can muster, then add a little flattery. "Mrs. Ryan speaks so highly of you."

Theresa Ryan hasn't said a word to me beyond emailing instructions about brunch, but Donald doesn't need to know that. "How kind of her," he says, but there's a reserve to his response that I can't quite read.

"I didn't tell her I was coming here," I say, in case that's his concern. "And I wouldn't tell my grandmother, either. She'd never have to know we talked about this."

Donald sits straighter in his chair, frowning, and I realize I went too far with that last line. "I would never violate your grandmother's confidence, Milly. It's not only morally wrong but also illegal. I am her counsel, after all."

"Okay, but . . ." I keep my fake smile firmly in place and take another tack, even though I know I'm losing him. "But couldn't you suggest that she talk to us about what happened? Clear the air? Maybe she'd be healthier, and happier, if everything was out in the open."

Donald regards me steadily. "Milly, will you take a word of advice from an old man?"

*Definitely not.* "Of course."

"Leave the past where it is. You and your cousins seem wonderfully well-adjusted—which was not, to be frank, the case with your parents when they were your age. There's nothing to be gained from reopening old wounds, and a lot to lose." He smiles at me with what he probably thinks is grandfatherly charm. "Now, can I put in a call to my friend and confirm you and your cousins for the *Agent Undeclared* set?"

He's obviously not going to tell me anything useful, but at least I get the satisfaction of watching his face drop when I say, "No."

It's hot and crowded at Dunes, and hard to carry on a conversation because the Asteroids are covering Journey at top volume. Chaz is in the shadows, on a stool toward the back of the stage. All I can see clearly are his jean-clad legs and the edge of his guitar.

"Milly! Question for you," Brittany shouts into my ear above the music. We're crowded around a small table with Efram, Aubrey, and a couple of other kids from the Towhee program. Behind us, Jonah is playing pool with an older guy I don't recognize. Probably somebody from here, since the crowd at Dunes is much more townie than tourist. Efram snuck a flask of rum in and has been doctoring all of our Cokes, except for Aubrey's. I'm at that pleasant, slightly buzzed point of the night where everyone around me seems more likable than usual, so I beam cheerfully at Brittany even though we don't usually talk much.

She taps my arm, and I realize I owe her an answer. "What?" I yell back. The band wraps up their song and the crowd cheers loudly, shouting for more.

"Does your cousin have a girlfriend? He's so cute." I follow Brittany's gaze to where Jonah is lining up a shot, dark brown hair flopping into one eye and the lean muscles in his arms flexing. Objectively, yes, that's an attractive pose for him. And his face hits all the right notes: straight nose, full lips, square jaw. It still feels weird, and a little wrong, to notice that. Just like it did on the ferry, when I realized the hot guy on the staircase I'd been checking out was my cousin.

But now he's not.

Jonah looks up and meets my eyes, then winks and flashes a wicked grin before taking his shot. My cheeks warm and I glance at Brittany, who's looking between us with a confused expression. "You should go talk to him. He just winked at you," I say.

"I don't think he was—" Brittany starts.

I swirl the ice in my drink before finishing it. "You know what, I don't actually know if Jonah has a girlfriend or not. We're not particularly close, but I'll find out. For you."

The distinctive piano opening of "Don't Stop Believin'" rings out as I slide off my stool, and the crowd goes wild. Jonah is finishing the last of his rum and Coke, glaring at the cue ball like it betrayed him, when I nudge his arm with mine. "Don't tell me you missed a shot," I say.

The townie guy Jonah is playing against descends on the table, cue in hand. "Excuse me, small-town girl," he says loudly as the lead singer of Chaz's band screams the same lyrics behind us. I roll my eyes and step aside.

Jonah squints at me with a half smile. "I was distracted," he says.

"Stop that," I hiss.

"Stop what?"

"Flirting with me."

"I'm not flirting with you." Jonah props his pool cue against the wall and leans beside it with a lazy grin. The alcohol is obviously hitting him as hard as it is me, because I've never seen him this loose before. "You're kind of full of yourself, aren't you?"

"You *winked* at me!"

"That was a cousinly wink. The kind that says, *Hey, cuz, hope you're having a good time stalking our grandmother's bartender.* Not *Hey, Milly, you look really pretty tonight.*" He dips his head toward mine. "Even though you do."

"You're ridiculous," I mutter, fighting off a smile. Damn it. I haven't been interested in anyone for nearly a year, and I can't start now. This summer is enough of a mess without adding that particular complication. "I'm going back to the table."

"Don't." Jonah's hands briefly circle my waist and he spins me to face the pool table as I studiously avoid whatever incredulous look Brittany must be sending our way. I can't even blame her. "He already missed, so it's my turn again. And you're good luck."

I should leave. This is beyond weird to the casual observer. But while I can handle asshole Jonah and imposter Jonah, I'm completely unprepared for this version. I stand rooted in place while the band plays on and Jonah circles the table like he owns it. He sinks four quick shots plus the eight ball, and just like that, the game is over. Jonah's opponent puts his hands together in a praying motion, bowing in an exaggerated manner that, somehow, still seems kind of respectful. Then he extends his hand for a fist bump before melting back into the crowd. The band wraps up to loud applause, but instead of launching into their next song, they start conferring onstage.

"One of these days you're going to explain how and where you acquired your mad skills," I say as Jonah places his cue in a wall rack. I mean it as a compliment, but the confident smirk drops from his face like I just wiped an eraser across it.

Before I can apologize—for what, I don't even know—the Asteroids' lead singer leans into his microphone. He has the same Gull Cove townie look about him as the guy Jonah just beat: deeply tanned, weather-beaten, and older than he probably is. "Evening, all, and thanks for coming out," he says. "We're just about done for the night, but before we take off, we'll be switching things up a little. Our guitarist, who's usually a stay-in-the-shadows kind of guy, has asked if he can close things out with his favorite song. So please give it up for Chaz!"

"Let's go listen," I say to Jonah, starting for the table where Aubrey, Efram, and Brittany are still sitting. He follows me, so closely that when I suddenly turn, I nearly bump into him. I should probably back up, but I don't. "Oh! One more thing. I was supposed to find out whether or not you have a girlfriend." My voice comes out breathier than I'd intended, and I try to inject a more businesslike tone when I add, "For Brittany."

Jonah stares at me for a beat, brown eyes sparkling with reflected light from the stage. "No," he says. "I don't have a girlfriend. But I'm not interested in Brittany."

My face is way too hot. "All right. Noted," I say, turning before he can pick up on my blush. We reach the table just as Chaz steps into center stage, blinking like he's not quite sure how he

140

got there. Even from this distance he looks rough, and I have no problem believing he's still on that days-long bender everyone at Gull Cove Resort keeps gossiping about.

I slip back onto my stool, avoiding Brittany's gaze. Chaz mumbles, "This one's for my family," his voice crackling against the mic, and strums a familiar chord. The band kicks in seconds later, and Aubrey straightens in her seat.

"Is that—" she starts.

"Weezer," Brittany says. " 'Africa.' "

"Not originally." Efram leans forward. "Toto did it first. This band is all about the eighties, remember?" He frowns a little. "This song is really . . . a product of its time, isn't it? Like, they'd probably never been to Africa, but they decided to sing about it anyway. In a supremely cringey way."

He's right, but that's not what I'm thinking about as I try to catch Aubrey's eye. Was this song as much a part of her childhood as mine, or did Uncle Adam not share this particular bit of Story lore? Has she seen the video of my mother, her father, and their brothers, singing this song at the top of their lungs when they were kids?

Aubrey is staring intently at the stage, so I shift my gaze from her to Chaz. He tilts his head and closes his eyes as he sings the chorus and— *Ohhhh.*

Oh my God.

I'm on my feet in an instant, shouldering my way through the crowd until I'm almost at the front of the stage. I've been closer to Chaz in The Sevens than I am here, but I can see him clearly beneath the bright lights of the stage.

I can't believe it took me this long to figure it out.

As soon as the song finishes to loud applause, Chaz drops

his guitar onto the stage and lifts one hand in the air, signaling to the bartender as he walks offstage. I turn and head for the bar, too, but get stuck behind a group of guys my age. I have to start breathing through my mouth when the smell of too many competing colognes overpowers me.

"Hey, Milly, how's it going?" Reid Chilton says, smiling widely as I crane my neck to see past him. Chaz looks slightly panicked, but also determined. Like he just realized he needs to escape, but isn't willing to leave without a drink in hand.

"Great, but I can't talk right now," I say shortly, pushing between him and another boy in a blue polo shirt. The second boy laughs as I pass.

"Damn, Reid. She's not feeling you *at all*."

I keep weaving through the crowd until I'm close enough to grab hold of Chaz's sleeve. I tug hard, and he turns. The eyes that meet mine are so familiar that I'm annoyed with myself all over again for not seeing it sooner. Conversation buzzes loudly around us but I still lower my voice, bringing my lips close to his ear so he can hear me.

"Hey, Uncle Archer," I say. My mother's youngest brother's eyes widen in alarm as I add, "Are you the one who brought us here?"

# CHAPTER ELEVEN

## AUBREY

"I'm nowhere near drunk enough for this conversation," Uncle Archer mutters, running an unsteady hand over his mouth.

"Oh yes, you are," the band's lead singer says grimly. We're in his house now—or, more accurately, the bungalow *behind* his house where Uncle Archer lives. It doesn't look like much from the outside, but inside it's surprisingly large and clean.

The singer's name is Rob Valentine, he told us back at Dunes. He runs a painting business on the island, and used to be a friend of Uncle Archer's in high school. Without him, Uncle Archer probably would've escaped through the back door of Dunes as soon as Milly used his real name. "Come on," Rob said as he half wrestled Uncle Archer toward a battered Honda SUV in the parking lot. Milly, Jonah, and I trailed behind them, too shell-shocked to do anything except watch. "No more hiding. Tell the kids what's going on."

"I will at the house," Uncle Archer mumbled when he finally

gave up and let Rob push him into the Honda's passenger seat. Then he promptly passed out, or pretended to.

The drive to Rob's house was short, just enough time for him to awkwardly ask after our parents before we reached his driveway. Then we went through another lengthy production of getting Uncle Archer out of the car, into the bungalow, and onto a small sofa. He's sitting upright now, but sagging against the plaid cushions as Rob takes a seat at the opposite end of the sofa. Milly, Jonah, and I are lined up on a futon across from them, waiting.

Uncle Archer finally clears his throat and says, "So . . . this isn't exactly how I'd planned on introducing myself to the three of you." His glance skitters in our direction without ever really settling on us. "In retrospect, I shouldn't have . . ." He trails off, and Milly fidgets beside me. Her impatience for getting some kind of explanation is coming off her in waves. "Played that song," he finishes.

Milly sits up straighter, frowning. "*That's* what you're leading with? Song choice?"

"It's kind of my signature song," Uncle Archer says, as though Milly were looking for an explanation instead of expressing frustration. "Well, my family's signature song, back when we lived here. I guess your mom told you that. And people here . . ."

He trails off, and Rob finishes for him. "Remember. So much for being incognito, *Chaz.*"

"My cover was already blown," Uncle Archer mutters. "Blew it last week."

"You don't know that," Rob says. His tone is one of patient forbearance, like he's made the same argument more than once. "He hasn't said anything yet, has he?"

144

Milly and I exchange confused glances. "Who hasn't said anything?" she asks. "What are you talking about?"

"Tell them, Archer," Rob says. "From the beginning."

Uncle Archer's head just droops in response. We all wait for him to speak again, until Rob heaves a sigh and shoots us an apologetic glance. "This might be one of those nights that we need to let him sleep it off," he says.

"So tired," Uncle Archer mumbles.

Milly gives them both an assessing look before getting up and heading for the kitchen. When she comes back, she's holding a glass half full of water. She stands in front of Uncle Archer, raises the glass, and throws the water in his face.

His head jerks up and his eyes pop open, shocked but alert. "What the hell?" Water droplets cling to his beard and soak into his shirt as he wipes a sleeve across his face.

"You owe us answers," Milly says.

"Hey, now." Rob's voice is gentle, but firm. "I understand that you're frustrated, but your uncle isn't being difficult by choice. You're dealing with someone who has a disease, and unfortunately, sometimes this is what addiction looks like."

Milly opens her mouth, then closes it and drops back onto the futon, red-faced. It's the first time I've ever seen her look chastened, and I have to admit—I'm glad she does. Normally I like her hard-charging style, but seeing Uncle Archer like this makes my chest hurt. Milly said on the way over that we should've realized who he was earlier, but I don't see how we could have. My last memory of Uncle Archer is of him handsome and laughing, crouching on the floor with me to build a Lego town when I was a little kid. There's nothing familiar about this version unless you know to look for it.

"I'm sorry," Milly says quietly.

"It's okay," Uncle Archer says, blinking through still-wet eyes. "I deserved that. And hey, what do you know? It might've done the trick." He laughs shakily and swipes the last of the water droplets from his beard. "I owe you an apology, too. All of you. You asked me, in Dunes, if I brought you here. Truth is, I did."

And there it is: the answer to a two-week mystery. But it only raises more questions, and for once, Milly seems reluctant to ask them. Jonah's basically useless, since he's too worried about saying the wrong thing, so I guess it's up to me. "Why? And how?"

Uncle Archer looks longingly at Milly's discarded glass, like he wishes it were still full and holding something stronger than water. "It started with Edward—you remember Edward Franklin?" He looks at us questioningly, and we all nod. Milly recovers enough to elbow me in the side with a self-satisfied smirk, since she's been trying to follow the Edward Franklin thread all week. "Well, Edward and I were introduced by a mutual friend in Boston last winter, and we hit it off. When I found out where he worked, it seemed like fate. I'd been thinking a lot about family, and home, and I just—I wanted to come back. But I knew I couldn't waltz in here as Archer Story. I asked Edward to set me up with a bartending job at the resort, and Rob if I could pose as a friend from out of town while I got my bearings."

"Bearings?" I echo, and Archer sends me a wry smile.

"I had this silly fantasy at first that I'd run into Mother at some point, and all the anger she's been holding on to would melt away. That she'd realize she wants to be reunited just as much as I do. But that didn't happen. I haven't even caught a glimpse of her the entire time I've been here. She keeps herself very isolated. Even when she comes to the resort for business reasons, she only sees a handful of people."

I inch a little closer to the edge of my seat. "Uncle Archer, do you know what the letter meant?" He furrows his brow, and I clarify. "The *you know what you did* letter that Donald Camden sent. Do you, um . . . know what you did?"

"I have no idea." He spreads his hands in a helpless gesture. "I've never been able to understand what she meant. I'd give anything if I could."

It's the same answer Dad has always given, and that I've always accepted without question. But now that I know how duplicitous my father can be, I've been considering his response through a different lens—his eyes would shift just a little, his jaw tighten, and his nostrils flare. Small tics that make me wonder what he might have been hiding. When I search Uncle Archer's face, I don't see any of that, though. All I see is sadness, and confusion.

"Did you ever think about trying to see Gran?" I ask.

"Constantly," he says. "But the longer I was here, the more I realized I'd been kidding myself to imagine that I could become part of her life again. Me, Adam, Anders, Allison—none of us can. Whatever happened to change Mother's feelings hasn't faded in more than twenty years. Our chapter of the Story legacy ended a long time ago. And then I saw an article about *you*, Aubrey."

I tilt my head, confused. "Me?"

"Yeah. Your swim team was in that national meet that *USA Today* covered. I read the article, and it hit me all over again how fractured our family is. It felt like such a waste, to know so little about you that I hadn't even realized you'd become an elite swimmer."

"I'm not elite," I say, my cheeks warming. "It was a team thing."

"It's a tremendous accomplishment!" Uncle Archer insists, and I have to blink back sudden tears. My father didn't even go to that meet. He said he wasn't feeling well, but he probably just didn't want to run into his girlfriend with his wife there. "I was proud of you, and I wanted to congratulate you. But I was afraid that would seem strange and out of the blue, since we hardly know one another. Then I thought about Mother, and how she's never met any of you. I told Edward that if she did, maybe she'd realize what a mistake she'd made cutting off her entire family tree. That's when the idea took hold of me, and wouldn't let go."

Milly's held her tongue the entire time Uncle Archer and I were talking, but she can't keep quiet any longer. "To bring us here under false pretenses?" she blurts out.

Her words are harsh, but her tone isn't, and Uncle Archer smiles ruefully. "It seemed a lot more virtuous in my head, but—yeah. In a nutshell, I guess that's it. Edward was planning on leaving Gull Cove anyway, so I convinced him to invite you guys under Mother's name." He clears his throat. "I, um, don't have the best of relationships with any of your parents, so I didn't clue them in. I figured they'd forgive the deception if things worked out like I hoped."

My head is starting to hurt from all the new information I'm trying to process. "Were you the one who tipped off the *Gull Cove Gazette*?"

"Yes," Uncle Archer admits. "I thought it would buy you some time, since Mother cares a lot about appearances. I didn't expect you'd run into her on the very first day. But I'm glad you did, because—I was right, wasn't I? She *does* want to know you. She's invited you to Catmint House, and to the Summer Gala, hasn't she?"

"Well, yeah, but only after ignoring us for two weeks. Which seems more like she's trying to save face than mend fences." Milly frowns, shaking her head. "I mean, what's the long-term plan here? Did you think she'd never find out that you're the one who brought us here?"

"Oh no." Archer looks shocked at the suggestion. "I've been planning to tell Mother everything after the gala." He rubs a hand across his face. "In a letter, probably. It's highly unlikely she'd agree to see me."

Milly stares at him like he's just sprouted a second head. "But she'd be furious at you for pulling something like that. You'd never get re-inherited."

Uncle Archer's brow creases. "Re-inherited?"

"You know. Back in the will. An heir once more," Milly says. "Isn't that what you want? It's what my—it's what our parents were hoping," she adds, glancing first at me and then at Jonah. "Right?"

Jonah clears his throat. "It's definitely what my, um, parents were hoping."

"Mine too," I say.

"Well." Archer blinks. "This is going to sound naive, I suppose, but all I really wanted was for her to get to know you. And vice versa."

We're all quiet for a minute, absorbing that. I almost don't believe it—a Story who doesn't care about his lost fortune? That goes against everything I've ever known about my father's family. But the thing is, I can't imagine any scenario where this situation turns out well for Uncle Archer. Even if Gran ends up happy to have us here—which feels like a big *if*—she'd still have been duped by her youngest son. And we already know she's not the forgiving type.

"Anyway, I'm sure I'll be fired the next time I show up at work." Uncle Archer sighs and looks at the floor. "Which is why I've been avoiding it. So to speak."

"Why?" I ask, and then remember his conversation with Rob from earlier. *My cover was already blown.* "Did someone recognize you?"

Uncle Archer grimaces. "Fred Baxter, of all damn people. He was our family doctor when I was a kid, and he has dementia now. I ran into him in Mugg's Pharmacy last week. He was by himself, looking lost, and I figured he'd given his nurse the slip. I offered to help him find her, and he said, 'No thank you, Archer. I could use some time alone.'" Uncle Archer shakes his head. "Here I am thinking the guy can't even find the door, and he's the only person on the entire island to see through the Chaz Jones facade. He asked me where I was staying, and I . . . I was so rattled that I actually *told* him."

"Well, he might've forgotten," I say consolingly. "We've met him. He does that a lot."

"You met Dr. Baxter?" Archer asks, just as Jonah says, "Does he, though?"

I look between them, but Jonah doesn't say anything else, so I answer my uncle. "Mostly we met his granddaughter, but he was . . . there." And then I shut up, because there's no way I'm heading down the rabbit hole of sharing Hazel's ugly rumors.

Uncle Archer looks nonplussed. "Okay, well . . . whether Fred Baxter remembers seeing me or not, once I tell Mother the truth, my time here is up." He leans forward, elbows on his knees, looking suddenly exhausted. "You guys probably think I'm out of my mind. Maybe I am. But I really did mean well."

My phone buzzes then. I pull it out of my pocket automatically and without much interest, but my eyes widen when I see the name on my screen. *Thomas: What's up?*

I almost laugh. How much time do you have, Thomas? And why is he getting in touch *now*, after two weeks of silence?

But I know why; it's because I stopped thinking about him.

Thomas has a sixth sense about stuff like that. For years, I've showered him with attention while getting scraps in return, and the only time that dynamic has ever shifted is when I pulled back. Even unconsciously. Like sophomore year, when he wasn't going to take me to the spring dance because "dances are boring," until I got partnered with a new boy in biology and couldn't help noticing what a nice, deep brown his eyes were. I never even mentioned the boy's name, but Thomas could tell I wasn't as fixated on him as usual. And suddenly, we were going to the dance as if he'd been planning it all along.

Because Thomas only really pays attention when the adoration he thinks he deserves starts to fade. Just like . . .

Oh God. When it hits me I want to throw up. Not only out of disgust with myself for putting up with him for so long, but because it never occurred to me until *right now* that I've basically been dating the Ashland High version of my father.

Milly's elbow digs into my side again, bringing me back to the present. "Are you okay with that, Aubrey?" she asks.

I blink around the room. Everyone is looking at me except Uncle Archer. He's slumped against the sofa cushions, as though whatever burst of energy carried him through the conversation has deserted him. "With what?" I ask.

"We're going to sleep on this and talk more tomorrow," Milly says.

"I'm just—" Uncle Archer gestures unsteadily with one hand, knocking a pile of envelopes from the end table beside him onto the floor. "Damn it. What are those?" he asks as I crouch down to gather them up.

"Your mail," Rob says, showing the first hint of impatience all night. "In the exact same place I put it every time I bring it by."

"Eh, it's all junk anyway," Uncle Archer mutters. "Dear Occupant, blah blah."

I shuffle the mail in my hand. "You got a letter," I say, holding out an envelope with *Archer Story* written neatly across the front. There's no stamp or address, as though someone simply slipped it into the mailbox.

"I did?" Uncle Archer takes it with a bemused expression and opens the flap. "Who the hell would send me a letter? No one even knows I'm here, except . . ." He pulls out a single sheet of paper, the crease between his eyes deepening as he reads. "This is—I don't understand this."

"What is it?" I pluck the paper from his unresisting hand and turn it over. I scan the brief lines, then meet my uncle's eyes. His confusion mirrors my own as I say, "I guess he remembered after all."

"Who?" Milly asks. "Remembered what?"

I raise my eyebrows at Uncle Archer in a silent question, and when he nods, I read the note out loud.

Archer,

    I have not been able to rest easy since seeing you the other day.

    There are things I should have told you long ago.

    And I fear my time is running short.

    Would you be so good as to meet with me?

Yours,
Fred Baxter

## ALLISON, AGE 18

### JULY 1996

"Hey, Matt, it's Allison. So, *Independence Day* is playing at Gull Cove Cinema, and I was thinking about going next weekend. Can't get enough of those alien invasions. Let me know if you want to come with? You can call me here, or whatever. Okay, talk to you later. Bye."

Allison hung up the phone and immediately started pacing her bedroom in a haze of mortification. *Can't get enough of those alien invasions?* What was wrong with her? But then again, it hardly mattered what she said or didn't say. Matt hadn't returned her two previous messages, so he'd probably delete this one without even listening. It was time to face facts: what she'd considered a romantic, possibly life-changing (or at least summer-changing) night on the beach at Rob Valentine's party was just a one-night stand.

Matt Ryan was blowing her off.

She'd only seen him once in the three weeks since Rob's party, when he was delivering flowers to Donald Camden's waterfront office. Allison had actually followed him inside, rehearsing the *Oh, I was just dropping something off from my mother* excuse she'd use when he noticed her. But Kayla Dugas, who was working that summer as part of the office's cleaning crew, got to Matt first. "Hey, stranger," she called, pushing her mop toward him with a little shimmy that made Matt laugh. Even in a shapeless blue smock and plastic gloves, Kayla looked gorgeous. Allison ducked behind a pillar, but she might as well have been invisible. Neither of them took their eyes off one another, and Allison ended up slinking right back outside.

She'd told herself all kinds of stories to explain Matt's silence. *He's playing it cool. He's worried about what his mother will say. He's intimidated by my family.* But too much time had passed for any of those to be true.

Which sucked, but wasn't even close to her biggest problem right now.

Allison's room suddenly felt too small and too lonely. She stepped into the hallway, listening for signs of life in Catmint House. Her brothers were on the beach, an invitation she declined because she'd wanted to be alone while she called Matt. On the off chance that he would pick up, which seemed ridiculous now.

Mother had to be around somewhere. She barely left the house anymore.

Allison padded downstairs and, sure enough, her mother was seated at the window table in the kitchen, poring over home design catalogs. She'd recently redone the backsplash behind the Viking double stove with hand-painted tiles from Italy, then decided they were too "showy" and needed to be replaced with something else. "Allison, what do you think of these?" she asked, turning the catalog face out as Allison approached the table.

Allison gazed down at a page's worth of unremarkable white tiles. "You're going to break Theresa's heart, you know," she said. Theresa had recommended the Italian tiles, and Allison happened to agree with her that they were stunning—little works of art that brought color and vibrancy to the kitchen. But Mother needed a distraction that didn't require her to leave the house, and she'd chosen redecorating.

"Well, Theresa doesn't live here, does she?" Mother asked, taking the catalog back.

"Actually, she does," Allison reminded her. And then, because she was at that point of unrequited crushdom that she'd take any excuse to mention his name, she added, "Matt must be lonely without her."

"Boys that age don't miss their mothers," Mother said. "Or listen to them. That's a universal truth I know all too well." Her voice hardened as she turned a page in the catalog. "Anders is seeing that girl again, isn't he?"

"What girl?" Allison asked, even though she knew perfectly well that her mother meant Kayla. And Mother was right; despite whatever Kayla might have going on with Matt, she had fallen right back into old patterns with Anders.

Mother's lips thinned as she flipped pages faster. "He's getting too old for this nonsense. There are so many wonderful girls at Harvard, the kind he could build a real future with. Your father and I were engaged by the time we were sophomores."

Allison would have laughed if her mother hadn't looked so serious. "Anders is nineteen, Mother. He's not thinking about marriage."

"I guarantee you *she* is," Mother sniffed. "He'd better watch out if he doesn't want to find himself trapped."

The conversation was becoming uncomfortable on too many levels. "I'm going to see if the boys are back," Allison said, getting to her feet.

"I expect you all home for dinner tonight," Mother said without looking up from the catalog.

"We will be," Allison promised.

She hurried out of the kitchen, down the hallway that led to the foyer, and nearly bumped into Theresa, who was accepting a delivery at the front door.

"Hi," Allison gulped, pasting on a smile. God, she hoped Theresa hadn't heard any of that kitchen conversation.

But Theresa just smiled distractedly. "Hi, Allison. Right over there," she told the delivery man, who wheeled his dolly containing a large, rectangular cardboard box into the foyer. "New sculpture," she added as an aside to Allison. "Another bronze."

"Ah." Enough said. Allison's mother was having a bronze moment lately, and each sculpture was uglier than the next. It was heroic, really, that Theresa managed to keep a straight face when talking about them. "Have you seen the boys?"

"Driveway," Theresa said, pointing to the still-open door. Adam's cherry-red BMW convertible was visible through the frame. "I think they're headed downtown."

"Really?" Allison perked up. Downtown was a useful destination. She dashed through the door, waving wildly at Adam as he started to back up.

"What?" he asked impatiently, hitting the brake.

"I'm coming with you," Allison said, climbing into the backseat with Archer. "I have an errand to run."

* * *

157

Hurley Street was packed, and Adam had to slow to a crawl to accommodate all the tourist traffic. Allison watched her brother adjust his Ray-Bans in the rearview mirror, and flex the tanned bicep that he'd draped out the car window. Adam liked nothing better than performing for an audience, and he considered all of Gull Cove his personal stage.

"How is there no parking?" he complained, as if it wasn't the height of vacation season. "I hope Sweetfern isn't a zoo."

"I'm going to the comic book store first," Archer said, with a sideways glance toward Allison. Only she knew why: because he was crushing on the cute guy working the register this summer. Archer had told Allison over Christmas that he was gay, and she'd been touched that he trusted her with information he hadn't shared with anyone else in their family. He'd intended to approach their mother next, but Father had died soon after. The timing, Archer said, was never right after that.

"Save me a seat?" he asked her now.

"I'm going to Mugg's first," Allison said.

Anders yawned loudly in the front seat. "I'll come with you. I need a razor."

"I'll get you one," Allison said quickly.

He made a dismissive noise in his throat. "You'll get the wrong kind."

"Not if you tell me what you want."

"It's easier to get it myself. Plus I don't have any cash to give you."

"I'll pay for it," Allison said, trying to keep her voice casual. She desperately didn't want Anders trailing her through Mugg's Pharmacy, but if he knew that, she'd never get rid of him.

Anders twisted in his seat to look at her. "It's an artisan-made razor that costs more than two hundred dollars. You want to cover that for me?"

"Sure. Fine," Allison muttered. Thank God for credit cards. Anders recited details about his ridiculously overpriced razor as Allison kept her eyes on the street.

"Got it," she said.

"Oh, sweet! Look at that." A car pulled out of a prime parking spot right in front of them, and Adam expertly parallel parked the BMW. "The streak continues," he gloated as he shifted into park. Parking spots always opened up for Adam. It was annoying, actually.

"Congratulations," Allison said flatly. "See you at Sweetfern." As soon as Adam turned off the engine, she launched herself out of the car without waiting for her brothers. They had parked just a block from Mugg's Pharmacy, and Allison strode quickly down the crowded sidewalk until she reached the distinctive brown-and-white striped awning. She pulled the door open to the discreet jingle of a bell.

"Hello, Allison. What brings you here today?" Mr. Mugg's twentysomething son Dennis was behind the cash register, because *of course* he was. It couldn't be a college student here for the summer whom she'd never see again.

"Hi," she said, forcing a smile. "Well, first off, I'm getting the Zephyr AS single-edge razor for my brother. He said it would be behind the counter?"

"Indeed. Excellent choice," Dennis said, unclipping a set of keys from his belt loop. He unlocked the glass case behind him and removed a black velvet box, as though Allison were buying a piece of jewelry. "It's a solid block of stainless steel with a satin matte finish," Dennis said, opening the box to reveal the razor inside. Allison had to admit that, as far as razors went, it was a good-looking one. Maybe Anders could hang it on his wall, since he barely needed to shave. "Very slim and ergonomic. Will you be wanting a set of blades with that?"

Anders hadn't specified blades, and since they were probably another two hundred dollars, he could buy them on his own. "No, just the razor."

"Anything else?" Dennis asked, putting the box into a brown-and-white paper bag.

"Yes, but I'll get it myself and come back." Allison unzipped the top of her bag, then said the words that would guarantee Dennis wouldn't try to extend the conversation when she returned. "I need some tampons."

She ducked into an aisle before Dennis could turn red and start stammering. He hadn't mastered the art of the poker face when it came to feminine hygiene products.

At least Mugg's Pharmacy was empty. Tinny music piped through the speakers as Allison worked her way to the back of the store. She grabbed a box of Tampax, then moved farther down the aisle to find what she'd really come for.

*Early pregnancy test*
*Results in five minutes!*
*Accurate within two weeks of conception*

Allison said a silent prayer of thanks that Mr. Mugg was too old-fashioned to install security cameras, before she plucked a pregnancy test off the shelf and dropping it into her bag. Then she turned, and froze.

"Well, well, well." Anders was standing a few feet from her, with a smirk that left no doubt he'd seen exactly what she was about to shoplift. "What do we have here?"

160

# CHAPTER TWELVE

## JONAH

A persistent ringing wakes me up Saturday morning. My room is stuffy and hot, and I push aside the tangle of sheets weighing me down before reaching for the floor to pick up my phone. Efram is gone, probably working an early shift at the pool. I'm not due at The Sevens until noon, so even though it's past ten I don't need to get up for another hour. And wouldn't have, if it weren't for . . . Oh hell.

My dad. I want to let it go to voice mail, but I can't. I know why he's calling. "Hey, Dad," I say, heaving myself into a sitting position. "How was bankruptcy court?"

"Postponed," he says.

"Sorry, what?"

"Your mom and I need a little more time to finish the re-structuring plan we're proposing. So we asked the trustee for an extension until next week, and he said yes."

"Okay," I say cautiously. "Is that good or bad?"

"It's good. Gives us a better shot at hanging on to Empire."

Empire is Empire Billiards, named after my mother's favorite movie, *Empire Records*. My parents bought it when I was too young to remember what life was like before Empire became the family business. My first memory of it is the two-year anniversary when I was five; my dad carried my mother through the door with me trailing behind, into what felt like the biggest party I'd ever seen. Even though, looking back on it more than ten years later, it was probably just our relatives, a few of the construction workers and plumbers who'd become Empire regulars, and a lot of balloons.

It didn't matter. I loved that place. It felt magical to me; someplace where I could learn a new game and where grown-ups were always happy. It took a lot of years for me to recognize how much of that good mood came from the bottles behind the bar, and how many times the bartender, Enzo, diplomatically cut off regulars when they'd had too much. But nothing ever got out of hand at Empire. It was my dark, musty, sticky-floored second home.

"Jonah?" Dad's voice yanks me back into the present. "You still there?"

"Yeah," I say. "You said you'll have a better shot at hanging on to Empire. But it's not a sure thing, right?"

"None of this is for sure. We're doing the best we can."

I had prepared myself, when I worked the late shift at Empire the night before I left for Gull Cove, that it might be shut down by the time I got home. I thought I was ready. But every time one of my parents calls with an update, I get hit with the same stomach-curdling mix of resentment and anxiety. Nothing ever seems to get resolved; it's always delays, and meetings with creditors, and a bunch of legal terms I don't understand. It's death by a thousand cuts, and even though I told my parents I wanted them to keep me in the loop, I'm starting to wish they'd spare me the details.

"But you're still open, right?" I ask.

"We are," Dad says. "We've been working on a few different ways to cut costs." Something about the way he clears his throat makes me positive I'm not going to like whatever he says next. "We had to let Enzo go, unfortunately."

I've never hated being right more. "Dad, come on!" I protest. Enzo's been the bartender at Empire since it opened, and he's the only guy there who can still beat me at pool. He's also funny, loyal, and more like an uncle to me than a guy who works for my parents. "How can you fire Enzo? He's an Empire institution! He works his ass off!" My voice sounds harsh and unfamiliar to my own ears, like I swallowed something sharp.

"He's expensive, Jonah. Tough decisions have to be made."

"He's a *person*. You can't put a dollar sign on him and be done with it!"

"If you think for one second—" Dad's voice rises to match mine, and then he stops. Breathes in and out, composing himself. When he speaks again it's in a tone that's almost normal, except for the brittle edge. "If you think it didn't break my heart, and your mother's, to let Enzo go, you're mistaken. We had no choice."

*You had a choice not to listen to Anders Story,* I almost say, but stop myself just in time. It's not like he doesn't know that. "Okay, so . . ." I trail off as a loud rap sounds on my door. "Hang on, somebody's knocking. Let me get rid of them and I'll be back."

"No, go ahead and get on with your day," Dad says, sounding as relieved as I feel at the possibility of ending this call. "That's all the information I have right now anyway." He clears his throat again. "Maybe I'll just text the next update."

Shame at giving him a hard time stabs at my chest, but I have too much residual anger about Enzo to turn it into an apology. "That works," I say, and disconnect. I let the phone drop onto my pillow with a frustrated grunt and shove my hands into my hair, tugging until it hurts. Another knock sounds at the door, louder than before.

"Coming," I snap. "Hold your horses." That's an Enzo saying, one he'd always throw at me when I'd bug him to take a break and play pool with me. *Hold your horses, kid. I have work to do.* Goddamn it. If I keep thinking like this, I'm going to be useless all day. I force myself to take a couple of deep breaths, then stand and head for the door, running a hand over my disheveled hair when I catch sight of myself in the mirror over my dresser. Not that it matters. It's probably Reid Chilton wanting to borrow toothpaste again.

I've barely opened the door a crack when someone pushes it all the way open. Not Reid.

"Have you seen this?" Milly demands, shoving her phone at me.

"Good morning to you, too," I grumble, but my mood lifts a notch at the sight of her. I grab a T-shirt off the back of my chair, and Milly's cheeks color as she registers that I'm only wearing boxer shorts. Serves her right for barging in at the ungodly hour of—okay, ten-thirty. Maybe I should've been up by now. "Where's Aubrey?" I don't usually see one of them without the other.

"Lifeguarding," Milly says. She looks great like always in a lacy white top, tan shorts, and complicated sandals with lots of straps. When my head emerges from my T-shirt neck, her eyes are trained on a spot over my shoulder as she continues to hold out her phone. "Uncle Archer was right; he messed up by playing that song. The *Gull Cove Gazette* is at it again."

"At what again?" I take her phone and angle the screen so I can read it. My heart sinks as soon as I see the headline at the top of the Lifestyle section.

THE STORY CONTINUES: HAS ESTRANGED SON ARCHER BEEN HIDING IN PLAIN SIGHT?

"Well, shit," I say, scanning the article. It's all about how "various sources" spotted a man resembling Archer Story perform at Dunes last night. "How is this news? And did people really figure him out just because he sang a freaking Toto song?"

Milly sighs. "This is Gull Cove Island, remember? People are obsessed with the Storys."

"I better let JT know," I say. "I was going to keep quiet till Archer had a chance to talk to Mildred, but now that it's out . . ." I send the link to myself and give Milly back her phone. Then I pick mine up from the bed and forward the article to JT with a text telling him to call me. "Do you think he's read it?"

"JT?" Milly asks doubtfully.

"No. Archer."

"I don't know." She chews on the knuckle of her thumb. "I've called and messaged him a bunch of times this morning, but he hasn't answered."

"It's early. He's probably still asleep," I say, then worry that it sounds like I really mean "passed out," so I add, "I wouldn't be up either if you hadn't knocked."

"Yeah, but I thought . . . I don't know. I thought he'd want to talk to us again as soon as possible," Milly says. Her shoulders slump, and I get that weird, tight feeling in my chest that happens any time Milly looks sad.

"We'll hear from him soon." I say it with more confidence than I feel, because there's a fifty-fifty chance that the stress of last night sent Archer Story on another bender. And if that didn't do the trick, today's news story definitely will.

"Maybe he's talking to Dr. Baxter," she says. "I wouldn't be able to wait, if I were him. That note was so strange."

Dr. Baxter is strange, period. Milly and Aubrey were so upset that day at his house that I never told them what I thought I saw—him knocking into the table on purpose to interrupt the conversation about Story sibling rumors. It didn't seem important at the time, anyway. We were all uncomfortable, and I was grateful he broke things up. It didn't occur to me, until Aubrey read the note from him last night, that he might've done it because Hazel was about to share something he didn't want us to hear.

*There are things I should have told you long ago,* the note said. If I were Archer Story, and I'd spent the past twenty-plus years wondering why I'd been cut off from my family fortune, I'd sober up enough to knock on his door first thing.

"You're probably right," I say. Milly raises a hand to tuck a strand of hair behind her ear, and that big watch she always wears slides down her arm. Dr. Baxter and Archer Story both fade from my mind as I step closer, brushing my fingertips along the burnished gold band. "You ever think of getting this resized so that it actually fits?"

"No." She slips it off easily and hands it to me. "It was my grandfather's. It doesn't actually tell time anymore."

I turn the watch around in my hand. It's heavy and still warm from her skin, the metal smooth and glowing. "Why do you wear it if it doesn't tell time?"

"I just like it," she says.

There's an inscription on the back of the watch's face: *Omnia vincit amor. Yours always, M.* "Was this a gift from Mildred?" I ask. Milly nods. "What does it mean?"

"Love conquers all." Her lips twist as she lifts one shoulder in a shrug. "Unless you're talking about her kids, I guess. Or her grandkids."

When it comes to how she presents herself to the world, Milly doesn't mess around. I dragged her giant suitcase far enough to realize she cares *a lot* about appearances. So it's interesting that the one thing she wears every single day is a broken reminder of being shut out.

I take her hand and slide the watch back onto her wrist. "Mildred's out of her head for never giving you guys a chance till Archer forced her to. You get that, right? She's the one with the problem, not you."

"I'm aware." Milly rolls her eyes. "Thanks for the free psychoanalysis, though."

"There's more where that came from." I still have her hand in mine. "Did you know that sarcasm is a defense mechanism?"

She gazes around my room, looking everywhere except at me. "Did you know your room is a disaster area? You realize you have a dresser, right? And that clothes can go in it?"

"Deflection is *also* a defense mechanism."

Her lips quirk. "Defense against what?"

"Feelings of abandonment, probably." She laughs a little, giving me one of those looks from beneath her lashes that always makes my pulse speed up. All of a sudden, I'm reminded of a conversation I had a couple of days ago with Efram, when he told me how he'd asked out his now-girlfriend while she was stopped next to him at a red light, bobbing her head along to the music he was playing. *You gotta shoot your shot when it comes,* he'd said. *Who knows if you'll get another chance?* I'd thought of Milly then, and how impossible it is to have a shot with someone when you have to pretend to be their cousin in front of the entire world.

But for once, it's just the two of us.

I keep my voice light, because I don't want to freak her out. "Or maybe you're experiencing feelings of attraction toward someone inappropriate."

"Oh?" She raises a brow. "Like who?"

"Red Sox fan," I say, and she snorts. "Elderly townie, maybe? Pretend relative. Could be any one of those, really."

Milly tugs her hand away, but not like she's mad. "Hardly."

"Don't fight it," I say in my best professional voice. "Repression is unhealthy."

Now she laughs for real. Almost a giggle, which isn't like her. It's so cute that I rack my brain trying to think of something else funny to say. But then she crosses her arms, her eyes returning to that spot over my shoulder. "You're doing it again," she says accusingly.

"Doing what?"

"Flirting with me."

"No I'm not." I wait a beat. "Unless you're into it. Are you?"

She fights a smile. "You should really be wearing pants for this conversation."

That feels like the opposite direction of how I'd like things to go, but I'm not about to argue with her right now. "Fair point. Could you—" I gesture toward her, and she turns around so she's facing the door. I grab my jeans from the end of my bed and pull them on. It's too hot for jeans on this island, but I've never been a shorts guy unless I'm playing basketball. And I haven't played basketball since I had to start working double shifts at Empire. Which I'm not going to think about right now, because Milly is in my room, and—

She lets out a gasp. When I turn, she's staring at her phone, eyes wide. "What's up?" I ask. "Archer finally get in touch?"

Milly shakes her head, her hand at her throat. "No. Oh no."

My shoulders tense. I've never seen Milly look this rattled before, and I've been with her through two fake-identity reveals, including my own. "Everything okay?" She doesn't answer right away, so I start lobbing guesses. "Is something going on with your grandmother? Your parents? Aubrey?"

"Yes," she finally says. "I mean, no, it's not *about* Aubrey, but she texted me from the pool. Carson Fine just gave her some news." Her eyes, still round and glassy with shock, meet mine. "About Dr. Baxter. He died this morning. Drowned in a creek in the woods behind his house."

# CHAPTER THIRTEEN

## MILLY

We see the gate well before we see the house. It must be fifteen feet tall, made of thick wrought iron, flanked by an equally tall stone wall that stretches as far as I can see in either direction. There's no way into Catmint House except for this gate, unless you want to try scaling the oceanside cliff that flanks the back of the house.

"Almost there," our chauffeur says, pressing the brake as he rolls down his window. I'm immediately overpowered by the scent of honeysuckle. He extracts a slim silver rectangle that looks like a credit card from the sun visor, and holds it up against a sensor attached to a wooden post. There's a loud clicking noise, and the gate doors slowly swing open.

We're riding in a Bentley Mulliner that has four seats in the back, two on either side facing one another, with a chrome and walnut table between them. The seats are buttery espresso leather and equipped with dozens of buttons that let us adjust temperature and seat position. Jonah has been fiddling with his controls for the entire ride, but he looks up now as the car proceeds slowly down a winding driveway. Flowering honeysuckle bushes climb tall trellises on our right, and lush green trees that I haven't seen anywhere else on Gull Cove Island are on our left.

Aubrey sighs. She looks stiff and uncomfortable in a striped shirtdress, the only article of clothing with a skirt that I've ever seen her wear. "I got a text from Hazel this morning. She said the funeral is going to be Wednesday. We should ask Carson for the day off."

"Yeah, of course." I run my fingers down a seam in the smooth leather of my seat. "Do you guys think Uncle Archer got a chance to talk to Dr. Baxter before he died?"

"I think . . ." Jonah hesitates, like he's weighing how ready we are for bad news. Then he just goes for it. "To be honest, I think he's been drunk since he saw us."

He's probably right. It's been thirty-six hours since we left Uncle Archer's bungalow, and we haven't heard from him once. All our texts have gone unanswered, and any calls go straight to voice mail.

"Gran must know about Uncle Archer by now, right?" Aubrey asks. "I mean, she has to have seen the article."

"I'm sure she did," I say. I can't imagine a piece of gossip like that not being brought to her attention straightaway.

Aubrey chews her lip. "Should we tell her that he's the one who brought us here?"

"No," Jonah and I both say at once. Then he grins at me, head cocked, and my stomach flutters. I'm not sure what would have happened in his room yesterday if we hadn't gotten distracted by the news about Dr. Baxter. A not-small part of me wishes I'd found out.

"I know *my* reason," he says. "I'm trying to hang on to this job as long as possible. JT's already in a panic about the Archer thing. What's yours?"

I lift my chin. "We don't owe Mildred anything. She can figure it out on her own, just like we did." It hits me, as I say it, that I really do think about Aubrey, Jonah, and me as a "we" now; an odd little team, caught up in something that only the three of us can understand. This summer keeps twisting in ways I never expected, and it's a relief to have them along for the ride.

Aubrey and I are sitting side by side, facing forward, and when her breath hitches in her throat, I can tell she's been distracted by the sight of Catmint House. "Oh, wow," she says. I crane my neck so I can see what she's seeing, but within seconds there's no need. The driveway straightens, and the house is directly in front of us.

The back of the house that we glimpsed from the road was all sparkling windows and modern lines, but the front is pure New England mansion. Two symmetrical wings, each the size of a typical house on Gull Cove Island, flank a midsection dominated by vast white pillars leading to a Juliet balcony. The roof is dark slate and dramatically sloped, with a widow's walk on top framed by four stone chimneys. All of the windows—I lose count as we approach—are tall, white-paned, and green-shuttered. A four-door garage attached to the left wing is constructed of the same stone as the chimneys, with a trellised wall covered with contrasting pink shades of honeysuckle. Behind the house, dark-blue ocean meets a paler blue sky that's dotted with lacy white clouds.

I've seen pictures, but they didn't prepare me for the real thing. It's stunning. For a second I can't breathe, imagining an alternate universe where I'd spend every summer here under the watchful eye of a doting grandmother.

A woman in a shapeless gray dress and clogs stands between the columns flanking the front door, looking out of place amid all the grandiosity. The chauffeur parks, and Theresa Ryan waves as we exit the Bentley. "Welcome, welcome," she calls. Aubrey is the first to reach her, and Theresa grasps Aubrey's hand in both of hers. "You must be Aubrey. And this is Jonah, of course." I hang back as they exchange greetings, since I've already met Theresa.

When I talked to Mom last night, she sounded wistful about her mother's assistant. "Tell Theresa I'm feeling good about the Yankees bullpen this year," she'd told me. "It almost reminds me of 1996." But when Theresa extends a welcoming hand to me, the words won't come. It feels too much like I'm trying to kiss up to her. She's the most pleasant person in Mildred Story's inner circle, but she still picked her side years ago. And it wasn't ours.

Theresa puts one hand on the doorknob, but doesn't turn it. "If I could have a quick word before we go inside," she says, her brow knitted in concern. "This has been a very trying weekend. Fred Baxter was one of your grandmother's oldest and dearest friends. She's devastated by his death. And on top of that, I suppose you've seen coverage about your uncle being back in town?" She gives us a searching look, and I keep my expression carefully neutral.

"Yeah," I murmur. "So strange." Aubrey and Jonah both look at the ground.

"It's a lot to take, all at once," Theresa says. "I hope you understand that we may need to keep brunch brief."

I nod. "Of course."

She pushes the door open, and gestures us into a grand foyer. The walls are pristine white, the ceiling soaring, and the space is full of the most exquisite collection of paintings, sculptures, and vases that I've ever seen outside of a museum. A slim man dressed all in black is peering intently at one wall, jotting something in a Moleskine notebook. I've spent years hanging out at my friend Chloe's mother's art gallery, and I'm pretty sure he's looking at an original Cy Twombly painting.

When the man sees us, he snaps the notebook closed. "I'm sure we can work something out," he says to Theresa. "I'll be in touch."

"Wonderful, thank you," Theresa says, backtracking to open the door for him. They converse briefly in low tones, and when she returns, she smiles brightly at us. "Your grandmother is considering divesting some of her art collection."

*Divesting.* That's a word I recently learned when Mom berated me into studying for the ACT; it means *rid oneself of something that one no longer wants or requires.* That painting Mildred is about to *divest* might be on the smaller scale of Twombly's works, but it would still pay for all of our college tuitions at Ivy League prices.

Not that I could get into the Ivy League. But still.

The bitter thought distracts me until Theresa leads us through a set of glass French doors. We step onto an expansive porch overlooking the ocean, framed by a stainless steel railing. I feel a sense of déjà vu, even though I've never been here, because Mom has described this porch in so much detail. It was her favorite spot in the entire house.

"Mildred, the children are here," Theresa calls.

My grandmother is sitting at a teak table, shaded by an enormous, gauzy umbrella set up behind her. There are four place settings, and three tiered trays holding a mouthwatering array of sandwiches, pastries, and fruit. Mildred is wearing a sun hat despite the umbrella, and a beautiful patterned scarf over a long-sleeved, cream-colored linen dress. Her gloves are the same cream color, short enough that I can see the stack of gold bracelets on her left arm. Her white hair is loose and wavy, and she's wearing a pair of large black sunglasses.

*Not fair,* I think as I take a seat. I thought sunglasses would be rude, or I would've brought my own. I could use some camouflage right about now.

"Aubrey. Jonah. Milly," Mildred says, inclining her head toward each of us in turn. "Welcome to Catmint House." Theresa steps away as a man in a black apron materializes behind us, offering coffee, tea, or juice in a hushed tone. "Please help yourselves to whatever you would like to eat," Mildred adds.

"Thank you," we chorus, but nobody makes a move toward the food.

"Unless nothing appeals to you?" she asks dryly, and then silverware clatters as we all try to fill our plates at the same time. *Damn her,* I think, stabbing a slice of melon with my fork. We haven't even been here two minutes and she already has us jumping to do her bidding.

Jonah, who's sitting beside me, is staring at the sandwiches with an expression of mild dread. "They're all full of lettuce," he whispers. "And nothing else."

"Here." I poke one with my fork. "I think that's roast beef." Jonah grabs it gratefully. Aubrey plays it safe by piling her plate high with mini pastries.

"So." Mildred folds her hands under her chin. I wait for the obvious question: *Why are you here?* But it doesn't come. Instead, she tilts her head toward Jonah and says, "I must confess, Jonah, that I see nothing of Anders in you."

Jonah tries to buy time by biting off half of his roast beef sandwich and then—disaster. His face turns red, his eyes water, and he gags before lunging for a napkin and spitting gobs of half-chewed food into it. "What was that?" he gasps, reaching for his water glass. I look at the uneaten sandwich half on his plate, and catch sight of a creamy white substance nestled between the layers of roast beef.

"Oh, um. Looks like horseradish. Sorry about that," I say as Jonah drains the entire glass of water in two gulps. "He's not a fan," I add, to Mildred.

"So I see." She plucks a plump blackberry from the top of a miniature tart and pops it in her mouth. The gesture is startling, like this person actually *eats*? I wouldn't have been surprised to learn that she just feeds off decades-old resentment.

When Mildred has chewed and swallowed, she finally takes off her sunglasses, setting them on the table beside her plate. Her eyes, ringed with heavy eyeliner like the first time we saw her, remain on Jonah. "Tell me," she says. "Is Anders doing well?"

Jonah goes still, except for the slight twitch of a muscle in his jaw, for so long that I wonder if he misunderstood the question. Then he reaches for the pitcher of ice water and pours himself a fresh glass, taking his time like there's no awkward silence whatsoever. When he finishes, he looks at Mildred and inhales a slow, deep breath. Almost as though he's about to give a speech. "Do you want me to answer that honestly?" he asks.

His voice is calm, with a hint of a challenge. It's like all of his earlier unease has suddenly vanished, and for some reason that makes *me* uneasy.

Mildred arches a brow. "I do."

I let out an involuntary, nervous cough. Jonah blinks, catches my eye, and a deep flush stains his cheeks. He turns back to Mildred and mutters, "I guess he's okay. I don't know. We're not close."

An emotion I can't decipher flits across Mildred's face as she turns toward Aubrey. "You also look very little like your father, although I see traces of him in the shape of your eyes, and your chin." Aubrey looks surprised, and gratified, at the comparison. "How is Adam nowadays?"

Aubrey tugs at the collar of her shirtdress and wets her lips. She hasn't touched her pastries yet or any of the three beverages in front of her. She's nervous, but her voice is steady as she says, "He's pretty much the same as always."

Mildred takes a delicate sip of tea. "In other words, he thinks the sun rises and sets on him, and surrounds himself with people who agree?" she asks.

I can feel my eyes pop as Aubrey goes red. *Jesus, lady,* I think. *If he's like that, don't you think you might've had something to do with it?*

Aubrey's obvious agreement with Mildred's jab is at war with loyalty her father doesn't deserve, and the conflict is written all over her face. Mildred relents, going so far as to briefly pat Aubrey's hand with gloved fingertips. "Forgive me," she says. "This has been a difficult weekend. I didn't mean to lead with—well. Let's talk of happier things. I understand that you're a competitive swimmer?" Aubrey nods, gratefully, as Mildred adds, "Your father must be proud of you. He always prized athletic ability."

Aubrey hesitates, like she suspects a trap. "I . . . I hope so."

Mildred turns back to Jonah, who's been quietly cleansing his palate with miniature fruit tarts. "I hear your grades are excellent, Jonah. Will you be applying to Harvard?"

Jonah takes his time swallowing the tart, but looks relieved at the relatively easy question. "Yeah, probably."

It's a good fifteen minutes later before I fully grasp the pattern of the conversation. There are a half-dozen fascinating things we could be talking about right now, like our parents' disinheritance, Dr. Baxter's death, Uncle Archer's reappearance, and, of course, the question that has to be foremost in Mildred's mind: *Why the hell are you three here?* But none of those come up. My grandmother is dividing her laser-like attention between Aubrey and Jonah, asking them questions about their lives, their accomplishments, and their fathers. Sometimes her interrogation borders on the uncomfortable—she's clearly fishing for *something* related to her two oldest sons, although she won't come right out and say it—but her attention never wavers.

Jonah looks deeply uneasy the entire time, but he doesn't give himself away. Aubrey unfurls like a flower in the sun, basking in the light of our grandmother's unexpected interest.

I might as well not even be here.

My whole life, I've imagined what it would be like if my grandmother and I finally met. Yes, the shopping fantasies were silly, but beneath that, I used to think that me being her namesake might mean something. That looking so much like my mother might mean something. That wearing my grandfather's watch every day might mean something. That caring about art and fashion the way she does might mean something.

And now, sitting in my mother's favorite spot in the legendary Catmint House, watching whitecaps skitter on the horizon as I eat more than my fair share of brunch because I never have to answer any questions, all I can think is this:

None of it means anything at all.

Maybe she's a racist who can't be bothered with her only nonwhite grandchild. Maybe she's sexist and only cares about her sons. Or maybe she just doesn't like me.

"I need the bathroom," I say, standing abruptly.

Mildred gestures at the French doors. "Take a left at the hallway. There's a powder room two doors down."

"Okay," I say. But when I leave the room attached to the balcony, I turn right instead. To hell with Mildred's directions. I've never been inside my mother's house before, and I'm going to have a look around. I slip my sandals off and hold them in one hand, padding quietly through vast, beautifully furnished rooms that look like something out of a magazine. Art and fresh flowers are everywhere. When I peer into the kitchen, I marvel at the top-of-the-line appliances that sparkle as if they've never been used for anything as mundane as cooking. Then a soft voice catches my attention, and I follow it back into the hallway.

"I think it was excessive," Theresa Ryan is saying. She's in a room adjacent to the kitchen, and from my spot in the hallway I can see an entire wall of built-in bookshelves. "We've been down this road before. You think you're getting rid of one problem, but all you're doing is creating a dozen more."

She sounds angry, which isn't an emotion I associate with my grandmother's placid assistant. I edge closer.

"They're here now," she says. "I'm trying to keep things short, but I'm not sure how soon I can pry her away. She has an almost—morbid curiosity, I suppose." There's a long pause, and then Theresa adds, "Well, what do you think? The same old obsession. And now is not the time for her to be distracted like this." Another pause. "It would be best for everyone, I agree. All right. Let's touch base later this afternoon."

I hear the click of footsteps and quickly backtrack into the kitchen so I can duck behind the island. Theresa makes her way down the hallway without pausing, humming to herself. When I can't hear her any longer, I ease out of the kitchen and peer into the room she exited. It's an office, filled with books, filing cabinets, and an enormous carved wooden desk. I'm dying to look around, but I've already been here too long. I have just enough time to check something.

There's a landline phone on the desk, the kind with a screen on the handset. My mother has something similar in her office; she can't seem to let go of outdated technology. I press Menu on the handset, then Last Call.

A name pops up on the screen: *Donald Camden.*

# CHAPTER FOURTEEN

## AUBREY

Milly is a dream client for Kayla's Boutique. "Everything looks so good on you!" the owner exclaims, hands clasped in front of her, as Milly steps out of the dressing room and onto a dais in front of a large mirror. "But I do believe we've found it. *This* is the dress."

I think she's right. Milly is wearing a stunning sleeveless gown with a plunging yet still tasteful black top and a billowing white skirt. At least a foot of fabric pools around her feet, which are encased in black high heels, but other than that she looks Oscar-ready.

Except for her face, which is closed off and remote. She's been like that ever since our weird brunch at Gran's two days ago, which ended abruptly when Gran declared a sudden headache. I thought shopping would for sure cheer Milly up, but she looks like she's just going through the motions. Polite, but not really interested.

"We'll need to take up the hemline, of course, but the rest fits perfectly," the owner says. She's an attractive woman in her late thirties with dark hair and olive skin, wearing a simple tan sheath that's dressed up with layers of necklaces. She closed the shop when we came in, and she and the saleswoman on duty have been giving us the royal treatment for almost an hour.

I've never been in a store like this before. The interior practically glows with flattering white light that makes everyone's skin flawless. The chairs are cream leather, the mirrors are antique silver, and the floor looks like luminous mother-of-pearl. Red roses are everywhere, filling the air with their soft, heady fragrance. The overall effect is like being inside a comfortable, expensive jewelry box.

"You look incredible," I tell Milly from my chair beside the mirror. I've been sitting here half curled into the fetal position ever since trying on a single, horrifically unflattering dress.

"I agree," the owner says. "If you like it, we can start the alterations right now."

"All right," Milly says. The owner waves toward the front of the store, and the saleswoman heads our way with a seamstress in tow. She wasn't here when we arrived, so she must've been called in especially for us. The seamstress crouches beside Milly and starts pinning the dress's hem with quick, deft hands. The attention seems to revive Milly, who offers the owner a genuine smile. "Thanks for all this. I love the dress."

"Your mother would be thrilled," the owner says.

"You mean my grandmother?" Milly asks.

"Well, yes, I hope so. But your mother, too. I knew Allison a little way back when. I was too young to run with the Story crowd, but my sister was friendly with all of them."

I glance at the front of the store, where *Kayla's Boutique* is written in stark black lettering above the cash register. "Are you Kayla?" I ask.

Her face droops a little. "No, I'm Oona. Kayla was my sister. She died when I was in high school, so when I opened this shop I named it after her."

"I'm so sorry," Milly and I say in unison, and I can feel my face get hot. Leave it to me to turn our fancy shopping trip depressing.

Oona smiles reassuringly. "Thank you. It was a long time ago. But I remember both of your parents very well. Allison was so beautiful. And Adam, well—" She lets out an almost girlish laugh. The teen version of my father seems to have had that effect on everyone. "Adam was quite dreamy, back in my day."

For once, I don't want to hear about my father. "Did you know Archer, too?" I ask.

It's been two days since our brunch with Gran, and we still haven't heard from Uncle Archer. He hasn't been to work at the resort, either, and I'm starting to wonder if he took off once he realized his cover was well and truly blown. The thought leaves me feeling empty and unsettled, like I've lost something before I even knew I had it. I keep remembering the younger version of my uncle sitting amid a sea of Legos with me years ago, patiently searching for a policeman's hat after my father, tired of my whining, sniped that I'd probably lost it. "The right hat is important," Uncle Archer had said, unperturbed. "We'll track it down." And eventually, we did.

"Of course I knew Archer," Oona says. Light and conversational, as though the entire island isn't a boiling pot of rumors about him. "He was always friendly with the residents of Gull Cove Island, almost as though he were one of us. We've stayed in touch throughout the years. Lovely man, despite some . . ." Oona hesitates briefly before finishing with "challenges."

"Did you know our Uncle Anders, too?" I ask.

"Oh yes. Better than any of them. Kayla dated him off and on throughout high school, and while he was at college." Milly and I both blink in surprise, and Oona laughs ruefully. "I don't think your grandmother ever approved."

"Did you?" I ask, and Oona raises a brow. "I mean, did you like him?" Uncle Anders is still a mystery to me, the Story sibling I know the least about.

Oona shrugs. "He was very intense," she says as the seamstress gets to her feet. Milly's skirt just brushes the tips of her shoes, and Oona nods approvingly at the length. "That's perfect. Linda, could you help Milly out of that dress so we can get started on the hem?"

The saleswoman ushers Milly off the dais and into a dressing room. The seamstress heads for the front of the store, leaving me alone with Oona. She raises a perfectly shaped eyebrow with a kind smile. "You're not quite as comfortable with this process as your cousin is, are you?" she asks.

My eyes drag toward the pile of fabric on the chair next to me. It looks so innocent now, nothing like the pink monstrosity it was when I tried it on. "Dresses don't look good on me."

"Nonsense." Oona lowers her voice and leans her head toward mine. "Linda is still relatively new, and she hasn't fully mastered the art of picking the right dress. That pink was a wonderful color for you, but I have something different in mind. Why don't you head into a dressing room and let me bring it to you?" I nod half-heartedly, but she's already charging toward a rack. "Take off everything except your undergarments!" she calls over her shoulder. "I'll be right back!"

That's the downside of personal shopping—zero privacy.

Behind the curtain, I strip off my T-shirt and shorts with a feeling of dread. Milly is going to look incredible at the gala. Jonah, who's off in some tuxedo shop down the street, will undoubtedly be dashing. And I'll be the frump in the corner making everyone whisper, *Are you sure she's a Story?*

"Here we go!" Oona appears with a dress draped over her arm. The color is a gorgeous twilight blue, but I catch sight of some kind of beading and—I don't know. The simpler, the better, usually. But Oona hangs the dress from a hook on the wall and starts unzipping the back with total confidence. "What do you think?"

"It's nice," I say hesitantly. I want to distract her from the moment when I'll have to stuff myself into what looks like an unforgiving column of fabric, so I add, "You said before that my uncle Anders was intense. What did you mean?" She furrows her brow at me in the mirror and I add, "I haven't seen him in years, and I barely remember him."

"Well." Oona slips the blue dress off its hanger, letting the silky fabric run through her hands. "It was a long time ago, of course. All I remember, really, is that it was all very *dramatic*. He and Kayla broke up a lot, and each time Kayla swore she'd never take him back. Then she did. It was hard, in those days, to resist a Story." Her eyes get a little unfocused. "Kayla was a townie at heart. I think she knew she'd never be able to keep up with Anders in the real world."

I feel awful, then, for making her talk about her sister again. "I'm sorry. I shouldn't have brought it up."

She pats my shoulder. "It truly is fine, Aubrey. It's been twenty-four years since Kayla died, and I enjoy talking about her."

Something prickles up my spine then. Twenty-four years is

185

1997, the year my father and his brothers and sister were disinherited. *That's where it all started to go wrong.* I haven't thought about Cutter-slash-Cutty Beach in a while, or that strange line about it in his novel, but I'm struck with the sudden urge to ask Oona if something happened to Kayla there. I can't bring myself to do it, though. It's one thing to talk about her sister's ex-boyfriend, and quite another to relive the way her sister died.

Anyway, Oona is brandishing the blue dress at me with a determined expression. "This is going to look stunning on you."

"It can't look worse than the first one."

"That was the wrong style," Oona says, positioning the dress in front of me. "Step into this, would you? You have such wonderful arms and shoulders, we want to show them off."

I don't move. "We do?"

"Absolutely!"

I fold my arms across my faded sports bra. "I kind of hate my shoulders, though. And my arms. I wore a long-sleeved dress to prom."

"Well, that was a tragic waste," Oona says, shaking the dress. "Go on, step in."

I do as I'm told, clutching her elbow for balance. "My boyfriend said I looked like a kid playing dress-up." I don't know why I just told her that, other than that the fake intimacy of the situation is making me strangely confiding.

Oona's dark brows draw together in a frown. "He doesn't sound like a particularly worthy date." She tugs the dress over my hips, then holds the bodice up so it covers my chest. "Go ahead and take that bra off. You'll need something strapless with this neckline. We have a lot of lovely bras that will work perfectly."

"Um, okay." Once again, I do as I'm told. I almost feel a

compunction to defend Thomas, except—she's right. He's *not* a particularly worthy date. "I think he might be an ex now," I say as she zips up the back. "My boyfriend, I mean."

"You *think*?"

"Well, for a while he wasn't returning any of my texts. Now I'm not returning his, so . . ."

I trail off, and she finishes, "That's how it's done nowadays, huh? Goodness, I feel for you kids. Life is complicated in the digital age. But he doesn't sound like the catch you deserve. And—there!" She smooths her hands over my hips and beams. "Look at you! Perfect!"

I stare. All I can see is shoulders filling the mirror in front of me. *They're broader than mine,* Thomas said to me once. Despite all my time in the sun I'm still pale, my arms an unbroken stretch of freckled white until you get to the wine-colored birthmark. This dress is a lot more clothing than the bathing suit I wear to swim meets, of course, but when I'm in my bathing suit I don't think about looking *good*. It's just functional. My eyes prick as embarrassment floods my veins, and I wish I had something to wrap around me. Like a parka. "I don't—I think it's too revealing on top," I stammer.

"Oh, honey, not at all. You have a wonderful upper body. You're like a Greek goddess! We'll pull your hair into a twist, give you some amazing drop earrings, and you'll be the belle of the ball."

"My cousin will be," I say. I'm not jealous. It's just fact.

Oona pats my arm. "Your cousin is beautiful. But so are you. Anyone who can't see that isn't worth your time."

I try to see the dress like she seems to. It's a great color, definitely. There's just one beaded strap, which runs across my right shoulder and down the bodice. The dress is fitted, which I usually try to avoid, but the fabric is so rich—some kind of heavy silk, I think—that it flows across my body a lot better than my cheap prom dress did.

"You need the right accessories, of course," Oona says. "Linda?" She raises her voice. "Could you grab a pair of the sapphire drop earrings? And one of those mother-of-pearl hair-combs we just got in. Let's try to re-create the final styling as best we can."

"My ears aren't pierced," I say.

"Clip earrings, Linda!" Oona calls.

I blink at myself. *You wouldn't be a swimmer if you took after the Storys,* my father used to say. *My mother and sister could never build up that sort of arm strength. They're far too delicate.* I always took that as a subtle insult, which it probably was. A backhanded reminder that the Storys are special, ethereal, and too precious for this world. But I'm tired of hearing Dad's voice, and Thomas's, running through my head every time I look in the mirror. Every time I do *anything*. Maybe it's time to start listening to someone else.

I meet Oona's kind dark eyes as she loops her arm through mine and squeezes lightly. "I wouldn't steer you wrong, Aubrey. I promise. This is beyond lovely on you."

I still hate my reflection, but the more I look at it, the more it seems like I'm looking into a fun house mirror—a distorted image that doesn't reflect reality. I don't know how to see beyond it, yet, but I want to try.

"I'll take it," I tell Oona.

188

# CHAPTER FIFTEEN

## JONAH

We're too early for Dr. Baxter's funeral on Wednesday because *someone*—thanks, Aubrey—insisted we leave an hour early. It took two minutes to get downtown, and they're not letting anyone into the church yet. So Aubrey drags us, sweating in our funeral clothes, to the air-conditioned Gull Cove Island Library a few blocks away.

"We could've gone somewhere that serves coffee," Milly mutters, dropping her purse onto an empty table. She's wearing a sleek black dress and heels, her hair pulled back into a high ponytail. Aubrey is in the same dress she wore to brunch on Sunday. I brought nothing appropriate for a funeral and had to borrow a button-down shirt and a pair of khakis from Efram. The pants are too short, and the shirt is just a little too tight. Every time I move my arms, I feel like a button's about to pop.

"I want to look something up," Aubrey says, scanning the room until her eyes land on a row of big, blocky monitors. "Did you know that back issues of the *Gull Cove Gazette* are only online since 2006?"

"I neither knew nor cared," Milly says, at the same time as I say, "Yeah."

Aubrey cocks her head at me, and I shrug. "I used their website to research your family before I left. There's not much about your parents in the past fifteen years, though."

"Right," Aubrey nods. "So I need a microfilm machine." She heads for the monitors, and Milly and I follow, bemused.

"A what?" I ask.

"Microfilm," Aubrey says, looping the strap of her handbag across a chair in front of the nearest monitor. "It's, like, pictures of old newspaper articles."

"They're inside that machine?" I ask. It looks like a 1980s computer.

She laughs and opens the middle drawer of a towering file cabinet. "No, they're stored on reels in here. I have to load the reel onto the machine to read it."

"How do you know all this?" Milly asks, in the same brittle, impatient tone she's been using ever since our Sunday brunch with Mildred Story.

Aubrey sorts through rows of small boxes crammed into the filing cabinet. "I looked it up on the library website last night."

"Okay, but why?" Milly asks, as Aubrey extracts one of the boxes. She opens it and pulls out a blue plastic reel about the size of her palm.

"Remember what Oona said at Kayla's Boutique?" she asks. She might as well be speaking Greek right now, because half of that doesn't make sense to me, but Milly nods. Aubrey turns toward me to explain. "Oona is a woman whose sister used to date Uncle Anders, and Gran didn't like her, and she died twenty-four years ago, which is . . ." She pauses, frowning at the machine until she locates a peg where she can attach the reel.

Milly finishes for her, looking suddenly pensive. "When our parents got disinherited."

"What's Kayla's Boutique?" I ask, and Milly catches me up while Aubrey feeds one end of the film into a chute beneath a glass surface on the machine. Aubrey hits a button, causing the blue reel to spin, and the screen comes to life with the front page of a 1997 issue of the *Gull Cove Gazette*.

"So you think—what? Those things are related?" I ask, as Aubrey twists a dial to bring up a different page.

"I don't know," she says. "But I'm curious about what happened. These editions are from November, a month before our parents got the *you know what you did* letter." We're quiet for a few minutes while Aubrey runs through the reel, weeks' worth of newspapers scrolling in front of our eyes. "I don't see anything," she finally says, pressing a button to reverse the film. When it's all back on the reel, she removes it from the machine and stuffs it back into its box.

My mind's been somewhere else while the newspaper pages flashed before us. "Do you guys remember that day we went to Dr. Baxter's?" I ask. "All that stuff Hazel was saying?"

Milly's mouth twists. "I've been trying to forget, but yes."

"Sorry. But you know how Dr. Baxter almost knocked over the table?" Aubrey nods distractedly as she replaces the box in the filing cabinet and takes out another one. "He did that on purpose."

Aubrey pauses halfway through pulling the reel from the box. "What?"

191

"He was watching you guys, totally clear-eyed, and then you said something—I don't remember what—and he banged his knee on the table and started acting all confused."

Milly puts her hands on her hips, frowning. "You never said anything about that."

"I thought Dr. Baxter was doing us a favor," I say as Aubrey starts up the process of loading the blue reel onto the microfilm machine. "Getting everyone out of an uncomfortable situation. But then Archer got that letter, and—I don't know. Maybe we were talking about something he didn't want anyone to know."

Milly's face goes splotchy. "Look, my mother was not *impregnated* by one of her *brothers*. That's—"

"That's not what we were talking about," Aubrey interrupts. Her eyes are on the screen as she spins the dial to keep pages moving.

"Yes we were," Milly says testily.

"At first, yeah. But Dr. Baxter didn't do anything until I said, 'I'd more easily believe they all killed somebody than *that*.'"

There's a long beat of silence. I can't think of a good response—I'd completely forgotten about that until right this second—and nobody speaks again until Aubrey says, "Here it is. December twenty-second, 1997." She twists a dial to enlarge an article on the screen with the headline LOCAL WOMAN DIES IN TRAGIC ACCIDENT. Milly and I lean over her shoulder to read the rest of the article.

Milly speaks first, her voice breathless with relief. "It was a car accident," she says. According to the coverage, Kayla Dugas, who was then twenty-one, left a downtown bar one night and drove her car into a tree a half mile from Cutty Beach. The autopsy report showed she had a blood alcohol level over the legal limit, but just barely. "She was alone."

"Cutty Beach, though," Aubrey murmurs, her eyes locked on the screen.

"*Your* father is the only one who ever talks about that," Milly says. "And Kayla's car accident didn't happen on the beach. It happened near it. It's a reference point, that's all."

"Hmm." Aubrey is still staring at the article. "It says here that Dr. Baxter was the attending physician after the accident."

"Of course he was," Milly snaps. "This is Gull Cove Island we're talking about. He was probably the *only* physician."

Aubrey finally looks up, her brow creased. "Are you . . . *mad* about something?"

"I'm just—what even is all this?" Milly asks, gesturing between the filing cabinet and the microfilm machine. "What are you trying to prove? That our parents *murdered* some girl and Mildred kicked them off the island because of it?"

Aubrey blinks. "I'm just trying to understand what happened."

"Why don't you ask Mildred?" Milly says. "Since the two of you get along so well."

"We don't—" Aubrey starts, but I break in.

"We're going to be late. The funeral starts in fifteen minutes," I remind them. This conversation isn't headed anywhere good, and we've already been here too long.

"I'll wait outside," Milly says. She spins toward the door, ponytail flying.

Aubrey watches her go, hurt and confusion written all across her face. "What is going *on* with her?"

"Come on, Aubrey. You know," I say. I always thought Aubrey was pretty in tune with other people, especially Milly, but she just stares at me blankly until I spell it out. "Your grandmother basically ignored her on Sunday and spent the whole time talking to you and me. It made Milly feel like shit."

"Did she tell you that?"

"She didn't have to."

"But Milly doesn't care about Gran!" Aubrey insists. "She doesn't even have a grandmother name for her."

"You really think that?" I ask. "You think Milly wears that watch every day because she doesn't care about her grandmother? Because she doesn't want your grandmother to care about her?"

"She . . ." Aubrey bites her lip, her face conflicted. "She's *Milly*. She's already the best grandchild. The best Story out of all of us. Well, you don't count—no offense—"

"None taken."

"But JT's horrible and I'm . . . Nobody's ever thought I was anything like my father. Milly is beautiful and glamorous and stylish and—"

"And none of that mattered to Mildred," I finish.

Aubrey's face crumples. "Oh God. I could tell something was off when we were shopping for dresses. But it didn't hit me, till you said it—Gran *was* ignoring Milly." She twists her hands. "I was just happy that she seemed to like *me*. I never thought she would."

"It's not your fault. The more I see of your grandmother, the more I think JT might've been right all along. She likes to play games." I almost add what I've been thinking since Sunday; that Mildred wasn't interested in *us* so much as Adam and Anders. All of her questions were just a roundabout way of forcing us to talk about them. But Aubrey doesn't need to hear that; she already believes she'll never be as important as her dad. Instead,

I point toward the clock on the wall. "Look, we really have to get out of here. I haven't been to a funeral in a while, but I'm pretty sure it's bad form to walk in late." I reach for the machine to start the rewinding process, but Aubrey stops me.

"Hang on. I want to print this page."

I wait, impatient, while the machine takes what feels like ten minutes to crank out a single page. Milly's gone by the time we get outside, and I feel a sharp stab of regret that I stayed with Aubrey instead of going after her. We walk the few short blocks to the church, out of place in our funeral clothes among all the tourists. When we arrive at St. Mary's, a familiar, silver-haired figure greets us somberly at the door.

"How good of you to come," Donald Camden says.

I haven't seen the guy since he tried to bribe us with movie jobs. It already feels like that happened months ago. He looks older and more tired than he did at lunch that day, with bags under his eyes that I don't remember seeing then.

Aubrey blinks at him like he's a mirage. "Aren't we late?" she asks. Donald looks at her with a quizzical expression, and she adds, "I mean, I would've thought you'd be inside already. With our grandmother or something. The funeral starts at eleven, right?" She's babbling now, and turning red, but Donald just holds out his arm.

"I'm an usher for the service. Fred Baxter was one of my oldest and dearest friends." The phrase sounds like an echo, and it takes me a minute to remember where I heard it last. On the steps of Catmint House, spoken by Theresa. *Fred Baxter was one of your grandmother's oldest and dearest friends.*

*And then there were two,* I think as Aubrey takes Donald's arm.

She peers into the open door. "I think Milly is already here. . . ."

"She is. I put her at the end of a crowded pew. She said she was alone."

"Okay," Aubrey says, her mouth settling into a thin line. We walk through the church vestibule and down the center aisle; we're a lot closer to the front than I would have thought we'd be after showing up this late. An organ plays softly in the background, but our footsteps still echo loudly. A girl in the first pew turns at the sound, and I recognize Hazel Baxter-Clement. I nod and give her a tight-lipped grimace of sympathy, and she smiles faintly. Donald finally stops, gesturing toward a pew where four black-clad people shift to their right to make room for us.

"Thanks," Aubrey whispers, releasing his arm. "And—I'm sorry. I'm really sorry that you lost your friend."

"He's at peace now," Donald says in a low voice, his face grave. "And in the end that's all that any of us can ask for, isn't it?"

## ALLISON, AGE 18

### JULY 1996

Allison took stock of herself in her bedroom mirror. She looked better than she had in a while, but then again, almost everybody looked better in a ball gown and diamonds. She'd been worried about wearing white when she was so pale, but something about this particular shade—the shimmering blue white of snow on top of a frozen lake—brought color back to her cheeks.

She'd had no trouble zipping the dress up and immediately thought, *See? I haven't put on any weight. I can't be pregnant.* Then her traitorous brain reminded her that her period was still weeks overdue, and that her stomach wouldn't stop rolling with unfamiliar queasiness.

She didn't know for sure, though. The test she'd stolen from Mugg's Pharmacy sat unopened beneath a pile of sweaters in her closet. She was going to get through the Summer Gala tonight and then, finally, she'd take it.

Probably.

"Knock-knock!" came a cheerful voice at her door, accompanied by a loud rap on the wood. "You decent?"

"Yes. Come in," Allison said. The door opened to reveal Archer in a tux, his bow tie already loosened. He grinned when he caught sight of her.

"Don't you look fancy. Nice diamonds. Hey, guess what I found?" Archer let himself in and closed the door behind him, brandishing a green and gold bottle in one hand. "Dom Pérignon got separated from his friends."

Allison frowned, her stomach filled with the now-familiar nausea at the thought of drinking anything alcoholic. "Can't you wait till we get there?"

"You know what they say about a dream deferred," Archer said. When she didn't reply, he added, "It dries up like a raisin in the sun. Or festers—"

"I get it," Allison snapped. "I took English composition with Ms. Hermann too, remember? All I'm saying is, maybe for once this summer, you could show enough restraint that you don't make a fool of yourself or pass out before midnight. Or both."

"Ouch," Archer said, looking hurt.

"Mother spent a lot of time planning the gala, you know. It's practically the only thing that's made her even a little happy this summer. So how about you try not to ruin it?"

"I'm not *ruining* anything. God. Next time, a simple *no thanks* will do." Archer shot her a reproachful look, and Allison was instantly sorry. She had no reason to lash out at her youngest brother like that. And no excuse, other than that she was a ball of jangled nerves every second of every day. That wasn't Archer's fault, though.

"I just meant——" she started, but Archer was already halfway through the door.

"Never mind. Message received. Dom and I know when we're not wanted."

Allison sighed and let him go. She didn't know what to say anyway.

When she'd touched up her lip gloss as many times as she could stand, she left her bedroom and started down the hallway. As always lately, she was drawn to a door she usually avoided. She rapped lightly on the frame, and Anders's impatient voice called, "Come in."

He was fully dressed except for his tuxedo jacket, and the bow tie that he was working on while standing in front of the full-length mirror across from his bed. Allison's reflection caught his eye, and he raised one sardonic eyebrow. "To what do I owe the pleasure of your company?"

Allison closed the door and sat on the edge of Anders's bed. "I'm just restless."

"You take it yet?" he asked without preamble.

She didn't have to ask what he meant. "No."

He rolled his eyes. "Jesus Christ, Allison. At this point you're going to give birth before you even acknowledge there might be a problem. Oh, screw this tie to hell and back." Anders undid the entire thing and started over.

Allison wanted desperately to confide in someone about her fear of being pregnant, but she couldn't bring herself to tell her mother, Archer, or any of her friends. She'd fantasized briefly about telling Matt—maybe he'd finally return *that* call—but her pride wouldn't let her. That left her with two options: keep bottling it up, or talk to Anders about it.

Anders, of all people. Who'd been born without the empathy gene. But maybe, Allison thought, he could rise to the occasion if the stakes were high enough.

"I'm scared," she said.

Anders snorted, tugging at his bow tie. "I'd be scared, too, if I were about to introduce the Ryan gene pool into this family. Our collective IQs would drop like a stone." Allison stared reproachfully at her brother, cheeks burning, as he added, "I don't know why you ever slummed it with that guy anyway."

"That's all you have to say?" she asked.

He shrugged. "Take the damn test, then take care of the problem. And don't be such an idiot the next time some townie loser pays attention to you."

Okay. Rising to the occasion wasn't going to happen. "You should talk," Allison snapped. "High-and-mighty Anders Story, so above it all until Kayla crooks her little finger. Then you come running."

Anders finished his tie and ran a hand through his hair. It was all spikes and cowlicks, nothing like the thick waves both Adam and Archer had. "I don't *run* anywhere. I'm having fun. And I've managed to do it without knocking anyone up, so— you could learn a few things."

"Was it *fun* when Kayla dumped you for Matt?" Allison knew her words had finally hit their target when Anders stilled, eyes narrowing at his reflection in the mirror. Part of her brain realized she should stop talking, but another part was viciously glad that he felt as badly as she did. Even if it was only for a minute. "She probably will again, you know. I've seen them flirting more than once this summer. Ironic, huh? We have all this"—

her hand swept around Anders's vast bedroom—"but it seems like the only thing those two want is each other."

"That would be a mistake," Anders said calmly. He picked his tuxedo jacket up from his desk chair and shrugged it on. "Now get the hell out of my room."

Allison obeyed, already regretting letting her mouth run away with her. Anders would be impossible to deal with for the rest of the night. She went back to her room and shut the door, tracing the now-familiar path to the pile of sweaters in her closet that hid the pregnancy test. She opened the box and pulled out the slim piece of plastic inside.

*Results in five minutes!*

Before she could think too much about what she was doing, Allison headed for her bathroom with the test clutched in one hand. It wasn't easy to pee in a ball gown, but it wasn't impossible either. Then she set the test on the back of the toilet, washed her hands, and waited.

Barely a minute passed before the second line appeared, as strong and dark as the first. Allison's stomach lurched, and the nausea that had been plaguing her for weeks couldn't be contained any longer. She retched loudly into the toilet, over and over until her sides ached and her throat was raw.

When her stomach finally stopped heaving, she flushed the toilet and picked up the pregnancy test. She wrapped it in thick layers of tissue and tossed it in the trash. Feeling light-headed, she plucked her toothpaste and toothbrush from their holder and brushed her teeth for three minutes. Then she gargled with mouthwash, reapplied her lip gloss, smoothed her hair, and straightened her pendant.

She didn't have the luxury of falling apart. It was nearly time to leave for the Summer Gala, and Allison knew the image her mother wanted to project for the family: still mourning Abraham Story, of course, but strong and united, bright futures stretching endlessly in front of them. Not afraid, not rejected, not bitter, and definitely not pregnant.

Allison made her way down the curving staircase into the foyer, where Mother kept all of her favorite artwork. A man stood in front of the newest bronze, his head cocked as though he was trying to figure out what it was. Allison recognized Mother's lawyer, Donald Camden, even before he turned at the sound of her approach.

"It's a mother and her children," Allison said, lifting her skirt as she negotiated the final two steps. "Mother had it flown over from Paris."

"Your mother has interesting taste," Donald said diplomatically, returning his eyes to the sculpture. "Though I must admit, I don't see a family here."

Not surprising, Allison thought. Donald Camden was the classic lifelong bachelor. He probably didn't see families anywhere. "Are you Mother's escort for the evening?"

"I have that honor, yes," Donald said with a small bow.

Allison pursed her lips against another wave of nausea that, thankfully, passed. She gave him her best smile. "We're all looking forward to tonight."

"As you should be," Donald said formally. "The Story family never shines so brightly as it does during the Summer Gala."

# CHAPTER SIXTEEN

## MILLY

I can't resist. Once I'm all decked out for the Summer Gala, in a perfectly fitted dress and borrowed diamonds—actual *diamonds,* for crying out loud—I text a picture to my mother. *Headed for the gala,* I type.

Her reply is instantaneous. *Oh, Milly, that's wonderful! You look beautiful! How is Mother?*

I stare at my screen for a while before replying. That's a loaded question. In the end, all I type is, *We haven't had much chance to talk yet.*

*Tell me everything once you do!* Mom writes back.

*I will,* I reply, before slipping my phone into the pocket of my dress. This dress is the most perfect article of clothing I've ever worn—not only because it's beautiful and fits me like a dream but also because it has deep pockets that hold a phone and a lipstick without ruining the line of the skirt.

Aubrey comes back from the bathroom, where Brittany,

who's working as a server tonight, took her to apply makeup because the lighting is better. I wasn't sure what to expect, since Brittany's a big fan of smoky eyes and bold lips for herself, but she used a light hand with Aubrey—just mascara, a hint of rosy blush, and lip gloss. It's perfect, but Aubrey's eyes are clouded with doubt when they meet mine. "Too much?" she asks.

"Not at all," I say. It hits me then, like a punch to the stomach, that *I* should've been the one to do Aubrey's makeup. I should have offered in Kayla's Boutique, after I saw how uncomfortable she was with the whole process. But I didn't, because I was still twisted with resentment over what had happened at brunch with Mildred.

It's made me snappish all week, and Aubrey defensive, and now there's this distance between us that I can't seem to close. Even though I want to—much more than I want to be Mildred's favorite grandchild. That feels like the poisonous apple in "Snow White"; a gift given with malice that I'll instantly regret accepting.

So why does it still hurt that I can't have it?

I push the thought away and tell Aubrey, "You look beautiful."

She smiles shyly. "So do you. Are you ready?"

"As I'll ever be."

I have a sudden urge to grab her hand, to shake off all the tension of the past week and go back to being a team. I don't know how either of us will get through tonight, let alone the rest of the summer otherwise. But before I can, Aubrey plucks a handbag off her dresser and darts into the hallway.

Jonah has already left. Carson Fine told us this morning that Mildred was sending a different type of car tonight—one that would accommodate ball gown skirts without wrinkling them—but that it would only fit two in the backseat. "You'll need to be driven separately," he explained. "Aubrey and Milly in one car, and Jonah in another."

"Why don't I just ride in front?" Jonah had asked.

Carson looked scandalized. "That's not how it's done."

The whole thing is ridiculous, especially considering the dorms are a five-minute walk from the resort. But whatever Mildred wants, Mildred gets. So when Aubrey and I make our way outside, a gleaming car is parked right out front, and a chauffeur in full uniform—white gloves included—pulls the back door open. "Miss Story. Miss Story-Takahashi," he says, nodding to us in turn. "Good evening."

I stifle an inappropriate laugh. "Good evening," I echo, sliding into the seat. The interior of the car smells incredible, like a combination of expensive leather and winter forest. Across from me, a console holds two chilled glasses of champagne. I settle my skirt around me as the chauffeur closes the door, then escorts Aubrey to the opposite side of the car.

When I'm satisfied that my skirt won't wrinkle, I grab one of the champagne glasses and take a long sip. It would be rude not to.

Aubrey lowers herself carefully into the seat beside me, eyes widening when she spies my glass. "Do you think that's a good idea?" she asks.

I know—I *know*—that she's only asking because she's nervous about tonight. Not because she's judging me, or thinks she's better than me, or any of the other uncharitable things that start buzzing through my head. But I down half the glass before answering coolly, "I think it's a *great* idea."

"Milly." Her open, freckled face is troubled. "I hate this."

"Hate what?" I ask, even though I know exactly what she means, because I hate it too. Somehow, though, the same resentment that's been curdling our interactions all week makes me tip my head and gulp the rest of the champagne. "Lighten up. It's supposed to be a party," I say, putting my empty glass down next to Aubrey's full one. Then I see the tears forming in her eyes.

Another gut punch hits me, and this time, I grab her hand. "Don't cry," I say urgently. There are at least a dozen things I should say after that, but all I can manage to get out is, "Your mascara will run."

Aubrey sniffs. "I don't care about my *mascara*."

"We've arrived," the chauffeur says smoothly. I turn to look and we're pulling up on the lawn in front of the resort's side door. That was literally a ninety-second drive.

"I'm sorry," I whisper to Aubrey, but that's all I have time for before my door opens to reveal Donald Camden in all his silver-haired, tuxedo-clad glory.

"Good evening, ladies. I'm your escort to the gala." He and the chauffeur help us out of the car, and then Aubrey and I are on either side of Donald and heading inside. We can't talk, except to answer his polite questions as we make our way through the resort, and I feel restless and anxious about how we left things in the car.

"And here we are," Donald says, pausing at the entrance to the ballroom. The room is filled with music and laughter and beautifully dressed people, the crystal chandeliers sparkling and making the tapestries on the wall glow a rich gold. A string quartet is set up on a small stage at the center of the windows, and circular tables are evenly spaced at one end of the vast room.

For a second my spirit lifts—I really do love a party—and then Donald says, "Your grandmother requested that I bring you by one at a time so she can speak with each of you individually before dinner. She'd like to start with you, Aubrey."

*Of course she would.* I swallow the words, but Aubrey sees them on my face anyway. "Maybe Milly should go first," she says.

"No, it's fine," I say tightly, disengaging myself from Donald. "I'll mingle."

"Milly—" she says unhappily, but Donald is already ushering her toward the head table. I grab a glass of champagne from a passing server and take a much longer sip than etiquette would recommend. Then I work my way farther into the room.

*The Summer Gala.* I used to think it was a magical event, the absolute height of glamour. I loved looking at pictures of my mother in her white dress, and imagining myself transported in her place. Now I'm finally here, and all I can think is that I hope she wasn't as miserable that night as I am now.

"Hi, Milly." The quiet voice at my side startles me, and I turn to see Hazel Baxter-Clement looking tired and drawn in a wine-colored gown. Her dark hair is piled high on her head, and she's holding a full champagne glass.

"Hazel, oh my gosh." I grab her free hand with mine. "I'm sorry I didn't get to talk to you at the funeral." The burial after the Mass had been private, family only. "And I'm so sorry about your grandfather. He was a really sweet man."

"Thanks," Hazel says. "The good thing, I guess, is that he had a long life. And his dementia was getting worse, so . . ." She heaves a sigh. "Mom says maybe it's a blessing that he doesn't have to go through the late stages of that. I don't know. I just wish he would've died in his sleep, or something more peaceful."

I can't think of anything comforting to say in return, because she's right. Drowning in the woods behind your own house is a horrible way to go. I finally settle on, "I know I only met him a couple of times, but I could tell how proud of you he was. And you took great care of him."

Her expression darkens. "I don't know about that. I let him go outside on his own that morning, and I shouldn't have. But he was having one of his better days, and he said he was meeting a friend, so . . ."

The back of my neck prickles. "Do you know who?"

"No. I wish I did. Nobody's come forward, and it would be nice to know how he spent his last morning."

I pause, thinking about Dr. Baxter's letter to Uncle Archer. *There are things I should have told you long ago.* "Had your grandfather, um, mentioned my uncle Archer recently?"

Hazel blinks. "About him possibly being back in town?" Some of her usual energy returns as she adds, "Is he really? People keep insisting they saw him last Friday, but nobody's spotted him since. I'm not sure Granddad knew, though. He never said anything. Did you guys see him? Archer, I mean."

I hesitate. It's been over a week since we talked to Uncle Archer, and Aubrey is convinced he hightailed it off the island. We stopped by the bungalow a couple of times, but the shutters were always drawn and no one answered the door. So she's probably right, and there's no harm in feeding Hazel's curiosity, especially after the week she's had. "We did. He'd been staying in a little bungalow behind his friend Rob Valentine's house, but—"

"Sweetheart." A woman materializes beside Hazel, looking like her middle-aged doppelgänger. "One of Granddad's classmates from medical school wants to meet you. He's at Mrs.

Story's table. Can I steal you away?" She turns to me with an apologetic smile, and her eyes spark with recognition. "Well, goodness, speaking of Storys. You must be Milly. I'm Katherine Baxter, Hazel's mother. I saw a lovely picture of you and your cousins leaving my father's funeral in the *Gull Cove Gazette*."

"Yes, hello," I say, shaking her outstretched hand. "It's nice to meet you. I'm so sorry for your loss."

"Thank you. I appreciate that. I didn't mean to interrupt—"

"It's fine," I promise, glad for the escape. I like Hazel, but there are more than enough rumors swirling around Uncle Archer without me adding to them. I probably shouldn't have said as much as I did, so now seems like a good time to cut my losses and run. "I need to find my cousins, anyway. I'm sure I'll see you both later."

I scoot away, nearly bumping into a server holding a bottle of champagne. He tips it toward my almost-empty glass. "Can I top that off for you?" he asks. I don't answer right away, trying to count how many I've had already, and he does it anyway.

Well. When in Rome. I gulp the fizzing bubbles and keep moving, my eyes roving across the well-dressed crowd. Directly ahead of me, I see a familiar blond head: Reid Chilton, fellow Towhee and senator's son. I have zero desire to talk to him, so I spin on my heel and almost collide with the person behind me.

A hand reaches out to steady me. "Whoa. Sorry. I was just trying to . . ." It's Jonah, handsome in a tuxedo, and his eyes widen as he takes me in. He doesn't say anything for a beat, his Adam's apple rising and falling a few times before he finally adds, "I forget what I was trying to do, because—all the blood left my head just now." He swallows again. "You look incredible, Milly."

Something warm and fluttery nips at my chest. "Thanks. So do you." It's true. Maybe it's because the best tailors on Gull Cove Island were at his beck and call this week, but Jonah looks born to wear a tux. His dark hair is smoothed off his forehead for once, and while I kind of like his usual tousled look, I can't argue with how the current style accentuates the angles of his face. I hold up my glass before taking another sip. "Have you tried the champagne?"

"No. I had cocoa." I raise a brow, and he shrugs. "It was, like, made from chocolate they flew in from France and hand-ground with a mix of cinnamon and nutmeg. And also a little bit of chili, I guess? That's what Carson says anyway."

"Was it good?"

"The best cocoa I've ever had in my life," Jonah says, so fervently that I smile.

"Mildred knows how to throw a party. You have to give her that." I feel myself relaxing for the first time all night, and press my fingertips against his sleeve with a sudden rush of affection. "I'm glad you're here."

He grins, looking both pleased and confused. "Well, I had to be, right? Mildred's orders."

"I know, but I don't mean just *here* here. I mean in general. On the island." Jonah still looks a little uncertain, and I can't blame him. My thoughts aren't as organized as I would like right now. "What I'm trying to say is—I'm glad I met you."

As soon as the words slip out, my face heats with embarrassment. That's not the kind of thing I usually say, and while I'm not *sorry*, exactly, because I mean it . . . it's possible that the third glass of champagne was a mistake.

Jonah's deep-brown eyes get soft. "I'm glad I met you, too.

210

Really glad." He licks his lips, and I have the sudden urge to trace the movement with my finger. Okay, the third glass of champagne was *definitely* a mistake. That realization does not, however, stop me from grabbing a fourth when a server passes by. Jonah's gaze shifts to my glass, and he tugs at his cuffs as he adds, "The thing is—"

"There you are!" A voice interrupts from behind us. "I've been looking all over for you, Milly. Hello, Jonah." It's Reid Chilton, wearing an extra-large bow tie and a smarmy grin. The bigger, butterfly bow tie is in this year, according to *GQ,* and I kind of hate myself for knowing that. It's the sort of useless information I've been accumulating for years, just waiting for the opportunity to dazzle my neglectful society grandmother. Joke's on me.

"What?" Reid asks, frowning. Jonah is also looking at me strangely, and I realize I said that last part out loud.

"I said, I like your tie."

I very obviously did not say that, but they're both too polite to contradict me. "Thank you," Reid says smoothly. "But nobody in this room can hold a candle to you."

*Oh, barf,* I think. Then I freeze. Did I say that out loud, too? But Reid is still smiling at me, so probably not. "I think we're at the same dinner table tonight," he continues. "My mother is here as a guest of your grandmother. Perhaps you've heard of her. Senator Genevieve Chilton? Democrat from Massachusetts."

"My mother is a Democrat from New York," I say. "But not a senator. And not here."

Jonah mumbles something under his breath that sounds like *This is going well* as Reid's smile gets a little strained. "Your family history is fascinating," he says.

211

I didn't intend to drink any more champagne, but somehow the glass in my hand emptied itself while Reid was talking. I blame him for being long-winded. "That's one word for it," I say. I mean to accompany the words with a sophisticated light laugh, but it comes out as a snort. Which makes me laugh even harder. Reid stares, brow furrowed, as Jonah grips my elbow.

"My cousin and I were just going to get some air," Jonah says. I'm still laughing. Who knew Reid was this *funny*? "It's getting really hot in here. You ready, Milly?"

"Absolutely," I say, angling for a regal tone but failing when I slur the *s*.

"See you at dinner," Reid says.

"Not if I see you first," I giggle before Jonah steers me away.

"How much champagne have you had?" he asks quietly.

Too much. That becomes clear as the room wavers around me. I'm used to sipping cocktails with my friends over the course of a couple of hours—not downing four glasses of champagne on an empty stomach. Or was it five?

"It doesn't matter," I whisper. "Mildred already hates me."

"She doesn't hate you."

"She does. She likes Aubrey better than me. She likes you better than me, and *you*"—I stab one finger into his chest for emphasis—"aren't even related to her."

"Shhh," Jonah mutters. He steers me around a small knot of Donald Camden clones, all silver-haired and ruddy-cheeked, chuckling in a genteel sort of way as they clutch tumblers of amber liquid. I almost point that out—*Look at all the Donalds!*—but Jonah is still talking. "Milly, you can't let her get to you. I don't think your grandmother is an especially good person. Maybe she was once, but not anymore."

We're at a big gold curtain now, and when Jonah parts it there's a French door behind it. Jonah unlatches the door and—oh, blessed cool air. We step onto a stone balcony, and when Jonah closes the door behind us, it's as close to privacy as we're going to get at the Summer Gala.

I lean against the balcony's rail, pushing my hair back with an unsteady hand. It's a clear night, and the stars look low and bright against the blue velvet sky. "Are you having a nice time at my grandmother's extremely important party?" I ask.

"Are *you*?" Jonah asks.

"Super," I say, and have to bite my lip to keep from laughing again. "It was totally part of the plan to get hammered. Mission accomplished."

"You just need some air," Jonah says. Unconvincingly.

I turn to face him. The motion makes the balcony spin, and my hand shoots out to clutch at the railing. I don't find it, but Jonah catches my arm before I stumble. "This floor . . . should be straighter," I tell him gravely, and he nods.

"I was just thinking the same thing."

"It's an old hotel," I say. "Needs updating."

Jonah clears his throat. "Listen, while we have a minute alone, there's something I want to tell you. About why I'm here."

I'm still light-headed, and he looks reassuringly stable, so I loop my arms around his neck to anchor myself in place. Much better. "Is it to keep me upright?"

"Not exactly." Jonah laughs a little. "Happy to do it, though. The thing is . . ." He trails off, licking his lips again. This time, I give in to the impulse and detach one hand from behind his neck so I can trace his bottom lip with one finger. He tenses, but doesn't pull away. "You're making it hard for me to concentrate."

213

"You talk too much," I say, and reach up to brush my lips against his.

I pull back, just enough to see his eyes widen and then go a little unfocused as his hands cup my face and pull me closer. "Well, I tried," he murmurs before his mouth covers mine. It's warm and searching, and I feel a jolt of desire so strong and unexpected that it roots me to the spot. I mean, I wanted this, obviously, because I'm the one who started it. But I didn't understand, until right this second, how *much.* My arms go around his neck again, my fingers twining in his hair and my heart hammering in my chest. Jonah's tongue slips into my mouth, and the taste of him, all chocolate and spice, makes me swoon.

"Oh my God!"

The voice that interrupts us is loud and shocked, and in the split second it takes Jonah and me to break apart, I sober up completely. His gaze holds mine, and I see my own question mirrored there: *What did we just do?*

The answer comes soon enough. I turn to see Donald Camden gaping at us, a red-faced Aubrey by his side. The curtain we slipped behind has been pulled aside, the French door leading to the balcony is open, and every single person behind Donald— and there are *a lot* of them—is staring at us.

Including my grandmother.

# CHAPTER SEVENTEEN

## AUBREY

I've never seen a train wreck in real life, but I finally understand the metaphor. Looking at Milly and Jonah is unbearable, but I can't *not* look, either.

Especially since this is kind of my fault.

I knew Milly was upset when Donald brought me to Gran's table. The whole time Gran and I were talking, I tried to keep an eye on Milly as she moved around the room, but I kept losing sight of her. My last glimpse was of her disappearing onto the balcony with Jonah. So when Gran asked Donald to bring Jonah by, I said, *He just stepped outside, I can get him.* Then Gran replied, *Fresh air sounds lovely, Donald and I will join you.*

And here we are.

I should say something. I'm not sure what, but anything would be better than the horrified silence of two hundred black-tie party guests who think they just caught a couple of long-lost first cousins making out. In fact, now would be the ideal time to explain that they're *not* cousins. But I have no idea how to open that conversation, and before I can start, Gran speaks.

"I suppose this is what comes from not listening to my instincts," she says coldly. "Your parents were nothing but disappointments, and you are entirely the same." Heat rushes to my cheeks at the blanket statement as her eyes narrow in on Jonah. "I shouldn't be surprised that Anders's son is utterly *depraved.*"

Jonah, who has looked like he was in a fog since he and Milly broke apart, snaps out of it at the mention of Uncle Anders's name. His face settles into an expression of intense hatred as he steps away from Milly and through the French door, stopping within a few feet of Mildred. "Yeah, well, I have a message from *Anders,*" he says. His voice is low and angry, but it carries easily through the silent ballroom. "He fucking hates your guts and always has."

Shocked gasps run through the room as Gran's face turns a mottled purple. I gape at Jonah in confused astonishment, half believing that I must have heard him wrong. Why on earth would he take a horrible situation like this, and make it *worse*? Donald inhales sharply beside me, looking as though he'd like to hurl Jonah right off the balcony.

The *balcony.* Where poor Milly is still standing, frozen, all by herself. I'm about to push past Donald and go to her when another voice rings out over the buzzing hum surrounding us.

"What a vicious lie. But what else can you expect from an *imposter.*"

I turn at the voice, but can't see the speaker. Gran stiffens beside me and clutches Donald's arm, her eyes going wide and almost terrified. "Go," he says to her in a low voice. "I'll take care of this." And Gran just—leaves. Turns on her heel and heads back in

216

the direction of her table, walking as quickly as her dress will allow.

The speaker breaks through the crowd, pausing as he catches sight of Donald. He's short and slight but still oddly imposing, and crackling with suppressed energy. He has a shock of dark hair and a thin, ferret-like face. I recognize him instantly.

"Hello, Donald," he says, stuffing his hands into his tuxedo pockets with a smirk. "Nice to see you again."

"What the hell are you doing here, Anders?" Donald growls. "Who let you in?"

Uncle Anders shrugs, hands still in his pockets. "Security here isn't what it used to be. You should thank me, though, for setting things straight before this entire room has a meltdown at the thought of cousinly incest. This boy?" He jerks his head toward Jonah. "Not my son. *This* is. JT!" He raises his voice, and another figure steps reluctantly forward. Even without the name, I would have known my actual cousin anywhere. He's a carbon copy of his father, except instead of an arrogant smirk, his narrow features are pinched into a shifty, furtive expression. "Donald, let me introduce Jonah Theodore Story."

"Holy crap." Someone breathes into my ear as the ballroom erupts into low, urgent chatter. I turn to see Brittany beside me in her server's uniform, and make a grab for her arm. I feel a surge of gratitude when I actually make contact, because all of this has such a dreamlike quality that I wouldn't have been surprised to grasp thin air. "Jonah's not Jonah?" she says.

"He is. Sort of," I murmur back. "It's complicated."

"So he and Milly aren't actually . . ." Brittany starts nodding as her eyes dart between Jonah and JT. "Everything makes so much more sense now."

"What in God's name are you pulling, Anders?" Donald asks.

"Me?" Uncle Anders puts a hand over his heart. "Absolutely nothing. I'm afraid, though, that you've all been the victims of fraud. My son, JT, is the only one of the next generation with a conscience." I start getting a sick feeling in my stomach as Uncle Anders continues, "I'm sure you're under the impression that my mother invited her grandchildren here. You couldn't be more wrong. Let me explain what's really going on."

He has the room's undivided attention, and he plays to it with a deep sigh. "My brother Archer approached the children and offered them jobs under false pretenses, hoping to worm his way back into our mother's good graces. JT was the only grandchild who refused to accept, so Archer found a replacement. I had no idea any of this was going on until I saw a picture of our neighbor's son at Fred Baxter's funeral. I said to JT, 'What in God's name is Jonah North doing with your cousins?' And we realized what must have happened."

I squeeze my eyes shut for a second, frustration humming through my veins. Busted, by the *Gull Cove Gazette*. We should've realized our parents would be keeping an eye on the local paper. Once Uncle Anders saw the photo, he must've known JT had put one over on him. I can only imagine how quickly he forced a full confession out of JT—not just the switch with Jonah but also that Uncle Archer was behind the original invitation. After that, all he had to do was throw us under the bus with a bunch of lies to salvage his shot at reconciling with Gran.

And it seems to be working. The crowd around us is eating up Anders's performance, whispering and murmuring behind their hands.

"You lying sack of shit." Jonah finally speaks, practically spitting the words. "You're trying to manipulate the entire room, just like you manipulated my parents. Your *son* put me up to this, and he—"

"Honestly, Jonah," Anders interrupts with a smile that manages to be both pained and patient. "Quit while you're ahead. No one here is going to believe a word you say."

"He's right," I blurt out. I let go of Brittany's arm and grab Donald Camden's, shaking it to force him to look at me. "I mean, Jonah North is right. JT paid him. And we didn't know Uncle Archer brought us here until last week. He was . . ." I trail off, because from the way Donald is glaring at me, I'm pretty sure I just made everything worse.

"Really, Aubrey? It's Aubrey, isn't it?" Uncle Anders turns his condescending smile on me. "So you're admitting you knew this boy wasn't your cousin, and that you knew Archer brought you here, but you never bothered to inform your grandmother? And now you want people to believe that the rest of what I'm saying is a lie? Come on." His voice turns silky smooth. "I can understand why you went along with it. Your father is a tough customer. It's so hard to earn his love, isn't it?"

The words suck all the air out of my lungs. Somehow, despite not having seen me since I was a little kid, Uncle Anders knew exactly where to hit. Meanwhile, he's spinning everything to make him and JT sound blameless, and the rest of us sound like conniving gold diggers. And the worst thing is, what he's proposing isn't much more ludicrous than what actually happened.

"Where is Mother?" Uncle Anders asks. He scans the crowd with a frown, finally realizing that his audience is missing its most important member. "She needs to know that she has at least one grandchild who values honesty and respect."

"Your mother left, thank God, before she had to listen to any of this travesty. And I've heard more than enough," Donald says. He raises his hand and snaps his fingers. "It's time for you to leave." Men in dark suits seem to materialize out of nowhere, grabbing hold of Uncle Anders by both arms. His face flushes a deep, angry red.

"What's the matter with you, Donald?" he yells. "I'm *saving your ass.*"

"His son, too," Donald says to the men in suits. "And the other boy. Get all of them out of here."

It's chaos around us suddenly, a tangle of movement and shouting. Uncle Anders is straining against the men dragging him toward the exit, screaming, "This is my fucking home, Donald! Not yours! *Mine!*" at the top of his lungs. More men in suits appear, surrounding JT and Jonah and pulling them away as Milly watches with a blank expression.

Oh God. Milly.

She's still on the balcony. I push through the crowd, making my way through the French door until I'm beside my cousin. One look at her glassy eyes, and I know the combination of shock and champagne has rendered her sharp tongue useless. Any other night, Milly would've gone toe-to-toe with Uncle Anders. But when I thread my fingers through hers, she just stares down at them like her hand is an alien appendage she's never seen before.

"I should've known," she says, her voice thick with alcohol. "I'm so *stupid.*"

"No you're not." I brush a strand of hair from her face. "Should've known what?"

"That it was Jonah's parents."

"Huh?" I'm still not getting it. I know Milly's more than a little drunk, but I need her to focus. "Can you explain things to me like I'm in kindergarten?"

She presses a hand to her forehead, like that'll help her collect her thoughts. "I read an article in the *Providence Journal* about how all these families lost money because of Uncle Anders's financial advice. One man said he'd declared bankruptcy, and he— *God.* His name was Frank North. But I didn't make the connection." Her face hardens, eyes flashing with a shadow of her usual fire. "Because Jonah didn't tell me. Didn't tell *us.* All this time we've been protecting him, keeping quiet about who he really is, and he never bothered to let us know that oh, by the way, he has a massive grudge against our family."

"Ohhh," I breathe. Jonah's *just like you manipulated my parents* comment—which had flown right over my head in the heat of the moment—suddenly comes back to me, and his whole demeanor makes a lot more sense. No wonder he Hulked out at the name *Anders.* "So he hates Uncle Anders."

"And us, probably." Milly folds her arms tightly across her chest. "He's been using us for cover. Stringing us along till he could do something like this, and humiliate our entire family. I gave him the perfect opportunity, didn't I?"

"No," I say quickly. "He wouldn't do that." Milly doesn't respond, and I squeeze her arm. "Milly, come on. Even if Jonah were a complete jerk, which I don't think he is, he's not that good of an actor. You saw through him in a flash, remember?"

"I didn't see this," she says dully.

I want to find the right words to comfort her, but before I can say anything else, Donald Camden leans through the doors, his face a cold mask of fury.

"You two. You're going back to the dorms. I'll deal with you tomorrow."

# CHAPTER EIGHTEEN

## JONAH

Of all the ways I thought my time on Gull Cove Island might end, I didn't picture two guys in suits standing over me in a dorm room while I stuff everything I own into my duffel bag.

"Am I under arrest?" I finally blurt out.

Suit No. 1 huffs out a laugh. They're both blond guys in their thirties, but he's taller and broader. He's holding the bag with my rental tuxedo, which they told me to change out of as soon as we got to the dorm. At least they waited in the hall while I did it. "We're not cops, kid. We're security detail. Our job is to get you off resort premises and into a hotel downtown. You get one night to make arrangements with whatever parent or guardian is responsible for you. Mrs. Story expects you to be off the island by tomorrow afternoon." His tone is even, almost bored, as he adds, "What happens to you after that isn't our problem."

I zip my duffel in response, which Suit No. 2 takes as his cue to grab my arm again. "All right, let's get moving," he says.

"I'm coming," I say tersely, shaking free. "But I need to send a text. I have to get in touch with my *parent or guardian,* right?"

His neutral expression doesn't change. "Make it fast."

He propels me toward the door and shuts it behind us. I blink in the fluorescent lights of the hall, too bright after the dim dorm room, until the dark spots in front of my eyes fade to reveal a half-dozen curious faces. Every Towhee who's not working or attending the gala is in the hallway to watch my walk of shame. News travels fast on a twelve-mile island.

"So long, Jonah," Reid Chilton's roommate calls. "If that *is in fact your name.*"

"Get back in your rooms," Suit No. 2 says. "Show's over."

Nobody listens. I keep my head down as the Suits lead me outside, scrolling through my contacts. But I'm not looking for father's number; I'll deal with that later. Instead, I pull up Milly's.

*I'm sorry,* I text once I'm buckled into the backseat of the car. *I screwed everything up.*

Every time I think about what I did tonight, I feel sick. When Donald Camden burst in on my kiss with Milly, my time as Jonah Story was officially up. I knew it, and part of me was even relieved. What I should've done next was this: grab Milly's hand and tell everyone within earshot that I wasn't her cousin so they'd stop looking at her with shock and disgust, and focus all that negative energy where it belonged—on me. Then I could've taken the brunt of what happened next, or maybe Milly and I would've dealt with it together. Which is what I've wanted ever since she snagged my wallet and called me out.

Instead, I launched into my Anders Story revenge fantasy. Even though I'd already decided, that day we had brunch at Catmint House, that I needed to let it go. It wasn't worth putting

Milly and Aubrey in a bad situation. But tonight, when I was humiliated and stressed and goaded by Mildred, I let my bitterness take over. And not only was that a shitty thing to do to Milly, but it *didn't work*. All I managed to do was give Anders an opening to spew lies.

I'm so caught up in my thoughts that I don't even notice we've arrived downtown until I see the bright lights of the dock. Suit No. 1 is driving, and Suit No. 2 is on the phone as we pull in front of a redbrick building. "All set," he says into the handset, then lowers it and twists to face me. "This is the Hawthorne Hotel, your home for the night. You can order from room service, with a cap of fifty dollars. You've got an open one-way ticket for tomorrow's ferry waiting for you at will call. The earliest leaves at seven a.m., the latest at four p.m. Understood?"

"What if I miss it?" I ask.

His voice doesn't shift from the monotone he's been using all night. "I wouldn't advise that. Come on, I'll check you in."

Suit No. 1 stays in the car with the engine running as we head inside Hawthorne Hotel. If the clerk at reception thinks it's strange that a guy in a suit is checking a teenager in at nine o'clock at night, she doesn't show it. "You're in room 215," she says, eyes on the computer in front of her. "The elevator is down the hall to your left, or you can take the stairs around the corner to your right. Do you need help with your bags?"

I hitch my duffel higher on my shoulder. "I'm good."

"One room key or two?" she asks.

Suit No. 2 answers before I can. "Just the one."

She hands it to me with a bright smile. "Enjoy your stay!"

I thank her and turn away, Suit No. 2 right on my heels. The front door opens, and I stop in my tracks when I see Anders and JT coming through it. They're alone, not flanked by security guards like me, and that makes my temper spike all over again.

"You fucking liars," I snarl.

Anders Story looks cool and collected. You'd never guess that he'd just gotten thrown out of his own mother's party. He peers past me to a silver bowl on the reception desk, and grabs a plastic-wrapped mint. "I took a shot, Jonah," he says, unwrapping the candy and popping it into his mouth. "It was the only one you and JT left me with."

I glare at JT, still skulking in his father's shadow. "This whole thing was *your* idea."

JT shrugs with a ghost of Anders's bravado. "You're the one who couldn't manage to lie low. Getting your picture taken at a funeral and making out with my cousin weren't part of the deal. Technically, all of this is your fault."

"Technically, it's his," I say, shifting my gaze to Anders. "I wouldn't have gone along with this if you hadn't ruined my parents. You're a liar *and* a thief."

I wait for him to deny it, but he just lifts a shoulder, chewing and swallowing the mint with deliberate slowness. "Your parents are adults, making decisions about how to manage their money of their own free will. Stop shifting blame. It's pathetic."

"Enough." Suit No. 2 tugs on my arm. "Time for you to get to your room. We taking the elevator or the stairs?"

"I'll go on my own," I say, trying to wrench free.

It doesn't work. Suit No. 2's grip is like a vise. "My orders are to get you safely to your room so that's what I'm doing," he says mildly. "Elevator or stairs?"

"Stairs," I grit out. Because the only thing worse than getting sent to my room in front of Anders and JT would be waiting for an elevator while they watch.

Suit No. 2 and I climb the stairs silently, pushing through the door on the second floor into an empty hallway. Room 215 is easy to find—it's right next to the stairwell and across from a vending machine. Probably the noisiest and therefore cheapest room in the place. A light on the door panel flashes green when I insert my key, and I pause after turning the handle.

"Please tell me we part ways here," I say.

"We do." Suit No. 2 allows an amused glint to enter his eyes. If nothing else, tonight must've been a break from routine. "Good luck, kid."

I heave a sigh of relief when the door shuts behind me. Alone at last. I pull my phone from my pocket, hoping for a text from Milly or Aubrey, but there's nothing. I think about sending one last message to Milly, but I can't bring myself to keep bugging her. If she wanted to talk to me, she'd have answered by now.

This room isn't as luxurious as the ones at Gull Cove Resort, but it's better than the dorms. There are two twin beds with nautical-striped bedding, a small desk in front of the window, and a large-screen television that takes up most of one wall. The air-conditioning is noisy and set so high that goose bumps rise on my arms. The bathroom is clean and bright, and the muscles in my shoulders ache at the thought of a hot shower. I should call my father, but that can wait another five minutes.

It ends up being more like twenty. A shower was a brilliant idea because it lets me shift into autopilot, going through motions I've done thousands of times before. I can pretend for a little while that everything is fine. Normal, even. But eventually, when I've used up every tiny bottle available and the entire bathroom is enveloped in a cloud of steam, it's time to leave the cocoon of the shower stall. I step out and towel off. Carson Fine had our clothes washed and pressed yesterday, so I actually have something clean to wear. My sweatpants are weirdly stiff with starch, but whatever.

Once I'm dressed, I can't put it off any longer. I sit at the foot of one of the beds, phone in hand, and debate how to start the conversation. *So, Dad. About that sweet summer job . . .*

Maybe I should start with a text. I open my messages, and blink when I realize that I missed one from him earlier today. The preview reads *Hey, Jonah, bankruptcy court went,* and I groan. I was so worried about the Summer Gala that I forgot my parents' hearing had been rescheduled for today. "When it rains, it pours," I mutter, opening the message. It's classic Dad: one giant paragraph instead of a bunch of individual texts.

*Hey, Jonah, bankruptcy court went better than expected today. Looks like your mom and I will be able to keep Empire open after all. More to come, but we're feeling optimistic for the first time in a while. Enzo's working at Home Depot. We talk to him every day and we're hopeful that we'll be able to bring him back before the year is out. Try not to worry, ok? Enjoy your weekend and we'll talk soon.*

I drop the phone onto the bed, put my head in my hands, and let out a deep, shuddering breath. My eyes sting as I press my palms against them. I hadn't been letting myself hope, but . . . they did it. My parents have been working nonstop trying to show the bankruptcy trustee that they can pay back their creditors and still run a business, and I guess he listened.

*Stop shifting blame.* Anders Story might be an asshole with no conscience, but maybe he's not wrong. "You can't prove fraud. And you can't get your money back," the lawyer my parents consulted said. "All you can do is dig yourself out and move on." My parents didn't want to hear that for a long time, and neither did I. It felt *good* to be angry. But it didn't help, and it didn't change anything. I feel another sick stab of regret when I think about Milly, and how differently tonight might've gone if I'd let go of all that useless rage sooner.

A sharp knock interrupts my thoughts. "Oh, come on," I grumble, my head still in my hands. "Now what?" The knock sounds again, louder this time. "Hold your horses," I call, managing a slight grin at the homage to Enzo. When I open the door I expect to see Suit No. 2, making sure I haven't crawled out the window or something, but that's not who's standing in front of me.

I almost don't recognize him. He's clean-shaven, dressed neatly in a long-sleeved T-shirt and jeans, with clear eyes and a tired smile.

"Hey, Jonah," Archer Story says. "Can I come in?"

Archer raided the minibar before we started talking, and now he has four small bottles lined up on the desk in front of him. Only one of them is open, the vodka, and he's taken two small sips. "I apologize for drinking in front of you," he says. "I'm trying to get back on track, but I can't go cold turkey, especially for difficult conversations. I'll just backslide if I do." His eyes stray to the row of bottles. "I'm not intending to have all of these. Or even most of them. There's just something comforting about knowing that I could."

"It's fine," I tell him. "How'd you know where I was?" There's limited seating in the room, so I'm sprawled across one of the twin beds, while Archer sits in the desk chair.

"I still have friends at the resort," he says. "I don't deserve them, but I have them." He rubs one hand over his thin, angular face. I can't get used to the lack of mountain-man beard. "Just to keep things straight, because I've been hit with a lot of new information tonight: you are not, in fact, my nephew. Correct?"

"Correct," I say. He gives me such a regretful smile, like maybe he wishes that I was, that I find myself telling him the whole sordid story about how I got here. When I finish, he shakes his head and takes a small sip of vodka.

"Gotta admit, you as Anders's son never really fit."

"So I keep hearing," I say. "Were you at the gala tonight?"

"Oh no. I was distinctly not invited. But I heard all about it. Including my brother's return." Another small sip. "I need to try to contact Milly and Aubrey. As far as I can tell they're back in the dorms. But I'd like to make sure they're okay. And to apologize," he adds, his voice getting heavy. "Which is why I'm here. I owe you an apology too. I dropped out of sight after we talked. I saw the article about me in the *Gull Cove Gazette* the next day, and it hit me hard. I felt like I'd ruined everything, and I panicked. And when I panic, well . . . I tend to lose what little control I have."

Archer looks like he desperately wants another sip of vodka, but he doesn't take one. "I brought you guys here, and then I abandoned you. Which is unconscionable. You're just *kids*. I'm sorry that my refusal to act like an adult human at any point in the past few weeks—or the past two decades, really—led to the horrible evening you've just experienced."

I'm quiet for a moment, absorbing his words. "That's a pretty far-ranging apology."

The ghost of a smile flits across his face. "I felt like I needed to cover a lot of bases."

"It's okay. I mean, I was lying to you the whole time, so I guess we're even." I wait until Archer picks up the vodka bottle again, then ask, "Did you get a chance to talk to Dr. Baxter about that letter before he died?"

He pauses before taking another drink. "No. I was too much of a wreck to leave the house that day."

"What do you think he wanted to tell you?"

Archer sighs heavily. "No idea."

"So now what? Are you going back to Rob's?"

"Yeah, but not for long. I've taken too much advantage of his goodwill already. I just need a few days to get my act together, and then it's time for me to leave the island." He sighs again. "Return to real life, whatever that is."

An idea hits me, so suddenly that I sit bolt upright. "Can I come with you?" I ask.

Archer blinks. "Say what?"

"Can I come with you?" I repeat. "I haven't called my parents yet. And I—I left things really bad with Milly." I flush, remembering her frozen face after I went off on Mildred. "I need to apologize."

"I understand the compulsion," Archer says cautiously. "But you can do that long distance, after tempers have cooled. I think it's in your best interest to head out as planned."

"Please? Just for a day or two."

He regards me steadily. "Jonah, in case this wasn't perfectly clear—I'm an alcoholic."

"I know," I say.

"You can't depend on me. And I can't be responsible for you."

"I'm almost eighteen." In ten months, but close enough. "I'll be responsible for myself. I have been since I got here." Archer hesitates, and I press. "Come on. Do you want your mother to get her way every time she orders Donald Camden to kick somebody off Gull Cove Island?"

"Well." A smile tugs at the corners of Archer's mouth. "I'll say one thing for you: you know how to make an appeal."

# CHAPTER NINETEEN

## MILLY

I'm feeling energized when Aubrey and I walk into Carson Fine's office first thing in the morning. Being summoned from the dorms this early doesn't bode well, but I've had three cups of coffee and I'm wearing my mother's red dress. I'm not sure what's about to get thrown at us, but I'm ready to fight it.

Unfortunately, the man behind the desk isn't our friendly, nautical-tie-wearing head of hospitality. "Have a seat," Donald Camden says. He flashes his teeth or, more accurately, bares them. "Let's discuss last night."

God. *Last night.* I can't even think about it without wanting to throw up. After Jonah got escorted out, Aubrey and I were rushed back to the dorms by a couple of women I'd never met before. Not surprisingly, I passed out as soon as Aubrey wrangled me out of my dress. I woke up to two texts from Uncle Archer—surprise, surprise, he's still on the island after all—and six from Jonah.

*I'm sorry.*

*I screwed everything up.*

*I never should have said that.*

*Can we talk?*

*I owe you an apology.*

*And an explanation.*

I sent a single text back: *Did you come here to get revenge on Uncle Anders? Yes/no answer only.*

He answered within seconds. *Yes.*

Then he sent a bunch of other stuff, but I haven't looked at it. He's as big a liar as any Story, so I can't trust anything he says.

I still can't believe I didn't put two and two together about Jonah's family. And I can't believe . . . but no. I'm not going to think about him when I have to keep my mind clear for whatever's about to go down with Donald.

Who's currently looking at Aubrey and me with undisguised irritation, waiting for us to take the seats he ordered us into. We both remain standing. "Uncle Anders is a liar—" I start, but Donald holds up a hand.

"Yes, he is. And so are the two of you. So here's what's going to happen. As of this morning, you are no longer employed at Gull Cove Resort. You will be paid for the full summer, which in my view is very generous." His lips purse on the last word. "You're expected to make arrangements with your parents for your return within three days, and you have an open ferry ticket for today, tomorrow, and Tuesday. However, before you leave, Mrs. Story wishes to see *you*, Aubrey." His gaze locks on her, and she stiffens beside me. "A car will pick you up at one p.m. sharp from the resort's front entrance and take you to Catmint House."

"What?" she asks, at the same time as I ask, "Just Aubrey? Not me?"

"Mrs. Story wishes to speak with Aubrey alone, as a representative for the cousins," Donald says. His nostrils flare. "I advised against any further contact, considering the damage all of you have already done. But she was insistent."

Aubrey looks horrified as I ask, "A *representative*? What does that mean? Why not me?"

Donald's lip curls. "She didn't say. If I were to guess, your behavior last night renders you . . . less suitable."

"Suitable for *what*?" I practically yell the words, which probably proves his point.

"I don't want to go," Aubrey says.

"That is, of course, entirely up to you," Donald says. "The car will be there at one o'clock, and it will wait for fifteen minutes."

"What if we don't leave?" I ask. "The island, I mean."

It gives me an ounce of satisfaction when Donald's smooth expression briefly gives way to surprise. "If you don't leave? Well that's . . . I mean . . . you must."

I fold my arms across my chest. "I don't think we *must* do anything. You're not the boss of us. And neither is Mildred anymore. We can stay here if we want."

Aubrey darts a nervous glance toward me as Donald's mask of composure returns. "As I stated, your rooms at the resort dorms are only good through Tuesday morning. After that, we will be taking your keys and you will no longer have access to the building."

"There are other hotels," I say.

"Most of which your grandmother owns," Donald points out. "Further, your severance package is contingent on you agreeing to the terms laid out by Mrs. Story."

"We don't want her money," I say. "You can keep it." Then I look apologetically at Aubrey, realizing that I spoke for her without thinking. I know things are a lot tighter financially in her household than in mine, especially with the threat of divorce looming. But she's nodding right along with me.

Donald's neck flushes a deep red, and it's a beautiful sight. But he merely says, "You have nowhere to go except home."

"Then you don't have anything to worry about, do you?" I turn for the door, and Aubrey does too. It's as good an exit line as I'm going to get, especially since he's right.

Aubrey clutches my arm as we speed-walk down the hallway. "You weren't serious, were you?" she whispers. "About staying on the island?"

"No," I admit. "I wanted to give Donald a hard time, but he's right. We don't have anywhere else to go." I pull out my phone, getting ready to send a text to my mother, and one flashes from Uncle Archer. I frown in momentary impatience, until a new idea hits me. I hold my screen up to Aubrey with a grin. "Or then again, maybe we do. Want to go for a drive? I never did return those keys to the Jeep."

An hour later, we're sitting in the bungalow's living room, fully caught up with Uncle Archer. Unfortunately, he comes with an unexpected roommate who was supposed to be *gone already*.

I accepted Uncle Archer's apology. I stopped Jonah's attempt with a look. Every time I think about him abandoning me on the balcony so he could settle a grudge against Uncle Anders that he'd never bothered to tell me about, hurt stabs at my chest.

"So you're going home?" Jonah asks.

"I guess we have to," I mutter. When I'd imagined Uncle Archer's bungalow as a temporary port in the storm, I didn't realize we'd have to share it with Jonah.

"What does your mother think about all this?" Uncle Archer asks me, then inclines his head toward Aubrey. "And your father?"

Uncle Archer looks much better than he did the last time we saw him. There's a red Solo cup in front of him half filled with clear liquid that he's been sipping from the entire time we've been talking, and his hands never quite stop shaking, but he's been coherent throughout the conversation.

"They don't know," I say. "And we're not telling them. Not yet." Uncle Archer looks conflicted, and I add, "First we want to see what Mildred says to Aubrey."

Aubrey pales. "Only one of us wants that."

A knock sounds at the door, and Uncle Archer frowns. "Now, who could that be?"

"Maybe it's Uncle Anders. Coming back for another round," I say, shooting a baleful look at Jonah. He has the grace to blush, and I hate how good it looks on him.

"Oh God," Uncle Archer says as he heads for the door. "I hope not. I'm really trying to stay on track here, and that would—oh, hi." He steps back in confusion to reveal Hazel standing in the doorway. "Are you . . . do I know you?"

"No," she says. She's clutching a brown envelope to her chest, her pensive expression clearing a little when she spots me, Aubrey, and Jonah. "But I know who you are, and I know these guys. I'm Hazel Baxter-Clement, Dr. Baxter's granddaughter?"

"Of course. Welcome." If Uncle Archer is surprised that Hazel knew where to find him, he doesn't show it. Since I'm the

236

one who told her, I'm hoping he'll gloss over that small detail and just assume she found out from her grandfather. "Please come in, have a seat," he adds, gesturing to the living room. "I'm so sorry for your loss. Fred was a wonderful man."

"Yeah, that's kind of why I'm here." Hazel moves a few feet into the bungalow as Archer closes the door behind her, hovering beside the couch instead of squeezing into the space Aubrey and I try to make for her. "I just—I didn't know where else to go."

Uncle Archer cocks his head, concerned. "Everything okay?"

"I don't know." Hazel fumbles at a string on her envelope. "I found this in my grandfather's desk yesterday. It was addressed to me, but . . . it's about you."

I exchange glances with Aubrey as Uncle Archer asks, "Me?"

"Well, part of it. It's, um . . ." She opens the envelope and pulls out a sheet of paper. "Maybe I should just read it." She clears her throat. "'Dear Hazel, I am so proud of the young woman that you have become. You are kind, thoughtful, and hardworking. Quite frankly, you are a legacy that I do not deserve. There are things you don't know.'" Her voice falters, and she swallows hard before continuing. "'I'm afraid to face the consequences of my actions, but even more afraid that soon I won't remember them. So perhaps I should start with something that might yet be put right. I have done a grave injustice to Archer Story.'"

She stops. I don't think anyone in the room is breathing. I wait as long as I can stand it, to let Hazel collect herself, then burst out with, "*What* injustice?"

"I don't know," Hazel says. "The letter ends there."

I groan as Uncle Archer runs a hand over his face. "Your grandfather asked to meet with me, right before he died," he tells

Hazel. "I didn't get to him quickly enough. I have no idea what he wanted to talk about, or what he thinks he did to me. There's nothing, on my end, that's ever been a problem. He was our family doctor and always kind to me. That's it. May I?" He gestures toward the letter, and Hazel hands it over. Uncle Archer scans it quickly, frowning. "He never said anything to you before this?"

"No," Hazel says. "He'd never even mentioned you. There's something else, though." She reaches into the envelope and pulls out a thin sheaf of paper. "This was here, too."

Uncle Archer takes it, his brow furrowing. "An autopsy report?"

"Yeah. It's, like, twenty years old." My nerves start prickling as Hazel adds, "Twenty-four, to be precise. It's for someone named Kayla Dugas."

"Kayla?" I echo, looking at Aubrey. "Oona's sister Kayla?"

Uncle Archer looks up. "You know Oona?"

"She sold us our dresses," I say. "And told us about her sister. How she dated Uncle Anders in high school and college. And then she died. Right around the time you were disinherited. We noticed the timing." I look sideways at Aubrey and flush, remembering how rude I'd been to her at the library. "Well, Aubrey did."

Uncle Archer frowns at the report. "There's no note or anything attached to this? No context for why he'd want you or me to have it?"

"Nothing," Hazel says.

"Maybe I should get in touch with Oona," he says. "It seems like this should have been left for her, not me. Although I would've thought her family got a copy long ago."

Aubrey speaks up. "What about the timing, Uncle Archer?

You got the *you know what you did* letter from Donald Camden right after Kayla died, didn't you?"

"Before," he says. "I don't remember the exact timing, but it was a one-two punch. First the letters, then Kayla died. We came back for her funeral, and Mother refused to see us."

"Huh." Aubrey chews her lip. "I thought it might've been a cause-and-effect thing. Like, something about Kayla's death made Gran angry enough to disinherit you."

"No." Archer looks puzzled by the idea. "Just coincidental timing. Mother was never Kayla's biggest fan, to be honest. She wanted Anders to find a nice Harvard girl. Which he did, eventually." Archer turns back to Hazel. "Was there anything else in your grandfather's things addressed to you, or to me?"

"Not that I've seen. I can look again. I have to get home anyway." Hazel sighs and puts the letter back into the envelope. "We're packing up Granddad's stuff."

"Would you mind if I hang on to this?" Uncle Archer asks, holding up the autopsy report. "I'd like to show Oona. Maybe she'll pick up on something I haven't."

"Sure," Hazel says. "See you guys around." She tucks the envelope beneath one arm and slips past Archer out the door.

Aubrey plucks at my sleeve. "We should go in another ten minutes or so," she says. "Gran's car will be on its way soon. Unless you want to stay here."

"No, I'm going with you," I answer.

"Will you come back?" Jonah asks.

"Probably not," I say, my words clipped. A small part of my brain registers that I sound an awful lot like my mother when she's about to freeze someone out for disappointing her. The rest of me is too upset to care.

"Milly, please." Jonah leans forward, his voice low and urgent. "Can we just talk for a minute?"

Uncle Archer clears his throat. "I'm going to make coffee, if anyone wants some," he says, heading for the kitchen.

"I do!" Aubrey, that traitor, jumps up to follow him.

The seat beside me is empty now, but Jonah's smart enough not to move there. "Milly, I'm sorry," he says. "I should've told you about my parents and Anders. Believe it or not, I was actually going to—"

"I *don't* believe it," I interrupt.

"I was actually going to tell you the night of the gala," he continues. "I tried, when we were on the balcony. But you, um." He tugs at the collar of his T-shirt. "You wanted to talk about other things."

My cheeks flame. That night is more than a little hazy, but not so much that I don't remember that I was less *talking* on the balcony than stumbling around drunkenly and hitting on Jonah. "Kind of late, don't you think? You should've told us from the start. Aubrey and I deserved that much, after we kept your secret. But you couldn't, right? That would've spoiled your *revenge*." I pull my eyes up from the floor so I can glare at him. "I'm surprised you bothered waiting till the gala. You could've laid into Mildred at Catmint House."

"I was going to," Jonah says, and that surprises me into silence. "When she asked how Anders was doing? I had a whole speech planned. But I couldn't say it. I didn't *want* to say it. I didn't care anymore about hurting Anders. Not if it hurt you, too."

I ignore the warmth blossoming in my chest. "You didn't seem worried about that last night."

"I screwed up," Jonah says simply. "It was a nightmare moment and I just—I let my temper take over. You don't know what it's like, to have someone like Anders—"

"No, I don't know," I interrupt, getting to my feet. "Since you didn't tell me." Ugh. I don't want to keep going over this with him, but I can't just drop it, either. "First you lied to me about who you are, and when I caught you in *that* lie, you lied to me about why you're here." I hold up a hand before he can protest. "A lie of omission is still a lie. You told a bunch of half-truths, and you let me think we were . . . friends. . . ."

My voice catches on the word and then all of a sudden there are tears in my eyes, which is infuriating. I never cry. I'm Allison Story's daughter, after all.

Jonah stands too, and grabs both my hands. "We *are* friends," he says urgently. "Friends is like the minimum of how I feel about you. I care about you so much, Milly, you have no idea—"

I pull away just as Uncle Archer and Aubrey reenter the room. "No, I don't. Because once again? You didn't tell me."

Aubrey looks chagrined as she holds out a red Solo cup filled with milky brown liquid. "Coffee to go for you, Milly. I'm sorry, but if we don't leave now—"

"Fine," I say, brushing at my eyes. "I'm ready."

Uncle Archer comes up beside me and pulls me into a one-armed hug. Almost like he knows that's as much contact as I can stand right now. He steers me a little ways from the others, and bends his head toward mine.

"It's all right to be mad, Milly," he whispers. "You're entitled to that feeling. But give some thought to forgiveness too, okay? If there's one characteristic I wish the Story family had more of, it's that."

# ALLISON, AGE 18

## AUGUST 1996

"Go on," Anders said irritably. He poked Allison from their window seat in Arabella's Coffee Shop, directly across the street from Brewer Floral. "He's right there. He's alone. Do what you came to do."

Allison swallowed hard as she watched Matt place flowerpots onto shelves. She couldn't believe she was going to ask this, but . . . "Will you come with me?"

"Oh, for God's sake," Anders groaned. "No. I gave you a ride. My job is done. Don't drag me any further into this."

Allison's gaze stayed locked on Matt, her stomach churning. She didn't know what she was going to do about the pregnancy. Some days, she was sure abortion was the only answer. Other days, she imagined going off to college pregnant without Mother knowing, and giving the baby up for adoption when it was born. Sometimes she even thought about keeping it. Why shouldn't she? She had the kind of resources most people only dreamed of.

The only thing she didn't consider was not telling Matt. This was both of their problem. She wasn't going to face it alone.

"I just . . ." Allison paused as Matt opened Brewer Floral's front door, then turned to lock it and stepped onto the street. "Never mind. He's leaving. I'll have to do it another time." Relief washed over her, quickly replaced by panic when she saw where Matt was headed. "He's coming over *here*. Oh no. I can't talk to him in the middle of a coffee shop." She slid off her stool and tugged on Anders's arm. "We have to go."

"Don't be ridiculous," he snapped. "You'll just trip over Matt if you leave now. Stop being such a coward and ask him to take a walk with you."

"Okay. Yes. Good idea," Allison said as Matt came through the door. There was no way he could miss seeing her and Anders—they were directly in his line of vision—but he strolled right past them.

"Matt," Allison called. Her stomach hurt. She hated everything about this already.

He turned, reluctantly. "Oh, hey, Allison. Didn't see you there."

"Bullshit," Anders coughed. Because he was helpful like that.

Allison wanted the floor to swallow her up, but she also wanted to get this over with. "Do you think we could, um, take a walk real quick?" she asked.

"I can't," Matt said. "I'm just grabbing a couple of coffees and then I have to be somewhere."

"How about I come with you, then?"

Matt heaved a sigh. "Look, Allison . . . I had fun hanging out with you at Rob's, but that's all it was. Fun. So maybe you could stop calling me, okay?" Allison just stared, struck silent with humiliation, and he added, "I'm not interested."

"*You're* not interested?" Anders snorted out a rude laugh. "Oh, that's rich. You should be thanking my sister for giving you the time of day, you townie piece of shit."

Matt's jaw twitched. "Here's a question for you, Anders. If I'm such a piece of shit, why'd Kayla pick me over you?"

Anders narrowed his eyes. "She didn't pick you. You hooked up once. Big deal."

"We didn't hook up *once*," Matt said. "We're together. We have been for weeks. Haven't you noticed that she stopped returning your calls?"

Allison stole a look at Anders. The tightening around his mouth was almost imperceptible, but she saw it, and she knew Matt's words had hit their mark. Anders would've died before letting him know that, though. "I don't keep track of Kayla's calls," he said dismissively. "She always comes crawling back to me eventually. Have fun while it lasts."

"She's not going to . . . no, you know what?" Matt shook his head, like he was disgusted with himself. "I'm not getting into this with you. You think you own people just because you have money, but you don't. There's a whole island full of people who don't give a rat's ass about Anders Story. About *any* Story," he added, and Allison felt a gut punch of shame at being included like that. What had she ever done, except like him?

"You're so wrong that it's almost funny," Anders said.

"Whatever. I'm out," Matt said. He turned and left without his coffee, not sparing a backward glance for Allison.

"That *asshole*," she seethed as the door closed. Hurt sent a sharp, stabbing pain through her stomach.

"Finally, we agree on something," Anders said.

And yet, she *still* had to talk to Matt. She lifted her bag from the counter as she watched his rigid back through the window, then froze as he suddenly held his arms out to catch a girl who was flying toward him from across the street. Kayla Dugas.

*Just grabbing a couple of coffees,* Matt had said. Oh God. He was on a date.

Matt and Kayla kissed in the street, right in front of them. It felt like Matt was putting on a show, and Allison could feel the resentment coming off Anders in waves. "Come on," Anders growled, getting to his feet. "I changed my mind. I can't wait to go out there and tell him you're knocked up."

"No!" Allison hissed, digging in her heels. "I'm not doing this in front of Kayla."

Kayla turned, and for a second Allison thought she'd heard them, even though she was too far away for that to be possible. But she definitely *saw* them. With one arm looped around Matt's neck, she blew a dramatic kiss toward the window. Then she went back to making out with Matt even more enthusiastically than before.

Allison had never seen Anders so angry. His face was red and his jaw clenched as he said, "She's going to regret that," in a low, dangerous voice.

"Let's just go," Allison said. She looped her bag over her shoulder, then gasped as she caught sight of her leg. Her right thigh was streaked with blood beneath her tan shorts. "How did I . . ." She scanned the stool for something sharp that might

245

have cut her, and nearly doubled over as a wave of pain hit her abdomen. Then she understood.

She wasn't sick about Matt's behavior. This was something else entirely.


It took a week for the bleeding to stop. On the night when she'd finally gone a full day without it, Allison took another pregnancy test. One line. She should be relieved—and she probably would be soon—but at the moment, she just felt empty.

She wandered downstairs afterward, drawn by the sound of voices. Her mother, Donald Camden, Dr. Baxter, and Theresa Ryan were sitting around the kitchen table with a bottle of wine between them. Allison paused in the hallway as Donald lifted his glass. "A toast to you, Mildred, and your indomitable spirit," he said. Everyone clinked glasses, and then Donald lifted Mother's hand and kissed it.

Allison frowned. Anders's latest theory, which he shared constantly with his siblings, was that both Dr. Baxter and Donald Camden were pursuing Mother now that she was a wealthy widow. Never mind that Dr. Baxter was already married. "That's what divorce is for," Anders pointed out. "You can't tell me he wouldn't ditch his wife at a moment's notice."

"Mother's not interested," Archer always countered.

"They're patient men," Anders replied.

Allison cleared her throat now, and Mother beamed at her. "Hello, sweetheart. I didn't hear you. Come join us."

Allison wanted company, but she couldn't keep up a smiling front right now. She wished, fiercely, that her mother was alone.

If she had been, Allison felt sure she would've finally unburdened herself. "I was looking for the boys," she said.

"Archer is out with friends. Adam and Anders are on the beach."

With one of their father's five-hundred-dollar bottles of Scotch, no doubt. "I think I'll join them," Allison said.

When Mother smiled, she almost looked like her old self. Being around people was good for her, even if it was only these three. "Take a sweatshirt. It's chilly out there."

"I will."

Allison left the house and headed for her father's favorite indulgence: the outdoor elevator that allowed them to bypass the long, steep, twisting path to the beach. It hummed quietly on the way down, and opened with a soft whooshing sound. Allison stepped onto the sand and headed for the small, protected cove that was her brothers' favorite drinking spot.

She heard them before she saw them.

". . . could get them both fired, you know," Adam was saying.

Anders snorted. "Who cares if they lose a couple of minimum-wage jobs? Not me." There was the clink of a bottle hitting glass. Her brothers couldn't bring plastic cups to the beach like normal people; they brought crystal tumblers. Half the time they forgot them and Allison would find them embedded in the sand. "They deserve worse."

"It's bullshit what he did to Allison," Adam said, and Allison froze. *No,* she thought. *Please don't let Adam be referring to Matt. Don't let Anders have told him.*

"Allison shouldn't have screwed that loser in the first place," Anders said dismissively.

Of course he told. Anders told Adam everything. Allison wanted to bang her head—or better yet, Anders's head—against a rock.

"He shouldn't have dared touch her," Adam said. Even though it was none of Adam's business, Allison felt a small surge of warmth at Adam's protectiveness. Then, unfortunately, he kept talking. "It's like it didn't occur to him that our family is completely out of his league. Imagine Mother sharing a bastard grandchild with her *assistant*. That's not how the next generation is supposed to start. Thank God it's done with."

Allison closed her eyes against the prick of angry tears. She shouldn't have expected any better, but it still hurt that Adam managed to make even her miscarriage all about him.

"It's not over," Anders said. "He's still with my whore of a girlfriend."

"You have a one-track mind," Adam yawned.

Allison had heard enough. She turned back for the elevator, Anders's reply floating toward her just before she stepped out of hearing range.

"The world would be a better place without them in it."

# CHAPTER TWENTY

## AUBREY

"Here we go again," Milly murmurs as Gran's chauffeur pulls the Bentley onto the main road leading to Catmint House.

"Thanks for coming," I say gratefully. "I'm so nervous."

"No problem. I don't think she'll let me in, though. She did specify *just* you."

"I know. But why does she get to call all the shots, all the time?"

Milly's lips quirk. "Probably because she has all the money."

My cousin has been dry-eyed and composed ever since we left Uncle Archer's, and she's refused to talk about anything except this meeting with Mildred. Still, there's a melancholy air about her that tugs at my heart, so I try again. "Do you think Jonah—" I start.

Milly shifts her eyes out the window. "Not yet, okay?"

I study her profile. I wasn't surprised by her kiss with Jonah at the Summer Gala; if anything, I was surprised it hadn't happened sooner. And I'm not mad at Jonah for keeping quiet about Uncle Anders. I came here with my own secrets after all, and I'm not sure I'd have told Milly about my father and Coach Matson so quickly if she hadn't caught me in a crisis moment. There's something dangerously seductive about Story secrets; they snake their way into your heart and soul, burrowing so deep that the very idea of exposing them feels like losing a part of yourself. If anything, Jonah plotting against Uncle Anders while falling for Milly makes him more one of us than a borrowed birth certificate ever did.

But I understand Milly not seeing it that way.

We lapse into silence as the car glides smoothly along. I scroll through my messages, reading a new one from my father about how ungrateful and disappointing I am, plus an update from my mother sharing the kind of news he won't: Coach Matson has gone public with her pregnancy. Mom doesn't come right out and say that everybody knows who the father is, but she doesn't have to. I know how our town operates; nothing stays quiet for long.

Oh, and the baby is going to be a boy.

*I hope it's okay to tell you this via text,* Mom writes. *You've been so hard to reach, and I didn't want you to hear it from someone else.*

I feel a sharp pang of guilt. She's right; ever since I stopped talking to Dad, I cut back on returning calls from my mother, too. Not because I'm angry at her—God no, not even a little bit—but because stepping away from the misery of Coach Matson's pregnancy has been a massive relief. With everything that's been happening this past week, I almost managed to forget about it.

It's around ten in the morning in Oregon, so Mom's at the

hospital, at work, and won't check her phone for hours. Still, I fire back a series of texts:

*Thanks for telling me.*

*I'm sorry I've been out of touch. There's a lot going on here.*

*I'll call you soon to explain.*

*Also, just so you know, whatever you decide to do next in this mess: I'm with you.*

*Figuratively and literally.*

*Like, I will move out with you, if that's what you want.*

*GLADLY.*

*I'm sorry I haven't said that before now.*

*I love you lots.*

Just as I hit Send on the last one, my phone rings, and I stare disbelievingly at Thomas's number. "You have got to be kidding me," I mutter.

"Who is it?" Milly asks. I hold up my phone, and she makes a face when she sees the name. "Ugh. Are you going to answer?"

"Might as well," I sigh. "I'm ripping off all the Band-Aids today. Hi, Thomas."

"Dude." The word sets my teeth on edge. I've never liked that Thomas calls me *dude*, like I'm one of his volleyball team-mates. "Did your dad seriously knock up your swim coach?"

We're approaching the gate to Catmint House. The chauffeur eases to a stop and pulls the silver card he needs to open the gate from his sun visor. He's about to get an earful he never asked for, but oh well. "Did you *seriously* just ask me that?" I say to Thomas.

"Dude, come on. That's, like, insane."

"Nice speaking with you too, Thomas. Work has been fine, thanks for asking. What have *you* been up to all summer?"

Milly smirks across from me as Thomas launches into an excruciatingly detailed monologue. Unsurprisingly, he took my sarcasm as actual interest. "Thomas," I finally interrupt. "That's great. I'm glad things are going well at Best Buy. But why are you calling me?"

"Because your dad—"

"Okay, no." For the first time ever, I have zero patience with Thomas. "I get that you want the inside scoop. But you and I are broken up."

"We are?" Thomas says uncertainly. Not like he's upset about it. More like he's surprised I brought it up.

"You ignored every single one of my texts as soon as I got here," I remind him.

"I was busy," he says defensively. "Anyway, when I *did* send some, you ignored them right back."

"Right," I say, thinking of Oona's words in her shop. *Life is complicated in the digital age.* "Which means we're through, doesn't it?"

"So you *want* to break up?"

"Don't you?"

"Well, yeah," he finally admits. "I have for a while, actually. But I didn't think *you* did."

I suppress a sigh. We could argue back and forth about how crappy it was of him to leave me hanging like that, but I don't exactly have the time right now. And it doesn't matter. It's been creeping up on me ever since I got to the island what my relationship with Thomas really is: something that should've ended a few months after it began in eighth grade, when he started treating me like an afterthought. But it didn't end, because there was something almost *comfortable* about that. I was used to it.

The chauffeur eases the Bentley to a stop in front of Catmint House. "Well, I'm glad we got that cleared up," I say into the phone. "Enjoy the rest of your summer." I disconnect, and Milly starts clapping softly.

"Can we just take a minute to appreciate how much better you've gotten at telling people off over the phone?" she says with a grin.

I execute an awkward seat bow. "Thank you."

"Allow me to get your door, Miss Story," the chauffeur says. He does, and doesn't bat an eye when Milly climbs out the other door, unassisted.

"Let's see what Mildred wants, huh?" she says, linking her arm with mine as we make our way to the wide slate steps. Before we get to the top, the door swings open to reveal Theresa.

"Hello, Aubrey. And . . . Milly." Her placid smile falters as she takes in my cousin. "Mrs. Story is expecting you, Aubrey. Please come in." She steps aside, then right back in front of us as Milly moves to cross the threshold with me. "Milly, this invitation was for Aubrey only."

"Oh, I'm sorry," Milly says sweetly. "We thought there must have been a mistake."

"There wasn't," Theresa says. "You can wait in the car. It won't take long."

Well, that doesn't sound promising.

Milly gives her an ingratiating smile. "Are you watching the game? Maybe I could join you until Aubrey's done." Theresa looks blank, and Milly adds, "The double-header? Yankees versus Red Sox? First one's already started."

"I don't watch baseball," Theresa says irritably. "I really do need to ask you to leave. Come along, Aubrey."

253

I give Milly a helpless look as Theresa practically drags me inside, shutting the door in my cousin's face. "Mrs. Story is on the balcony," Theresa says, leading me to the same place where we had brunch. It's like déjà vu all over again: Gran seated beneath a gauzy umbrella, dressed to the nines and sipping tea.

"Hello, Aubrey," she says. "Please sit down."

"I'll be right inside, Mildred," Theresa says, and closes the sliding glass door behind me.

I sit in the chair farthest from Gran, heart pounding. I might've handled Thomas with an ease that impressed even me in the car, but that doesn't mean I'm ready for *this*. There's a large tray in the center of the table that holds a teapot, a steaming carafe of what looks like coffee, and porcelain bowls of milk and sugar. No food, though. This is clearly not a brunch situation.

Gran gestures toward the table. "Help yourself to tea. Or coffee, if you prefer."

"Coffee," I mumble. I don't know how to work the carafe, though—it's one of those awkward tops that you have to twist a bunch of different ways before it opens—and Gran lets me struggle with it. When I finally start to pour, the coffee gushes out so quickly that my cup immediately overflows into my saucer. We both pretend not to notice.

"I suppose you're wondering why I asked you here," Gran says, taking a delicate sip of tea. Her hat today is smaller than usual, a jaunty sort of fedora pulled low over one eye, in a brown color that complements her plaid suit. Her gloves are a light tan, instead of the usual white. She looks like she's taking a break from a World War II spy mission.

"Yeah," I say, taking a big gulp of black coffee so I have room for milk. And then I nearly choke, because it's *scalding*.

254

My tongue burns and my eyes water, but I manage not to spit anything out.

"I'm speaking to you alone of your cousins. You seem like a sensible girl. Milly strikes me as unstable, and as for the *other one*—" Her expression darkens. "JT is clearly just as much of a viper as his father ever was."

Surprise mingles with my nerves. "You don't believe him and Uncle Anders, then?"

"I don't believe any of you." Gran takes another sip of tea, then sets her cup carefully on its saucer. She folds her hands under her chin, gazing at me so intently that I have to drop my eyes. "I should have sent you away as soon as you arrived. It's what Donald and Theresa wanted, and they were right. But I was curious to meet you. *Especially* you." The emphasis forces me to look up again, and I flinch. If I was ever under the impression that Gran was paying attention to me because she liked me best—wow, that was wrong. She looks like she hates me. "Adam has always held a unique place in my memory. I've wondered, over the years, if you were like him."

My mouth is bone dry. "I don't think I am."

"No." Gran's stare doesn't waver. "He must be quite proud of you."

*Not really,* I think, but I don't say it.

She waits for a response, and when none comes, she lets out a small sigh. "At any rate, my curiosity has been satisfied. What I'd like to tell you now is that the ties I severed with my children twenty-four years ago are absolute. It was a mistake to allow you into my life, and it's not one I'll make again. I can't force you to leave the island, of course, but I hope that you do. This is my home, and you are not welcome here."

I was ready for this, so I'm not sure why her words land like a slap. Maybe it's because I've never had anybody say, so plainly, what I've always felt about being part of the Story family. *You are not welcome here.*

Gran sips her tea while I grapple for an appropriate response. Finally, I just say what I'm thinking. "Don't you even want to get to know us? Or our parents, the way they are now?"

My grandmother's eyes are cool and appraising. "Do you think your father is a man worth knowing?" she asks.

My phone sits heavy in my pocket, full of all the reasons why he's not. My father is a cheater, and a liar, and he's never—not *once*—failed to put himself first in any given situation. But then I think back to the picture of him and Gran in Sweetfern: her hand placed lovingly on his cheek, both of them beaming real, genuine smiles. The kind I've never gotten from him, no matter how hard I tried to please him. "He could have been," I say.

Gran refills her cup. "We don't live in the world of 'could have been,' though, do we? We live in this world."

"You *made* this world." My directness surprises us both.

"I had no choice," my grandmother replies, looking me up and down. "You should understand that. As I said, you strike me as a sensible girl."

"Sensible," I repeat. The word hangs between us, and I know what it really means. *Docile.* I'm the one who won't cause trouble—who won't try to manipulate her like JT, or challenge her like Milly. I'm the safe bet, someone who'll swallow whatever she tells me and dutifully report it back. I have a sudden urge not to do what she expects and *not* to leave quietly. "Okay,"

256

I say. "I'll go. But maybe you can tell me one thing before I do?" She lifts both perfectly arched brows. "Is there something unusual about how Kayla Dugas died?"

I wish Milly were here to see the expression on Gran's face. She stares at me in utter shock, putting her cup down so swiftly that tea sloshes onto her gloves. "How do you . . . ," she breathes. She makes a visible, mighty effort to compose herself. "What on earth are you talking about?"

I pause, not sure how much to reveal. I don't want to get Hazel or Uncle Archer in trouble. To buy time, I reach for the carafe of coffee. But I'm too nervous to aim properly, and my hand knocks hard against its side. For a half second it tilts precariously, and I almost manage to right it. Then it topples, spilling its scalding contents directly onto Gran.

"Good Lord!" The words are shrieked as my grandmother rises in an instant, ripping off the gloves that got the worst of it and holding her skirt away from her body. I stare at the mess for a few horrified seconds before I have the presence of mind to jump up myself.

"I'm sorry! I didn't mean it! I'm so sorry!" I babble, shoving my napkin at her.

"Mildred?" Theresa appears in the doorway. "What happened?" Then she takes in the scene and rushes to the table, dumping ice from an otherwise empty glass into a napkin and wrapping the napkin around Gran's hands. "Are you burned?"

"I may be," Gran says tightly.

"Let's get you somewhere where I can take a look," Theresa says. She turns toward me. "Aubrey, please show yourself out. *Now.*"

"Okay," I gulp. Gran's face is a mask of pain. "I really am sorry."

Theresa hustles Gran inside, and I try to retrace my steps. I make a wrong turn, though, ending up in a library-like room with floor-to-ceiling bookshelves and a massive desk stationed directly in front of the windows. There's an ornately carved side table right inside the door, holding a variety of vases and decorative bowls. When I glance over them, I spot something familiar nestled inside a bronze salver—a slim silver card, just like the one the chauffeur used to open the gates leading to Catmint House.

I don't think twice. I just do what Gran would never have expected of me, and slip it into my pocket.

# CHAPTER TWENTY-ONE

## JONAH

By five o'clock on Sunday, I've officially missed my ferry back to Hyannis. I'm not sure what comes next in the big scheme of things, but for the here and now we're having a cookout. Which seems strangely normal given the past twenty-four hours, but it's summer and we have to eat.

"I'm not much of a cook," Archer says, flipping burgers on the grill he found in the gardening shed and managed to start up. "But these are hard to get wrong."

Milly and Aubrey are here too, brought over in the resort Jeep by Efram. Carson Fine finally confiscated the keys, which would've come across as a Donald Camden move if he hadn't immediately handed them over to Efram so he could give the girls a ride. I wish I'd had a chance to say good-bye to Carson, who all in all was a pretty great boss.

Efram declined Archer's invitation to stay. "Seems like a family thing," he said, then grinned at me. "And pseudo family.

But thanks anyway." Before he left, he helped me pull all the chairs that were strewn haphazardly around the yard into a circle on the concrete patio. Milly's still not talking to me, but she's sitting next to me, and I don't think I'm wrong that her overall posture is less chilly than it was earlier today.

The wooden door on the fence enclosing the backyard rattles, then swings open to let a woman through. She's dark-haired, maybe a little younger than Archer, and carrying a large, foil-wrapped pan.

"Oona!" Archer calls. "Thanks for coming. You didn't have to bring anything, though."

"Well," the woman says, crossing over to the patio and putting her pan on the wrought-iron table. "I wasn't entirely sure what you'd be feeding these poor kids."

"I'm doing my best," Archer claims, flipping a burger straight into the grass.

Oona shakes her head and smiles warmly at Milly and Aubrey. "Hello again, girls. I was sorry to hear how everything turned out at the gala." My face flames with fresh guilt as she adds, "You both deserved better than that."

I brace myself for another death glare from Milly, but it doesn't come. She just tosses her hair and says, "At least we looked good while we were getting thrown out."

Oona takes a seat and turns to me. "And you must be Jonah."

"Yeah," I say, grateful that she leaves it at that.

She leans forward, lifting the rock that's been keeping the autopsy report from blowing off the table. "Is this what you wanted me to look at?" she asks Uncle Archer.

"Yeah," he says, scooping up a burger and placing it carefully on an open bun sitting on a plate beside the grill. "Sorry if that's weird, or morbid, but I couldn't figure out why Dr. Baxter would want me to have it." He repeats the process with another burger. "And Aubrey mentioned that my mother had a strange reaction to Kayla's name this afternoon."

"Strange how?" Oona asks, her eyes roving over the report.

"Well." Aubrey purses her lips. "I asked if there was anything unusual about how Kayla died, and she seemed . . . I don't know. Not *surprised*, exactly, like you would be if something like that came at you out of the blue. More as though she was alarmed that I'd asked. But I spilled coffee on her before she could answer."

"That's odd," Oona says, still staring at the paper. "And so is this."

Archer shuts off the grill and starts handing burgers around. "So is what?" he asks.

"This says Kayla had lorazepam in her system. That wasn't in the report my family has."

"Loraza-what?" I ask, before taking a big bite of my hamburger.

"Lorazepam. It's a sedative, I believe," Oona says, brow wrinkling. Milly has her phone out and is already looking it up.

"Yeah, it is," she says.

Oona's frown deepens. "I don't understand. Kayla was a drinker—she was drinking that night, unfortunately—but she didn't take drugs. I don't know where she'd even get something like that. And why is it in *this* version of the report, but not ours?"

"What if . . ." Milly hesitates, toying with the edge of her hamburger bun. No one except me is eating. "What if someone gave it to her? The drug, I mean." She darts a worried look toward Oona, who blanches. "And Dr. Baxter covered it up? He said he'd done 'a grave injustice,' didn't he?"

"To *me*," Archer says. "And I wasn't . . . I mean, I cared about Kayla, of course I did, but if a grave injustice was done to any of us, it would've been Anders. He was gutted when she died. Even though she'd just dumped him again."

"I remember that," Oona says. She puts the autopsy report down with a trembling hand. "She went to see him at Harvard that Thanksgiving and came back so upset. She wouldn't tell me why. All she would say is, 'I have to talk to Mrs. Ryan.'"

"Mrs. Ryan?" Milly blinks. "My grandmother's assistant?"

Oona nods. "Yes. I don't know why. They weren't particularly close. Kayla dated Theresa's son briefly, but . . ." A corner of her mouth lifts in a wry smile. "It wasn't the kind of relationship where they spent time with one another's parents."

"Wait. Hold up." Milly looks like her brain is about to explode. "Mrs. Ryan has a *son*?"

"She did," Archer corrects. "His name was Matt. He died, too. The year before Kayla."

"So Anders dated Kayla, who dated Matt, and now . . . both Kayla and Matt are dead?" Milly asks. She turns wide eyes to Archer. "How did Matt die?"

"Drowned at Cutty Beach," Archer says, and Aubrey makes a choking noise. He reaches over to pound her on the back before he realizes she's not eating. "What's wrong, Aubrey?"

"Cutty Beach?" she gasps. "My dad, he . . . he sort of wrote about that beach, in his book. And my mom said he's never liked the place."

"Well, Matt's death was very traumatic," Archer says. "It happened at a party, and we were all there. It was this wild, stormy night, and everyone had been drinking. No one realized Matt was gone until it was too late. We looked everywhere for him, and Allison got so worried that she insisted we call the cops, who ended up bringing in the Coast Guard, and . . . well. They searched all night, but didn't find Matt's body until the next day. It was horrible." He runs a hand over his face. "Why are we talking about this, again? I'm losing track of the conversation."

"I'm not sure either," Oona says. She keeps getting paler. "But I'm afraid I've lost my appetite. The idea that Kayla might have been *drugged* by someone—"

"We don't know that she was," Archer says quickly. "All we know is that Fred Baxter had two copies of an autopsy report. Maybe this version is a mistake."

"Maybe," Oona says, her expression troubled. "All these years, I've felt so guilty about Kayla's death. I knew she was struggling with something, but instead of trying to help, I got angry with her for drinking too much. And then, to have her die like that . . ."

Archer turns tired, compassionate eyes toward Oona. "There's nothing you could have done," he says. "Nobody can stop a person who's determined to drink from doing it."

She holds his gaze, a sad smile playing across her lips. "Perhaps not. But they can try, can't they?"

# CHAPTER TWENTY-TWO

## MILLY

Uncle Archer nods off on the futon after Oona leaves, so Aubrey, Jonah, and I tackle cleanup from the cookout. There's not much to it beyond scrubbing the grill, putting away the few utensils we used, and shoving paper cups and plates into a trash bag. When we finish, Jonah goes off in search of a bin to put the trash in, and Aubrey and I head back to the patio.

"I'm tired of sitting in these chairs," Aubrey says, surveying their rigid metal backs with distaste. "They're not very comfortable. Hang on a sec." She slips into the house, and comes back a minute later holding a large, fluffy blanket. I help her spread it over a patch of grass, and we both collapse onto our backs, staring up at the stars.

"You know, it's actually pretty nice here," I say, a yawn creeping into my voice. "Too bad we're leaving."

"Yeah," Aubrey sighs. Her knuckles knock lightly against my arm. "I'm going to miss you."

A lump forms in my throat. "I'll miss you, too." We're quiet for a few beats, lost in our own thoughts, until practical matters start creeping into mine. "Have you thought about how we're going to get back to the dorms tonight?" I ask.

Aubrey giggles. "Not really. Maybe we could text Efram?" Her voice turns considering. "Or we could just stay here. There's an extra room."

"We don't have anything to sleep in," I object.

She plucks at her mesh shorts. "That's only a problem for you."

The grass rustles beside us, and I turn to see Jonah's sneakers approaching the blanket. He pauses. "Is this just a cousin hangout?" he asks.

I sit up, brushing my hair behind my shoulders. Which is my instinctive, go-to, notice-my-hair flirt move. My subconscious isn't mad at Jonah anymore. And maybe I'm not, either. "No. Come on, join us."

He sprawls beside me, and Aubrey sits up too. Her phone falls out of her pocket when she does, along with a thin silver card. She retrieves the phone but doesn't notice the card, so I pick it up and hand it to her. "You dropped this."

"Oh. Thanks." Even in the moonlight, I can see her grimace. "I forgot I took that."

The guilt in her voice makes me pause. "Took what?"

"Um, so. It's the keycard that opens the gate at Catmint House. I think. It looks just like the one the chauffeur used. I grabbed it out of Gran's house when Mrs. Ryan told me to leave."

"You *took* that?" I ask, as Jonah starts to laugh.

"Damn, Aubrey," he says. "That's some next-level petty revenge. Were you planning to go back in the middle of the night and loot the place?"

"I didn't actually have a plan," Aubrey admits. "It was a

spur-of-the-moment thing." She puts the keycard back in her pocket and stretches her arms over her head. "What a weird day. And night."

"I can't even keep track of all the stuff that came up," Jonah says.

"Interesting how we keep going back to Anders, huh?" I ask. While we were cleaning up, I couldn't stop thinking about my uncle's smirk at the Summer Gala last night. How he seemed to almost relish telling all those lies.

I expect Jonah to loudly agree, considering how much he hates Uncle Anders. But he says, "Not just him." I turn to him in surprise and he adds, "We keep going back to Theresa Ryan, too. And unlike Anders, she's never left the island. She's been here the whole time. Whispering in your grandmother's ear."

I shift on the blanket. "What are you saying?"

"Look, maybe the woman is—unbalanced. Maybe losing her son pushed her over the edge, so she did something to Kayla Dugas and made Dr. Baxter cover it up. And maybe your grandmother learned what it was, but she's too dependent on Theresa to do anything about it. Like, she already cut ties with all her kids, so who else is gonna take care of her?" He shrugs at my dubious expression. "It's no weirder than anything else that's happened here over the past twenty years, is it?"

I have to admit he has a point. "But why would Mrs. Ryan hurt Kayla?"

"I don't know," Jonah says. "But your grandmother freaked when Aubrey brought up her name, right? There's something going on there."

Aubrey tries unsuccessfully to suppress a massive yawn. "I'm exhausted, you guys. I can't keep my eyes open. Do you mind

266

if we crash here, Milly? That spare bed is calling my name. It's a double, so we can share. I don't kick, I promise."

"Sure," I say, plucking at the skirt of my red dress. It's not ideal for sleeping in, but I guess I can handle it for one night.

Jonah takes in the gesture and says, "You can borrow something of mine if you want. It's all clean," he adds hastily.

"Yeah, okay," I say, and Aubrey gets to her feet with a relieved sigh.

"I'm out, then. See you guys tomorrow."

I watch until she opens the sliding glass door and slips through. Then I turn toward Jonah with a small smile. "Thanks for lending me a change of clothes. I wasn't looking forward to sleeping in a dress."

"Especially not a family heirloom, right?" Jonah says. I cock my head, puzzled, and he adds, "That's your mother's dress, isn't it?"

I let out a surprised laugh. "Yeah, but how did you know?"

"You told us, that first day. You wore it on the ferry."

"I can't believe you remember that."

"I remember more than that," Jonah says. "You wore sunglasses, even though it was raining. You referred to me as a J. Crew model and a constipated gnome in almost the same sentence." I snicker a little, because that was one of my better lines. "Then you bought us all gin and tonics, and tried to get us to spill some secrets. I had three. The first was that I'm not actually your cousin. The second was that your uncle led my parents into bankruptcy, and I had the ridiculous idea that I was going to make him pay for that."

"It's not all that ridiculous," I admit. "I might've helped if you'd told me."

"I should have." He faces me head-on, and the sudden intensity of his expression makes my breath catch. "But I kept getting distracted by my third secret, which was that I thought you were the most beautiful girl I'd ever seen. So, you see," he says, his hand brushing mine, "I remember everything."

The combination of his words and his touch make my skin buzz, but I draw back. "You don't want to get mixed up with a Story," I tell him. "We're a mess."

He smiles crookedly. "Yeah, well, so am I. I even failed at being one of you. And I got us kicked out of the Summer Gala because of it."

Yes, and no. What did Uncle Archer say earlier? *Give some thought to forgiveness too, okay? If there's one characteristic I wish the Story family had more of, it's that.* He was right, but it hits me all of a sudden that he didn't only mean that we should forgive other people—the way Mildred never could. Based on the exchange he and Oona had earlier, I think he was also talking about forgiving *yourself.* And you can't do that without acknowledging you did something wrong in the first place.

"That was my fault, too," I admit. "I threw myself at you when you were just trying to help me. I mean, Uncle Anders was coming along to ruin everything anyway, so we would've been toast no matter what. But things would have been a lot less embarrassing if I hadn't planted one on you in the middle of my grandmother's party."

Jonah grins. "That's the only part of the night I *don't* regret."

My pulse picks up as I reach out and play with the hem of his T-shirt. "I don't regret it either, except for the overdose of champagne. And the audience."

"Well, nobody's here now." His thumb traces my cheekbone and sends a chill down my back. "If you happen to feel like trying again."

And I do.

# CHAPTER TWENTY-THREE

## AUBREY

As soon as I slip between the sheets in Uncle Archer's spare room, I can tell I won't be able to fall asleep right away. That happens to me sometimes; I get so overtired that an unwelcome second wind kicks in, keeping my eyes open even when I desperately need them to close. But I don't want to go back outside, since I'm pretty sure Milly and Jonah would rather be alone.

I pick my phone up from the nightstand. The battery's low, and I didn't bring a charger with me. I can probably make it through one phone call. It should be to my mom, to explain everything that's happened and make arrangements to get home. Especially since I need to give her time to figure out travel logistics. My plane ticket back to Oregon isn't until late August, and I have no idea how easy it will be to change.

But my frustrated tiredness fuels a low, buzzing resentment that makes me dial a different number. I'm even glad when he answers. "Well, this is a surprise," he says.

"Hi, Dad," I say, propping the thin pillow against the headboard so I can sit up. "I wanted to tell you that I'm really angry at you for cheating on Mom, and for doing it with my swim coach. I think you should apologize to me. If you would do that—and mean it—then maybe I could start trying to forgive you."

"You have no idea the complexity of the situation," my father says. Just like I knew he would, but my chest still tightens at his tone. "It takes more than one person to keep a marriage going, and your mother—"

"No." I cut him off without hesitation, which is something I'd never have dared to do a month ago. It feels good. "You don't get to blame her."

"If you're not going to listen—"

"I'm not." I interrupt again and I'm strangely calm, my heart thumping steadily instead of pounding like it did the last time I spoke to him. "What did you do to Gran?"

"Excuse me?"

"What did you do to make her disown you?"

A bitter edge creeps into his voice. "I've told you a hundred times. Not a damn thing."

"I don't believe you." My mind's eye is split in two; on one side, I see that old picture of Dad and Gran from Sweetfern, her smile glowing with maternal love and pride. On the other, I see Gran like she was today on the deck, her face full of remembered pain even before I spilled scalding coffee all over her. *Do you think your father is a man worth knowing?* "What happened to Kayla Dugas?"

"How the hell do you know who Kayla Dugas is?" he demands.

"People here keep talking about her."

"She got drunk and crashed her car into a tree," Dad says. He sounds impatient and irritable at the question, but not particularly rattled. So I try a different tack.

"What happened at Cutty Beach?" I ask.

A pause. "What happened—where? You're all over the place tonight, Aubrey. You must be overtired. I think you should go to bed."

"You put a beach just like it in your book. It's the only place on Gull Cove Island you've ever written about. Why is that? Does it have anything to do with Matt Ryan drowning?"

Dad's sharp, shocked inhale is loud in my ear. "How do you—? Aubrey, you need to get a grip. I don't know why you're suddenly fixating on decades-old tragedies, but what happened to Matt was a terrible accident and has nothing to do with my mother."

"I think you're wrong," I say. I don't know *why* I think that—there's something creeping around the edge of my subconscious telling me so, but it's refusing to show itself fully. My father is right about one thing: I *am* overtired. My eyelids are starting to droop like they did outside, but I force the sleepiness from my tone. "Why don't you tell me what happened, Dad? What did you do? Be straight with me for once in your life."

"Aubrey." His voice is pure ice. "Nothing. *Happened.*"

"You're lying," I say, before I disconnect and drag the pillow back down to the mattress. I might be only seconds from crashing into sleep, but I'm sure I'm right.


When I wake up, Milly is sleeping soundly beside me. Whatever might've happened between her and Jonah wasn't an all-nighter,

271

at any rate. My phone is half buried under her hair, and I free it carefully and put it in my pocket. Then I slide out of bed and pad my way into the living room.

Uncle Archer isn't on the futon anymore. He must've gotten up at some point in the night and made his way into his bedroom. There's a red Solo cup on the end table, half full with clear liquid. I take a tentative sniff; definitely not water. I'm tempted to dump it, but I put it back down instead. My low-level interference won't make a difference in the battle Uncle Archer is having with himself.

The house is silent except for the loud ticking of a grandfather clock in one corner. It's eight o'clock, too early to wake anybody else. I go into the kitchen and search the cabinets until I find coffee and filters. I don't need coffee in the morning, but I know Milly can't function without it. Once I have a pot brewing, I slip on the sneakers I kicked off at the sliding glass door last night, and pull it open.

It's beautiful outside. A perfect cool summer morning, the sky a brilliant blue swirled with wispy clouds. Last night, when we went looking for the grill, I noticed a bike propped against the wall of the garden shed. I can't remember if the bike was locked up or not, but if it isn't, I could ride around the neighborhood while everyone sleeps. Maybe even down to the nearest beach.

I grin when I see that the bike is free for the taking. The tires are nice and full, and the seat's the perfect height for me. I wheel it out of the shed and into the backyard, feeling a hum of anticipation to get moving and stretch my legs. Probably the best memory I have of my father is him teaching me to ride a bike when I was six years old, his big hands covering my small ones as I clutched the handles of my pink Huffy and— *Oh*.

I almost drop the bike as I stare at my hands and a shocked understanding rushes straight into my brain. I almost had it last night, when I remembered the Sweetfern picture of my father and grandmother, but I'd put the wrong mental image next to it. I'd been thinking about Gran's face: half shaded like always by her hat, tight with sadness. I should have been thinking about her *hands*. Bare of gloves for once, wrinkled and age-spotted, but otherwise unblemished.

I fumble in my pocket for the keycard to the Catmint House gate. It's still there. Then I grab my phone, which is down to one percent battery. I've never been that low before, though surely I can still send a few texts? But I only get one out to Uncle Archer before the screen goes blank.

It doesn't matter. I'll get what I need to prove that I'm right, and then I'll tell them everything. I push the bike through the gate, hop onto the seat, and take off.

# CHAPTER TWENTY-FOUR

## JONAH

I wake to the smell of bacon frying, and that gets me out of bed immediately. When I enter the kitchen Archer is standing in front of the stove, and Milly's sitting at the table holding a steaming mug of coffee in both hands. She's wearing the T-shirt I loaned her last night, her dark hair a little mussed and loose around her shoulders.

"Where's Aubrey?" I ask, taking a seat beside Milly.

"Unclear," Archer says. He uses a pair of tongs to transfer slices of bacon from the frying pan to a paper-towel-covered plate on the counter beside him. "She's not here, and she sent me a strange text that raises more questions than it answers."

"What did it say?" I ask.

Archer crosses over to the table and puts the bacon plate next to a rolled-up edition of the *Gull Cove Gazette*. "It said, *There wasn't a birthmark*."

Milly snatches a slice of bacon before Archer has time to draw his hand away. I help myself to two and ask, "What does that mean?"

"We've been puzzling about it all morning," Milly says, breaking her bacon in half and nibbling at one of the edges. "I mean, Aubrey *has* a birthmark, so . . ." She shrugs. "There's no reason she'd text us about it."

Archer takes a seat, looking pensive. "I wish she'd answer her phone."

"It's probably dead," Milly says. "Mine nearly is."

Archer opens the *Gull Cove Gazette* and starts flipping through it. "When I leave, I won't miss that half the daily news is about my mother," he mutters.

Milly cringes. "They're not talking about the gala again, are they?"

"No. Some painting she sold at Sotheby's went for a small fortune." He turns a page. "You know, Mother always had terrible taste in art. We used to joke about it. Theresa must've been guiding her all these years to turn her into a connoisseur."

Milly and I exchange glances, and I can read an echo of what I'm thinking on her face: *Theresa, again.* We got more than a little distracted last night, but I think I was on to something about Theresa being unbalanced. There's something creepy about a woman who spends most of her life in a seaside mansion with only her boss for company. But before either of us can say anything, the doorbell rings.

Archer's brows pull together as he rises to his feet. "Maybe that's Aubrey."

"Is the door locked?" Milly asks.

"I didn't think so, but . . ." He trails off as he leaves the kitchen.

My attention snaps back to Milly, who's still eating her bacon slice. "Hi," I say, feeling a quick, electric thrill at the thought of being alone with her again. Even if it's only for a minute.

She swallows and takes a sip of coffee. "Hello."

"I like your shirt."

"Thank you. It's very comfortable."

My eyes stray to her legs. "It's giving me . . . thoughts," I admit.

"Keep them to yourself." But she smiles when she says it.

The background murmur of indistinct voices grows louder, and Archer steps into the kitchen, with Hazel close at his heels, midsentence, ". . . sorry to interrupt your breakfast," she says, then spots Milly and me and waves apologetically. "All your breakfasts. Hey, guys."

"Hi," we both say as Archer waves to an empty chair.

"It's no trouble at all," he says. "Do you want to join us?"

"No thanks. I just wanted to give you this." Hazel unzips the tote bag slung across her shoulder and digs into its depths. "You asked if there was anything else in Granddad's files that was addressed to me or you. Well, I went through a bunch of stuff last night, and this had a Post-it with my name on it so—here." She pulls out a sheet of paper and hands it to Archer.

Milly leans forward. "What's that?" she asks.

Archer scans the sheet of paper, then flips it over and keeps reading. "It looks like a medical report for my mother," he says. "It's a diagnosis for . . ." He breaks off, frowning. "That can't be right."

"What?" Milly gets up to peer over his shoulder. "What

276

is . . . hypertrophic cardiomyopathy?" she asks, pronouncing the words slowly and clearly.

"It's a condition where your heart muscles are abnormally thick," Archer says. "It can be mild or deadly, depending on the degree. My father had it, but nobody knew until he died. So this must be a mistake. My mother's name on a postmortem diagnosis for my father."

"When did he die?" Hazel asks.

Archer pauses, thinking. "Toward the end of 1995."

"This is from 1996," Hazel points out. "There was an echocardiogram done and everything."

"Huh," Archer says, the crease between his eyes deepening. "So, if I'm reading this correctly, my mother has the same condition my father had. But she's lived with it for . . . what? Twenty-five years? She must be managing it fine. I'm not sure why Dr. Baxter would have wanted you to see this, Hazel." He hands the paper back to her with a kind smile. "I've been wondering—do you think his letter to you, and the autopsy report, might just have been the dementia talking? Confusion and disorientation is part of it, right?"

"I guess," she says uncertainly.

"Donald Camden did say Mrs. Story was sick," I volunteer. "The first time we ever talked to him. He wanted us to leave the island because of it. She seemed okay every time we saw her, though."

Milly rolls her eyes. "I don't think we can believe anything Donald says unless it benefits Donald, and the only thing he seems to care about is . . . *Oh.* Wait," she adds in a quieter tone, clearly working something out in her head. Her face is suddenly suffused with color, her eyes sharp and bright. "Uncle Archer, you said this morning that Mildred's taste in art has gotten better over the years, right? That it used to be horrible?"

"Yeah. So?" Archer asks.

"And yesterday—I didn't really think anything of it because everything else was so weird, but yesterday at Catmint House, I asked Theresa if she wanted to watch the Yankees–Red Sox game with me and she said no, that she doesn't watch baseball."

"Really?" Archer blinks. "That's weird. Theresa was a huge Yankees fan when we lived here. She and Allison were the only ones."

"I know," Milly says, her voice gaining in urgency. "And Kayla had something to tell Theresa, right? Then she died. And Dr. Baxter had something he wanted to tell you, and *he* died. So what if . . . Uncle Archer, what if they're not the only people who died?"

Archer's face is a total blank. "I'm sorry, Milly, but I'm not following you."

She grabs the medical report from Hazel's hand and waves it at him. "Mildred had a deadly heart condition, right? Diagnosed in 1996. One year later she cuts all of her children out of her life and you've never known why. Well, what if she didn't? What if she *couldn't*?"

Archer and Hazel are both looking at Milly like she's lost her mind. But I'm starting to grasp what she's implying. I look at Archer's phone, abandoned on the kitchen table, and it hits me like a tidal wave. "The text," I say. For a second, I can't breathe. "Aubrey's text. It said, *There wasn't a birthmark.*"

"I know," Archer says. "I read it to you."

Milly whips around to face me. "Oh my God, you're right. She was talking about *Mildred.*" She turns back toward Archer,

her voice breathless. "Aubrey spilled hot coffee on Mildred yesterday, and she pulled off her gloves. I'll bet Aubrey didn't see a birthmark. That big wine-colored birthmark that Mildred has on her hand, and Aubrey has on her arm? Aubrey must've realized it wasn't there." She pauses, waiting for understanding to break over Archer's features, but it doesn't come. "Because I think . . . maybe . . . that the woman living at Catmint House isn't your mother. She's not my grandmother. She's someone else. Someone who took Mildred's place."

The kitchen goes so quiet that I can hear my heart pounding in my ears. "Took her place," Archer finally says in a dead voice. "Milly, that's insane. You can't . . . a person can't *just take another person's place*."

"Why not?" Milly asks.

"Because . . . because . . . ," Archer sputters. "Because people would know!"

"Not if you refused to see them anymore," Milly points out.

Archer's face is tight and haunted. "Stop it, Milly. You're out of control." He barks out a shaky laugh, running a hand over his mouth. "I need a drink. This is—you are—I can't—" He turns, and starts rummaging through the cabinets. "My mother isn't dead, for God's sake. People would know. Theresa, and Donald Camden, and Dr. Baxter—"

"Do you hear the names coming out of your mouth?" I interrupt. Milly needs backup, because Archer is losing his shit. "Donald Camden? Seems like his entire job is making sure nobody with the last name Story ever gets close to Mildred. Dr. Baxter? He was trying to tell you something's wrong. And Theresa? She—"

"*Why?*" Archer spins and nearly screams the word. His eyes

279

are wild, his hands clenched into fists at his side. "Why would anyone do something like that? To her, and to us?"

"Well." Milly's voice is low and calm, like she's trying to soothe a frightened animal. "Money is a big motivator, isn't it? It would motivate Donald Camden, I'll bet. And maybe . . ." She turns toward Hazel, who looks utterly shell-shocked. "Sorry, but there's no polite way to say this. Did your grandfather come into a bunch of money twenty-four years ago?"

"Milly, *stop it*," Archer says harshly. "You're taking this too far."

Hazel wets her lips. "He did, though."

Archer mumbles something incoherent and starts rooting through the cabinets with new fervor. Milly's eyes get wide. "Really?" she asks.

"I mean, I wasn't around, obviously, but my mom told me Granddad had a huge gambling problem when she was in college. It was so bad that they were going to lose the house, and she wouldn't be able to pay for school, and my grandmother was threatening to divorce him. But then he started winning." Hazel swallows hard. "She says he won all the time, after that."

"Huh," Milly says thoughtfully. "And Theresa would get money too, of course, but maybe there's more to it with her. Maybe you're right, Jonah, and she was never the same after her son died. Or maybe it's like Aubrey said . . . oh my God." For the first time in this entire bizarre conversation, panic hits her voice. "Oh no. Aubrey. Aubrey is *there*."

"At least she's not here," Archer says with a strangled laugh. He finally locates a bottle of vodka and untwists the cap, filling a red Solo cup nearly to the brim. "Here is the bad place."

"Uncle Archer, no! You don't get it." Before Archer can

lift his drink, Milly grabs his arm and spins him with all her strength. "Aubrey has a keycard to the gates of Catmint House. She found one when she was there yesterday, and she grabbed it." My pulse starts racing as fast as Milly's must be, because I know what she's thinking. "Aubrey went there, I'm sure of it," Milly continues, her voice turning desperate as she takes hold of Archer by the shoulders. "She's at Catmint House *right now*. Her father's been telling her all summer that she needs to be more proactive. She wants to confirm what she saw."

Archer is silent. Milly shakes him by his shoulders once, hard. "Even if you don't believe anything else I've said this morning, please believe this is *a bad situation*," she says tightly.

"Jesus." Archer's face goes slack. He twists in Milly's grip to look longingly at his drink, and I half expect him to shoot out an arm and grab it. Instead, he sucks in a breath and turns to Hazel, who's still frozen in place. "Did you drive here?"

Hazel blinks like a sleepwalker trying to wake up. "Car's parked next to the curb. It's a Range Rover." She digs into her pocket and tosses Archer the keys. He catches them in one hand, then lunges into the living room and out the door.

## ALLISON, AGE 18

### AUGUST 1996

Archer's friend Jess had gotten a new dog, and Archer was in love. "I would kill for you, Sammy," he said in a singsong voice, crouching beside the small terrier on the coarse sand of Cutty Beach. Sammy, ecstatic at the attention, tried to lick his face. "Yes, I would."

"That seems extreme," Allison said.

"Well, not, like, a person," Archer amended, scratching behind Sammy's ears. "Or another dog, obviously. Or a cat. I would kill a rodent, though. One that was already sick and going to die anyway."

"Take note, Sammy." Allison sat beside Archer as the dog crawled into his lap. "If you're ever tormented by a diseased rat, your champion is here."

She gazed at the crowds milling along Cutty Beach and clustered around two small bonfires. For the past few years, Archer's friend Jess Callahan, who lived in the house closest to the beach's crescent-shaped center, had held her birthday party here. Jess's older brother was on the Gull Cove Island police department, and he was their insurance that as long as they didn't let the party get out of hand, they'd be left alone. Chris Callahan even dropped off a couple of kegs before leaving for his shift at the station.

"Three cheers for Gull Cove's finest," Archer had said at the time. Now, he observed, "I think we're the only ones here who aren't drunk."

"Probably." Allison knew why she wasn't drinking—and why she was behind a rock with her brother and a dog instead of joining the festivities—but she wasn't sure about Archer. "Why do you suppose that is?"

"Well. You weren't entirely wrong, before the Summer Gala, when you reminded me that I have a habit of turning into a drunk asshole."

"I didn't say *exactly* that," Allison said. "And I apologized, remember? I was just nervous before such a big night. I didn't mean it."

"It's true, though. I've been overdoing it," Archer said. "Every party is the same. I think I'm only going to have a couple of drinks and the next thing I know, I'm out of my mind." Sammy flopped onto his back, legs in the air, and Archer obliged by rubbing his belly. "Maybe I just want to see if I can have a good time without it."

"And are you?"

"Not really, no." Archer grinned crookedly. "No offense."

"None taken." Allison wasn't, either. She hadn't wanted to come tonight, but she also hadn't wanted to *not* come. She knew Matt would be here, and she didn't want to stay away because of him. Part of her thought that maybe she'd even talk to him, finally, and tell him about the baby. But as soon as she arrived at the party she realized it was a lost cause. Matt was stumbling around and asking everyone if they'd seen Kayla, too drunk to remember that she worked the late shift at Donald Camden's office on weekends.

"The waves are out of control," Archer said.

"It's the cold weather," Allison said, pulling the sleeves of her sweater over her hands as a particularly strong gust of wind whipped around them. "Makes the tidal patterns wild."

Archer was only in a long-sleeved T-shirt, and he shivered. "I left my sweatshirt in the car. I'm gonna grab it." He got to his feet, Sammy dancing around him. "Are you coming, buddy?" he crooned to the little dog. "Yes, you are. You're such a good boy."

"You're a sap," Allison said, laughing.

"You need anything?"

*I need to go home,* Alison thought, but she said, "No, I'm going to look for Adam." Maybe he'd be willing to leave the party for fifteen minutes and take her back to Catmint House. She'd managed to make an appearance for close to an hour, and that felt like a minor victory.

She scanned the crowd as she walked, keeping a cautious eye out for Matt, but he was nowhere in sight. Neither were her older brothers. Allison circled the crowd around the bonfires twice, but she couldn't find them. Archer had returned at this point, his sweatshirt draped across his shoulders and a cup in one hand as he talked to Rob Valentine. Only Adam, Anders, and Matt were missing. She would have thought they'd left for the night if Adam's BMW and Matt's bright green moped weren't still in the beach parking lot.

Unease pricked at Allison as she walked farther down the

beach, the surf crashing loudly against the shore. She hoped her brothers weren't going to pick a fight. She was still angry with Matt about how he'd acted in Arabella's Coffee, but two on one wasn't fair.

She reached the edge of the party area, a cluster of rental cabanas that created a dividing line between another, rockier stretch of beach. People often used them as a hookup spot, but they were deserted. She passed them, wincing as the wind whipped sand into her face.

Past the cabanas, a pier jutted into the ocean, small rowboats bobbing against its side. And here, finally, Allison caught sight of two figures standing at the pier's edge. She recognized Adam's height towering over Anders's smaller frame, and quickened her pace.

They were staring at the churning waves, oblivious to her approach. "You see anything?" she heard Adam call over the howling wind.

"No. And we won't. Not with this undertow," Anders said.

"Jesus Christ, Anders." Adam's laugh sounded harsh and on edge. "Remind me never to piss you off."

The brief exchange, coupled with her brothers' laser-like focus on the raging water, made the hairs on the back of Allison's neck stand on end. She wasn't sure she wanted to know what Adam and Anders were talking about, and nearly turned to go back to the party. But something made her pause, and reach out a hand.

"Hey!" Allison shook Adam's shoulder as she yelled in his ear, and he jumped a mile. "What are you guys doing?"

Anders turned, his eyes glittering in the moonlight. "Taking care of a problem."

# CHAPTER TWENTY-FIVE

## AUBREY

Once I'm through the gate, I park my bike behind a thick tangle of honeysuckle shrubs and approach the driveway leading to Catmint House, considering my next steps. I can't exactly waltz up to the front door all *Hey, hi, could you spit into a cup for me? Just need a little DNA and I'll be on my way.*

Even thinking the words makes me feel like I'm losing my mind. Sane people don't break into mansions looking for evidence that their grandmother is an imposter. I kept asking myself, as I pedaled here, if there might be an explanation for the lack of a birthmark on my grandmother's hand.

*Maybe she had it lasered off?*

I'd asked about laser removal when I got teased mercilessly as a preteen. "You should be proud," my father said. "Your grandmother was. She wouldn't remove part of herself to please other people." Which was actually good advice, for once, but my mother agreed to let me consult with a few plastic surgeons.

They all said the same thing: the color was too dense and too deep. It might fade a little, but it would never go away completely.

*Maybe she was wearing makeup?*

But then why the gloves? Why the gloves, always, even on a hot summer day?

*Maybe you just missed it.*

I hadn't, though. I know that birthmark like the back of my hand, and that's exactly where it should have been on her. It's the only characteristic my grandmother and I share, and it wasn't there. I'm sure of that.

The lush landscaping of the grounds lets me skirt behind bushes all the way up the driveway and then around to the back of the house. Then I pause, looking at the sun-drenched yard. It's surprisingly big, given how close to the cliff Catmint House looks from a distance, and not as well maintained as the front. The grass is too long, the bushes too wild, and the flowers are unkempt and overgrown. I can hear the roar of the sea crashing against rocks behind the house, and the faint cries of seagulls circling above.

*What am I doing?*

I start to back up, suddenly horrified with myself. I'm trespassing, is what I'm doing, with the intent to break into a house whose owner explicitly told me to stay away. I could get arrested for this, and for what? I should just tell somebody my suspicions and leave it to the police, or whoever, to sort everything out.

And then I see it: a first-floor window barely five feet off the ground, half open. It almost looks like an invitation.

I creep forward until I'm beneath the sill, then raise myself on tiptoes to peer inside. It's a beautiful room, with crown molding and an elaborate chandelier, but it looks as though it's being used for storage space. It's empty except for piles of boxes, rolled-up rugs, and chairs stacked neatly one on top of the other. The hallway behind the open inner door is silent and dim.

Am I really going to do this? *Can* I do this? I curl my palms around the sill, debating. I haven't worked out here like I did while I was swimming competitively, and it doesn't take long to lose muscle strength. But I've always been good at pull-ups.

I take a deep breath and hoist myself up, surprised at how easily I rise. My feet scramble for purchase on the side of the house and I almost lose my grip, but I manage to get one arm up and over the windowsill, which gives me enough leverage to pull myself halfway through. I stay there for a few seconds, panting, then crawl the rest of the way inside.

I land in a crouch, flexing my sore palms. *Take that, Dad,* I think as I rise. *Arm strength comes in handy sometimes.*

I have no idea what part of the house I'm in. I slip off my sneakers and leave them beside the window, then pad across the hardwood floor until I get to the doorway. I move silently down the hall, pausing after every step, until I come to a staircase. I stand there a long time, straining my ears for any signal that someone's near the top, but there's nothing.

I navigate the stairs carefully, stepping lightly until I'm on the upstairs landing. I don't know what part of the house I'm in, but it's so quiet that I become a little bolder and move more quickly. Maybe I got lucky, and nobody's home.

I climb a second set of stairs, steeper and narrower, and pause at the door at the top. I place my hand on the knob and turn slowly, as far as I can. Then I push. It swings open with only the tiniest creaking noise, and I peer into a wide hallway.

There are doors on either side, and my heart starts pounding when I realize that I might've found a back stairway to the bedroom area. Which is where I need to be, because the only way I can be sure that I'm grabbing something of Gran's is to take it from her room.

I approach the first door noiselessly and open it quickly, stepping inside. Right away, I know this isn't anyone's current bedroom; it has a deserted, musty feeling to it. Not to mention outdated curtains and bed linens that look like they haven't been changed in years. There's a red blanket at the foot of the bed that reads MARTINDALE PREP in bold white letters, and two lacrosse sticks propped in one corner.

Wait. Could this be my dad's old room? I creep in a little farther and spy a framed photo on the wall beside the window. It's the same picture of my father and Gran that I saw in Sweetfern: the two of them holding that ugly painting and beaming for the camera. I zero in on my grandmother's hand, dominated by that prominent birthmark.

"Lovely picture, isn't it?"

I spin to see Gran—or whoever she is—standing in the doorway. At first, all I take in is that for once she's not dressed to the nines or wearing gloves. Then I noticed the small, pearl-handled pistol in one of her hands. It's so pretty, it almost doesn't look—

"Oh, it's real. And it's loaded," she says, stepping into the room. "Two elderly women living alone can't be too careful." The look she gives me is almost sympathetic. "Did you honestly think we're not alerted when the gate opens?"

I lick my lips, which have gone suddenly dry. "So . . . what? You let me come in?"

"I opened the window for you."

*Stupid, stupid, stupid,* I berate myself. "Well, you caught me," I say, affecting a guilty laugh. It comes out like more of a wheeze. "I wanted to see this place one more time. Try to find my father's room. And I did, so . . . I'll just leave now."

"No, you won't." My heart sinks as she takes another step forward. "I wondered yesterday, if you got a good look at my hand. I take it you did?" I'm too frozen to even nod. "And now here you are. Adam's daughter. It would be quite a poetic tragedy if I mistook you for a burglar and shot you in his old room, wouldn't it?"

"I told people." I blurt out the lie as convincingly as I can. "I told everyone what I saw. Uncle Archer and Milly and Jonah and . . . everyone."

Gran, or Mildred, or—I don't even know what to call her anymore—tilts her head to one side. "And yet, you're here all alone."

My blood runs cold. I got one text off to Uncle Archer, and there's not much chance that he'll know what I meant. "What did you do to my grandmother?" I ask, my voice trembling.

"Nothing," she says, with such quick certainty that I actually believe her. "Your grandmother died of natural causes twenty-four years ago. I found her here. She liked to spend time in Adam's room while he was gone." Her eyes flash. "He was always her favorite, even though he was the least attentive child."

"You're Theresa," I say. She doesn't deny it. "And . . . and the other Theresa . . ." I have no idea how to finish that sentence.

She doesn't satisfy my curiosity. "It's odd," she says musingly. "I took everything I could from Adam, and for all these years, it's never felt like enough. Maybe taking his only child would be." My heart drops into my feet and I almost blurt, *I'm not his only child,* before she adds, "After all, he took mine."

The world tilts on its axis. "My father . . . killed your son?"

"In a manner of speaking."

A loud, crashing noise startles us both. I move instinctively toward the window, reaching its edge before Theresa's commanding "Stop!" makes me pause. But I can see enough to make out a large black SUV barreling across the lawn. It's such a bizarre, out-of-context, yet blessedly welcome sight that I almost laugh out loud.

"Tess!" A woman's voice, loud and agitated, calls from downstairs. "Tess, someone is driving up to the house. *Tess!*"

"I see," Theresa calls back. She looks remarkably calm for someone whose house might be plowed into any second. But the car stops a few feet from the front door, and, with a mix of relief and apprehension, I watch Uncle Archer get out of the driver's seat.

"So you weren't lying," Theresa says. "Well. We had a good run, I suppose." The hand holding the gun drops slightly, and I feel a surge of hope until her face hardens. "May as well see things to their inevitable conclusion. Come along." She steps into the hallway, gesturing for me to follow, and crosses to the balcony staircase overlooking the second floor of the house. "Show our guest into the sunroom," she calls downstairs. "Tell him Aubrey will be right there."

"What are you going to do?" I ask anxiously. "Please don't hurt him." The thought of anything happening to Uncle Archer because he came after me makes me sick to my stomach.

"Downstairs," she orders. The look in her eye is so deadly

that I do what she says. She directs me—left at the foot of the stairs, right into the hallway, another right—until I'm in the doorway of a room that's floor-to-ceiling windows on three sides. At its center, Uncle Archer stands beside the woman I thought was Theresa Ryan.

"Aubrey!" he cries. He strides forward, mouth open to say more, until the real Theresa appears beside me, gun in hand. Archer stops short, his eyes boring into hers. "Oh my God," he says hoarsely, one hand curling into his chest. "It's true. It really is true. I thought there had to be some mistake, but . . . you're not my mother." The muscle in his jaw jumps. "If I'd ever gotten within ten feet of you before now, I would have known in an instant."

"Possibly not," Theresa says. "We see what we expect to see. But you understand now, I suppose, why I had to cut off contact." Her voice doesn't soften exactly, but it's less steely when she adds, "Even with you, who's relatively innocent in all this."

"All *what*?" Archer asks. "Why would you do this? What did we ever do to you?" His gaze flits between Theresa, the gun, and me. "Is this about what happened to Kayla? Or to Matt?"

"Paula," Theresa says. I have no idea who she's referring to until the second woman steps forward. "There's a chill in the air. Why don't you light a fire in the south parlor, and then leave us to talk about—" She pauses, eyes glinting. "What happened to Matt."

"Tess, are you sure?" the other woman says nervously.

"Positive," Theresa says. Paula brushes past us into the hallway.

Uncle Archer takes a deep breath. "Matt drowned, and that's awful, but—"

"Matt didn't *drown*," Theresa says sharply. "He was killed. That night at Cutty Beach? Matt would never have gone into the water on his own. He might have been drinking, but he wasn't a fool. He knew what the undertow could do on a night like that. Your snake of a brother, Anders, told him that Kayla had been swept away by the tide and needed help."

"Kayla?" Uncle Archer looks bewildered. "She wasn't even there."

Theresa's lip curls. "No. And Anders was perfectly aware of that. He lied to get Matt in the water. He knew he'd probably never come out. And Adam—Adam was standing right next to them, and he let Matt go." She's shaking now, her eyes wide and shiny. "Adam just let him go."

*Adam just let him go.* The words ring so loud in my ears that I almost miss Uncle Archer's next question. "How could you possibly know that?"

"Kayla," Theresa says. "Anders got drunk one night and spilled everything to her. I don't think he even remembered doing it. But she told me. Said he'd always been jealous of Matt, and resented him even more when Matt got Allison pregnant the summer he died." She laughs bitterly at Uncle Archer's shocked expression. "You didn't know? Me either. My grandchild, imagine that. And your mother's. But Allison miscarried."

"She did?" Uncle Archer asks blankly.

"Yes." Theresa's mouth presses into a thin line. "And she knew what happened to Matt. Anders told her that night, and I'll say this for her: at least she sounded the alarm that he was missing. But then she protected her brothers. She let everyone think it was an accident."

"Kayla told you all this," Uncle Archer says slowly. "And

then—what? You killed her? Drugged her and put her in her car?" Theresa startles, and Uncle Archer presses. "Fred Baxter gave me the original autopsy report. There was a sedative in her system the night she died."

"So that's why she asked about Kayla," Theresa says, looking at me. I've become *she* all of a sudden; a prop in the conversation.

"You killed an innocent girl and you have the nerve to play victim?" Uncle Archer asks, his voice rising.

"That wasn't me," Theresa insists. "It's just—everything happened at once. I found out about Matt. I was devastated and furious. The only thing I wanted in the world was to make your brothers and sister pay, somehow. And then your mother died." Her eyes get a faraway look. "She and I had been alone in the house. I called Donald Camden, because, well—we called Donald for everything back then. He said something about how you children would burn through Abraham and Mildred's fortune in no time flat. And I got an idea."

The edges of her mouth curve into a smile, and it's a gruesome sight. "It seemed ridiculous at first. But Donald loved it. He'd always wanted to get his hands on your parents' money. We looped in Fred Baxter, who was drowning in debt, and promised to make all that go away if he'd keep acting as my physician. We buried Mildred here, on the grounds of Catmint House, and I brought my sister, Paula, here to take my place. Then Donald wrote to all of you."

Theresa's face tightens. "But Kayla kept trying to see me. She wanted to know if Mrs. Story had disinherited the children because of what I'd told her. I talked to her on the phone a few times, trying to placate her, but she just became more agitated. I stopped taking her calls, and she went to Fred Baxter. He urged her not to worry about it, to keep quiet. But then she asked Donald. And Donald—well, he thought it would become a problem if she kept talking. If people knew I had a reason to hate the Story children. So he took matters into his own hands." A defensive note creeps into her voice at Uncle Archer's horrified expression. "Fred and I wouldn't have condoned that, but by the time we realized what had happened, it was too late."

"Well, aren't you and Fred just a pair of ever-loving saints," Uncle Archer says icily. Then he draws in a sharp, shocked breath. "Holy shit. Is that what happened to Fred, too? He started talking this summer, trying to piece together a confession in that addled brain of his, so Donald *took matters into his own hands*? Drowned the man in his own backyard?"

He takes a step forward, and something cold and hard presses into the side of my neck. I whimper involuntarily, and Uncle Archer freezes.

"Let's not forget who's in charge here," Theresa says.

Uncle Archer raises both hands in a gesture of surrender. "I'm not coming any closer, okay? But it's over. You have to know that. You can't put the genie back in the bottle this time."

"Probably not," Theresa says. "But I beg to disagree with you that it's *over*. Because here's the thing." Her voice turns musing. "Adam is the worst of them, I think. Anders never had a redeeming quality to speak of, and Allison is weak. But Adam—I adored Adam. I always stood up for him when the pressure from his parents got to be too much. I would have done anything for that boy. And then, when he had the chance to keep my son safe, he didn't take it. All Adam would have had to do is say *stop*. Either to Anders or to Matt. They would have listened to him, and Matt would still be alive."

*Foolish boy. Could've changed it all with a word.* Finally, I understand what Dr. Baxter meant when he said that about my father, and I feel a sudden rush of sympathy for the woman standing next to me. Then, an ominous click beside my ear drains away every emotion except fear. "The problem with Adam is that he hasn't suffered *enough*," Theresa says tightly. "He doesn't know what it's like to lose a child."

Uncle Archer's eyes grow round and alarmed. "Theresa, no."

"What else am I supposed to do with Adam's daughter?" she asks. "Just let her walk away? Like Adam let Matt walk away?" My breath starts coming shallow and fast. Somewhere in the back of my panicked mind, I register the smell of gasoline. Or is it smoke?

"You're angry with my family, I understand that. You have every right to be," Uncle Archer says urgently. "But if you think there's still a score to be settled—settle it with *me*. Not Aubrey." His hands, which have been up all this time, fold over his heart like he's offering her a target. "Take it out on me. I was there. I could have done something to help, and I didn't. That's the story of my entire goddamn life."

"Don't," I say. My heart is threatening to crawl into my throat.

"Kayla said you didn't know," Theresa says sharply. The smell of smoke is getting stronger. "Are you telling me that you did?"

Uncle Archer's gaze darts between Theresa, me, and the gun before finally settling on me. The tense lines of his jaw soften. My heart constricts and then swells, painfully, when I recognize the look on his face. It's one I've never seen on anyone before. It's *fatherly*.

Then he says, very simply, "Yes."

Everything happens in a lightning-quick blur after that. The gun leaves my neck. Theresa's arm shifts, and I react instinctively. I crash my shoulder into hers, knocking her off-balance and to the floor. A deafening blast fills the room, followed by a high-pitched scream of anguish. Sharp pain shoots through my elbow when I hit the ground, half on top of Theresa, and someone screams again. Red pools on the floor beside me as I twist my neck left and right, my eyes scanning wildly for Uncle Archer.

"Aubrey!" He's above me, Theresa's gun dangling from one hand, and I almost pass out in relief. "Are you hurt?"

"I don't think so." I lift myself from Theresa, and she groans. Her left leg is covered in blood, and so is the floor beneath her. Her face is buried in the crook of her arm, and she's not moving other than breathing heavily. "I think I shot her."

"She shot herself," he says grimly. "We'd better call for help. Do you have your phone? I forgot mine."

"It's dead." I stand, the adrenaline that's been coursing through me draining fast, and the stench of smoke finally hits me in full. The air outside the sunroom looks thick and hazy.

*Paula, why don't you light a fire in the south parlor?*

That's what Theresa had said, just before her sister left the room. I step halfway through the door and peer into the hallway. There's a crackling, hissing noise coming from somewhere. The floor is slick and wet.

*Tess, are you sure?*

*Positive.*

"Something's wrong," I say.

Then the hallway explodes into flames.

"Jesus!" Uncle Archer shouts as I stumble backward into the sunroom. "We have to get out! Come on." He reaches down to haul Theresa to her feet. She moans in protest, limp as a rag doll, and he heaves her into his arms. "Stairs, Aubrey! To your left."

"We can't!" Within seconds, the scene in front of us has transformed. Fire is everywhere, flames dancing and rolling through the hall. Smoke billows toward us and I choke when the first wave hits me, sending me back into the sunroom, my eyes streaming.

"We have to," Uncle Archer says, pushing past me with Theresa in his arms. He backtracks just as quickly, gasping. "Okay. New plan." He drops Theresa into one of the leather armchairs in a corner of the room, then picks up the second chair and hurls it at the nearest window. The glass shatters, flying everywhere.

I cover my nose and mouth with my hands as more smoke pours into the room. Uncle Archer picks up a long, old-fashioned umbrella from a decorative stand and swings it against the edges of the pane, clearing away jagged chunks of glass. I grab another umbrella to help, and look down at the ground. My heart plummets. "It's too far."

"We'll make a rope," Uncle Archer says, pulling a blanket from the back of the couch. I rip gauzy curtains from the window and turn to see what else might be in the room. There's a roaring sound at the door, and I watch in horror as flames zip up the crown molding that surrounds it, then spread to the nearest bookcase. At first its's just a small orange line running along the top shelf, and then the books catch fire.

The couch nearest the broken window is old-fashioned and

heavy. Uncle Archer ties an end of the blanket to one of the couch's legs in a tight double knot and the other end to the curtain I'm holding. It feels weightless in my hands. "Will this work?" I gulp. He knots the ends firmly, tests the hold, and doubles the knot. "Is it strong enough?" I ask.

Uncle Archer looks around the room. The bookcase is consumed in fire, the ceiling above it also alight. The smoke is gray and black now, stealing breath from our lungs even with fresh air streaming in through the window. Flames lick an area rug and spread across its surface. "It'll have to do," he says, tossing the loose end of the knotted material out the window. "You first, Aubrey. Keep your body relaxed and try to land on your feet."

There's no time to argue. I grab hold of the blanket beneath its knot near the couch and haul myself over the edge of the window. Shards of glass slice my arms and my wrists, spattering the pale-green blanket with blood. I lower myself as fast as I can. Before I know it I've run out of blanket, then curtain, and I haven't gone far at all. I don't know how close I am to the ground, but it doesn't matter. There's nowhere to go but down.

I let go of the curtain and I fall.

I slam into the ground feetfirst, my knees giving way as I tumble hard on my side. Everything hurts, but nothing so badly that I can't roll over and look at the house. The ground floor is fully alight. Smoke is pouring out the window I just came from. The curtain hangs loose, the bottom about six feet from the ground. There's no sign of my uncle or Theresa.

I cup my hands around my mouth and scream, "Uncle Archer! Come out!" Fighting back rising panic, I try to stand. Pain shoots up my right leg, forcing me back to my knees. "It's okay, it's not far. Hurry!"

The window stays empty. My lungs hurt, making it hard to yell. But I keep at it, calling my uncle's name over and over and over until my throat is raw.

And then, thank God, he appears. Theresa is slung over his shoulder, making his crawl out the window agonizingly slow. She's either unconscious or refusing to help, and as I watch him struggle through the billowing clouds of smoke, a furious thought sears my brain.

*Drop her. Just drop her.*

He doesn't. He inches down the makeshift rope until what's left of the window glows orange and the rope goes slack. They fall, and I hear a sound like the terrified scream of a dying animal. It takes a few seconds to realize it was me.

"Uncle Archer!" I crawl toward the motionless lump of limbs and clothing that landed a few feet away. Theresa's face is turned toward me, her eyes empty and staring. I let out another involuntary animal sound, and scramble past her until I reach my uncle's arm. "Please," I whisper, tugging at his wrist to turn it palm up. "Please."

When I feel a pulse beat faintly against my thumb, I start crying for the first time all day.

# CHAPTER TWENTY-SIX

## MILLY

Catmint House burned to the ground that day.

Theresa's sister, whose real name is Paula Donahue, had soaked it with gasoline before striking a match and taking off. Police have spent all week combing Gull Cove Island and staking out local airports, but there's no sign of her. I'm convinced she made it out of the country on a fake passport and is living off money that she and Theresa stole from Mildred and stashed away offshore. It's infuriating. At least Donald Camden, who didn't have the benefit of a head start, was arrested in his office and is in jail awaiting trial.

Aubrey sprained her ankle in the fall from the window, and Uncle Archer suffered a concussion and dislocated his shoulder. According to medical examiners, Theresa Ryan probably died from smoke inhalation before she hit the ground.

The land surrounding Catmint House is a crime scene now, so we're not allowed anywhere near it. But the day after the fire, Aubrey, Jonah, and I drove to the bend in the road where we'd first glimpsed the house. None of the destruction was visible from a distance, but there was something deeply unsettling about seeing an unbroken stretch of sky where the house used to loom. All of that history of Abraham and Mildred's legacy, and my mother's childhood home just—gone.

Mom arrived the next day, taking charge like she always does. "You can't stay here," she insisted as soon as she set foot in Uncle Archer's bungalow. "It's not private enough. The media is in a frenzy." And just like that, we moved into a swanky Story rental house. Since then, Mom's been acting as a liaison with police, medical examiners, reporters, and lawyers trying to untangle more than two decades of fraud.

The one thing she hasn't done, though, is talk about what happened to Matt Ryan on Cutty Beach that summer night twenty-five years ago.

I wanted to ask as soon as she stepped off the plane that brought her to the Gull Cove Island airport. But she pulled me into a stiff hug and said, "No questions, okay? Let's just get through today."

She's been saying that every day since. I'm trying to give her space, because I know that in addition to everything else she's handling, she has to come to terms with the fact that the mother she'd always hoped to reconcile with has been gone for twenty-four years. And that Mildred Story wasn't a villain after all, but a woman who got taken from her children without having a chance to say good-bye.

Uncle Anders took off from Gull Cove Island as soon as the first article appeared. He's done a single interview since, with

Fox News. "It's all lies," he said about Kayla's story. "Made up by a bitter ex-girlfriend. May she rest in peace, of course."

Uncle Adam isn't granting interviews, but he said the same thing through a spokesperson. Ironically enough, sales of his decade-old book went through the roof when the story broke. Just now, at 5 p.m. sharp, Aubrey got a text from him saying that he'd made the *New York Times* paperback bestseller list.

She tosses her phone aside with a frown. "I guess there are no consequences for some people, ever," she mutters.

Everyone except my mother is in the kitchen, making guacamole for tonight's dinner. It's the last week of July, so there's still plenty of summer season left on Gull Cove Island, but not for us. Aubrey and Jonah are both leaving tomorrow, and I'll follow soon after. My parents want me to stay with Dad and Surya while Mom deals with the fallout here.

"I don't know," Archer says, wincing as he awkwardly chops avocados one-handed. His shoulder bothers him a lot, but he refuses to take pain medication. "Your father still has to live with himself. I have a feeling that's been his problem all along."

It looks like that's the only punishment for Matt Ryan's death that Uncle Adam and Uncle Anders will ever get. Because Uncle Anders is right; the words of a girl who's been dead for twenty-four years, spoken to a woman who committed massive fraud before dying in a fire she told someone to start, isn't enough to convict anyone.

The court of public opinion has been harsh, though. The *New York Post* splashed the question IS IT MURDER? across the front page a couple of days ago, and social media has answered with a resounding *hell yeah*. Uncle Adam might be getting a temporary boost in book sales, but for most people, it's a hate read.

Aubrey still looks glum, so Uncle Archer changes the subject. "Tell us about your new place," he says, scooping uneven avocado chunks into the food processor.

She brightens. Her mother flew in for a day and then had to leave, to finish making arrangements for the apartment she and Aubrey will move into when Aubrey returns to Oregon. "It's a really cute three-bedroom condo. About halfway between school and the hospital where Mom works," she says.

"Sounds perfect," Uncle Archer says.

Aubrey gives him a shy smile. "Maybe you can visit. If you want."

She and Uncle Archer have been spending a lot of time together since they rescued one another from Catmint House. I know part of Aubrey is always going to wish for the kind of father-daughter relationship that Uncle Adam isn't capable of having, but there's something to be said for the uncle-niece bond, too.

"I absolutely will," Uncle Archer says. "But not for a while." Aubrey's face falls, and he quickly adds, "I'm going to be checking into a rehab center on Cape Cod next week. Not sure how long I'll be there, but at least a couple of months."

"That's great," Aubrey and I say in near unison.

"It's overdue," Uncle Archer says. His red Solo cup is on the kitchen island, like always, but he hasn't touched it since we sat down. "After that—I'm not sure. One day at a time." He looks exhausted suddenly, and heaves himself off the stool. "You mind finishing up? I'm gonna try to take a nap."

We murmur our assent, and he leaves. Silence falls for a few minutes until Jonah asks, "So. What are you guys doing when you get home?"

"Physical therapy," Aubrey says promptly. "Turns out swimming is good for a sprained ankle. And I want to keep at it." She reaches for a clove of garlic and starts to peel it. "Maybe even get back on the team."

That startles me enough that I pour too much olive oil into the food processor, and have to scoop some out with a spoon. "Really?"

"They're getting a new coach," Aubrey says. "Since the old one is going on *maternity leave.*" Her expression darkens momentarily, but then her good cheer returns. "It's a woman who ran a summer program I did once. She reached out to say hi and that she hopes I'm coming back. I really like her." She nudges me with one shoulder. "What about you? What are you doing at Casa Dad? He's in New York too, right?"

"Yeah," I say, recapping the olive oil. "My instructions are to lie low."

"What does that mean?" Her eyes widen in fake innocence. "No more paparazzi shots of you making out on the beach?"

"One time," I say, cheeks burning. The beach here is private, but helicopters keep hovering above us, angling for a shot. One of them caught a surprisingly clear close-up of me and Jonah kissing in the ocean. "That happened once."

Jonah clears his throat. "Probably wouldn't even be an issue if we were someplace more crowded where we could blend in." I raise my eyebrows at him, and he adds, "Like a city. Providence and New York aren't that far from one another. There's a bus that only costs thirteen dollars. So I've heard."

"By obsessively checking the Greyhound site?" Aubrey asks brightly.

He shrugs. "Possibly."

I fight off a smile. "I thought you had to work all summer."

"Not *all* summer," Jonah says. His expression turns pensive. "Although, you guys are practically heiresses now, so . . . I don't know. Maybe it'd be too weird."

The Story estate isn't something we've talked much about since Theresa and Donald were exposed, but it's always in the background. When Mom came to the island, she brought that diamond teardrop necklace she had promised me, but I've only tried it on once. Somehow, it didn't look as good on me as I'd thought it would. I put my grandfather's watch away, too. It's strange, but not in a bad way, how much lighter my arm feels without it.

Nothing about the Story fortune seems real yet. But Jonah does, and I'm not ready to say a permanent good-bye any more than he is. "It wouldn't be weird. At all," I tell him.

He grins, and I pick up a spoon and point it at him for emphasis. "I'm not taking a bus, though. Ever. That part is non-negotiable."

Hours later, after Aubrey's gone to bed and Jonah is locked into some multiplayer video game with friends from home, I wander outside and see my mother and Uncle Archer sitting on two Adirondack chairs arranged on a strip of beach near the house. I almost go back inside, not wanting to bother them, but my mother catches sight of me and waves me over.

"Let me get you a chair." Uncle Archer half rises before I motion for him to stop.

"It's okay. I don't like those chairs anyway." There's a towel draped over the edge of my mother's seat, and I spread it on the ground to sit at their feet.

"I was just telling Archer how happy I am that you and Aubrey have gotten close," Mom says. There's a table between her and Uncle Archer, holding a single glass of wine. Mom lifts it and takes a sip before adding, "She's a gem. It's hard to believe now how little effort I expended over the years to help you know your cousins."

I put on a breezy tone, because I'm trying not to think about Aubrey flying across the country. Our long-distance chats are going to be nonstop. "Well, in JT's case, that was a good call."

Uncle Archer shakes his head. "I'm still holding out hope for that kid. He was just trying to do his own thing this summer. I'll bet part of him is sorry for what happened."

"A very small part," I say. "An earlobe, maybe."

"You always did refuse to see the worst in people, Archer," Mom says.

It's been strange watching her and Uncle Archer slip into old patterns this week—*very* old patterns, from their teenage years—as opposed to the strained politeness I remember from my childhood. I'd observed closeness between the two of them in old videos, but never in real life, and I almost believed it was a trick of the camera. But it's not.

"I guess we have that in common," Archer says. He makes a fist with one hand and bops it gently against my mother's arm. "Couldn't even see it in our own brothers."

Mom stirs restlessly in her chair. "Have I used up all my *let's discuss that later* chips?"

"You don't have to talk about anything you don't want to," Uncle Archer says. "But I do want to tell you that I'm sorry for what you went through that summer, with the pregnancy and all. I knew something was wrong, but I had no idea it was that."

"Well, how could you?" Mom asks. "I didn't tell you. And it was over almost before it started." She takes another sip of wine. "I was both sad and relieved. I felt for a while like I hated Matt, but I didn't, really. I was just angry about how he acted. And then Anders told me what he'd done, and Matt died so horribly, and I just—I had no idea what to do."

Uncle Archer waits a beat, and when my mother doesn't continue, he asks quietly, "Did you ever think about telling anyone?"

"Every day." Mom grips the stem of her wineglass so hard that I'm afraid it might break. "I was so conflicted. I felt guilty, because I'd provoked Anders by telling him about Kayla and Matt. And because Anders almost made it sound as though he'd done it *for* me, and all I could think was—did I communicate, in some way, that I'd *wanted* this? Was it my fault? It took more than a year for me to understand that Anders was, as always, acting in his own self-interest. By that point I couldn't think how to bring it up again, or what good it could possibly do. And then Donald Camden sent that letter."

Mom finishes her wine and sets the glass down with a trembling hand. "It felt like we deserved it. Well, all of us except you. Even though I thought Mother couldn't possibly have known about Matt. And of course, she didn't." Mom huffs out the least mirthful laugh I've ever heard. "Now all I can think is—what if

I had said something back then? Would everything be different now? Maybe Mother would still be with us and—"

"Allison," Uncle Archer interrupts. "She wouldn't. She had a heart condition."

"I don't know. It feels like the butterfly effect." Mom's voice gets thick. "Especially now, knowing that Kayla's gone because of what I did—"

"Kayla's gone because Donald Camden is a greedy, soulless bastard," Uncle Archer corrects. For the first time all night, he sounds angry. "And if anyone set that particular butterfly effect in motion, it was Anders. Which is horribly ironic. I think he really did love Kayla, as much as Anders is capable of loving anyone. It has to hurt, knowing that what he did to Matt ultimately caused her death." Uncle Archer taps his fingers rhythmically against the wooden arm of his chair, one after the other. From his index finger to his pinkie, then in reverse. *One, two, three, four. Four, three, two, one.* "I don't judge you, Allison. I'm angry at Adam for not saying something when it would have made a difference, but not at you for keeping quiet after it wouldn't. I'm not sure what I would have done in that situation. You know what Father used to say. Family first, always."

Mom still sounds on the verge of tears. "Father would have been horrified."

"At *them*." Uncle Archer's voice softens. "You didn't set out to deliberately hurt anyone. Forgive yourself, Allison. Twenty-five years is a long time to hang on to guilt."

"I'm trying," Mom says.

A cellphone on the table between her and Uncle Archer rings. "Who's Charlotte?" Mom asks, looking down.

"An associate in Donald Camden's office," Uncle Archer

says. "I asked her to get in touch if she heard about any interesting developments. On the down low, of course. So don't tell." He puts a finger to his lips as he picks up his phone.

"How do you know everyone?" Mom asks wonderingly.

"I talk to people. You should try it. Hey, Charlotte," Uncle Archer says, getting up and walking toward the beach. "What's up?"

Silence falls between me and my mother. Then, to my surprise, she reaches down and strokes my hair. I can't remember the last time she did that, but I definitely wasn't more than six years old. "Being pregnant that summer was so lonely," she says reflectively. "I couldn't bring myself to tell my mother, but I kept wishing that she'd guess, somehow. Milly, if you are ever in a situation like that, I hope you know that you have my full support."

I push aside my natural inclination to say, *God, Mom, please don't talk about that,* because I *want* her to talk about it. Just not in relation to me. But I'll take what I can get at the moment. "I know."

"Do you?" Her laugh is brittle. "I'm not sure I've done a very good job of showing you my support over the years."

"Well, you've had a lot going on," I hedge.

"I'll take that as affirmation that I could improve my parenting," she says dryly.

"Mom, did you . . ." I hesitate, then decide to plunge right in. "Did you ever tell Dad what happened?"

"Not all of it." Mom tucks a strand of hair behind my ear before withdrawing her hand. "Your father is the kindest man I've ever known. He did so much over the years to help me come to terms with what happened to Matt, and with the pregnancy. But I couldn't finish the story. I never could tell him what Anders had done, or that I'd protected him." Her voice dips low. I twist my neck to get a look at her face, but the moonlight is too dim. "The truth was like a cancer inside me by that point, and I'd shoved it down so far that it wouldn't come out. It just . . . festered, and made me angry. Your father took the brunt of that without ever knowing why."

Sadness settles over my chest, at the thought of what life could have been like if my mother had ever unburdened herself. "I think he would have understood."

"I think you're right," she says quietly.

We're silent for a minute, listening to the waves lapping against the shore and the indistinct murmur of Uncle Archer's voice. Then Mom clears her throat and says, "I've been meaning to tell you, Milly, how impressed I am with the way you pieced the truth together. You have a sharp mind." I wait for the inevitable follow-up—*if you applied yourself that way at school you'd have an A average in no time*—but it doesn't come. "And a good heart" is all she says, and I feel the soft sting of tears behind my eyes.

Uncle Archer comes back then, holding his phone and breathing hard. Mom gets to her feet and hurries toward him. "Are you okay?" she asks. "Does your shoulder hurt? You keep overextending yourself."

"I—no." Uncle Archer's voice is strained. "That was Charlotte."

"I know," Mom says. "You told us."

"Right. The thing is . . ." He stuffs his phone into his pocket and runs a hand through his hair. "I asked her to let me know if anything important came up. It has. The bigwigs aren't telling

311

us yet because there's still a lot of paperwork to go through, but—Allison, Catmint House wasn't insured. Neither was any of the art or jewelry or furniture."

I turn toward my mother, who's blinking in confusion. "What? Why?" she asks. "How on earth is a house like that not insured?"

"Nothing is," Uncle Archer says. "All the policies have lapsed. No bills have been paid on anything for more than a year. The other houses our family owns—including *this* house—are in foreclosure. The investment accounts are empty. Donald and Theresa have been selling art to live on. Anything they hadn't sold yet went up in literal flames last week."

My mother doesn't say a word. Uncle Archer puts his hand on her shoulder and speaks slowly and patiently, his voice full of kindness and concern, like a doctor delivering a diagnosis that's going to hurt like hell, but not actually kill you.

"They spent it all. Every last penny. The Story estate is gone."

# EPILOGUE

## JONAH
### FIVE MONTHS LATER

Milly breaks, and balls go flying across crisp green felt. She just keeps getting better and better at pool. The last time I visited her in New York—when she took me to some swanky "entertainment complex" where all the tables were rimmed with fluorescent lights—she came uncomfortably close to beating me.

"Somebody's about to give you a run for your money, Jonah," Enzo calls from behind the bar. He returned to work at Empire Billiards right after Thanksgiving, although he still does a couple of shifts at Home Depot every week. Just in case.

"You've been practicing without me, haven't you?" I ask as Milly watches the last of the balls drop into a corner pocket.

"I'm stripes," she announces, giving me a coy glance from beneath her lashes.

There it is. That's the look that gets me every time. I forget where we are and reach for her, plucking the pool cue out of her hand so I can pull her close. Her silky hair is long and loose, and I brush it from her face before I kiss her. She lets out a soft sigh and melts into me, and I forget all about the endless three weeks since I saw her last.

I also forget about Enzo, until he coughs. "Parent. Parking lot," he says, and I release Milly a few seconds before my mother walks through the door.

Not that she'd mind. She loves Milly, and she's the one who invited her to stay with us after Christmas. But I'm trying to keep the awkward factor low so that Milly won't ever hesitate to come back.

By train, of course. She wasn't kidding about the bus.

"Mail came," Mom says to Enzo, dropping a thick pile of paper on the bar. "There's a new catalog from ServMor Bar Supply, if you're interested."

"I *am*," he says, plucking it from the stack with reverence. Ever since his stint at Home Depot, you can't keep Enzo away from DIY projects to improve Empire Billiards. We don't open for another hour, but he got here early to install what he claims is a more durable bar rail.

Mom turns to Milly and me. "I'm going to make myself a burger and some fries before we open. You two want anything?"

"Same," I say, with a questioning look toward Milly.

"Me too," she says. "Thanks, Mrs. North."

"Of course! Anything for you, Enzo?"

"Nah, I'm good."

"Okay. Just give me ten or fifteen minutes, kids." Mom disappears into the kitchen. Enzo tucks the catalog and the rest of the mail under his arm.

"I'll be reading this in the office for the next ten minutes," he announces, ducking out from behind the bar. "Do with this empty room what you will."

I moved a respectable distance from Milly when Mom came in, but close the gap now with a grin. "Where were we?" I ask, circling her waist with my hands.

She stretches on her toes to peck me on the lips, then pulls away. "We were about to call Aubrey, remember? I promised I'd FaceTime her at four."

"Goddamn it," I say, but I don't mean it. I'm looking forward to catching up with Aubrey, too.

I wasn't sure what would happen when the three of us left Gull Cove Island at the end of July. We'd just lived through the wildest, weirdest month imaginable, and it was hard to tell whether the intense relationships we'd formed with one another would last in regular life. Especially with all the estate stuff in such a colossal mess. It turned into a Story sibling showdown: Allison and Archer on one side, trying to untangle what was left and settle it fairly; and Adam and Anders on the other, dodging creditors and accountability while slapping nuisance lawsuits on anyone who'd ever worked with Donald Camden.

At first, I couldn't believe all the money was gone. But in the end, it very nearly was. Donald, Theresa, Fred Baxter, and Paula had lived high on the hog for twenty-four years, surrounding themselves with the kind of luxury I can't even imagine. They took extravagant trips, bought priceless art and other collectibles that they didn't bother to insure, and renovated the Story properties so extensively that even those mile-high hotel rates couldn't keep up. Dr. Baxter's gambling problem never went away, so he lost millions in Vegas every year. Donald Camden barely worked; he kept a shell of an office and a skeleton staff so he'd look respectable, and spent more on that every year than he came close to taking in.

By the time the dust settled, the amount left over for Adam, Anders, Allison, and Archer to split was, relatively speaking, minuscule. "Just enough to pay for rehab," Archer likes to say. But at least, since he's been sober for five months, it was *good* rehab.

Archer cares less than anyone about being broke. He's back on Gull Cove Island, working for Rob Valentine, and he's oddly serene about painting buildings that his family used to own. "Greed pulled this family apart," he told Milly when we visited him over Veterans Day weekend. He looked good: clear-eyed and clean-shaven, if a little on the thin side. "And honestly, if there'd been anything of significance left at this point? It probably would've happened all over again. I don't want to spend my life fighting with Adam and Anders over the family fortune, and I don't want to see it warp you like it did us. And Donald, and Theresa, and the rest of that messed-up crew."

"Maybe," Milly said grudgingly. "But still. It wasn't their money to spend!"

"No, it wasn't," Archer agreed. "Let's look on the bright side, though. I don't want it. I really don't. I'm happier living a quiet life back home than I've been in years. Allison doesn't need it. She's built a fantastic career all on her own. Megan's done the same, so Aubrey will be just fine. Not to mention all those swim scholarships heading her way. And as for Adam and Anders . . ." He permitted himself a small smile then. "They don't deserve it."

Adam Story's book fell off the bestseller list after two weeks. For a while, we were sure he'd be asked to write another, but the only story that people are interested in hearing from him is his own. And that's the one he refuses to tell.

Anders Story and his family still live in Providence, but JT and I don't go to the same school anymore. He's finishing his senior year at some charter school outside Newport. Long commute, but it has the benefit of being full of kids who don't know him. Except by name. The Story scandal was a big deal on the East Coast for months, so he can't escape it entirely. Anders is starting a new company, which I know nothing about other than what he shared with the *Providence Journal* last week.

"Everything I've learned, everything I stand for, and everything I have, will be poured into this new venture," he promised.

My mother tossed the newspaper aside with a disgusted snort after she read that. "In other words: nothing," she said.

Theresa's sister, Paula, is still at large. I have to admit, she's the one who interests me the most—the dark horse of the group, always in the shadows, who had so little going on in her life when Mildred Story died that she could give it up to pose as Theresa. The media keeps trying to profile her, but there's not much to go on. Twenty-four years ago, she was a fifty-year-old woman living in a suburb of New Hampshire and working for the electric company. Then one day she just—left. Quit her job, gave notice on her apartment, and said she was moving out of state. No one cared enough to ask why.

I told Milly once that I thought that was sad. She glared at me. "Lest you forget, you're talking about the woman who burned down Catmint House," she said. "She could've killed Aubrey and Uncle Archer! Don't you dare feel sorry for her."

"I don't," I said, and it's true. I hate the idea of Paula sipping cocktails on some foreign beach as much as Milly does. It's just . . . I can't help but remember how hard it was to pretend to be someone else, even for a short time. Occasionally, I wonder how she pulled it off for as long as she did. And the same answer hits me every time: because there wasn't a single person in the world, aside from the sister she agreed to impersonate, who would miss her.

Okay, maybe I feel a weird pang of sympathy. But I'm sure as hell not telling Milly that. Because Milly—God. That I get to call her my girlfriend still feels like a miracle. We see one another as often as we can, and when we talk about what we're going to do postgraduation, it's always about *how* we're going to wind up in the same city. Not *whether.*

And who knows, maybe our trio will reunite. Aubrey was offered a swimming scholarship to Brown, which is incredible, but she was also offered several a lot closer to home. Milly's making it her mission to lure Aubrey to the East Coast. Starting now.

We settle ourselves on the same side of a booth behind the pool table area, and Milly props up her phone between us. Once she's dialed Aubrey's number, she pulls off her moto jacket to reveal the Brown University T-shirt we picked up this morning.

Aubrey appears on screen, holding a tiny, squirming baby in the crook of one arm. "Hey, it's Aedan," I say, then do a double take when I get a good look at the kid's face. The last time I saw him via FaceTime, he was a newborn. Now he's two months old, and starting to resemble an actual person. One in particular, as it turns out. "Holy shit, Aubrey, he looks exactly like you."

She grins. "I know, right? It drives my father crazy, especially since he's always insisted that I only have my mother's genes."

She strokes the baby's tufty blond hair with her free hand. "I guess there's more than one way to look like a Story."

It shouldn't have surprised me, Aubrey being Aubrey, that she fell in love with her half brother straightaway. It's not like the mess he came out of was *his* fault. Still, it's pretty cool of Aubrey to be as involved with him as she is, when she could've easily held a grudge.

Milly crosses her arms over her chest, forgetting her T-shirt as she eyes Aedan warily. Babies make her nervous, even when viewed through a screen. "Is he going to cry?" she asks.

"He never cries," Aubrey reassures her. "He's the happiest little guy."

Milly settles back in the booth, looking unconvinced but willing to give the baby the benefit of the doubt. "And how are his parents?" She spits out the last word like it tastes bad.

"Well . . ." Aubrey jiggles Aedan meditatively. "Everyone says babies are hard on a relationship, right? Let's just say, as easygoing as he is, this little guy has been *especially* hard. They're not talking marriage anymore. Coach Matson got a new position a few towns over, but she really wants to stay home with Aedan. Dad, of course, refuses to get a job, and he's already burned through the settlement money and his royalties. I think Coach Matson is finally starting to realize what she signed up for with him, and she is *not* happy."

Milly leans toward the screen, her baby trepidation entirely gone. "I'm gonna start calling you *karma*, buddy," she coos. Aedan offers a toothless grin as Aubrey tries, unsuccessfully, to smother a laugh.

"You're terrible," Aubrey says, then shifts her glance to me. "How's business?"

I give her a thumbs-up. "Better all the time."

She beams. "I can't wait to visit. I'm so sorry I couldn't this week. Our meet schedule is killing me right now. But spring break should definitely be doable. I want to go to Gull Cove and see Uncle Archer, too."

"Perfect," Milly says, straightening her shoulders. "You'll have accepted Brown's offer by then, and as you can see"—she sweeps a hand across her chest—"I'm preparing my celebratory wardrobe."

Someone taps my shoulder, and I turn before I can see Aubrey's reaction. "Postcard for you," Enzo says, handing it to me.

"Really?" I ask, bemused. I never get mail. "Thanks." The front of the postcard shows the New York City skyline, and I immediately think of Milly. I tug on a lock of her hair and ask, "Did you send me a postcard?"

She swats me away, eyes on her phone. "Hold on a sec. I'm in recruiting mode."

I flip the postcard, scanning my name and Empire's address. It's not Milly's neat, loopy handwriting. The words are all cramped together, reminding me of the note we got from Mildred when we first arrived on Gull Cove Island, telling us she'd been called away to Boston. Although I guess it was actually Theresa who wrote that. Or Paula.

Holy hell. *Paula*. Dark horse Paula. The woman nobody would miss.

All of the hairs on the back of my neck stand up as I glance at Milly. She's still deep in conversation with Aubrey, so I shift my eyes down and read the note.

Jonah,

I hear that you, Milly, and Aubrey are doing well, and I am glad. Truly.

I bear you no ill will, and while I suppose it is fanciful to imagine that you and your "cousins" might reciprocate that sentiment, I hope it is the case.

From one imposter to another, I'd like to give you some words of advice: keep your parents far away from Anders Story's new venture. I have a strong suspicion that it will one day, as they say, go up in flames.

Family first, always.
P.

# ACKNOWLEDGMENTS

Publishing is an industry full of change, but I've been fortunate to work with an incredible team for four books straight. I'm so grateful for the ongoing support, and to everyone who made *The Cousins* such a joy to create.

Endless thanks to Rosemary Stimola and Allison Remcheck for your careful guidance of my career, and for always pushing me in the best ways possible. Thank you also to Pete Ryan, Erica Rand Silverman, and Allison Hellegers at Stimola Literary Studio.

Thank you, Krista Marino, editor extraordinaire, for your uncanny ability to see directly into the heart of every book I write. After four books with you, I'm a much better writer, but one who still relies on your sharp eye, keen insight, and unflagging support to inspire me to dig deeper. I'm so proud of what we create together.

The entire team at Random House Children's Books and Delacorte Press is truly amazing, from the strong leadership to the thoughtful planning of marketing, publicity, design, production, sales, and more. Thank you to Barbara Marcus, Beverly Horowitz, and Judith Haut for giving my books the best home I could ask for, and to the team that brings them to life: Monica Jean, Kathy Dunn, Dominique Cimina, Kate Keating, Elizabeth Ward, Jules Kelly, Kelly McGauley, Jenn Inzetta, Adrienne Weintraub, Felicia Frazier, Becky Green, Enid Chaban, Kimberly Langus, Kerry Milliron, Colleen Fellingham, Heather Hughes, Alison Impey, Kenneth Crossland, Martha Rago, Tracy Heydweiller, Linda Palladino, and Denise DeGennaro. Thanks also to Kelly Gildea of Penguin Random House Audio & Listening Library for brilliant production of my audio books.

I'm fortunate to work with many outstanding international publishers. Penguin UK has allowed me to meet and work with so many talented people, including Holly Harris, Francesca Dow, Ruth Knowles, Amanda Punter, Harriet Venn, Simon Armstrong, Gemma Rostill, Ben Hughes, and Kat Baker. This year I was able to visit more of my international publishers than ever before and I'm thankful for the hospitality of Christian Bach and Kaya Hoff of Carlsen Puls in Denmark; Nicola Bartels, Susanne Krebs, Birte Hecker, Julia Decker, and Verena Otto of Random House Germany; and Susanne Diependaal, Jessie Kuup, and Arienne Huisman of Van Goor in the Netherlands.

I'm indebted to Jason Dravis, my tireless film agent, and to the agents who help my books find homes around the world: Clementine Gaisman and Alice Natali of Intercontinental Literary Agency, Bastian Schlueck and Friederike Belder at Thomas Schlueck Agency, and Charlotte Bodman at Rights People.

Thanks to Erin Hahn and Meredith Ireland for your thoughtful feedback and your friendship, and to the wonderful YA community for all the energy and passion you bring to kidlit. I'm grateful for all of you, from the amazing authors I've had the good fortune to meet both online and in person, to the bloggers, educators, librarians, festival volunteers, and booksellers. And especially the readers, who make it all possible.

The setting in *The Cousins* was inspired by the islands of Martha's Vineyard and Nantucket, both of which I've visited many times as a child and an adult. I'm grateful for the hospitality I've always experienced there, and hope the residents don't mind that I created a fictional sibling for your beautiful homes.

Finally, thank you to my family, both Medailleu and McManus, for all your support. Lots of love to my son, Jack, and, in keeping with the theme of this book, to all of his cousins: James, Cassie, Mary, Nick, Michael, Max, Bri, Kelsey, Ian, Drew, Zachary, Aiden, Shalyn, Gabriela, Carolina, and Erik.

# ABOUT THE AUTHOR

**Karen M. McManus** earned her BA in English from the College of the Holy Cross and her MA in journalism from Northeastern University. She is the #1 *New York Times* bestselling author of *One of Us Is Lying, Two Can Keep a Secret, One of Us Is Next* and *The Cousins.* Her work has been published in more than forty languages. To learn more about her, visit karenmcmanus.com or follow @writerkmc on Twitter and Instagram.

# MURDER.

# LIES.

# DECEPTION.

## WELCOME TO BAYVIEW HIGH . . .

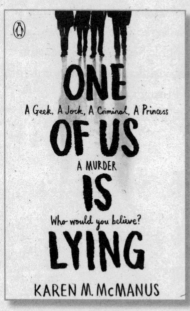

'McManus keeps the juicy subplots ticking over and drip-feeds reveals as clinically as an IV tube' *GUARDIAN*